City of Dragons
Blood Bonds

Adrienne Wilder

Dedicated to:

All the people who never stopped believing in me and didn't think I was crazy when I started this adventure.

And my mother—who always encouraged me to chase my dreams until I caught them.

Dear Reader,

Here you will find a much shorter version of the original Blood Bonds story. I have corrected many errors missed on the original E-book manuscript and I have done my best to cut any extra words. The first version of this novel was my first full length work and needless to say, I learned a lot in the following three years.

If this is the first time you have read Blood Bonds, thank you for purchasing this book. If you have read the earlier version, thank you for your commitment.

A special thank you to my GoodReads fans. You know who you are.

Terms and Definitions

Alchemy: Magical Science

Ancient: Any Kin older than three thousand years old.

Arena Fights: A cross between gladiator style fighting and sumo wrestling where Half-Breeds are pitted against each other for sport.

Become: The process of the Human body going from physical to metaphysical as they Shift and become Lesser-Bred.

Belong: To be bonded to another through metaphysical means. Humans who belong are not immortal, but they live a very long time and cannot live without the Kin they are bonded too. This term also refers to metaphysical bond between a Dominant and a Submissive. This is almost exclusively between Female who “owns” a Male.

Blood Rage: Loss of control due to not Feeding.

Bonded Pair: Two males who share metaphysical energy signatures. May or may not be Brothers. Always the same rank in the Food Chain.

Brother: Males who emerge from the hatching ground together.

Burn: Metaphysical surge. A feel good heat.

Chela or Chelae: Claws

Chetra or Chetrah: Humans. Olde Tongue for sweet meat.

Clicking: A rapid fire tick-tick sound emitted by Kin and Lesser-Breds. This sound is almost exclusive to submissives within a group or white-scales.

Dens: Territory owned by the Queen.

Dominant: Male that has established dominance in the Dens. Dominants can be “made” from birth or a Male can fight his way to the top. A “true Dominant” is a Male who obtains the position because he is metaphysically potent–rather than by skill and brutality.

dominant/dominance: social rank. One male maybe dominant over another. And may or may not be a Dominant.

EFH: Earth for Humans. Anti-Kin Political group.

Elder: Any Kin one thousand years or older.

Female: A title. The highest level of dominance. Refers to Kin who take on a Human female form.

Faerie: Singular version of Folk. Also a “slang” word for Folk.

Feed: The act of taking Blood, Flesh, or Metaphysical energy.

Folk: Faerie. Proper title for the species.

First RHage: A Queen's most powerful RHage. What she is imprinted with by her Mother. There are four: Fear, Flesh, Blood, and Violence.

Food: Lower than a submissive. Sole purpose is to Feed others. Usually do not survive the hatching grounds. Also a derogatory name to reference another Kin.

Food Chain: Dominance scale.

food: Substance that is consumed.

Food: When a Kin is a source of sustenance–a title.

Gray-Zone: The multi-block area surrounding the Dens. There are no real markers for the Gray-Zone but the area is very dilapidated and the city does not enforce codes, taxes, or provide police protection. Utilities and housing are almost always free in the Zone, as well as the basic needs such as clothing and some food.

Half-breed: Kin and female human offspring. Always male. Half-breed is not capitalized because the species views them as an abomination. Half-breeds cannot whirr-purr-or thrum. Some can whistle and click but most are mute. Half-breeds tend to have the intelligence of the average dog at best. Fertility is directly related to intelligence. The small number who are at a Human level of intelligence are the only ones which are fertile. Half-breeds do not *feed* but they can *feed* others because they heal Kin fast. The ability to be food is also linked to intelligence. Half-breeds are most often used by Humans and Faeries in the fighting arenas.

Halvsie: Slang for half-breed

Hatching Grounds: Where eggs are hatched and survival begins.

Hive: The Queen's domain. These are located below ground usually in major cities.

Hot Load: Reference to blood and flesh that is not safe to consume. Usually found in half-breeds. Results vary.

Impress: The act of acquiring phenotypic, genetic, and metaphysical, traits.

Impression: imprint (see above).

Kept: Term most often used when referring to Lesser-Breds who are under the protection of a particular Male. Lesser-Breds cannot *belong*, but they can be kept, scent marked and feed a Male giving them value and protection. Most often done by ferals who use Lesser-Breds as a source of income by selling their flesh, blood, and sexual favors.

Kin: Dragon. Proper title for the species.

Lesser-Bred: Half-breed and human offspring or any generation thereafter. Lesser-Bred should be capitalized. Because Lesser-Breds can be safely used as Food, which means they have value. Side note: The further away (genetically) a Lesser-Bred is from it's half-breed sire, the more likely they are to go through physical mutations. The closer they are to their Half-Breed Sire, the more Human they can appear. This is the general rule–although not set in stone. 4-8 generations removed usually have the strongest blood for feeding, and obtain some of the ethereal appearance of their Kin ancestors.

Link: Human Metaphysically tied to a Kin. Humans who "belong".

Made: To be designed through metaphysical and genetic manipulation.

Male: A title: Refers to all Kin who hold the shape of a Human male. Males can be high or low on the food chain.

Mark: Male Kin marked by a Female.

mark or marked: The scar left by a Kin, Male or Female.

Metaphysics: The energy emitted by all Kin and Lesser-Breds. It is also studied as a science.

MKFK: Man Kind For Kin: Kin activist group who view dragons as gods. Powerful political organization.

Mother: Term reserved for the Female who nurtured a Female or a Prince.

Need: The biological requirement to *feed.*

Nevus: Unique birthmark found on all Kin.

New: Same thing as the word young and more accurate because Kin are not born but made.

Owned: To be under the control/protection of another.

Pet: Humans who are owned by Kin often serve a Queen but are not her Link. A Female can "*own*" a Human and endow them with strength and longevity through her mark. A Male can only "*own*" a Human by scent marking them. Being *owned* by a Male does not increase longevity or health.

Physical form: Most often refers to a Human shape.

Purr: This sound is a cross between the purring noise made by a large cat like a lion or tiger and the churring sound produced by whales. It can be a continuous tone or rise up and down. Purring stokes metaphysical heat and can create a euphoric feeling. The sound has a positive effect on cellular reproduction and represses pain receptors.

Rage: Anger caused by a loss of control over instinct also a biological boiling point due to self-neglect or deprivation of meeting ones need.

RHage: A Queens preternatural power. There are four distinct types, Fear, Violence, Blood, Flesh. A Queen can only have one first Rhage, but she can posses all four.

Rise: Biological surge, the wave of metaphysical power or physiological changes as the body reaches a peak. Also refers to approaching one's need. Rise is also a term used by Lesser-Breds who are at the peak of their Shift when they go from Human to inhuman.

Roll: The act of a Metaphysical Feed. This is usually only done by Females. Dominant can also do it to lower ranking Males or Lesser-Breds. Lesser-Breds can perform this on Humans which is why Lesser-Breds are valuable as whores. Only the Female Roll is upper case. When a Male performs this act or a Lesser-Bred it is *roll* with italics.

roll: Act of domination of one Kin over another, can result in sex, feeding or both.

Scent: Act of drawing air over the palate to taste.

Shift: To change from Human form to Kin (dragon). Or go through the metaphysical transformation where Humans become Lesser-Bred.

Son: A Prince to a Queen. One Male, specifically designed for the purpose of supplying metaphysical variation, for breeding. Usually a gift to another Queen.

Stain: The metaphysical burn mark left on a Lesser-Bred's body where their Kin self attempts to rise to the physical world. This happens during the first phase of the Shift. The marks can be very small and well hidden, or they can be large enough to paint a significant amount of a Lesser-Bred's body. A stain can be physical, to the point the Lesser-Bred doesn't even look Human. Most commonly, are under the skin color splotches, and eye color change.

Submissive: Social rank within a group or pair.

submissive: social rank being lower than another. A Male may be dominant over one Kin and submissive to another.

Taste: Flavor.

Thrum: The proper term for the sound a Kin or Lesser-Bred makes when emitting metaphysical wave pulses with the purpose to assist someone in healing.

Thumping: Another sound which is more felt than heard. The purpose is unknown (and the dragons are not talking). It is a sound almost exclusively produced by a dominant Kin in a group. While the purposed is unknown the rate at which a Kin or Lesser-Bred thumps is in direct correlation to their heart beat. Side note: Sound is most often made when hunting.

True Form: A natural metaphysical state.

Ulysiss Gland: One located between the shoulder blades (upper) one located at the base of the spine (lower) under the skin. They cannot be seen. They fuel the biological engine which controls the Shift. Pushing it can have an orgasmic effect.

Wall: Structure surrounding the Dens. Man made.

Whirr: A higher pitched version of the purr, does not have as much of an effect on healing. The whirr is a sound usually associated with pleasure. Things that feel good will often make Kin and Lesser-Breds whirr.

Whistle: A high pitched sound, made almost exclusively by submissives within a group or white-scales.

White-Scale: Newly Hatched and not fully formed with a Human shape.

Wizard: People born leaking magic.

Chapter 1

This was it.

Haley Night's three inch heels clicked off her steps in the sterile, white, high-walled tunnel as she moved deeper into the Atlanta Draconian Prison Facility--the ADF, as it was known to the Humans and those who worked with them. All the while her emotions ricocheted between anticipation and dread.

Anticipation, because after fifty-some-odd years with the Center for Folk and Kin Relations--ten of them with official Agent status--Haley was finally flying solo. No escort. No babysitter.

Only because everyone else was too scared to go with her.

Whatever. She'd take the cards that she'd been dealt and run like hell. If she could show the Administration she could handle this on her own, they'd give her other assignments. Q and A with uncooperative Male Kin was getting sort of old.

But isn't that what I'm doing here?

Yeah, it was, but at least it wasn't going to happen down in one of the interrogation Tanks in the Center basement.

Nope.

This was way better.

So here she was, twelve stories down under millions of pounds of concrete, taking a long walk down a very narrow hall that led ... where else ... but the basement of basements in the ADF. And thinking about that fueled the dread. A thin sheen of sweat dotted her upper lip.

Now, Kin are cave dwellers by nature, but this wasn't anything like a cave. A cave has multiple tunnels, several ways in, several ways out, rooms, even hidden passageways. This place was nothing more than one giant roach motel. People check in but they don't check out.

Haley reminded herself she was here on behalf of the Bureau, at the request of the D.A. himself ... and because Niles Fury scared the piss out the Humans.

Literally.

Haley had to give the A.D.A. Bob Crane credit. At least he tried.

Niles scared most dragons, so it wasn't a surprise that Bob pissed his Mark Nasons full. It had been a bad idea to send a Human anywhere near Niles. They don't do well with the idea they're just snack food waiting to happen. After all, that's exactly why Niles was here. Crimes against Humanity. Specifically, eating them.

They should've sent Haley the first time. She had the experience and she was Female. It gave her the upper hand in the Tanks on a daily basis. Ten minutes in a room with the most difficult Male and she could have them eating out of her hand.

Or at least licking her palm.

It would have saved time and a good pair of shoes. 'Cause no one likes to ruin a good pair of shoes.

Haley stopped in front of the last of eleven steel doors leading into the depths of the ADF and hit the buzzer. She checked her watch. It was five after. Her appointment was at nine sharp. She was late and late wasn't acceptable.

The guard in the view screen ate his sandwich.

"I.D. please," he said around a mouthful of ... was that tuna? At nine in the morning?

Five after nine, chickadee. You're late.

"Look, I've just shown my I.D." Haley glanced over her shoulder and tried to remember how many check points she'd passed. "Six times? Seven? Can you just let me in?"

The guard gave her a bored look and sucked a wad of mustard off his thumb.

"I.D., lady. Regulation eight point eight..."

"I know, I know." Haley put down the brief case and fumbled with the ID fastened to the hem of her skirt. She undid the clasp and slid it out of the plastic sleeve, a battle all its own ... because regulation eight point nine something dictated that an ID could not be obstructed by foreign materials. 'Cause a clear plastic sleeve is really going to keep someone from being able to tell the difference between a fake ID and a real one from the other side of a monitor.

No need to rehash that argument. Door keeper number three had already made it perfectly clear he didn't give a flying flip. The regulation book was gospel and that was that.

Haley held her ID up to the screen. The guard on the other side was too distracted by his sandwich to even look at it.

Jerk.

The lock buzzed and the door, all nine tons of reinforced carbon steel, slid open with surprisingly little sound.

Haley wasted no more time and went in.

Inside it was just a whole lot more white, but the walls were easily twenty feet high. For decorations, they had cameras. The little red lights next to the lenses blinked down at her. Haley scanned the rest of the room. What the hell was it with Humans and the color white? She suddenly wished she'd worn something other than black. Both her skirt and blazer were black. Her blouse matched the paint job. Her shoes matched the skirt and blazer. Hey, at least she was color coordinated. Still, it was hard not to feel like a lost ink blot in a giant drawing pad.

The only real color in the room was the orange jump suit worn by Niles Fury. Prisoner 0984632 according to the numbers stamped on the back of his prison issued threads.

Nile's shackled arms were spread wide on the steel slab and building supports posing as a table. Its legs were bolted into the floor. Probably to keep him from picking it up and throwing it at someone.

Pleasant thought, that.

Haley's gaze went back to the chains going from his arms to his waist and then the floor. They could anchor a battleship.

I wonder if the Yamamoto is missing some gear?

Niles raised his head. His shoulders spread, and the orange jumpsuit strained to keep him covered. His skull was smooth except for a single black braid cultured from a patch of hair at the back of his head.

Haley was used to seeing big Human shapes on Kin. Most used it to gain a size advantage they didn't have in their natural form. It was a way to bluff wing span and strength.

But something told Haley nothing about Niles was a bluff.

She walked around the table, taking him all in. And, boy, there was a lot to see.

Niles's skin was smooth and evenly tanned in that artificial way that only came from million dollar plastic surgeries or, in this case, metaphysical energy. His face was all angles with a strong Greco-Roman influence and his eyes were Eastern. He was flawless. A regular *GQ* cover model.

The serial man-eater issue.

His *Nevus* was a mixture of reds and yellows. It crawled up from the collar of his jumper and traced his jaw line, stopping just under each eye. It looked like he was wrapped in fire. If his oh-so-godlike physical perfection didn't give him away for what he was, that birth mark would. All Kin had them, each one unique. A mark of bloodline, lineage, and metaphysical energy.

Niles' lips parted and nostrils flared as he inhaled her scent. Haley could smell his Male musk bloom in response to her presence. It tasted sweet. Like the *Nevus,* it was also unique.

She put her briefcase down by the metal chair and sat. The thing was so cold and hard it felt like she was planting her butt on a pizza pan. Niles flipped open his eyes and the color hit her like a pair of head lights.

Red. Ruby red. As dark as Human blood. The pupil in the middle was black. In a state of true Blood Rage they would have been blocked out.

"Niles Fury, I'm Haley Night."

He went still, staring at her with a dark expression. Males in the Tank never looked at her like that. Haley made herself turn her head. She smoothed out her skirt, adjusted her blazer, then pulled the file out of her brief case and set it down on the table. Niles Fury didn't even breathe.

Get a grip. You deal with Males every day in the Tank. Niles Fury is just like all the rest.

But sitting here in front of him, she knew something was different. Haley cleared her throat.

"I was hoping you'd still be willing to help the D.A. with a couple of things. I brought files." She tried to carry on but found herself watching him and wondering if he was even real.

Then he took a breath. One long slow inhale. It was like someone popped his top and poured life back into him. Niles blinked once. The movement looked artificial, like maybe he sat up late at night practicing in front of a mirror, trying to look more Human.

He needed practice. Lots and lots of practice.

Niles Fury was the kind of Kin that pissed Haley off. It was Kin like him that kept the rest of them in the dark ages: feared, hated, and generally despised. His selfish, pompous nature hurt the entire race. The Old Ones tended to be that way--stuck in their arrogance, unable to accept the times and quit eating the public.

And all that fed was prejudice.

But in four days, his reign of terror would come to an end. His death would save a lot of Human lives and, if the rumors were true, put a serious dent in the illegal flesh trade within the city.

Niles had evaded the Bureau for well over seventy-five years. Ever since they first caught wind he was here in the US, there had been a warrant out for his head. As technology got better, they got closer. Then six months ago, he'd been subdued. Maybe his death would set an example. For a people who believed in nothing after life, death could be an incredible motivator.

"Why are you here?" His words were accented with Olde Tongue, but his English was perfect. Mix that with his deep baritone and James Earl Jones might as well have been Mickey Mouse.

Maybe he'd forgotten about the appointment he'd made with the D.A. Oh, since yesterday?

"I told you I..."

Niles Fury cut her off. "You're not supposed to be here."

There was an odd lilt to his voice. Fear? If he had been any other Kin, maybe. But this was Niles Fury. Fear? Yeah. Right. Haley wasn't even part of the Dens and she knew about his reputation.

His arms flexed and the chain rattled. Heat rolled off his body and the air ignited with the scent of burning Alchemist magic. The Oisis pin in his back kept him from showing any of his Kin self.

Niles bared his teeth. Human teeth.

Haley managed not to roll her eyes. Barely. She was used to the theatrics. Lots of Kin liked to flash scales and teeth. While it was illegal to Shift outside of designated fly zones, a little show and tell was expected. A social display that was practically a language all its own.

"You're not supposed to be here," he said again.

"I heard you the first time." Haley spread out the reports she wanted him to look over, all of them unsolved homicides associated with the flesh trade. Some worse than others. The M.O.'s made it unlikely any of them were his, but if Niles could identify some of the bodies, maybe even name some of the people who were responsible, he could do something productive for once in his miserable life.

"I agreed to speak with one of the Bureau *Chetrah*. Not. You."

Haley tried not to wince. *Chetrah* was common enough Olde Tongue slang that even Humans had learned what it meant. Food. More precisely, "sweet meat". Throwing the word around in public was like an Aryan poster boy screaming the "N" word at a NAACP convention.

"I'm here because you scared the A.D.A into pissing his pants, and now no one else will come down here and talk to you." She pushed the first file under his right hand. "I'm all you've got. It's just you and me." Haley smiled and folded her hands.

Niles shut his eyes.

* * * * * * *

This was bad.

No, this is worse than bad.

Niles Fury tried to find some sense of calm, but there was just too much anger. Anger fueled him. Anger drove him. Anger had shielded him from the power of the Queens, and it had shielded him from the Alchemy the *Chetrah* used to try and control him.

Now, anger was quickly becoming his enemy. He'd planned on trying one last time to get out of here. His last attempt had failed. The A.D.A had been too weak-willed and Niles had pushed too hard.

The plan seemed simple. He'd agree to speak with one of the *Chetrah* and when they were close enough, he'd catch their mind. The problem was getting them close enough without shorting out their fear response. Unlike prey, he didn't want them immobile. He just wanted them to do as he said. The only command he planned on giving them was to pull the pin out of his back. Simple enough. Even a monkey could do it. Or in this case, *homo sapiens*.

After the pin was out, he'd kill the *Chetrah* and use their blood and flesh to heal the damage he was going to endure getting out of this place. But he had to do it from here--from this room. Any deeper and he'd never make it to the surface and wind up consumed by his own fire.

And the plan would have worked.

Colonel Dobson would die and the lab below would be lost. Niles would be safe, his people would be safe, and so would she. But that wasn't possible now. The plan had changed. Instead of the *Chetrah* with his briefcase, papers, and his stupid questions, it was the Female Niles Fury had been so careful to never meet. To never touch.

Haley's scent clung to the roof of his mouth and the inside of his nose. It did things to him, things that scared him, things he couldn't explain. In her presence, the anger inside him withered and cowered, leaving him helpless. That had only happened with one other, centuries ago, make that a millennia. It was stupid to think that there was rebirth after death just as it was stupid to think there were gods. Death was final, absolute. And yet...

Every atom, every molecule hummed in her presence. It always happened when Niles got too close. Just like before. Those were better times. The *Chetrah* knew their place in the world and had no Alchemy. His Brother felt it too, which was why they worked to protect her and keep the Queens at bay. The Queens didn't fear his softer sibling, but they feared him. They feared the *Fury* he could bring down on them.

The pin in Niles' back burned as his metaphysical energy surged. The *Ulysiss* gland between his shoulders felt like fire. It rivaled the starvation-fueled pain pricking over the rest of his body.

"When's the last time you *fed*?"

Haley's voice caused his hearts to jump, slamming the blood in his veins, and firing up all his senses. Niles opened his eyes and looked at her, captivated by her lack of perfection and her mastery at Humanness.

But then that's what she'd *Impressed* on instead of a Queen. No wonder she was so much like them. Haley's movements, her voice, her eyes and mouth conveying emotion just like the *Chetrah*. If it wasn't for her scent, she could pass for one. The idea repulsed and intrigued Niles Fury all in one breath.

Haley's hand moved near his and he held very still. Niles didn't know what he would do if she touched him. But touch was what he craved, what he needed. His starved metaphysical side screamed for it and clawed at his insides begging to be let out.

Does Dobson know she is here?

The thought sent the smallest lick of fear through Niles Fury. How long would it be before the colonel got word that his visitor was her and not one of the *Chetrah*? The colonel would find a way to keep her here. He would find some reason to trap her down in that lab and take what he wanted from her: blood and bone to finish his science. And all Kin would be dead before the month was out.

Niles Fury thought hard and fast. What were the options? Escape wasn't going to happen, but if that *Chetrah* Dobson found out Haley was here, then everything he'd tried so hard to protect would be lost. Niles Fury believed in no gods, no magical afterlife, and nothing supernatural. And yet he was driven by the inexplicable need to watch over Haley. He blamed that on his Brother, the source of all his weaknesses. That half of him who borrowed his anger--and no matter how hard Niles Fury resisted--managed to leak his own conscience back in its place.

And the constant trickle of loyalty and ethics being shed down to Niles Fury was a bother.

A regular fucking Jiminy Cricket.

Niles Fury had to get Haley out. He wouldn't be able to control the knowledge of her presence and his Brother would eventually leak the information to the Queen that owned him. For his Brother, the channels were always open. Niles Fury's anger kept them clogged full, which was exactly what he needed most of the time.

That way, the Queen couldn't get to both of them.

His Brother's bond with the Queen worried him. Niles Fury needed to get around that, so he could warn Haley Night. But the only time the bitch couldn't hear the thoughts between him and his Brother was when Niles Fury was deep in unconsciousness. A state that superseded sleep and bordered on death.

Just like that, Niles Fury's mind shifted gears and started planning. He didn't like the plan but he was helpless to stop it. His compulsion to keep her out of harm's way was unstoppable. He reworked his ideas of escape and shaped them into a scenario of death.

His.

* * * * * * *

The long stretch of silence started playing on Haley's nerves like a cat walking across a piano. But the problem was obvious. Niles Fury hadn't fed. It was unusual for a Kin this old to succumb to isolation and hunger so quickly. But then maybe he'd gone for a while without on the outside.

It was the only logical explanation.

"Niles, did you hear what I asked you? When's the last time you fed?"

His tongue stroked his lips and a small wicked grin made his ruby eyes fierce.

"Too long." He moved ever so slightly and the chains protested.

God of Man, how she hated those things.

"I'm sorry about..." Haley looked at the chains and didn't quite know how to put her feelings into words. "You must really scare them if they feel a need to lock you down like..." "A monster" went unsaid, but then maybe that's exactly what he wanted: to be feared. A lot of Kin wanted to be seen as predators. Haley didn't get it, but she'd been Impressed and raised by Humans.

Niles tilted his head ever so slightly. His eyes slid across her face, down her shoulders, lingered at her chest, and were diverted by the table which forced them to her arms, then hands.

Her fingers were a few inches from his. She'd started to reach for him, to give him comfort, but she also didn't want to send him the wrong signals.

She was, after all, out here on her own. Beyond the confines of the Bureau, there would be less tolerance for normal Kin behavior and a ton of bureaucratic bullshit if she acted inappropriately. Which, for Humans, meant anything touchy-feely or beyond the boundaries of personal space.

It was one of the biggest problems her people had working with man and was a constant Human Resource nightmare.

Even though the son-of-a-bitch sitting in front of Haley was a man-eater, it pained her to see him suffering. Her Human rearing said he deserved it, while her Kin nature argued he'd only been doing what came naturally. A few hundred years was not a lot of time for an entire race to alter a behavior based in biology.

Eat and survive.

And Human flesh and blood just happened to be extremely fulfilling. Like steak and fine wine, only better.

Still, it was wrong. Kin nature also dictated respect for the *Dominant* race. Intelligence had nothing to do with where you sat on the food chain. However, dominance meant the other species had carved out their niche and proven themselves able to fight and win.

Humans and their creative nature had made them a worthy opponent for Kin.

Unfortunately, there were still a few who refused to acknowledge they had been bested by a hairless monkey that had no power to fly, no fire, no metaphysical ties, and the life expectancy comparable to a house fly.

This was getting Haley nowhere. Most Males begged for her touch. There were very few Females to the number of Male Kin, and Females spent the majority of their lives holed up inside the Hive, catered to and protected by their selected Harem. That meant only a small number of Males ever got to *see* a Female, let alone touch.

Screw it. Paperwork be damned.

Haley closed the distance between them and touched his hand. Niles was on fire. His skin burned with metaphysical energy.

Niles Fury blinked again, long and slow, and his chest hitched like he was having trouble breathing. Haley pressed her palm against his fist and he responded by opening his fingers and accepting the touch. His lips curled, flashing bright white teeth that looked a little too jagged. She didn't pull away. You didn't offer your touch then reclaim it. It was bad, bad manners. The kind that could get your liver ripped out and handed to you.

Haley slid her fingers to his wrist and pressed her thumb to the pulse beating like a constant drum under his skin. For Humans, it would have been an intimate gesture. But for Kin, it was simply hello-hi-how-are-you-nice-to-meet-you.

Niles came forward and Haley's hand was swallowed up by his. He cradled her hand like it was a flower and raised it to his face, touched his lips to her palm, and left a wet hot line down the center with his tongue. His mouth opened and he breathed, drawing in her scent from across the skin. Haley could feel the metaphysical surge as it crashed over her, stirring her instincts.

She told them to sit and stay or she was getting out the rolled up newspaper.

A growl rumbled in his chest. "You should leave." But Niles didn't let go of her hand. He flashed his teeth again and there wasn't a Human one left in his mouth. It should have been impossible. Alchemist magic was a powerful force.

Haley said, "If you'll help me, I'll be out of your hair in no time."

Okay, that was a bad choice of words, considering he was doing a good impersonation of Mr. Clean. Haley cleared her throat and waited for him to let her go. Like every other movement it was slow and deliberate, as if he was trying to use limbs he hadn't gotten used to yet.

"Will you help me?" Haley asked.

Niles dropped his stare to the folder in front of her. She took it as an opportunity and slid it closer. He started slow, his eyes scanning the glossies, then his hand flipped them off to the side.

Haley watched him, feeling unusually sad. Niles' Human form was beautiful and she was willing to bet his true shape was even more stunning. What a shame he wasted so much potential, so many possibilities to help his race, all over illegal flesh trading. And why do it illegally? God of Man knew there were enough crazies with the Mankind for Kin group willing to donate blood and flesh to feed her people.

Haley had to admit, there was something seriously demented about the idea of Humans tattooing themselves up with the Olde Tongue script reading *Chetrah,* and standing around in the Dens like a walking all-you-can-eat-buffet.

All-you-can-eat until they die that is.

Niles stopped, his eyes lingering on one of the photos. Haley caught the splatters of bright red and high white contrasting dead Human flesh from the corner of her eye.

"How do you live among the *Chetrah* and not crave their flesh?" Niles' eyes were locked on the photo, his fingers petted the slick surface. He glanced up at her, his ruby eyes burning.

"I just don't." It was the truth. Haley didn't have any of the blood cravings that seemed to affect a lot of Kin. Okay, most Kin. Even her partner and best friend, Farley, dealt with a long standing addiction to the stuff.

However, a Human had raised her.

Although "Raised" wasn't really the right word, because Kin didn't begin life as infants. Life for them started as impressionable beings--white-scales--driven by insatiable hunger. The Human woman who took Haley in didn't fear the unruly beast still pale with hatching skin. She fed

Haley the meat and blood her newly hatched body craved, and she *Impressed* Haley with the images she would need to emulate a Human shape.

"The pictures, Niles."

His eyes narrowed. "My name is Niles Fury. Don't call me Niles."

Haley arched an eyebrow. A Kin having two names was unusual. It was respectful to use only the first name, disrespectful to call them only by the second. But a Male insisting on being called by the first and second together? That was downright bizarre.

He went back to the stack of photos, and it was silent except for the sound of pages being turned.

After a moment Niles paused at another and made a disapproving sound in the back of his throat. "I do not understand the fascination with fucking *food* before you eat it." He turned the photo one way then the next. The scene was nothing more than a collage of bodies and broken furniture. He pushed the stack back towards Haley.

"You haven't looked at them all." She stopped him by putting her hand on the folder.

"I never fuck my food before I eat it. I prefer it running. Screaming. Pleading for mercy. None of these bodies are mine. Too much meat left on the bones. Too much blood spilled. I eat what I kill. All. Of. It."

Haley flinched; she couldn't help it. Niles grinned, his shoulders flexed, and the heat of his trapped metaphysical energy surged like a south wind. Red scales flashed along his forearms and neck.

That just wasn't possible.

She flicked her eyes back up at his face. Niles's smile made her blood cold.

"I'm sorry. Did I offend the pet dragon?"

Yeah, he was sorry all right, just not in the way he fantasized about.

Haley shoved the files back under his hands. That bastard was going to give her something to take to the PD if she had to beat it out of him. Another mountain of HR paperwork, but the satisfaction might be worth a pack or two of Bic pens. He was a Male after all. Nothing special. Nothing she couldn't handle.

Maybe if Haley kept telling herself that she'd eventually believe it.

She frowned. "Respect the dead."

Niles slapped the file from the table top, turning the white-washed room into a cheap snow globe.

Haley stood and planted her hands on the table. Chains tightened with a sharp clack and kept Niles from standing to his full height as he met her challenge. Even at half-mast he was big. Really. Big.

Haley pegged him with a glare. "You're going to die in four days. And that means you have four days to do something with your life that shows the Humans that run this world you have some grain of sympathy for their loss of life."

"Or what?"

"There is no 'or what'. It would be the decent thing to do."

Niles threw back his head and roared in laughter. When he rolled his head back down his blazing stare hit her hard. "And you think I care about *decent*?"

Obviously not. Out loud she said, "Well, at least it would give your existence some sliver of value. Because as it stands, your life is worth nothing. You're worth nothing."

A long low growl trickled from the back of Niles' throat and he curled his lip.

Haley waved him off. "Save your theatrics. I am not a Human and I am not a lowly Male. There is nothing about you that scares me."

Niles leaned forward as far as the chains would let him. The metal groaned and the air ignited with the smell of burning magic. "Then you don't know me well enough, Haley Night." He opened his mouth wide, flashing too many teeth for a Human mouth. It didn't last very long; the Alchemy overrode his biology and pushed his metaphysical energies back down.

Haley glared at him. "How can you die knowing you've done nothing for your people?" Haley snatched up the photos and reports lucky enough to land on the table.

Niles fell still again and the room was plunged into an eerie silence.

When he spoke, his baritone voice was barely a whisper. "How can you live knowing the *Chetrah* you covet so much are planning the destruction of our people?"

Was he serious? More like delusional.

Haley shook her head. This interview was going nowhere. She had a class at noon full of new trainees for the Civil Peace Division. Unlike Niles, they weren't a waste of her time. "Your *need* has scrambled that gray matter trapped between your ears."

Niles snapped at the air in front of her. Haley refused to back away. As far as she was concerned, he was no different than any poorly mannered half-feral Male. Just bigger, older, and more stupid.

She flicked him a look. "You'd think being on such a short leash would instill some decency to quit acting like a dog."

Overhead, the intercom clicked on and a tinny voice addressed Haley Night with concern for her well-being.

"I'm fine. Just dealing with a few behavioral issues..."

And these were nothing that a session with the Dog Whisperer could straighten out either.

Niles snarled and snaked his neck in a way that suggested he had joints where no Human would. His eyes rolled up at the overhead cameras.

"Good morning, Romero. How's that hand working out for you? Are you able to beat off in the john again, or is your fuck buddy, Frank-O, still giving you lip service?"

The speaker crackled but the voice didn't reply.

Haley glared at Niles while she scrounged for a few more pieces of tossed paper.

Niles lunged at her when she leaned down close to him to pick up a report. She didn't even flinch and continued retrieving the contents of her folder. There must have been a hundred pages. The thing had been thick, but she never imagined there'd be so many. Haley continued with her private game of fifty-two pick up while Niles frothed and growled.

Pathetic, really.

The intercom kicked on again and the tinny voice asked her if she required any assistance.

Haley stood up with a half dozen rescued glossies. "I'm still okay, really." She put them back into the folder as neatly as she could. Organizing them would have to wait. She pushed back a lock of dark hair and eyed the mess.

"You know, you're a real pain in the..." Niles' hand flew out, slapping the folder out of her hand again. Then he did the unthinkable. He grabbed hold of her wrist and yanked her flush against his body. Touching a

Female without permission was an unforgivable act. Haley growled and Niles jerked her like he was trying to shake something loose.

Haley said, “Let me go.”

Niles ignored her.

Overhead, Romero or Frank-O barked orders for Niles to release his visitor and drop to his knees on the floor.

“Fuck you, Romero. Maybe I’ll just have one more little snack before I check out.”

“I’m not...” A hand closed around her throat cutting off the air she needed to speak.

Niles leaned in close. He ran his tongue across her cheek and raked his teeth across her ear, nicking it. “You do a really good job looking like the *Chetrah.*” His hot breath hit her neck. “Do you think they know? I’m betting even if they do, you’re pretty enough to draw them in here.” Niles’ ruby eyes came up to hers. He was so close their noses almost touched.

The tinny voice overhead trying to sound more authoritative, wound up sounding panicked.

“Scream for me, Haley. Bring the *Chetrah* to me so I can bathe one last time in their blood.” Niles’ grip loosened.

“Let me go or I’ll...” The vice closed down again.

“Make me, *Chetrah* pet. Control me like a proper Female. Demand that I bow to you and maybe I will.”

Haley squeezed his wrist and felt something crack. Niles laughed, throwing back his head and roaring like a monster.

“I like this one, Romero! Reminds me of you! Think I should start with her fingers and work my way down her toes? I haven’t forgotten about you, Frank-O. I’ll give you a special treat. Carve your daughter’s name in her back; pretend it’s your kid I’m tearing apart. Think you’ll have nightmares? I bet you’ll have nightmares till the end of your pitiful days.”

The screaming siren cut the air like broken glass. Small yellow security lights flashed from the recesses in the wall above. Niles snarled and Haley squeezed his wrist, snapping the bones. With a quick twist he had her around the waist and pinned to the table. His body pressed down on her back; his mouth was to her ear again.

“I wish we had more time together.” His scent spiked as he moved his knee up between her legs and inched her skirt higher. "But do not think I will waste this moment we have." To the Humans it would look like he was considering rape. But those kinds of things didn't exist for Kin. Niles was trying to get as close to her as possible, to *feed* his metaphysical side. Even the slightest bit of fabric made drawing on it difficult.

Haley strained to push him off her, but he had her too far over the table and her feet couldn't touch the ground.

Niles said, "I need you to scream for me, Haley."

His hand inched up her thigh, and slipped under her blazer. Niles' fingertips dug into the *ulysiss* gland in her lower back. The surge of pleasure ignited Haley's body. Niles released her throat just enough that her cries sounded strangled and desperate.

"Very good."

"Let go of me!" She kicked.

"Oh, nooo ... not yet." Sharp points raked against her ribs. "Do you fear me yet?"

"No." Haley bucked. Damn, he was strong.

Niles rubbed his cheek against hers. "I have so enjoyed your company. I only wish my bothersome Brother hadn't always been there to stop me from doing things..." His lips pressed to her ear. "Such glorious things..."

Haley whipped her head around to the sound of a metal door sliding open. At her back, Niles tensed. In a low, deep snarl he muttered, "Show time."

Niles Fury threw Haley like a broken doll and she hit the wall hard enough to crack a rib and see black fireworks. Human guards filed into the room, dressed in riot gear, armed with Plexiglas face masks, and were those...?

Stun guns?

They might as well be planning to poke a rattlesnake with a sharp stick.

The sound of chains screaming brought Haley's head up in time to see the metal links at the floor on Niles' left snap. A criss-cross of Taser barbs filled the air and hit Niles from head to toe, turning him into a walking pin cushion. The rapid fire sounded like it was coming from microscopic machine guns, and for all the good it did, they might as well have been.

Haley watched in horror as the massive Male launched the chair he'd been sitting in with one kick. It took out the closest guard, popping his skull wide like an over-ripe melon. With a heave of his shoulders once, twice, the chains on his left came free and became a new kind of weapon. Heavy steel whistled, gaining momentum, then with a flick it snapped like a whip. Bones cracked and the sounds of screaming men propelled Haley from the ground. Their fear made the blood they shed smell candy sweet. She had to stop this.

Shifting was out of the question. The confines were too narrow and too many Humans were in the way. But it didn't mean she couldn't tap into her metaphysical side, push just enough scale and muscle to back up her demands.

"Niles!" she screamed, but he wasn't listening. He'd zeroed in on the new game that'd just walked into the room. The kind of screaming and bleeding fun that was right up his alley.

Haley threw herself into the much larger Male and at the same time unsheathed her *chelae*. His flesh parted and his ribs snapped. Thick green *ichor* rushed over her hand and splattered on the white floor mixing with red.

Niles spun and Haley slammed her other fist into his chest. Her fingertips brushed the first of two hearts. Haley pulled on the preternatural energy created by her biology and channeled it down her arms. The smaller, half-shifted muscles and bones were not strong enough to withstand the adrenaline pumping through her body. Tendons and muscle shredded under her skin, which split as bone cracked. Anger and pain tore a cry out of her throat, but she succeeded in stopping Niles' forward momentum and sent him crashing to the ground.

Behind her, the guards scattered. "She's one of them! Holy fucking God!"

Don't run ... don't scream.

It was a battle to stay on top of Niles with her fists buried in his ribs and chest and not chase after the Humans. They smelled like *food.*

The *burn* of healing gave Haley something else to think about until they were gone. Niles tried to sit up and she shoved him back down, squeezing his lower heart in her grip. Air bubbled around the hole she'd made in his ribs. Niles' eyes rolled upward and his mouth opened and closed.

He tried again and she pushed him back. "Stay down, Niles."

The Alchemists were coming. She could feel them like an oncoming storm.

His ruby eyes blazed. "Finish it..."

"Shut up and lay still."

"Kill me, Haley."

"What?"

"Do it. Kill me." His hands locked on her wrist and he shoved her claws deeper. She retracted in time to avoid piercing the heart. Niles made a frustrated sound in the back of his throat. A thick green bubble formed on his lips and popped.

Haley shook her head. Kin don't request to die. Kin don't commit suicide. Kin fear death. Having the potential to live forever will do that.

"You are difficult to anger." Niles actually sounded exasperated.

"You did this on purpose?"

He grinned at her, flashing sharp teeth painted with blood.

"Why?"

"I have to die so you will be safe." He touched her cheek and pushed his fingers into her hair. His ruby eyes stared like he was seeing through her most private thoughts.

"Safe? Why would you dying make me safe?"

"He saw your blood. He knows. *Deviant Nuestrauss*." Niles slipped into Olde Tongue and Haley cursed her lack of discipline. All Females could speak the Mother language, but then all Females were raised by their Queens, protected and comforted, not thrown out into the Human world, denied the most basic Kin ways.

"Niles..." Behind her, heavy boots rose and fell, rhythmic, like a machine. The air crackled with the stench of magic as the *Oisis* pin in Niles's back responded to their presence.

Yeah, it would make sense that something so nasty would recognize its maker.

Haley looked up to see the black dressed figures surround them. A hand reached out and grabbed her by the back of the neck. Eyes, dark pits of nothing but magic stared at her through the protective helmet. Male or Female, she had no idea, but there were bits of blond hair sticking out from the edge of the facemask it wore.

A bark of pain escaped her throat as she was hurled into the table. Blue-white sparks illuminated the room as the Alchemists pulled their tritons. Torture devices, nothing more. Haley struggled for air; something sharp made her breaths come in short quick gasps.

Rib, she thought. The heat of healing was slow to rise. She'd spent a lot of energy taking him down, healed a lot of bones to keep him there. And now she was helpless to watch as they struck Niles, over and over, with the wide-pronged weapons.

One of the Alchemists stepped back from the team giving Niles's body an electric workout. Haley raised her head. Was it the one who had thrown her?

The eyes were black, same as any other Alchemist.

The Alchemist raised the triton and said, "Night-night, wyrm."

Chapter 2

Death was about being terrified.

A sensation of smothering in fear and darkness.

But Niles Fury could only feel the touch of Haley's flesh drowning in his blood. The beating of his heart against her fingertips. Even as the tritons punctured his skin he felt nothing but the hum of her metaphysical force left behind. A mix of their blood.

And he knew why the Queens feared her.

And understood why his Brother insisted that she be saved.

As death came, the walls of Niles Fury's anger fell. He clung to that moment between the end and now, pushing the thought to the farthest reaches of his mind and out.

Brother o'mine...

He could hear a voice. Angry, but nothing Kin, and it was shoving him toward consciousness.

For the first time in his existence, Niles Fury fought life. There had been a few times in his younger years where death and he were lovers. Once at the hands of a Dominant Male who took too much flesh and left him broken and feeding the carrion birds. Another time, a Queen. Her name long forgotten.

So the empty, godless space was nothing new to him. An endless, lonely blackness. More cruel than Queens or the Blood Rage of a hundred unfed hatchlings, the void was his source of terror. Pushed by fear and Kin instinct for survival, Niles Fury always fought his way back from the void. Until now.

Now he fought to get there, pleading for the bitter frozen fear to leach into his bones and render him helpless.

The predator becoming the prey.

Only this beast had no teeth and claws to rip and tear. Niles could understand those things. He could anticipate the jarring sting of tendons being ripped from joints, but the darkness gave nothing.

And nothing was far worse than any kind of pain.

"You will not die today, wyrm. You will only die when I say, and today is not your day."

Niles Fury knew the voice and ran from it, fleeing into the blackness. The veil of anger receded. So close ... so close to embracing the end.

Words drifted through breaks in the static.

"Jesus Christ, did you fucking idiots have to puncture him so many times? He looks like a goddamn pin cushion!" There was a commotion. "I've got to pull this pin. It's interfering with his natural healing abilities and right now those aren't much, but we need them. Fuck you ... you did this. Unless you want to tell Dobson his pet project is dead, get the hell out of my way!"

Niles Fury took a breath even though he didn't want to, then he was sucked back under the stillness.

"Pull up that vial of Dopram! Yes, the whole thing ... well, it's either risk a coronary or he's dead anyway."

Niles Fury's eyes came open and he thought he saw the sun.

"Shit! Do it! Do it now!"

The stench of magic replaced the memory of Haley's scent. The icy hot pin bit back down into his *ulysiss* gland, shutting off the biological process for the change. The upper gland provided the heat needed to fuel the process; the lower gland cooled the molecular changes so the body didn't catch fire.

With the upper gland rendered useless, Niles Fury couldn't fuel the change and he was trapped in his *Chetrah* shell.

The irony was not lost on him.

His lungs expanded, sucking the air from the tube threaded down his throat. His eyes rolled upward and he saw the whiteness of lab coats. They had him spread eagle on a steel slab, the cold of the room biting him deeper than it should have.

"I need those heating pads on him now. His DTs are starting. Do it now, ladies, before he rips his peroneus from his tibia." It wasn't just Niles Fury's leg muscles they were going to have to worry about. His ribs made an audible crack as his obliques spasmed. Niles Fury screamed, helpless to stop the onslaught of muscular seizures. Ichor poured from partially healed wounds sutured together as his spine bowed, pulling him off the table. His left hip dislocated and a fresh new pain raced down his leg.

He needed the touch of his own, not *Chetrah* science. The heating pads hit him like scorching sandpaper. A poor substitute for flesh on flesh and the warmth spread by the sharing of metaphysical energy. As pain wrenched his body he tried to think of Haley and how she'd felt under him. His weight pressed against her, the sensation of her hands buried in his flesh...

Blood.

Her blood caught fire in his veins.

"Callahan, he's slipping ... I need that propranolol *now* before we lose him...somebody open me a vein before I do it for you!"

Niles Fury felt his anger crumble and could feel beyond.

Brother, you were right. I have felt her blood in mine. She is our Augury.

Chapter 3

Colonel Dobson picked up the satellite phone on the third ring.

"Yes?" Formal hellos, how-are-yous and what-the-hell-do-you-wants were unnecessary. Only one man would be calling him from a number outside the Bureau military lines, and that was Richards, his head metaphysical biologist.

"I've got bad news both ways," Richards said.

Dobson pulled the tattered cigar from his lips and smashed the smoldering end into the glass ash tray.

Smoking on the plane was prohibited.

He pulled out another two-hundred dollar Cuban and contemplated lighting it. He only had three left. Thank God he only smoked on the plane. It would be at least three days before his next shipment came in.

And nothing was as good as a Cuban. He could almost taste the sweat of the caramel-skinned whore who rolled the thing.

Even though the Gulfstream five-fifty gave a flawless ride, it was still flying. And every cell in Dobson's body knew he was up in the air. No amount of fine furniture, luxury seating, or plush carpeting was going to change that. It bothered him, because wyrms were born with wings.

Down to three cigars, with six hours in his flight left to go, and now Richards was burning up his satellite phone with more melodrama. Probably the goddamned monsters eating each other again.

Dobson rolled the cigar with his tongue. "I told you, if you wait until they're as crazy as a shit-house rat, one of them would wind up killing the other. You can't starve these fuckers, Richards. It's not like your dog. They're eating machines. Keep em' fed or kill em'. But quit calling me because you decided to go home early and thought half a day wouldn't make a difference."

"We've got sample Zero."

Dobson grinned. "I thought you quit sampling the synthetics, Richards."

Richards was quiet. Dobson could just imagine him, standing there in his pristine white lab coat, sweating like a pig on a spit.

"Sir, I'm clean."

"Then what's with the horseshit about having Garrett's pet?"

"She's here, sir. She's here in the ADF."

Dobson leaned forward in his seat. He dropped his voice even though he knew he was alone. The stewardess knew to stay the hell out unless he yanked her leash.

"Do not fuck with me, Richards. I am not in the mood to be fucked with."

"I'm ... I'm not, sir."

"Then tell me how you just happened to have the golden egg land in your lap when I've been trying to get my hands on her without causing a shit storm with the higher ups?" For how long? Months. And even now that he was head of the Military section, they told him "no".

This had better be good. Real good.

Richards talked and Dobson listened. It was good, all right. She'd picked up the unwanted assignment of trying to get Niles Fury to confess a few more crimes before they lopped off his head this Friday.

For whatever reason, the son-of-a-bitch went AWOL and it had come down to a fight. The fact that he didn't kill her was a plus. The fact that she couldn't control him was disturbing. If a Female couldn't control Niles, then how the hell were they ever going to break the bastard? But then maybe she needed practice. After all, she'd been raised by Humans. There were sure to be some shortfalls.

Bad news, three guards had been critically injured. Bad news, one of the other guards had started calling friends and family about the hoe-down and now the ADF was fast becoming a Channel Five special report.

Good news, Niles Fury was still alive because they hadn't run out of Dopram or Propanolol yet. His body was slow on the healing scale because they couldn't risk pulling the pin for more than a few seconds.

Bad news, the strawberry blond with the tight ass wouldn't be doing Dobson any favors any time soon. Seems Niles Fury had a little more get up and go in him than they thought and managed to rip out the inside of her arm. They went ahead and let her bleed out. It was easier to dump a body than have to worry about her getting sour grapes and going to the press over a violation of ethical science.

Ethical science, my ass. These were goddamn monsters of the man-eating kind. Dobson was doing the world a favor.

Good news, sample Zero was alive: breathing, detained and waiting for his arrival.

Bad news, someone had squealed to Garrett, the Center's Senior Special Agent.

As far as Dobson was concerned, the Center for Folk and Kin Relations was nothing but a warehouse of minority reports. Someone needed to do the world a favor and burn that place down.

"How much time can you buy me?" Dobson was only--he checked the digital flight map on the display next to his chair--an hour and fifteen minutes outside of Atlanta. If he could get there before Garrett left, Dobson could pull rank, and send his wyrm-loving-ass right back to that cesspool he called a job.

"We've already stalled Garrett for an hour out front. He's heading downstairs right now. So an hour and thirty minutes tops if we make him do the paper work in triplicate."

"How fucking long has she been there?" Because even Superman didn't move that fast.

"Two hours, maybe three, I don't--"

"Three fucking hours? Three hours! Why the hell wasn't I notified?" Christ, he wasn't even off the ground when she'd shown up. Just fucking great!

"We were a little busy with Niles, sir. It took everyone on staff to..."

"Listen here, Richards, you keep him there two hours or I'm going to soak your ass in synthetic Temporal and put you in with those Males we've got in cell C."

Richards made a strangled, unhappy sound.

"Do it, Richards. You're only one of dozens of meta-biologists. I can replace you."

Dobson cut the call and sat there staring at the receiver, trying to decide what to do. He paged the cabin.

"And what can we do for you this fine morning, Colonel Dobson?"

"Turn the plane around."

Silence.

This was the problem with non-military men. They all had to stop and think about the orders he gave. Dobson didn't pay them to think. Hell, he didn't even pay them to reply. They were paid to do, and yet it never failed. They always found some way to make him repeat himself and sound like a goddamned parrot.

"Did you hear me or do I need to come up there so you can read my lips?"

"Yes, sir. Turning the bird around now, sir."

Dobson hung up and dialed the Bureau's switchboard.

On that line there was no automated 'press one for English, two for Olde Tongue' bullshit. The internal line went right to a real, I'll-be-go-to-hell, live person.

Unfortunately she sounded like a female version of Barney the Dinosaur with all her happy-to-help-you crap. In spite of that fact, it was better than a machine.

"This is Colonel Dobson, ID eight-four-five-seven-nine. I need you to give me the number, then connect me to Garrett. No matter where he is."

Little Miss Happy didn't dally. Must have been a military brat.

The line rang.

Dobson had sample Zero. With enough plasma and a core sample of her *ulysiss* gland, he could get the virus retrofitted into an airborne stage. That was the only way this was going to work. Beijing proved that. There were just too many survivors from trying to deliver it by direct contact and because of that Mount Everest-sized fuck up, Dobson was still dealing with the clean-up thirty years later.

Six rings and it clicked to voice mail. Dobson hung up and dialed again.

You'd think the Triads would be grateful for the ninety percent kill ratio. How the hell was Dobson supposed to know having a fifteen percent DNA complement with wyrms would kill just as quick as a pure-bred? Wasn't his fault they didn't do a better job screening members. You'd think they'd appreciate the clean slate. Preservation of the Human race and all that.

The voice mail clicked on again. That asshole was avoiding his calls. Dobson punched in the priority code and heard the beep-beep of the push-to-talk override.

"I know you're there, Garrett. I can hear your Senior Special Agent status echoing all over my holding facility."

"Good afternoon, Colonel Dobson. I was just standing here speaking to one of your guards. Seems he can't find the key code to open the cell you're holding my Agent in." The echo disappeared which meant he'd switched the walkie-talkie off. "Misunderstandings do happen."

Arrogant bastard.

"Way I hear it, your Agent was getting busy with my prisoner. I told you, Garrett. You cannot take the animal out of the forest, dress it up, and expect it to do anything but dump your trash and shit on your rug." He stood up, looked out the window and resisted the urge to motivate the pilot by putting a hole in the co-pilots head.

Never know when you're gonna need a spare.

"As you know, Colonel, Haley Night is Kin. The whole 'touchy-feely' thing is Kin. It's their nature. I saw the video tape--"

"Did you see all of it?"

"I saw enough of it to know she handled this interview like any other. If nothing else, she was conservative."

Conservative? Dobson stared at the phone. The cigar in his mouth rolled from right to left. Garrett said something, but he missed it. He was too busy trying to think of who he could call to hang his ass out to dry.

But the truth was, Garrett also had connections. Mr. Senior Special Agent of the monster squad somehow kept blocking any and all of Dobson's attempts to get Haley moved to I-O status. With I-O status, Dobson would be in charge of her miserable hide, and that meant if he wanted to make her disappear he could.

Dobson put the phone back to his ear. "Garrett, get out of my building."

"Not without my Agent."

"Do not start this pissing contest with me, soldier. You will not win."

"Colonel, with all due respect, Haley is property of the CFKR. And I'm the head of the CFKR. Last time I checked, my branch of the Bureau is completely separate from any and all military I-O operations. While you may have jurisdiction over the vast majority of Bureau affairs, this isn't one of them. You know it. I know it. And the Bureau knows it. So you have two options here. You can either release my Agent to me, or I'm going to make a phone call." His voice went dangerous. "And you will not like the results of that call."

Cursing, Dobson slung the satellite phone and sent it careening into the wet bar.

Chapter 4

Haley had the distinct feeling she was falling and came awake with a start.

If she had been falling, it was too late to stop it because the concrete floor was kissing the side of her head. She waited a moment, trying to get the feel of her body and assess the damage. There was only a dull ache in her chest. Probably where the Alchemist had hit her with the triton.

She tested her fingers, toes, and then went on to move a limb. Everything responded. Which meant the falling had been a part of the nightmare.

Although, after looking at where she was, maybe the falling had been the good part of the dream and this was the nightmare.

The room was large and looked more like a concrete hole than anything else. There was a pipe sticking out of the far wall. The concave circular dip and drain in the center suggested it was a shower. The large hole, a few yards over, could only be the other appliance normally found in the household bathroom.

Haley strained her ears, listening to the silence. It was an abnormal, manufactured sense of stillness. The kind which comes from extreme ground depth and about twenty yards of solid concrete. She turned her head hoping the view would change.

Nope.

Walls were just as gray on this side as they were on the other.

She pulled herself up. Her legs felt a little shaky, but what did she expect? Her body had used up almost all her resources healing the injuries she'd gotten from facing off with Niles.

Haley continued her self-inventory since nothing critical was missing. Her blazer was shredded, as was most of her blouse, thanks to the large burn hole in the front. And her skirt was *so* not coming back from the dead on this one. However, her nine-hundred dollar Pradas looked like they could do a round on the show room floor. Who says you don't get what you pay for?

The muffled sound of arguing trickled in from behind the only part of the wall that looked like it could function as a doorway. Haley moved closer and scented the air. Except for the smells she wore on her skin and clothing from the melee, the room offered nothing except damp concrete.

The arguing got louder.

Either the people involved were too far away, or the walls were a lot thicker than she imagined.

Haley was betting on thick walls.

Really thick walls.

Silence.

She strained her ears and heard nothing but the echo of her own body. Her hearts beating, her pulse moving ... the concrete door slid open with a sharp grind and she jerked back.

An Alchemist stood staring, pin rifle in her right hand and "fuck you" written all over her face. Her black eyes danced up and down like she was surveying the scene and trying to decide the most painful way to do the deed.

The burning phosphorus smell, associated with Alchemy, permeated the air around her like the tobacco scent of a two-pack-a-day smoker. Haley couldn't help it. She took a step back. The Alchemist didn't raise her weapon, but she did step away from the opening.

It took Haley a moment to recognize the almost seven-foot-tall-line-backer of a Human, her boss Pip Garrett, as he stepped into view.

Garrett's cold steely eyes did a quick once over of the room and his lips effectively disappeared into an angry slash across his square jaw. "You all right?"

"Yeah." Haley tugged at her blazer's remains. Humans had hang ups about flashing too much skin, along with all the touchy-feely stuff. Garrett was more used to dragon behavior than most, but there was no need push it. Especially not today. Especially not now.

"Are you sure?" His gray eyes gave her a quick scan. Not in a sexual way. Not Garrett. His expression said he was just checking to make sure nothing non-Human was hanging out anywhere. "Seems the Alchemy team in charge of this place is convinced you're in *rage* and need to be contained."

"I'm fine, sir." Haley felt her face flush. Garrett always could make her self-conscious about the nature of her people. Although, with the way so many of them acted, it really wasn't that difficult.

"That's what I told them. 'Haley Night has been with the Bureau almost as long as I've been alive. She has more control than most Kin I've seen. Haley Night doesn't *rage;* she's a professional, a Female, a Class Four and my Agent.'"

Haley ran a hand through her curls. It did nothing to help the serious bird's nest starting to form. She looked at Garrett. He was still staring at her.

The fact he had not asked her if she was ready to leave did not go unnoticed. Maybe he wasn't quite convinced she didn't belong here.

"Pip..."

"Don't call me that."

Yeah, Garrett did not like anyone using his first name. Whatever possessed his parents to call him that was beyond Haley. Pip was what you named a three pound Chihuahua, not a three hundred pound man.

Of course, Humans go through a lot of anatomical changes. Maybe he did look like a "Pip" when he was born.

"Garrett, sir. I'm fine." Haley crossed her arms and tried to forget the fact her clothes made her look like a contestant on Survivor.

Garrett gave her one more up and down then nodded. "Come with me."

Haley all but ran out of the room.

It took a lot less time getting out than it did getting in. The guards had suddenly gone A-OK with no ID inspection. Section eight point what-ever didn't seem to apply when it came to pissed off Senior Special Agents. And Garrett was pissed. His scent was hot like peppers.

When the last steel door slid open it took every ounce of dignity and professionalism Haley had to keep from throwing herself across the ground and rolling in the sunlight. Blue September skies never looked so good.

She looked at her watch. The face was smashed.

Garrett said, "It's three o'clock." He watched her from the corner of his eye.

"Damn. I missed my class."

"I told them you were sick. Put it off till next Wednesday. I figured you'd have your act together by then."

They stopped at the first series of external check points and waited for the chain link gate to slide open.

Haley looked at him. "What's that supposed to mean, sir?"

He didn't answer her right away; he waited for the buzzer to sound, the gate to open, and for them to get halfway across the walk to the second check point. "Three guards are in the hospital. One of them was taken out on Life Flight. He's messed up pretty bad. Won't ever be the same again. Has a wife and two kids." They stopped at the second gate and the Alchemists on the catwalk took their time letting them out. The exit was half the distance of the other two check points. With the guard tower in front and the barrier behind them, it formed a perfect box, effectively sandwiching them between two gates.

"I'm sorry about them." And Haley was. Niles might not have cared about Human life, but she did.

"I know you are." Garrett looked up and made an angry sound in the back of his throat. "Damn."

Haley saw it too. A crowd of people rushed around the edge of the prison yard, carrying large homemade signs slashed with red letters--kill the wyrm.

Garrett groaned, "Christ on a Cross, don't these people ever sleep?" His eyes flipped up at the Alchemists who were moving like molasses in January. Obviously giving the protesters enough time to make it around the yard to where they were about to exit.

Wasn't this a restricted zone? Unauthorized personnel will be detained and all that? Haley was pretty darn sure the Earth for Humans junkies were not authorized.

"Someone must have made some phone calls."

Garrett grunted in agreement. "Some of the guards here have life memberships."

"Great."

The first of the protestors slammed into the fence screaming obscenities. Garrett stepped in front of Haley and flashed his ID. If they saw it, none of them cared.

"Kill the wyrm!" The chanting drowned out any threats Garrett made.

"I'm sorry about this," Garrett said.

But this wasn't anything unusual. Sad to say it was pretty much standard operating procedure.

Haley side stepped a protestor's attempt to impale her through the fence with the sharp end of his sign handle. There weren't that many of them--fifty tops. But it didn't take long for all of them to join in. Pretty soon, Haley and Garrett had to step all the way back, to avoid getting hit.

"Where the hell is their security?" Garrett grabbed one of the sharpened sticks and yanked it through the chain link, shredding the sign and obliterating the photo of mutilated Human bodies that had been stapled to the front.

Someone spit and Haley caught it on the side of the face.

"Damn it." Garrett moved in front of her.

Haley wiped her cheek and scanned the screaming Humans. She caught sight of a white van pulling into the parking lot. "I think we're about to have bigger problems."

Through the breaks in the waving signs and flailing arms Haley could just make out the Channel Two logo on the side of the van.

Oh yeah, they were about to get some really big problems.

Garrett yelled into his cell phone, demanding they get the riot squad out.

"Cleanse the Earth!" The next round of chants began and someone got out the bullhorn. "No more Children of Cain!"

Humans and their Biblical references.

The Channel Two news van opened up and the reporters and camera crew filed out like well-trained SWAT team members. Instead of HK-416 they had the latest Sony HDs.

Protestors were shoved out of the way as the camera crew and head reporter made their way through.

Surprise, surprise, Sandra Munly was leading the pack. Seems she was always first on the scene when it came to anti-Kin news. Only thing stopping her from shoving the microphone in Haley's face was the twelve foot chain link wall. If there hadn't been razor wire at the top, she would have probably climbed it to get an exclusive.

Sandra spoke into her microphone, "Haley Night, is it true you attempted to aid serial man-eater,Niles Fury in an escape attempt today?" She stuck the end through the fence like she could skewer a reply.

Talking to reporters was about as effective as scratching poison ivy.

And yet you just can't help yourself.

"No. Nothing like that happened here," Haley said.

A camera lens hit the fence almost level with her face. Haley let Garrett push her back again. His hand came up in front of the lens.

"We have no comments."

Sandra Munly seemed to be having a hearing problem. She moved her microphone closer to Garrett.

"We've heard reports that as many as five guards are critically injured and three are dead. Can you confirm or deny this?"

"What part of 'no comment' did you not understand?" His eyes went up to the guard tower. "Tell me those bastards are not smiling."

Haley took a quick glance. "Looks like they are, sir."

Garrett flipped open his phone again and dialed.

Sandra Munly turned her mic and camera onto one of the protestors.

"Can you tell us why you're here today?" Haley caught the sneer the reporter flashed in her direction.

"To wake up America!" the protestor screamed. "We have to stop these things from polluting our planet, our gene pool, our chances of survival. They are a disease, they are filth, they are nothing but child killers and rapists..."

Haley turned away. It was better not to listen.

All of Garrett's yelling must have finally gotten to someone. The sound of foot falls echoed across the parking lot as an Alchemist team approached, their batons beating in time with every step.

Garrett growled. "About damn time."

Haley wasn't sure which were worse: the protestors and their bullhorn or the Alchemists and their magic.

The riot squad filed out and cut the crowd in half. Sandra protested as she was separated from her crew. The gate opened. Garrett led the way. The riot squad did their job but barely. The trail they cut was narrow but it got her to her car.

When Haley saw it the only thing she could say was, "Shit."

Her '65 Mustang had all four tires slashed and the words "cunt" and "wyrm" scratched into the primer paint. The back windshield was busted out and it looked like someone had backed their truck into the side. By the color of the paint it was most likely the silver suburban parked over on the other side. It was also the only other car within a hundred feet except for Garrett's state-issued sedan.

Something hit Haley in the side of the head. She recoiled from the wetness and slapped at the white bits clinging to her hair.

Eggs. The protesters were now throwing eggs. There were so many nasty meanings in that. Eggs were what they had smashed in Texas, back in the eighties, when the Queen of Houston was assassinated by the local people and the Dens were destroyed. Only those eggs had living Kin in them. While Kin accept the strength of the Dominant, the killing of that which has no chance to fight for life was an insult which almost caused a civil uprising--of Draconian proportions.

Garrett's coat came down over her head and she let him push her towards his car. The dull splats of bursting chicken eggs followed them. He shoved her into the driver's seat and she crawled across to the passenger side. Haley didn't come out from under the coat until she was sure all the doors were closed. Garrett fumbled with the key a second before the engine roared to life.

Well, at least they'd left *his* ride alone. Haley glanced back at her car in the rear view. One of the protestors stood on the hood and urinated through a brand new hole in her windshield.

She sighed. "My car..."

"You were going to get it repainted anyhow." Garrett threw the sedan in gear and hit the gas.

"It's not the paint job I'm worried about. Do you know how much it costs for leather seats?"

Garrett slammed on the brakes when one of the demonstrators stepped out in front. Haley caught herself before spilling onto the floor board.

The man shook his sign at them, screaming. At some point all the insults just blended together until it was nothing more than a rash of unintelligible gibberish. Garrett inched the car forward using the bumper like a cattle pusher until the guy had enough and got out of the way.

But not before taking one last swing with his military boot and taking out the mirror on Garrett's side.

The sedan pulled out into the two-lane and the ADF shrunk away in the distance. It was a while before Haley spoke. "Thanks."

"For what?"

"Back there. For coming to get me. They weren't going to let me out, were they?" Garrett didn't answer. He didn't have to. Haley knew when Kin wound up in holes like the ADF they usually didn't get out.

"They said you shifted without clearance."

Her hearts stuttered. If she was getting fingered for shifting, then Niles had to be dead. Why did that bother her?

"Is he dead?" Haley's throat felt too tight and her head too heavy. Garrett glanced at her then back at the road. "Garrett..."

"No, not yet. You didn't answer me."

"No. No, not full form." She knew better. It didn't matter if you killed in self-defense or the defense of others, even if it was one of your own. If you did it in full form it was an automatic death penalty. "I pulled a little strength is all. Some claw, scale, but I did not shift."

"I told them to send up the surveillance when they sent your briefcase."

"I did not shift." Saying it out loud made Haley feel better.

"I believe you. I think they were just trying to bide time for Colonel Dobson to get there."

"Why?"

"Because then I wouldn't have been superior on the scene."

"He'd pull rank?" As if that was new. Haley didn't know much about Dobson, but what she did know was bad. He was a little too Human-Puritan for her taste. And Farley hated him.

Garrett kneaded the steering wheel, making his knuckles turn white. His scent changed.

"What is it?" Haley asked.

He gave her a sideways glance then his eyes were back on the road.

"Garrett?"

The man shifted in his seat and the muscle in his jaw ticked. "Dobson's been sending me promotion forms with your name on it." Another quick glance as if he might be concerned she was still there.

"And?"

"I've been denying them."

There had to be a good reason for Garrett to deny Haley anything, because he knew she did her job and did it well.

"What kind of promotion are we talking about?"

"He wants to give you I-O clearance."

Haley leaned back and stared out over the dash. I-O clearance? That was pretty much a free ride card. She'd never heard of Kin having it. Only a few top Human military and Folk internal investigation team members had it. And she wasn't military and she sure wasn't Folk.

"Somehow I get the suspicion that being I-O isn't all that?"

Garrett nodded. "If you're I-O, the Bureau owns you, and the only ones using I-O members are the Director and the Military Branch. Dobson runs military operations. If you had I-O, Dobson would call the shots." Which meant she could wind up right back in a lab. That was not something Haley wanted to relive again. Sure, it had been done with the intentions of bettering both species, but living like that had been terrifying.

"And you told him no?"

"Yes."

"Good." When she glanced his way he smiled. "I have the feeling he wouldn't be the type to give me a corner office."

"No, he wouldn't. Dobson is a dangerous man." Garrett's hands flexed again and his knuckles popped.

"And?"

His smile fell and the tick returned. "After this little incident today, I've requested an investigation from upstairs. What happened today shouldn't have. No one in their right mind would have sent you in with Niles Fury."

"I got the email this morning. The D.A.'s office okayed everything with the Director and I went in. I left you a message with Claire." Haley shivered. "If you think I jumped the fence on this one..."

"No. That's not what I'm saying at all." He glanced at her again and this time his stare lingered. There was a little worry in those storm cloud eyes of his. Haley looked away. Other Humans showed weakness, never Garrett.

She stared out the window and watched the tree line start to shrink as it was replaced by more and more concrete. "Then what are you saying?"

"I called the Director after I got the call you were in holding. No one okayed anything with her. She didn't even know you were gone. I called the D.A.'s and asked around. No one knew anything about the request."

Haley stared, well aware her mouth was hanging open like a barn door. “I got the email directly from the D.A.’s office. It came from Marco’s email account. I swear.”

Garrett nodded. He flicked on the blinker, and took the I-20 off ramp and headed into downtown.

“The email came from the D.A.’s office. I checked it myself before I came and forwarded it to upstairs. Just in case. I had Ken in IT double check what I found. He said it came from the D.A.’s office, too.”

Good. If Ken said it came from the D.A.’s office, then this wasn’t some figment of her imagination.

“He verified it as coming directly from the D.A.’s account.”

Even better.

“So what’s the problem?” she asked.

“Paul Marco didn’t send you the request. He decided after Bob...” The “pissed his pants” went unsaid. “He decided whatever Niles had to offer wasn’t worth putting another person through that. They were worried Niles tried to make Bob do something...”

“You mean *push* him?” Haley shook her head. “He’s Male. Queens do stuff like that, but not Males. Males just don’t have that kind of metaphysical power.”

“He’s old, Haley, really old.” Garrett turned onto Industrial Street. “No one’s sure how old he is. Even the old Hatching records, preserved by census, don’t have an exact date.”

“You could ask his Brother.”

“What Brother?”

She shrugged a little. “Niles mentioned a Brother ... what?”

Garrett gave her a look. “While the dates of his hatching are fuzzy, the one thing that isn’t are the number of eggs in that clutch. And there was only one.”

Which was unusual. Clutches rarely had less than a hundred. Unless, of course, he’d once been a Prince. Still, why would Niles talk about a Brother he didn’t have? The records had to be wrong. If he really was that old, it was a distinct possibility. After all, it’s not like they make a spell check for stone tablet five-point-oh.

She glanced at Garrett, but he was watching the road. He took another right and headed up Peach. The CFKR building was only a few blocks on the right.

He said, “I’ve requested a full I.N.I. on the email, and the D.A.’s office has issued its own full internal investigation.”

Why would someone send her a trumped up email so she would meet with Niles Fury? What would it accomplish?

“What are you thinking?” Garrett pulled the car into the back lot and parked it in his usual spot. The thrum of the sedan’s engine made Haley miss her Mustang. Not because they sounded anything alike. Quite the opposite. It was a sad reminder of how good hers felt. She was going to miss the vibrations of the engine biting into her bones.

“How I’m going to miss my car.” It wasn’t a lie, but it also didn’t fool Garrett for a second.

“Before that.”

“Who would want me to talk with Niles and why?”

He gave a nod. A short quick one that said he was thinking along the same lines. Garrett opened his door and Haley followed.

“Here.” She started to hand him his jacket then looked down at herself.

“Keep it until you get changed.”

Yeah, it was no secret she kept a few extra clothes in the downstairs locker room. Getting bled on wasn’t all that uncommon of an experience when it came to interviewing her people.

“Thanks,” Haley said. “For everything.”

Garrett’s gaze was hard. “Nothing about you is ever boring, you know that?” A small dark smile replaced the thin slash of his mouth.

“Great. Is there an Employee of the Month award for that?”

The smile cracked and he almost laughed.

Almost.

Chapter 5

Haley was out of the shower in record time. She finished getting dressed and worked on getting her hair dry. Black dominated her wardrobe--it was easier to mix and match that way--but now she wore a red blazer with a black skirt.

Her shoes were the same three inch heels she'd started the day in. Garrett didn't approve of her choice in footwear. But at five-foot-three she needed the heels to give her an extra few inches. The neck cramps from looking up got old. Besides, they made her legs look good.

Haley knew she was not immune to the kind of vanity that infected Kin from coast to coast. But she hadn't had the choices of form and shape that so many of her people were given. She was by no means unattractive. The way Human men looked at her confirmed that ample hips and breasts were well appreciated, but she lacked the artificial perfection of god-like beauty.

Instead of being obsessed with unblemished beauty in her white-scale days, she'd been fascinated with the details of the Human body, such as the hair on their arms, the scars on their skin, the change of pigment depending how much sun their bodies were exposed to.

The results had been a less than perfect form, flawed in ways synonymous with Humanity. It also made her almost impossible to pick out in a crowd. Unless, of course, the one doing the Where's Waldo routine could sniff out the difference. Haley had long ago accepted that her lack of Kin perfection was fate, but it didn't mean she couldn't enjoy nice clothes and expensive shoes.

Very. Expensive. Shoes.

As Haley walked down the hall and through the front lobby, she knew the news of what happened that morning was already making its way around the office. She'd have to be blind, deaf and dumb to not notice the averted eyes, the cold glares and muffled whispers. Even though she'd been with the Center longer than the building had been standing, there were still people here who didn't trust her. Hell, a lot of them didn't even like her, especially the women.

Haley couldn't decide what was worse: the men who thought she was a whore, or the women who also thought she was a whore. Only worse because she wasn't even discrete about it. She'd given up trying to explain things years ago. Why bother? Her job was to deal with her people, which meant a lot of touching and palm licking.

And Humans just didn't do palm licking.

She walked into her office, dreading the next round of office rumors she was going to have to deal with. But it could have been worse.

I could still be down in that hole, who knows how deep, waiting for someone to realize I was missing.

"Hey..."

She looked up. Farley was sitting in her chair with his feet up on her desk. The floor was littered with Post-It notes folded into paper footballs. By the look of the place, he'd been at it for a while now.

Housekeeping was not going to be happy.

He slid out of the chair and glided across the floor.

Farley was the only other Kin who worked the Atlanta Bureau and he wasn't even an Agent. Garrett had tried to give him Agent status once, but Farley was Male. A relatively low-man-on-the-totem-pole-type-Male. Okay, even that was giving him a status booster. Farley was Food, which meant his control just wasn't what it needed to be.

After a few write ups he'd been dropped back down to an informant. The pay sucked, but at least it was a job. It kept him licensed and legal outside the Dens.

Still, he was better than average about working with Humans. But there was no mistaking him for one. Farley wasn't tall and broad like most Males, but his skin had the flawless ethereal look. His eyes were large with thick lashes. Too pretty for a man. Now that he kept his hair sheared short, he didn't have those lovely red curls to soften his facial features as much. If it weren't for the short hair, the tawny muscles and his squared-off shape, Farley would look feminine.

Haley hated to admit it, but she missed the curls.

"You okay?" Farley smiled in a crooked way which said he was thinking nefarious things. But then, he had a one track mind.

Haley pushed the door shut behind her and let out a sigh.

No, she wasn't okay. She leaned into her friend and he wrapped his arms around her and pressed his face into her neck.

God of Man, it felt so good.

A deep thrum kicked up in Farley's chest and the sound of it reminded Haley why she loved her Mustang so much.

He stroked her back. "Are you hurt?"

Haley didn't trust herself to speak, so she just shook her head.

His mouth touched her neck, his tongue pressed down on her pulse. The sensation was calming. Better than alcohol or tranquilizers. If Humans only knew what they were missing.

Haley turned her head so her nose was against Farley's neck and all she could smell was his scent. It was nothing like Niles. His scent screamed power, Farley's whispered comfort.

He pulled her to the small two seat couch and made her sit. Haley said nothing to the fact he'd broken about a hundred taboos about Males initiating contact.

The truth was she just didn't care.

No, Haley liked it that Farley didn't act like other Males. Oh, he knew how to revert to the mode of survival when it came to working the Dens, but when he was with her, he knew she wouldn't pull the dominance card.

She didn't want to pull it.

Farley drew her into his lap until she had one leg thrown over his thigh and her entire body was pressed into his. He stroked her back and rubbed his cheek along her jaw while she curled against him and listened to him purr.

Haley petted the soft cotton of his black T-shirt. Farley didn't have her hang ups about clothes, but then, he was usually in the Dens. At the office, Farley's choice of baggy skaters, black urban shit kickers, and various heavy metal T-shirts were out of place. But in the Dens, he fit right in. Haley touched his forearm and traced the gold and bronze pattern of his *Nevus*. Most Kin only had one. Farley had a rare trait and displayed mirror images, one on each arm. His hold tightened.

"How bad is it?" He'd know exactly what she meant. The media backlash for this kind of crap always got to her.

"Do you really want to know?"

When she looked at him, his dark brown eyes were flecked with gold. He smiled, flashing fang.

Typical Male. Low threshold.

She sighed. “Yeah, I do.”

Farley slipped right into reporting mode. “News has been on all morning. Lots of exclusives with EFH members.”

Great. Put the bigots on the news. Give them plenty of air time. Haley heaved another sigh and closed her eyes, wishing she could go back and start the day over. “What else?”

“Channel Five is flashing about eight seconds of security footage showing Niles doing a number on those Human guards.”

Haley moaned.

“Channel Two has that and another snippet of you getting top.” He grinned.

“I was holding him down.” She glared at him. “I had one hand around his heart and the other in his lung, for crying out loud. I don’t do sex in public.”

‘Cause that’s exactly what a large majority of her co-workers would think. Not to mention the public. Nobody would bother to take into consideration all the blood.

Farley’s grin widened. “I know. But I still like to hear you say it.”

Haley sobbed. She just couldn’t hold it any more. It was the worst of her Human impressed habits. Crying. Real crying, the shoulder-jerking, earth-shattering kind. Kin weren’t supposed to cry.

“Hey, hey, I was only kidding.”

“All I wanted to do was prove I could be trusted outside this damn building.” She didn’t resist when Farley pulled her face up and made her look at him. His thumbs erased the tears out from under each eye. He sucked them off one by one.

“Who says you can’t be trusted?” His eyes searched hers. There was more gold in them now and little flickers of copper-red. “You’re completely trustworthy, Haley. You’ve got control like no other.”

“And yet, every interview I do, I have someone leaning over my shoulder. The cops are afraid to be in the same room with me. The other Agents don’t want me on any case they deal with. I’m stuck here, in this building, every day.” And what made it worse were the restrictions the higher-ups put on her. She had to live in a certain area of the city, attend at least half of the office functions, and go to Human Sensitivity Training at least once a year. Not to mention she wasn't allowed past the Wall into the Dens.

Farley shushed her. The thrumming in his chest kicked up a notch, easing her tensions. His hand went to her throat and he stroked her under the neck with his thumb.

"Why do you do this to yourself?" He sounded so sad. "Why do you stay with them?"

She knew what he meant.

It was an old argument. It wasn't that Farley didn't understand. If anyone was capable of it, he was. He'd been her friend for a very long time. Haley's adoptive Mother needed a way to *feed* her. Fresh kill could only do so much. The metaphysical side of her biology couldn't be sustained by human standards of consumption.

Back then, it was common for Alchemists to used pinned Kin in the labor trade. Haley's adoptive mother picked Farley because he was small. If only she had known his reputation for being a man-eater. Farley stayed with Haley in the little town she was in and eventually the town became a city. With each passing generation of Human life he always asked her why she endured the hate to stay.

And for her the answer was simple.

She stayed because it was all she knew.

Besides, Medan had made it clear that she was not welcome in the Dens.

Haley wiped her eyes and sat up. She sniffled once, cleared her throat, then pulled herself off the sofa. She had work to do. There would be forms to fill out about the incident and she needed to check her voice mail. It was always full with requests from other Agents who needed her expertise in dealing with Kin. Expertise that was mostly book-learned and supercharged by genetics.

The rumors, glares, and ugly whispers would pass. They always did. At least here she had purpose.

Farley held onto her hand, and she looked down at him and smiled.

She pulled away, went to her desk and sat down. Haley pulled up her email. When she looked at Farley he was sitting on the edge of the couch watching her. "You work tonight?"

"Actually, I'm off. I was thinking about a movie."

A movie was a great idea. Just like cell phones, Haley had no idea how anyone ever lived without them.

She scanned her inbox. "Sounds like fun. What are we going to watch?"

"Um ... that's kinda what I wanted to talk to you about..."

When she looked at him he was digging the toe of his boot into the industrial carpet and staring at it like he might find a lost gold nugget or something equally impressive.

"Don't tell me--"

Farley held up his hands. "It's her birthday."

Haley rolled her eyes. Farley just couldn't seem to get it. He was playing with fire when it came to screwing around with the office help.

Farley peeled himself from the sofa and eased across the floor. It was hard not to watch him move. By nature all Kin moved with liquid grace, but Farley was downright breath taking. He slid onto the edge of her desk and stroked her arm as she hammered in her password.

"You're mad." It wasn't a question.

"No, I'm not."

"Then why are you abusing that keyboard?"

She stopped typing and looked up at him. His face was a careful picture of blank beauty.

Talk about a poker face.

She frowned. "I'm not mad."

"Jealous?"

Yeah, he'd enjoy that. Another Human hang up he could pick at her about. If only it were that simple.

Haley caught Farley's hand and made him quit petting her. "You're going to break Claire's heart."

"No, I'm not."

"Yes, you are." She finished hammering in her password and opened her inbox. "You'll break her heart just like you have all the other office help. And then they'll come to me, all boo-hooing and blubbering, wanting to know what aspect of Kin culture they got wrong. And I'll tell them, same thing I always say..."

"It's not you, it's him," finished Farley.

Haley glared at him, totally unamused. "And if I'm lucky, she won't have some jilted ex-lover who seems to think by trying to beat the living hell out of you, they can win back"--she put the back of her hand to her forehead and pulled a Scarlett O'Hara--"the love of their life."

Farley waggled a finger at her. "Hey, you're pretty good at that. Maybe you should consider acting."

She ignored him and continued, "Or a pissed off big brother who's bent on revenge because you broke his little baby sister's heart."

Farley snapped his fingers. "Don't forget the psycho, tire-slashing, stalker chick who thinks you're 'standing in the way…'" He even made air quotes.

"Trust me. Four sets of tires are not that easy to forget."

"And I still plan on paying you back for those."

"Riiight."

"No seriously, I'm working on it." Farley petted her arm again as she opened her mail.

"I just worry you're going to wind up losing your job because you keep sleeping with all the office help."

"Just the women..." Farley poked around on her desk. "Where's that jar of candy?"

Haley lifted the corner of a paper stack so he could see it.

Farley rescued the jar, then picked through the various colored wrappers."Did you eat all the green ones?"

"They're on the bottom."

He made short work of the wrapper and popped the candy into his mouth.

"Seriously, Farley, you really need to stop."

He shrugged. "I can't help it if they find me attractive."

Haley shook her head. It was more than that. As Food, he'd survived the hatching grounds by turning the hunger of others to something he could control, something that made him more interesting than a snack.

Pleasure. Sex.

For him it was a natural as breathing.

Four hundred years was more than enough time to perfect technique. No wonder every time he slept with a woman she wanted to *keep* him.

Haley sighed and went back to reading her mail. There wasn't much. Just a few internal memos, some spam mail, and one from an unknown sender. She clicked on it.

Beside her, Farley said, “Look, I’ll talk to Claire.”

“You need to break up with her now before it goes too far. Before she wants you to go with her to pick out drapes. Good grief, look at how messed up Deshi’s life is.”

Farley made a face.

“You know I’m right.” Her eyes were still on the email. She read it a few times trying to take it in.

“Unlike Deshi, I’m not delusional. Besides, if I break up with Claire, I won’t be able to tell you all the juicy stuff when we go out on movie night.”

Haley rolled her eyes. “Trust me. I can live without hearing your imitations of the sounds she makes when you ... hey ... when did Medan get email?”

Farley turned to look at the screen. “She’s had it ever since she put the Pit online. It has Wi-Fi now and everything.”

Haley read the email for the third time, but her brain flat out refused to process the words. “Seems like she wants me to meet with her.” She leaned back in her seat. That couldn’t be right. Not leave-forever-or-die Medan.

“Damn...” Farley whistled.

That was the understatement of the year. Even if Haley wanted to go--which she didn’t--she couldn’t. Because of her sensitive position with the Center she was forbidden from the Dens.

As in, her loyalties could be seriously compromised. Queens were notorious for head games, and they could really screw up a person’s brain matter, Female or not.

“Email her back and tell her you can’t,” Farley suggested.

Haley waved a hand at the screen. “I can’t. There’s no return address.”

“She’s clever, I’ll give her that.”

Yeah, in order to tell Medan she couldn’t meet her request, Haley would have to show up in person. Which put her right where the she-bitch would want her to be.

Haley bit her lip. “Maybe I could call her?”

“Good luck. Only time there’s anyone around to answer the phone is during club hours, and then the place is so loud you can't hear it ring." Farley gave her a pat on her shoulder. "You have my sympathies."

"Gee, thanks." Haley stared at the email a little longer. Maybe she could get Ken in IT to do a trace on the IP. And if all else failed there was always snail-mail.

Someone knocked on her door. Farley hopped off her desk and crammed his hands in his pockets. Human sensitivity training at its best.

"Come in," Haley called.

The door opened and she didn't need to look up to know who it was.

Speak of the devil. Claire Patterson. Her ears must have been on fire.

"Hi, there." Claire's voice was way too sticky sweet to be addressing anyone but Farley. "Did I interrupt?" Her cornflower blue eyes did a lap around the room.

So polite. Hard to imagine such dirty little things coming out of that mouth. Haley stared harder at her screen, not reading any of it.

"Um ... no. We were just talking about Agent stuff." Farley inched closer. His fists made lumps in his pockets. No doubt, he was just dying to reach out and touch someone. But of course that would have broken ten thousand Human sexual harassment rules.

Thank you God of Man, those kinds of Taboos didn't exist for Kin.

"I can..." Her hands made little butterfly motions. "I can come back later if you want. Becky said she saw you come in and..."

Haley glanced at the woman from over her monitor.

"Naw ... no way. I was ... I was just coming to find you." The expression on Farley's face was a cross between adoration and innocence.

"Yup, he sure was." Haley grinned wide, hoping it looked as painful as it felt.

Farley threw a glare in her direction and she shrugged.

He turned back to Claire, all smiles and bedroom eyes. "Hey look, I've got tickets to the movies tonight. I was hoping you'd want to go with me." Good one. Buy the tickets first, then ask. 'Cause if she did have any plans she'd feel guilty that he wasted part of his measly paycheck. "And I made reservations at that little Italian place you like so much."

Whoa, no wonder he didn't have the cash to pay for Haley's tires.

Claire smiled. "That's so sweet. Dinner and a movie. I'd love to."

Haley popped her head around the monitor and said, "I hear that new hack and slash is good ... *Friday the Thirteenth*, I think? Lots of T and A, if you get my drift." The suggestion earned her another searing glare from Farley.

She had to give him credit. He was getting good at the stink eye look. He gave her his back. Haley rolled her eyes and went back to not reading her email while Farley eased in for the kill. He slipped an arm around Claire's shoulders and walked her to the door. And Haley didn't fail to notice how he angled the Human on the other side so Claire wouldn't be able to catch any of the disgusted stares she might toss her way.

The door clicked shut and Farley's shadow rained all over her desk again.

"I think you're jealous." His tone suggested he was excited by the concept.

"No, I'm not jealous."

"Not even a little?" He pinched his fingers together.

Haley sighed and propped her chin on her hand. "Would it be a turn on if I was?"

"Yes" He eased a little closer to her desk.

"Then no."

Farley leaned in and raked his teeth across her cheek. "Don't wait up."

Haley growled as he sauntered out of the room laughing.

Damn him. Farley was going to wind up in some serious shit one day. He had no idea how possessive Human women could be. The thing was, it was never him they went after. It was almost always her.

Her door opened.

"I'm still not jealous, so you can take your happy ass--"

She snapped her mouth shut. It was Detective Bauer. The man leveled his dark eyes on her. She said, "Sorry, I thought you were--"

"Are you busy?" That's Bauer, right down to business.

"Um, no. What can I do for you?' Haley stood up and straightened her jacket.

"You sure? I know you had a bit of a rough start this morning."

Great. He'd probably been down in the common room watching it on the flat screen with the rest of the uniforms. The Center didn't have a common room; it had a break room, equipped with four vinyl chairs that had escaped from the sixties, and a half-working coffee maker.

"Yeah. About that..." Damn, how did she go about explaining this one? Especially to Bauer? "Nice suit." Oh great, that was brilliant.

Bauer smiled and touched the dark coffee jacket like he was still taking in all the new and shiny it was giving out. His large, equally dark hands adjusted the already perfect lapels. "The wife picked it out."

She'd done a good job. Haley had never met the woman, but she knew how to dress her man.

"It looks nice on you." An awkward silence lingered for too long.

Bauer cleared his throat. "Look, I've got a lawyer downstairs in the Tank with a busted nose screaming lawsuit. His supposed-to-be client is in interrogation room six, licking the blood off his fingers like he's just gone to KFC. So, I couldn't give a rat's ass what those idiot reporters blabber all over the news on things they know nothing about. And those boys at the PD know you keep their asses out of the hospital on a daily basis, so they won't dare talk smack about anything." He crossed his arms, uncrossed them, and then scrubbed a hand over his half inch brush cut.

Haley tried to knock the stupid grin off her face but it wasn't going anywhere. "Interrogation room six?"

"Yeah..."

She motioned to the door. "Lead the way, Detective. Lead the way."

Chapter 6

Detective Bauer gave Haley the stats on the detainee as they walked down the stairs and across the underground breezeway connecting the CFKR building and the Atlanta PD.

"His name is Creyal. Young, fifty years tops. Vice has been working tips on a new gang that just moved into the city."

"What's the name?" Names said a lot about a gang. Like whether or not they were Folk, Kin and what they were involved with. Faeries usually specialized in weapons (technological and magical), plant extracts, and sometimes endangered beasts or their parts. Kin usually dealt with illegal flesh trading, domestic slavery, and drugs. There wasn't much Haley could do about Folk because they were free Agents. However, Kin could be pressured by involving the Queen. More than likely, Medan was the biggest source of illegal activity, but she liked to keep that kind of business at an arm's length. If the problem people started attracting attention to her club, she usually made them disappear.

And that train didn't have a return track.

"No name," Bauer said.

That was unusual.

They came to the stairwell. Bauer pushed the door open and held it for Haley.

They headed down the stairs. He said, "We think they may be involved with a new kind of drug trade." At the next door leading into the Tank, he paused and pulled a vial from his pocket.

Haley took it and held it up to the light. The contents looked like liquefied gold.

"Temporal fluid?" That's what it looked like to her. She'd seen enough of the stuff from her own temporal glands. She used it to Roll Farley when they *fed*. It opened the lines for metaphysical contact. Farley wasn't strong enough to endure the exchange without it.

"That's what the lab boys thought until they tested it." Bauer pushed the door open.

"What is it then?"

"A synthetic." Bauer shrugged. "Seems like it's close enough to the real deal to give the desired high."

With Humans everything was a "high". The effects of metaphysics or Alchemy were rarely as simple as a "high."

Haley said, "Uh, temporal fluid doesn't make you high. Not like your normal street crud."

"Then what do they use it for? They're obviously injecting it intravenously. That Kin down there has track marks all over his arms."

If he wasn't healing needle holes, it meant Alchemy was involved.

Haley tried to think of an explanation she could give in thirty seconds and wouldn't break about fifty Human sensitivity rules. "It's the atom bomb of Viagra."

There. That should do it.

Bauer's eyebrows collided between his eyes and he looked at the vial like it was kiddy porn.

"Okay, that's not the best of explanations."

"You want to try again?" he asked.

"Not really. 'Cause no matter how I try to say it, you're going to get that same look on your face."

As they headed into the Tank, the walls became a dark olive green. It wasn't a pleasant color, but it didn't show ichor stains.

Interrogation Room Six was on the right. A tall skinny lawyer stood near the door, screaming hysterically, while stuffing wads of Kleenex up his nose in an attempt to stop the red geyser in the middle of his face. Two uniforms stood by looking concerned but smelling like they were just a few steps from pissed off.

Haley stepped up between the two cops and extended her hand at the screaming, bleeding pencil man. "I'm Agent Haley Night, with the CFKR."

The lawyer fell silent. It took him a moment, but he gave her his hand. She shook it, limp dish rag that it was.

Haley motioned toward the room. "I hear you're having a bit of a problem with your client? I'm here to help you with that."

The lawyer sputtered a moment then said, "He hit me!" His eyes went up to the two uniforms. "And they won't arrest him. I want to press charges. I want them to do something about it, and they keep telling me it was my fault! My fault!" His voice cracked.

Haley kept her smile in place and nodded like she completely sympathized.

Not.

Bauer was looking through the six by six inch port hole in the door. The expression on his face wasn't a happy one.

The lawyer waved a boney finger at the door. "That-that-that thing in there ... he hit me for no reason. I want an Alchemy unit down here now!"

Haley shook her head but kept her best shit-eating grin in place. The last thing they needed down here were any of those.

"Mister..." She waited for him to fill in the blank.

"Lemmons. James Lemmons."

"Lemmons." Haley put her hand on his arm like an old friend. With a small pull she had him inching down the hall. "How long have you been with Legal Aid?"

"Two weeks."

"And this is your first non-Human assignment?"

"I've handled dozens of defense cases..."

Haley patted his arm. "But those were Humans, am I right?"

Lemmons occupied himself with trying to cram another tissue in his nostril.

"Okay, this is my suggestion. The next time rotation comes around for Kin behavior, you might consider taking the free workshop."

"I've worked with some of the finest law firms in this city, Miss Night. I can promise you I know how to conduct myself with a client." Considering he'd just called her Miss Night, he needed some workshop time before he did that to a Male. It was going to be a lot harder to stuff Kleenex up his nose with one arm shoved up his ass.

Haley eyed the guy up and down while he rotated between trying to keep his tissue in place and pushing back his comb over. He smelled like day old bacon sprinkled with something bitter. Lots of Humans smell like food to Kin. Usually it was something boring like buttered chicken. But Mr. Lemmons had a very distinctive odor Humans only acquired under certain conditions. Those conditions being the illegal plants and flowers kind. Besides, lawyers didn't come out of cushy offices to trudge in the Tank for just any reason.

"You want to file a report." She made it a statement.

"Yes!"

Haley looked over at the two uniforms. They watched her, stony faced and completely calm.

"Um, gentlemen?" She waved them over. "Mr. Lemmons here wants to file an assault charge. You'll need to call Internal Investigations since he was injured down here in the Tank by a suspect." She did her best to sound oh-so-important and in command.

The cops exchanged a look and slowly unfolded their arms.

"Make sure you take Mr. Lemmons to the hospital. Get a full blood panel including all the basic extracts and implants."

One of them reached for Lemmons and he jerked back. Haley feigned surprise.

"I'm fine, I don't need a hospital." Lemmons tugged at his jacket.

Haley shook her head. "Sorry, but it's protocol. When an incident happens on city property and people start talking like they might sue..."

"But my nose is just broken." His hands fluttered at her. "Why would all that other stuff be necessary?"

Haley smiled. "Now, Mr. Lemmons. You're a lawyer. If our insurance is expected to pay out any kind of damages then they'll want to make sure you weren't, how do I say this, engaging in inappropriate herbal recreation at the time of the incident."

Lemmons' eyes popped and his watery gaze pinged at rapid fire between the three of them. One of the cops reached for the man again. Lemmons yelped and pulled back. He lost one of his Kleenex when it fluttered to the floor and he was left fumbling for a new one from his jacket pocket while his upper lip turned crimson.

"That won't be necessary. I'm fine. I'll be fine." He plugged the leak again.

"Are you sure?" Haley waved a hand up and down at the uniforms. "These officers want to make sure you're completely satisfied with their, services."

Lemmons nodded, crammed the tissue higher up into his nose, and then adjusted his hair. Twice.

"Really, really, just, just do whatever, I'm fine." His eyes went from the floor, the walls, the doors.

"Okay. I'll get Creyal straightened out. You wait here." Haley pointed to the spot he was standing on. He gave another nervous hand flutter and nodded.

Haley joined Bauer at the door. He still had that look on his face, the one that said he didn't approve of what he saw. "Thanks."

She shrugged. "No problem." After all, it was her job.

"You ready?"

Haley took off her jacket and handed it to one of the officers. No need to mess it up. It was easier to replace a blouse. The jackets had to be tailored to fit right. Sometimes cleavage could be an inconvenience. "I am now."

Bauer turned the handle and yanked open the door.

"You may want to close that thing." Haley pointed to the window and glanced at the lawyer. "I don't think he'd be able to handle the show." It wasn't really just the lawyer Haley was worried about. She stepped inside and the door shut with a heavy metallic thud.

The room was small like all the other interrogation rooms. A badly scarred wooden table occupied one half and was accompanied by two folding chairs that looked like they'd been run over a few times and hammered back out.

Chairs got broken a lot down here. Some days it was a regular WWF match. Especially if the cops tried to handle something on their own.

Creyal was doing an impersonation of a vulture on the edge of the table. One hand was up at his mouth and he was rotating between sucking and licking the blood off his fingers.

His lavender eyes rolled up to Haley and he grinned, flashing large lower fangs that were almost tusks. It was an unusual characteristic.

His tongue lolled out, a piercing dotted the center, and he pressed it against his thumb which he pushed too far into his mouth. Creyal had a lot of piercings. Most were in his ears, but there were some in his nose, lips, and eyebrows. He was missing his shirt, which gave Haley a good view of the posts in each nipple. And of course the tattoos covering every inch of skin.

The images were of scales and fire.

Some of Haley's people fought the anti-shift laws any way they could.

The ink was so dark and dramatic it almost concealed the small round *Nevus* set at the edge of his collar bone. Unlike the flat ink, its green color glittered and rolled even in the sickly florescent light.

"Well, well, if it isn't the domesticated Female I've heard so much about." Creyal unfolded himself and stepped off the edge, his body bending and rippling in a way only nonhuman creatures could.

He was no different than most. His body was tight, carved, too perfect to be real. His leather pants hung low, flashing a thin line of hair. He had a post piercing his skin right where a belly button should be. Not all Kin impress the same subtle details. Belly buttons were kind of like pubic hair, some had them, some didn't see its use.

Haley stood still while Creyal slinked around her, his mouth open, his nostrils flaring, as he ate up her scent. Heat rose off his skin and green iridescent scales rippled down his shoulders and across his arms and chest before disappearing back under his flesh.

Creyal stopped his body inches from hers. Haley met his gaze. Bits of gold joined in with the inhuman lavender shade. Creyal cocked his head one way, then the next. His hands hovered over her shoulder. His fingers worked like he could feel her skin.

Haley eyed the track marks in his arms and neck. She frowned.

The Male eased the rest of the way around her and dropped his shoulders. Haley stared, realizing part of her was hesitant to initiate contact. This morning had gone badly because she'd overestimated herself. But Creyal was no Niles Fury. He was a mid-ranked Male at best--new, reckless, and terrified of being pinned. Not much more than the average feral. She was stronger than him, faster. Even if he did move like liquid and look like he belonged on a calendar of World's Sexiest Band Members.

He'd play drums.

Haley lifted her right hand and Creyal dipped his head down, catching her palm. He went to his knees, submissive, but not quite surrendering himself completely.

His mouth pressed to her hand and he licked it, his teeth brushing her skin.

"I smell other Males on you." Creyal pressed her fingers to his chin using her hand to stroke his own jaw and neck. Covering the other scents with his own. In a Harem, only a Dominant would take top scent. Creyal was issuing a challenge for placement.

"Are they yours?" He looked at her with curious eyes, a small crooked smile on his lips.

It was a common question and Haley only had one answer. "No."

His face fell. It was unusual for a Female to not *own* the Males who had left scent on her skin. Creyal obviously didn't know what to make of that.

He pressed his shoulder to her thigh. His hands brushed her ankles, his fingers kneading the skin of her leg as he moved them upward. Creyal stopped halfway, his gaze pleading for permission to continue.

Haley put a hand on the top of his head. Creyal's black hair was pulled back in a ponytail and slick under her fingertips. She felt him shudder and his scent blossomed. He smelled sickly to Haley. Whatever Creyal was shooting into his arms was doing bad things to his body.

The hollowed out look to his cheeks and ribs may not have been so purposely designed after all.

Haley touched his cheek and that was all.

Creyal hesitated, probably hoping she would change her mind. Haley held her stance and he curled against her, his hands dropping to a point below her knee. His head went down between his shoulders.

Haley stepped back and he let her. Of course he didn't have much choice. She'd made it clear she wasn't interested.

These moments were always a battle between Haley's biology and her Human social lessons. In the Dens, even Females who weren't interested in sex at least brought blood.

"I've never touched a Female." His eyes rolled up at her, glittering more gold than lavender now. "I do not please you?"

"Creyal, I'm here to help the local PD. It's not about whether or not you please me."

He snarled, his eyes going dark, and his face becoming harsh. "What Female rubs skin with the *Chetrah*?" He uncoiled from the floor and moved away from her. "You really are domesticated. I thought they were stories. Do you fuck them too?" He dropped his jaw, flashing his strange tusks, and flicked his now forked tongue.

Haley crossed her arms and watched the display. It was typical, and nothing but hot air.

Creyal's hands slid to the front of his pants. He popped the button and pushed them downward, flashing enough that Haley could tell he was going commando.

"I can offer you a lot more than any walking snack-cake."

Haley didn't look away when he slid his hands down the front of his leather pants. Looking away was a sign of intimidation. A Male like Creyal was stupid enough to try and take advantage of that.

He rolled his head around on his shoulders, obviously enjoying himself.

"Creyal."

He paused in his massage. "Yesss…"

"I need you to cooperate with the Detective outside that door."

He pulled his hand out of the front of his pants and stroked his stomach. For Kin, the gesture was sexually explicit. A lot more brazen than rubbing his cock.

Haley did not avert her eyes, and she was careful to keep her expression bored. After a moment, he quit.

Creyal shrugged. "If I cooperate, will he bleed for me?"

She almost asked who. Bauer or the lawyer. Convincing the lawyer he might need to *feed* his client could prove interesting.

Might even be worth the disciplinary action.

Instead she said, "No."

Creyal shrugged, moved to one of the metal chairs, and melted into it. He swung his bare feet onto the table top; he wore a jade ring on his middle toe. Shoes were another thing a lot of Kin went without. Most were barefoot and shirtless until the middle of winter.

"Then why should I tell them anything? If I have something they want, then they should be willing to give me something I want." His hand rested on his stomach just above his unbuttoned pants.

"Creyal, this isn't the Dens."

"No shit!" His eyes were angry. Haley had insulted him by not acknowledging his perfection or his willingness to please her.

At least she didn't eat out his throat.

It was a good thing a lot of Males never got to touch a Female. Most of them wouldn't survive it. And Creyal was most Males.

Haley moved next to him. She smoothed out her skirt and pulled herself up on the edge of the table, scooting near him, but positioned higher up. At her height, sitting in the chair put her head lower, and he was unsocialized enough it would come across as an opportunity. And Haley really wasn't in the mood to throw away another skirt.

Haley touched his hand resting on the table edge. The Male froze. Unlike Niles, he didn't lose the look of something real or alive. Creyal just looked scared.

"Creyal." She moved her hand up his forearm and paused over the track marks at the crook of his arm. Profound sadness filled Haley's insides. Creyal was killing himself, slow and sure. He was filling his body with Alchemy poison and it was eating him from the inside out. When she looked at him his eyes were very wide, his face averted, his mouth parted so he could pant.

"Why are you doing this to yourself?" Haley asked. He almost looked at her but couldn't seem to pick up his head.

When he didn't answer, she let the weight of her palm press down.

"Creyal?"

He closed his eyes and shook his head.

Haley watched him. Something was off. Kin falling into drugs wasn't any more unusual than Humans, but Creyal didn't act like a Male using drugs to satisfy his needs. Something else was going on.

She could force him. Males expected that kind of thing. Here in the Tank Haley could do what she needed to without worrying who she was going to offend. It was the closest she got to the raw visceral nature of the Dens.

But sometimes it was just nicer to use honey instead.

Haley put her finger up to her mouth and sliced it wide with a quick flash of fang. The sweet taste of her own blood hit her palate. She held her hand out to him, the blood welling up on the end of the already closing wound. Creyal jerked back, his eyes very wide, his face pale. She was offering him blood. Females did not just give blood to Males and most certainly not lesser Males. When he started to shake his head she pushed her finger to his lips. Creyal's eyes fluttered. He was hesitant at first and then drew her deeper into his mouth. A deep thrum kicked up in his chest. His draw on her skin became desperate as the cut healed. Haley moved her finger over one of his bottom fangs and reopened the wound.

The Male made a pitiful sound and spilled out of the chair in front of her on his knees.

"Talk to me, Creyal, Kin to Kin." Haley pulled her finger from his mouth and he whimpered. His hands locked onto her calf and he pressed his face against her leg. His whole body shuddered. "I want to know why you're sticking Alchemy into your body."

He looked up at her, holding her so tight it was starting to ache. "Because that's what they pay me to do." He shut his eyes and stank of shame.

"Who pays you?" His grip tightened, but Haley didn't react. Lots of things hurt worse than Human hands gripping with abnormal strength. When he didn't answer she took his chin and made him look her in the eye. "Who pays you to stick poison in your arm and why?"

Creyal shut his eyes. His dark brows collided in the middle of his forehead hard enough to make a furrow. "These people, Humans and an Alchemist."

"Is it the stuff the cops found on you? In the vial?"

"No." Creyal pulled away and crawled to the far wall. His spine curved as he pulled himself over his knees. He averted his face and remained still. "The *sythn* is what they pay me with most of the time. The rest is cash."

"What are they putting in you?"

"I don't know. I don't ask. They take out samples as well." He unfolded an arm and looked at it. It was obvious he didn't like what he saw but accepted it.

"Where does the synthetic come from?"

"I don't ask, and they don't tell."

"So this gang is run by Humans."

He shook his head. "It isn't a gang. These aren't your usual dealers."

"Enlighten me."

Creyal leaned against the wall. He still wouldn't look at her. "They send word out in the Dens. A place and a time. The first ones who get there get the money and the goods."

"The synthetic?" Haley asked just to clarify. Creyal nodded. "So where do they meet you?"

"Different places. Usually warehouses. They bring in vans that have equipment. I don't know what they do. I'm usually too ... you know ... out of it." He ran a hand over the top of his head, pushing back hair that wasn't out of place.

"Can you give me any names?"

Creyal shook his head. "Even if I knew who these people were, they'd kill me. The Alchemist is especially scary." Most were. He looked at his arms. "I used to not ... not do it this much ... but lately they've been around more, offering more ... I figured what the hell." This time he did look up and his eyes were very sad.

Haley bit her lip and willed herself to stay where she was. "Why do you do it?"

"Why do any of us do it? I've sold sex. I've sold my freedom. What's a little blood? I need the money. Medan doesn't exactly give out enough to survive. This is easier than the ... other." He rubbed his arms like maybe he could erase the track marks.

"Creyal, whatever they're putting in you is making you sick."

He shook his head. "Kin don't get sick."

"No, we don't. At least not naturally. But whatever those people are shooting into your arm isn't worth the money they're giving you. I can smell it. You're sick. It's eating you up from the inside."

He looked away again and stared at the wall like drab green paint was suddenly the most interesting thing in the world.

Haley said, "There's a free wellness group run by a Kin named Loren. He meets three times a week with other Kin down at the old YMCA building on Morrison inside the Gray Zone. There's a meeting tonight, starting at seven. They'll have free food. Good fresh meat. It's a small group. They don't ask you your name. You just go. Talk. Maybe he can help you."

"What if I don't want help?" Creyal glared. "Maybe I like what I am, how this," he held out an arm, "makes me feel."

"If you like dying, then keep it up. 'Cause that's what you smell like, Creyal. Death. A slow kind that sneaks up on you and takes you apart piece by piece."

He snarled at her. Haley pretended not to notice. When she gave back her attention, his face was normal, Human. Even his tusks had withdrawn.

Creyal flicked his gaze up at her. "If I do that, can I *Belong* to you?"

It was Haley's turn to act nervous. She hopped off the table edge and fumbled with her blouse. "Creyal, I don't *own* any Males."

"None?"

"None."

His shoulders tightened and he heaved a deep breath. "Why not?" Haley blinked at him. No one had ever asked her before. Not even Farley. It wasn't normal for a Female to go without a Harem. But it wasn't a Male's place to question what a Female did. But now the question was out.

"I..." Haley tried desperately to think of a reason. Any reason. "I just never have. I guess I don't want one right now."

"What if you changed your mind?"

"I don't think that will happen."

"But if it did."

"Then ... then I guess I'd need a bigger apartment." She folded her arms, feeling extremely vulnerable. If Creyal noticed, he didn't show it.

"If you changed your mind, could I *Belong* to you?" God of Man, there was so much hope in that one question. Creyal looked at his arms. "Sometimes I think if I could *Belong* I wouldn't want to do this anymore."

Haley chastised herself for feeling guilty. It wasn't her job to feel guilty. Hell, it wasn't even in her biology. Sometimes Human influence could be such a bother. Saving the whales just delayed the inevitable.

What would it hurt?

It's a lie.

Not really. She just had to word it right.

"Creyal, you are a beautiful Male. Any Female would be proud to make you theirs." See, no lie. And by the look on the Male's face he seemed completely satisfied.

Chapter 7

Colonel Dobson didn't have to show his ID to get through the check points. As he approached, the doors just opened.

Like magic.

Taa-daa.

And he was wanting to taa-daa all over someone's ass. His sample Zero was gone. Walked right out of his facility. He had the means to pull rank and he could have kept her. With a little bit of work he could have brought her to rage, and then Garrett would have had to let her stay. No ifs, ands, or buts.

But there was more than one way to skin a cat ... er, Kin.

If that pompous-self-righteous-holier-than-thou-Kin-lover was going to refuse Dobson's requests to promote Haley Night, then he'd find a way to bring her here.

That plan was still in the cooker. In the meantime, she'd fallen right into his lap and he'd missed it.

Dobson fumbled for a cigar. He'd mangled his last one right after they landed. Now he had to make do with cheap substitutes. Rolled out in a sterilized factory, rather than off the sun-warmed thighs of Cuban whores.

Of course, there weren't many women who weren't whores in his book. Any of them would fuck you if you paid them enough, promised them enough, or knocked them around.

His own wife had proven that fact. A whore, born from a whore. Filthy bitch. If he'd known what she was, he would have killed her sooner.

Fucking cunt.

But no. She'd lied. They all lie. There wasn't one out there who didn't. They all told you they loved you. As if the lying wasn't bad enough, she had to go and steal from him. Take his hope, his dignity.

And then she took it from his son.

As if squeezing him out of that hole between her legs had given her some kind of entitlement. That was *his* son. His seed built that boy and she'd contaminated him. Now the boy was poisoned, defiled ... impure.

And it was her fault.

When the first signs had manifested back in '81, they'd taken William to the doctor like any concerned parents would. Back then, the information on Human genetics was grossly limited, let alone the genetics of the monsters.

William was a sophomore in high school. Star quarterback, top ten in his class, a regular hometown hero.

Then the leg pains started. The Whore had wanted to take him to the doctor, saying it wasn't normal, not at his age. But the boy was still growing. A big fine man he was going to be, too! Tall, like his paternal grandfather. The Whore had insisted there was something wrong. Obviously she was guilt-ridden. She'd known what was coming. She'd known and she didn't care!

The leg pain didn't stop and it progressed to other limbs. William had to stop playing football and pretty soon the pain kept him in bed, curled up and weeping like an infant. They'd taken William to the doctor, who had to sedate him to get x-rays. The x-rays had been frightening.

Something was seriously wrong.

The doctors called a staff meeting and they took turns looking at the films. William's bones were being twisted and broken, right through his muscle. Strange new spurs were forming in various locations as bits and pieces splintered off. They'd given it some fancy name. Osteo-metaphysical-manifestation or some shit.

Then the fever almost killed him.

After three weeks of hospital time, his body had been transformed into a caricature of something Human. The Whore wouldn't even look at him then. Dobson looked at him. Dobson was not afraid to look his son in the eye, even when he was begging him for death.

And one day the screaming just stopped. William was a mess but he didn't hurt any more. It was like his body had decided it would take a break. Another set of x-rays showed strange rounded areas in his spine and shoulders, like he'd grown joints for limbs he didn't have.

The doctors still didn't know what to make of it. They sent for specialists across the United States. Medical journals wanted to do interviews, and in desperation to help his son, Dobson agreed.

Looking back, it had been the wrong decision.

Not long after the bone changes stopped, William lost his hair. All of it. And it didn't happen slow. It was like someone had dosed him with a round of chemo. The nurses went in to roll him over and jarred him enough to shake it all loose.

Like a fucking Christmas tree that'd been left in the house till March.

Three days later, his teeth followed the same path his hair took.

Dobson knew then. In his gut he knew. In Beijing he'd seen half-breeds, quarter breeds. The half-breeds were bare of any hair, not even a patch around their nuts for crying out loud. Completely slick, from head to toe, like they'd been taking Nair baths or some shit. And they were always Male.

Then there were the Lesser-Breds. That's what the wyrms called them. Lesser, because they were mostly Human. As if wyrm blood was somehow better. Lesser-Breds were second generation down or greater from the beast blood.

The quarter breds or less were a little more difficult to spot. They looked Human. Hair, height, freckles and moles. And they could come in both sexes. Unless you caught a look-see at those devil marks they had on their body they could fool you. Some of the birth marks were large and obvious but a few had small ones which were easy to hide.

On occasion, the color of their eyes gave them away.

It seemed the last genes to want to let go would be passed down from any females in the line. The Kin gene equivalent of the X chromosome wouldn't be turned on in the presence of a Human X chromosome. But pair it with a Y and the switch was flipped.

'Course it wasn't the doctors at that backwoods hospital who figured it out. No, sir.

As soon as Dobson realized his son was somehow carrying Kin blood in him, he'd transferred him to a private military facility. The U.S. government owed him the favor. Once there, specialists in metaphysics examined the biological changes happening to William. A team of geneticists was called in for consult.

It was confirmed. William was a Lesser-Bred. The problem genes had traveled down from his mother's side of the family, attached to the X chromosomes, and now that there was a son in the Female line, they could be expressed.

Dobson took the news straight faced. By the time the white coats were done talking about pleiotropic effects, mobile DNA, sex linked traits, and recessives, he'd made up his mind to turn this problem into a solution.

They didn't know how long it would take. But William wasn't going to be William for much longer. Apparently, the further removed from the Kin sire, the more unstable the genes became. Results were, to say in the least, unpredictable.

Dobson went home and took his wife out for a ride. He punched her in the head, knocking enough skull into her gray matter she was never going to get up. Didn't matter. She wouldn't need to where she was headed.

He sold her for a hundred bucks to a flesh trader in the Dens.

Dobson had his son moved to the basement of the Atlanta Draconian Prison Facility and waited for the rest of him to disappear.

It took awhile, almost five years, but pretty soon he wasn't one bit Human. He'd transformed into some hideous combination of Kin and man. He wasn't as large as a pure-bred wyrm. About the size of a horse. His front legs were different, more Human in their construction, as were his back legs. But his head had changed, leaving him with a bottom jaw that jutted out too far and a knobby skull that looked like it belonged on an iguana.

From hell.

The rest of him was very Draconian. He even had scales, a tail, and wings.

His mind was the last thing to go. Dobson was grateful for the loss. He was tired of the thing asking him about the Whore every time he walked into the observatory. Now it just stared at him with its yellow eyes.

But his son had been the doorway.

Dobson was going to solve the world's problems. He was going to kill all those fuckers. Every last one of them, as well as any bastard offspring they'd managed to slip into the population.

There was just one problem.

According to his metaphysical biologists, Male Kin had highly varied DNA. There just wasn't a way to make the virus fit to any one series of nucleotide combinations. Unlike Humans, Kin had well over a dozen different types. And depending on location, some of one kind weren't found in another.

It put a little bit of a wrinkle in his plan.

No. It put a goddamn wrench in the thing.

In order to build a virus specifically coded for a certain species, it would have to recognize something unique and only found in that organism. Because of the wide variation in Kin DNA, there just wasn't a way to design a virus that would recognize all of them without putting Human lives at risk.

While some collateral damage is acceptable in any war, the margin for error in this battle just wasn't flexible.

The Human race depended on it.

Dobson's metaphysical-biologist theorized that while Male Kin were extremely varied in their genetic makeup, it was reasonable to believe Females might offer more consistency.

It had taken some work but he'd managed to arrange the raid on the Texas Dens. With some very powerful weapons and military genius, Dobson pulled off what no one thought was possible.

The fact Texas was the last state where killing Kin was as legal as swatting flies didn't hurt.

It took a little over eight-hundred military men, three hundred Alchemists, and a shit-load of napalm, but they managed to burn her out. Three of the Females were killed along with a thousand or more Males, but one other survived, including the Queen. Dobson's white coats had been right. Females held a series of nucleotides which could be universally patterned with any Male they sampled. And they had sampled thousands.

So they'd set to work designing the virus. Thanks to the prison system, Dobson had easy access to a constant supply of DNA. They tested the Female samples against everything that came through and it always worked.

Until they sampled Niles.

That wyrm sent the white coats scrambling. Richards suggested it was because of his age. Which was a reasonable theory. If certain lines had lost their maternal lineage, and those Males were never utilized, then there was the potential for rogue DNA sequences that might be missed.

Unacceptable. This new information threatened to undo over twenty years worth of preparation. Dobson was almost ready to accept the fact they'd have some survivors when a hit came up on sample zero.

The Institute for the Advancement of Kin and Human Relations was one of just many fronts Dobson used for routine population checks. He had a group in thirty-five out of fifty states. Not only did the front give him an easy way to do the research he needed on a massive scale, it provided income for his project. Which was by no means cheap.

Dobson's budget made the U.S. government look like the weekend *Penny Saver* ads.

One of the things the Institute did was set up med clinics to pay the poor and unfortunate for their willingness to donate to science. Sample Zero was cataloged at a local Burn Research drive. When her DNA was entered into the system it took about three weeks for it to be tagged.

Richards brought Dobson the news. And for the first time in over a year Dobson slept like a baby. He thought finding the donor would be hard, but Zero was Female, and by God, she'd left her real name and address on the donor information card.

Haley Night.

Occupation, CFKR Agent.

Fuckin'-A

The same Female Kin he'd been trying to get moved to the Military branch since it opened.

Now it was as if God himself had gift wrapped the wyrm and put her on his doorstep. There was no doubt in his mind creating the virus was providence.

Dobson entered the observatory, and anyone who wasn't busy made like they were. Richards barked orders to other white coats and the air filled with a lot of yes-sirs and no-sirs. The viewing room emptied as the colonel went in. He didn't have to tell them to leave. They all knew the rules. The external windows dimmed as if on cue. Dobson refused to hesitate, in spite of the revulsion squeezing at his throat.

He always made himself look at it.

Every day.

Looking at it reminded him what this was all for.

There was a small framed picture of "William-before" sitting on the ledge. He was in his gold and white jersey with the indigo number seven on the front. In the picture he was smiling, his blue eyes bright, his skin flushed from practice.

Dobson touched the photo and imagined his son graduating, going to college, entering the military, making him proud. But that's what every parent did when they lose a child. They imagine what things would have been like.

It took everything Dobson had to peel his eyes off the photo and look at the thing in the room below. It was thin because they couldn't get it to eat anymore. Its pale white scales were peeling and its once bright yellow eyes had gone cloudy.

Dobson knew it was dying but he didn't care. Richards had suggested they dispose of it years ago because they had more than enough samples and there was no need to keep it here. Feeding it. Cleaning up after it.

Getting rid of it would have been easy.

It was keeping it that was hard.

And Dobson was a firm believer the hardest things in life were what made a man.

Colonel Dobson put a finger on the intercom button and clicked it on. The sound of its sandpaper breathing filled the viewing room.

"Good afternoon, William." His voice was steady today. That was a good sign. The thing below craned its misshapen head and tried to look up at him. Its mouth parted and nostrils flared. He could hear it inhaling, trying to scent him out.

In one lumbering step, it shifted its weight and moved towards the observatory window. The head came up a little higher and turned so its better eye was tilted upward.

Dobson had seen a lot of horrible things in battle, men blown apart, men eaten alive, but compared to this, all that was a Hallmark card. Looking at the thing that had once been his son did something to Dobson's insides. It showed him weakness he'd never known he had.

But he was fine.

Doing great.

Till it uttered a single word from its jagged mouth.

"Daaaaddeeeee..."

Chapter 8

Haley headed home a little after seven and hailed a cab. She considered walking until the sky rumbled and spit out fat drops of rain here and there. The cabbie got her home in less than ten minutes. She was heading up the steps into the foyer of her building when the sky split and dumped everything it had.

The Browning Building didn't look anything like its name suggested. The wide, fat square, with its white stucco walls, looked like a cross between 1960's architectural art and a La Quinta Inn. It was ugly, and home to mostly retired couples, but it was clean and rat free.

Which was more than she could say for Farley's place near the Dens.

The elevator came to a stop and dinged. Haley headed up the hallway. Beautiful Deshi sat on the edge of a large clay flower pot next to Haley's door, picking at the skeletal remains of the petunias she'd neglected to death. He was dressed in a light brown Baroni, looking every bit of the Prince he was.

But then, with his looks, he could have made a paper sack look good.

He ran a perfect hand through his blond locks as he stood up. His eyes went to the floor. Deshi was a rare thing among Males. He was high up on the dominance ladder not because of his strength, but because of his breeding. He'd been a gift from his Mother, the Queen of Jersey City, to Medan. He was one of eleven Males presented to her by various ruling Queens as possible breeding prospects.

While almost all Kin are born from a Queen, very few of them ever have the pleasure of calling her Mother. Queens hatch their young, then they push them out of the nest into the heart of the Hive. Male Hatchlings learn at an early date to eat or be eaten.

Deshi was the exception.

While most hatchlings are exposed to various body types and allowed to choose their forms, Deshi had been designed. From the blond hair on the top of his head, down to his pinky toe.

It was the way for a Queen to display her reproductive and metaphysical strengths. Haley couldn't figure out why Medan passed him up. It definitely wasn't because of his looks.

"Hey, sorry I didn't call first."

"No problem." Haley fished out her keys and undid the dead bolt. "You hungry?"

"Oh, no ... no. I won't be staying."

She pushed on the door with her shoulder and it opened. "You sure?"

"Yeah. I just..." His baby blues came up then fell again. "I was on my way home from the office and I thought I would come by and say ... goodbye ... and thank you." Deshi shuffled his feet and crammed his hands into the pockets of his jacket. It wasn't hard to believe he was less than fifty. Maybe his youth was the reason he married Emily.

Haley watched Deshi for a moment, then retrieved her key from the lock and headed across her living room to her bedroom in the back. Deshi stuttered at the threshold before following her in. He closed the door she'd left open.

"I want to try again." He followed her across the room. "I love her, Haley. I don't want her to find out. She's suspicious already."

Haley held up her hand, stopping him. The Queen of Jersey City had centuries of experience with Human anatomy. Deshi was beauty personified. So much so, it hurt to look at him.

Beside the entry for the "world's most perfect Male specimen", was his face and body.

"Is she going to go through with the bonding or not?"

His eyes hit the floor. Well, that was a *ginormous* NO.

"Deshi..." She took a step towards him and he withdrew. When she stopped, Deshi's shoulders slumped and his head dipped. He'd just made a terrible social no-no, but Haley wouldn't hold it against him. She played with Humans, so chewing out throats just wasn't on her to-do list.

With a sigh, Haley went into her room and stripped off her office wear. The shoes went first, then the jacket and the skirt. Normally she'd hang it all up, but she was mad, and kicking her clothes across the room was better than kicking Deshi.

"Emily promised she'd think about it." He sounded hopeful. But then he always sounded hopeful.

Haley unbuttoned her blouse. "Look, I know you want to be with Emily."

"I love her."

Yeah, well, Kin don't love, buddy. So what you're feeling isn't little red and pink hearts. All the books on Kin behavior and psychology said so. She'd read 'em.

All of them.

"You want to *keep* her, Deshi. You want to make her *Belong* to you. That's not love, and the sooner you realize that, the better off you'll be."

"I do love her. I know you don't understand that, but I do. I want to make this work between us, and I can't do that if I keep coming to you."

Haley glanced at him over her shoulder, unsnapped her bra, and tossed it on top of the pile. She stood there and let Deshi look at her. She turned back to her drawers and rummaged for a T-shirt. "You know, I don't question that you feel very strongly for Emily." She slipped on the long white jersey. It fell almost to her knees. When she looked up, Deshi had moved a few steps closer. His eyes glittered silver and gold.

She hoped he'd just give in, but Deshi was strong-willed and extremely good at controlling what he was. Haley went to him and put a hand on his stomach. "There's no doubt in my mind you would do anything for her." He already had. Eight months ago she'd gone with him to a plastic surgeon who specialized in removing *Nevus*. The pale white birthmark tagging Deshi for who he was had been replaced by a long nasty scar.

Using Alchemy to burn it off was the only way to make it permanent.

The Prince put his hand over hers and she could feel heat rising off of him.

He said, "I love her..."

"But does Emily love you?" The look of desperation in his eyes turned to anger. Haley stepped away and walked back into the living room and into the kitchen. It was more of an attachment to the main room, since only a short counter top separated the two spaces.

Deshi followed, growling, "She loves me." He sounded like he was trying to convince himself more than her. "And she deserves to have me to herself. You, of all Kin, should understand that." Haley went to the fridge and pulled out the horse steaks she'd left to thaw. Horse meat was way better than cattle.

More protein, less fat, great taste.

"Yeah? And what are you going to do when she changes her mind *again*, about going through with the Link, and you wind up killing her because you *raged*?"

He flinched and he shook his head. "I'd never hurt Emily. Never."

"Never is a long time, Deshi. You're very young. You're very controlled, but still very young. You've been married to her, what, two years?" She counted off the months on her fingers. "Yeah, two years and two months. And how long have you been coming to my bed because Emily won't do what she needs to do to *feed* you?" Haley made a big show of counting down again. "Oh, gee, that's right, twenty four months. That's two years! What a shocker!" The steaks hit the counter with a thump and she shredded the plastic and threw it into the sink. Cabinet doors slammed and plates rattled. Haley pushed the meat onto a platter, opened the microwave and set it for thirty seconds. Just enough to knock the chill off.

"So tell me..." She put her hands on the counter. "Did you ever tell her what really happened to the dog? Or does she still think that Chihuahua ran off when you opened the door?" Deshi blanched. The dog was the reason the affair started. Barely two months into their marriage the issue of Emily *Belonging* reared its ugly head.

Linking meant Deshi and she would share a metaphysical tie transcending any kind of marriage vows. But *Belonging* to Deshi conflicted with Emily's constitution of women's rights.

What Emily didn't know was not long after their extended honeymoon, she'd almost become a midnight snack. All because Deshi wasn't getting fulfilled.

"That's not fair. You know how I feel about that."

"Well, how would you feel if it had been her instead? You ate her dog, for Christ's sake. Because it had her scent on it." Deshi crunched down, and hugged himself, looking more like a scared little kid, and less like a six foot six Male.

Haley growled and dug her fingers into the counter. She was careful not to extend her *chelae* or she'd shred the cheap aluminum. "I just don't want to see you executed because of Emily's selfishness." She took a breath. "I care about you, Deshi. You're my friend."

"I know." He sniffled and swiped at the sliding down his cheeks. It was a bad habit he'd learned from her.

"God of Man..." Haley came around the counter and made him sit on one of the bar stools. His baby blues spilled over and a sob escaped his lips. "Deshi..." She wiped the tears away but they kept coming. "Oh, Deshi, don't cry. Please..." Haley pulled him to her and felt him tremble. She hated what Emily did to him. It pained her to see that Human woman reduce the Male into a weak sobbing shell of himself. He was a strong Kin, strong about anything, except when it came to Emily.

Haley rocked Deshi and thrummed in her chest. She stroked his head and neck. His hair had been long once. But Emily had insisted he cut it off, too.

Emily had gotten everything she wanted in Deshi: a trophy husband, a sports car, a big house in a gated community, membership at the exclusive resorts, nights out on the town, and the bank roll of a Draconian empire. So far, the only thing Deshi had gotten was a lot of mental anguish and a serious case of bad self-esteem.

It was fact. Kin just couldn't deal with a monogamous Human relationship, unless the Human was willing to do what it takes to fulfill metaphysical needs, as well as physical ones. The Jersey City Prince needed Haley in ways he was still too young to understand.

The racking sobs finally stopped and the tears followed. Deshi's body relaxed under Haley's constant petting and deep purr.

Beautiful Deshi opened his mouth against Haley's neck and pressed his tongue to her pulse. She fell still. If he wanted to take from her, she would freely give it. But she didn't want to make any movements that would push him over the edge of his control.

'Cause right now it wouldn't take very much.

The Prince's hands tightened on her hips and he pulled her closer. She didn't resist, but she kept hers on the back of his head and neck.

"I love Emily." Deshi's teeth raked her throat. "I love her and I want to be with just her." Heat flickered across his skin and the scent of his *need* became over-powering.

When Deshi stood up he took Haley with him, making desperate noises in the back of his throat. Her butt landed on the counter and she rolled her head back, letting him know he could take whatever he wanted.

Haley straddled him while he rubbed himself against her core. She could feel the length of him under his expensive suit and knew from experience he'd be wearing silk boxers. Deshi snarled and pulled his face out of her neck. When Haley looked at him, everything Human was gone from his eyes. They swam solid gold. The color of *need.*

His lips drew back, flashing long sharp teeth. Every muscle in Deshi's body shook with resistance. Had he looked at Emily this way the night he killed her dog? What would have happened if he had woken her up and she had seen his beautiful face, contorted with fangs and dragon eyes?

She probably would have screamed, and without the bond, the Prince would have seen her as only one thing.

Prey.

But instead of killing and eating her while she slept, Deshi had grabbed that stupid dog from its sleeping place at the foot of the bed. He'd made it into the bathroom before losing control and chewing out its throat.

According to Deshi, he didn't remember actually eating it, only waking up covered in blood. He panicked at first because it was red. But the scent was unmistakable. Mitzi the dog had taken one for the team.

Deshi pawed at Haley's T-shirt. He almost lost it, and bit down on her shoulder, but didn't break the skin. Haley wished he'd just let go. Tear off his clothes and sink his teeth into her up to the gums. But his control was remarkable.

Lucky for Emily.

Deshi's grip loosened and he backed away. Haley put her knees together and watched him regain his composure.

He exhaled a shaky breath. "I should go."

No. You need to stay. Please. For your sake. Haley kept her thoughts to herself and watched him as he smoothed out his shirt, fixed his tie and adjusted his pants.

When he looked at her all trace of Kin was gone. "Thank you for everything." Deshi headed towards the door. Haley watched, wishing she could change things for him.

Deshi paused with his hand on the knob and Haley said, "If you need me, my door is always open for you. Key's still in the same place." He nodded once then left.

Chapter 9

Haley died when she went to sleep. But all Kin slept like the dead. It's why Humans were able to kill so many of them with primitive weaponry. It's also why Females surrounded themselves with dozens and dozens of Marked Males. That way there was always someone awake.

And willing to die in order to protect her.

By the time Haley hailed a cab it was ten after nine. She finished tucking in her blouse in the back seat. Her blazer was green, her skirt cream like the blouse. Haley tried to use the rearview mirror to fix her hair, but the cabbie kept getting in the way because he was using it to try and see down the front of her top.

She buttoned the last three buttons to make a point.

Late again. This was getting to be a bad habit.

Claire waved at her as she came through the front office and headed down the hall. Haley ignored her. She didn't have time for chit chat.

Bauer was in her office, standing there like he'd just walked in. Haley knew damn well he'd been waiting a while.

"I'm sorry, I overslept. I know I promised to be here at nine--" He held up a hand and stopped her. Great. This couldn't be good.

Bauer put his hands into his jacket pockets. It was no Baroni, probably a Men's Warehouse special, but it still looked nice. His wife really knew how to adjust them to fit. Today he was wearing soft gold tweed. It made his skin look like chocolate.

"I just came in. Thought I would wait. Everything went fine. Creyal met with Lemmons again this morning with the A.D.A. and he was a total gentleman."

"Total gentleman?"

Bauer laughed. "Okay, maybe that was a little too generous. But he didn't hit anyone, bite anyone, and he only made one request for someone to bleed, and took the rejection better than most."

"So what happened?"

"The A.D.A. took your suggestion and gave him six months mandatory counseling. Lemmons got him ninety days in a communal prison. If he behaves himself, he'll do thirty days at the most. If he agrees to work as an informant, and gets us a few locations, he'll never see a day."

This was good.

Haley said, "He'll do it."

"How do you know?"

"He's mid-ranked at the most. Doing time, even thirty days, could potentially kill him." And no matter how bad things got, dying wasn't something Kin embraced.

Haley tried not to think of Niles and how he'd begged her to kill him.

But then, he'd also imagined a Brother.

A knock on her door made her look up. Claire poked her little blond head in and tossed her eyes back and forth between them. Haley started to tell her to get lost, but Bauer excused himself before she could use him as an excuse not to talk.

"I'm busy, Claire." Haley turned to her desk and moved papers around. By the look on Claire's face, and the way she smelled, things must have not gone so well last night. But she didn't leave. In fact little-miss-secretary just invited herself right in and shut the door.

This was it.

The coming to Jesus moment where Claire would to cry all over Haley and demand to know if she and Farley were sleeping together.

Which was a capital Y-E-S.

Haley put down the file she'd been pretending to look through and faced the woman. Her cornflower eyes couldn't quite meet the Haley's stare. Haley sat back on the edge of her desk, crossed her arms and waited for Claire to get on with the show.

Her small bird-like hands fluttered and her thin face flushed until her nose glowed.

This was it. Any moment. Waiting ... waiting...

The dam burst and the tears spilled out. Right behind it was a flood of vocabulary, butchered by sobbing. Haley could only catch bits and pieces, something about *movies, dinner, friends, birthdays* and *bitch.* She gathered the bitch must have been a reference to her.

Haley handed Claire a couple of Kleenex from the box on her desk when it became obvious her sweater sleeve just wasn't cut out for the job.

Claire blew her nose into the extra aloe silky-softs, doing a very good impression of a goose.

Claire hiccupped.

"Claire, I'm sorry." Haley stood up and handed her another half-dozen tissues. "I'll tell you what I tell all the women who come in here crying. Farley is Kin. He's never going to offer you a ring. He's never going want to meet your parents. And he sure as hell is never going to get married. He'll have all the sex you want, whenever you want, but you're Human and I'm Kin--" The slap came out of nowhere. Just one hard blow which set Haley's cheek on fire. She slid her gaze over to Claire. Haley touched her hand to her lip to check for blood. It was clean. "I think you'd better leave now."

"Whore!"

Farley was right. When Claire was mad, her voice did sound remarkably like a cat caught in a blender.

Claire swung her hand, but this time Haley caught the woman's wrist.

Haley stepped forward until they were toe to toe. In two inch heels, they were the same height.

"As I was saying..." Haley gave Claire a little shake to emphasize each word. "Farley will fuck you, every day if you want it, but you cannot give him what he *needs.* You will never be able to give him what he *needs.* He can only get that from his own people. If you can't stand the idea of him sleeping in my bed, or in the beds of other Males ... look at me ... that's right, Males. If you can't share him, then don't initiate any relationship. He knows how to take no for an answer."

The tears flowed again and Claire's bottom lip trembled. Haley let her go, and Claire rocked back cradling her wrist.

"But why last night? Of all nights to keep him away from me..." *What?* "It was my birthday, Haley. It was my birthday, and instead of being with me, he stayed the night with you." She burst again, crying all over the place.

Haley rewound what she said and shook her head.

"Claire, Farley didn't stay at my place last night."

"Liar!"

"Look, Claire, Farley doesn't turn down free sex. Trust me. If he had plans for an all-nighter with you he would have been there." Haley stepped back, trying to think.

"He wasn't with you?"

Haley frowned. "No. Did you call him?"

"Are you sure he wasn't with you?" She sounded worried now. Like maybe she should have been more concerned for her date, instead of wallowing in her own self-pity.

"No ... no ... do you have your cell phone?" Claire shook her head. Haley looked around her office. Her briefcase was on the floor next to her chair. Garrett had lived up to his promise--now hopefully her phone hadn't gotten lost in the melee. She found it in the pocket where she kept her pens. It looked intact and the battery was still good.

Praise Nokia.

Haley quick keyed Farley's cell phone number and the line rang. If he didn't show at Claire's, it meant he'd probably never left his apartment. "Did you tell Garrett that Farley didn't show up?" The look on Claire's face suggested she would have died first. Haley rolled her eyes. "Look, go tell Garrett that..." The line picked up. Haley expected voicemail or Farley, but what she got was a Male voice she didn't recognize.

"Medan was wondering when you'd call." His Olde Tongue accent was heavy.

Haley said, "Who is this?"

The Male laughed. The sound suggested bad things done in dark places.

"Names aren't important. Her Greatness is very disappointed in you, Haley Night."

Haley looked up at Claire, who stared at her with wide eyes. Haley said, "Where is Farley?" The Male growled. There was a shuffling sound, then a rattled breath. "Farley?" She could barely say his name.

"Hey..." There was a lot of pain in that one syllable. Haley felt her heart stutter and leaned on her desk. Before Farley could say anything else, the unknown Male came back over the line.

"Why are you doing this?" Haley tried to think of protocol. Who did she need to inform? Who should she call? But her brain refused to form an organized thought. All she could think of was Farley's pitiful voice sounding ... broken.

"The Queen requested your presence and you denied her." The Male made a clicking sound in the back of his throat.

"I didn't deny her!" Not yet, anyways. "I just got the email yesterday."

"And yet you are still not here." Someone whimpered in the background.

"The email didn't exactly have a date and time. Look, tell Medan--"

The Male snarled and Farley screamed. "You will address her properly or this conversation is over."

"Okay ... I beg forgiveness." Haley's hands shook. She closed her eyes and pleaded with the God of Man to listen just this once. "Tell ... Her Majesty, that as an employee of the CFKR, I have been restricted to certain areas of the city. I'm not allowed in the Dens without clearance." The Male on the other end was quiet and so was Farley.

The he said, "The Queen is impressed with your survival among the *Chetrah*. She will grant you forgiveness..." Haley slid to her knees. "But you *will* come to the Dens."

"Yes..." Haley slumped against the desk. "Yes, I'll come to the Dens, but I have to have time to talk with my boss."

The Male was quiet again. "She will allow you to speak with your dominant. But do not take advantage of her kindness."

Kindness? Kindness would have been a warning. Or maybe even a threat.

Haley said, "Where should I meet with her?"

"The Pit." The Male said it like Haley should have known.

"What time?"

"Dark."

"Can I speak to Farley? If Her Majesty should so desire it? Please?" There was the sound of movement again. The scream which came over the line was so loud Haley had to hold the phone away from her ear. It didn't stop; it just kept getting more desperate until the line went dead.

"Hello?" Haley checked her signal. They must have cut the call. "Damn it!" She pushed herself off the floor.

"Was that Farley screaming?"

Haley looked at her. Claire stood in the middle of the room, her hands at her mouth, her eyes looking like they might pop out of her head. Haley couldn't help but feel angry. Claire should have called her when Farley didn't show. The woman knew he worked in the Dens. She knew it was dangerous for him. There was no telling how long they'd had him ... doing ... whatever.

Claire burst into tears. "Oh God, that was him ... that was him screaming ... what's wrong ... who has him ... what's...?"

Haley held up her hand. "Just shut up for a second. I need to think." She took one step, then two towards the door. Then she was running.

Haley tore down the hall. Garrett's office was a floor up and on the other side of the building. The elevator would be too slow. She took the stairs.

When she got to the top, she forced herself to calm. Her vision had gone all bright. She blinked once, three times. The ache in her teeth receded along with the auras of crystalline light.

Farley. Her chest ached.

What if Garrett didn't let her go into the Dens? What if he told her no?

But he wouldn't. He couldn't.

Yes, he could. As an employee of the CFKR, Haley was privy to a lot of sensitive information. She knew the names of snitches, undercover informants, and worse than any of that, she knew the Bureau's methods of watching the money flow, the flesh trading, guns and drugs. There was more, so much more, and all that knowledge suddenly weighed on her like a sin.

Haley knew in her hearts she would never betray Garrett, but she was Kin, Medan was Queen, and it's just fact that blood was thicker than pink slips, retirement, or even prison time. After all, Medan could make her talk if she wanted to. That power was what made her Queen.

When Haley was calm enough to trust herself, she opened the door and took a brisk walk down the hallway. She kept her eyes down, counting her steps. Two hundred and fourteen of them and she was standing at Garrett's door. Haley didn't knock; she just walked in.

Garrett hung up the phone. "Claire called."

Phones, right. Yeah. She should have thought of that.

"Medan has Farley."

"Explain."

"I received an e-mail yesterday. I really didn't take it seriously." And, boy, was she regretting that now. "It was from Medan. She requested to meet with me."

"Why didn't you tell me about this?"

Haley shook her head. "I forgot, I guess. Bauer came in and asked me for help, then I was tired, I went home." She clenched her eyes shut. "Why would she take Farley? He didn't ignore her request, I did." Garrett's hand touched her shoulder.

"Because she knew taking you is a Federal offense. She would open up a whole can of worms she isn't ready to deal with." 'Cause Haley was an Agent and Farley was an independent contractor: a specialized informant. Only he played both sides. Feeding information back into the Dens, as well as bringing it to the office.

It was a dangerous two-way game of chicken.

And Farley never blinked.

"But why? I mean, why would she even want to talk to me? She expelled me from the Dens..." Haley looked up at Garrett, hoping to find answers, but his stormy eyes were just as lost, just as worried. "I can't leave him there. If I don't show, she'll kill him." When Garrett didn't reply, she paced the floor. "I know Farley screws up here and there, but he's a good Kin. He loves his job. We owe him this. I owe him. I have to get clearance. You have to give me permission, or..." Garrett's face was still stone cold and blank. "Or I'll go in there without your permission, even if it means winding up in jail ... or worse ... Garrett..."

Her boss seemed to deflate. His eyes dropped, and he stepped back behind his desk. Garrett picked up the phone and tapped out a number Haley didn't recognize. He put the receiver to his ear. "Connect me to Greenville."

Greenville? Greenville, South Carolina was the Bureau hub. Garrett was going to make this happen.

"Transfer me to Moreland." He tapped a finger against the calendar on his desk. "Yes, sir. This is Pip Garrett with the Atlanta CFKR. I need to request a two-ninty-seven clearance." All clearances were referred to as numbers. "Yes, sir. Yes, it is, sir. Yes, sir, I have a five-oh-eight-I." Emergency scenarios were numbers and letters. Haley had never heard Garrett use so many "sirs" in one conversation. He was quiet for a moment. His lips thinned out. "Yes, sir. I understand, sir. Yes, sir." Garrett put the receiver back on the hook and stood there staring at it.

When his eyes shut, Haley knew. They'd denied his request. And still she asked, "They gave the okay, right?"

Garrett's jaw tightened. "I'm sorry, Haley."

"No ... I can't believe they would do this to him. After everything he's done for this office, for Greenville. God of Man, if it wasn't for Farley, the Green-Street Killer would still be out there hacking people up, and the Atlanta PD would still be looking for a Kin. What about the shipping manifests he was able to slip out last month? How many people did he save on that truck? How many innocent Human lives did Farley keep from becoming part of the flesh trade? In case you forgot, eighty-one. Eighty-one! Because Farley risked his life!" Haley took a breath. Her throat hurt and her lungs burned from yelling.

Garrett looked as his calendar again. "My anniversary is tomorrow. Becky and I will have been married forty years."

"What does that have to do with Farley?" Haley looked at the calendar where Garrett kept tapping his finger on the little square.

He acted like he didn't hear her. "I've got a really busy schedule today, meetings, a couple of debriefings. The usual." Garrett looked up at her and his eyes were sharp. "What did you help me pick out last year?"

Haley stared at him, gaping. Farley was in the Dens, his life on the line, and Garrett wanted to talk about what she picked out for Becky last year? "Sir, I don't..."

He cut her off. "I thought about flowers but those are too overdone. And besides, she needs something special for putting up with me for this long." He rifled through a small stack of mail sitting on his desk. "Been thinking about going all out this year." He pulled out an advertisement with a small "ah-ha."

Garrett pointed to the bright blue stone on the front. "That jeweler down on West Lane. You know, about a block or so from the south Dens? He makes these beauties by hand." He showed her the picture, but Haley didn't see it. She was too busy staring at Garrett like she didn't recognize him. "He makes the orders while you wait. Sometimes it can take hours. Unfortunately I just don't seem to have the time." His gray eyes hit hers like a Mack truck. "You're not busy today, are you?"

Haley shook her head. "I don't know how long I'll need."

"Then buy something really expensive and extravagant." Garrett fished through his pocket and pulled out his wallet and gave her a Visa card. "Just put it on that." He waved a hand at her. "And have him engrave it for me."

Haley took the card. "What do you want it to say?" She sounded as numb as she felt.

"You think of something. I'm not too good at those kinds of things." He sat back down.

"I'll get him out." Haley put the card in the pocket of her blazer.

"You do that."

"I'll do right by this, sir. I swear..."

He coughed and rubbed one eye with his large knuckle. "Wish it would rain soon, pollen is getting to me."

But it rained last night.

"Thank you." Haley didn't know what else to say.

"You'll need these." He handed her his keys. "Take the office car. It has GPS. And drive it home. You may be there a while. No need to bring it back here and then take a cab."

She knew where West Lane was, but the GPS was a Send-Receive. The data on all the cars was uploaded daily. If they were out on the road, the office could locate an employee at any time. Or if the car was parked somewhere, it was recorded for how long.

Haley closed her hand around the keys.

"One more thing, Agent. Don't be late tomorrow."

Haley said the only thing she could, "I won't."

Chapter 10

Farley flinched when something warm brushed the side of his face. He blinked, trying to clear the static from his head. He faintly remembered hearing Haley's voice. But that was impossible. He was in the Dens, and Haley never came to the Dens.

A hand stroked his cheek, then pulled his head up.

Farley recognized the face. It was one of the three Males who took him down outside his apartment. No, what Haley had was an apartment. What he had was a hole in the wall he shared with the rats.

And cockroaches the size of rats.

"Her Greatness is content with the arrangement. She has granted you a stay of execution."

Oh, right. Now Farley remembered why every bone in his body ached. Because they'd broken them. The lower caverns were cold enough to make Farley's breath turn white, but that wasn't what made him cold. His resources were running low. His welcoming committee had been at this for hours.

"Are you ready to dine yet, little dragon?" The Male's thumb stroked Farley's cheek and he leaned down close enough for Farley to get a real up close and personal view of his sharp and pointies. "Your *hunger* rises, does it not? You crave flesh, you crave blood?"

The hands of other Males worked to undo the shackles holding Farley down to the roughhewn table. His body contracted in rebellion from being stretched out so long. He screamed as his muscles pulled tight, and still broken bones tore through half-healed skin. Around him there was laughter.

Something hot touched Farley's leg. He cracked his eyes and watched as one of the Males ran his tongue from his ankle to his calf. They had taken his clothes somewhere between topside and the Hive, so there was nothing to get in his way. The Male smacked his lips, making a show of tasting him. Lots of Males liked the way Farley tasted. He used the natural born talent to stay alive.

"Are you ready to *feed* yet?"

"I'm fine. I had a big lunch yesterday."

Like hell he was.

The Human standing in the corner, looking like a food buffet, was making Farley's mouth water.

"Please, Your Greatness, let me be the life for which you need." And it sure as hell didn't help that she kept saying stupid shit like that.

The dark Male grabbed Farley's chin and forced his head to twist in the direction he was trying so hard to avoid.

"Look at her!" Farley clenched his eyelids tighter. Claws sank into his cheek and dug into the bone of his jaw. "Look at her or I will peel off your eyelids!"

He opened his eyes. Naked, clean, the pretty blonde just stood there like she'd been doing for the past several hours. There was a big black tattoo across her chest spelling out *Chetrah*.

Her name was Chrissy and she was a diehard MKFK member.

Emphasis on the "die".

Chrissy pushed back a lock of blond hair and smiled so sweetly at him.

Blond hair, thought Farley. Claire has blond hair. He tried imagining that Chrissy was Claire. He cared about Claire and would never hurt her. It wasn't too hard. Chrissy was pretty enough, but taller, with a little more shape. Claire was small, bird like, with narrow hips and a B cup.

Claire. Farley told himself. *You're looking at Claire.*

Both of them had C names.

Getting easier all the time.

Chrissy held out her hands to him.

Claire, Claire, Claire. It became Farley's mantra.

"Please, oh Great and Wise, take my flesh and my blood. I am pure. No Kin has ever fed from me. You will be my first and it will be my honor."

Maybe if she was scarred, Farley would find it easier to remember why he stayed off the Human flesh. Medan probably thought of the same thing when she'd picked the girl.

A sharp pain hit Farley in the back of the thigh as one of the Males latched onto him. Teeth pulled and tore at his skin, keeping the wound open and flowing. The little sucking noises the Male made caused Farley's hunger to kick, not to mention the ache between his legs.

Farley tried to close his eyes again, but the dark Male tightened his grip.

"You will heal faster if you will just *feed*," said another Male, close to his ear. "Look at you. You tremble. You grow cold." A hand stroked Farley's arm, traveled across to his chest.

"If you want me to eat, then why doesn't one of you offer up something?" The suggestion earned Farley a cuff across the side of his face. Something flopped against his cheek. He was pretty sure it was his ear.

"Maybe we should just fuck you and eat you?"

Farley didn't know who made the suggestion, but it sounded better than the alternative: him doing what his instincts demanded to the Human standing in the corner.

God of Man, she smelled good.

Claire. Her name is Claire.

Another set of teeth sank into Farley's thigh and a hand stroked his cock. Sex was better than thinking about food. Farley arched into the Male's grip. The shackles on his wrists gave him no slack, so he had to force himself to twist his lower half one way to keep his head tilted up at the Human.

He didn't dare close his eyes because he knew the dark Male would make good on his threat. Farley locked his eyes on a spot above the girl's head. They'd never know. Chrissy watched the torture show, a small sweet smile on her pretty little face.

Farley opened his mouth so he could pant. Between the hand job and the *feeding* he wasn't going to last much longer. He concentrated on the crack in the wall, the shape, the direction, how the dim light of the catacombs dulled the pyrite flecked along the edge. Farley's body shuddered and he forced himself to hold back. Every second he withheld, was another second Chrissy had to grow a brain and take off. Teeth hit Farley at the base of his cock and sank into the soft flesh of his groin. He bucked, losing himself and bringing another round of laughter from the Males. Farley came again from the sensation of being *fed* on.

Farley rolled his eyes, wanting so bad to shut them.

"Are you ready to give in yet?" The dark Male caressed his neck and back. His *chelae* left burning trails along the way.

Just a little bite. You can take it from her wrist or ankle. It will barely leave a scar.

I will not eat Claire!

"Actually..." Man, it was getting hard to think. "I was thinking you could undo these shackles and let my hands go, and I could show you how to give a proper hand job?" Farley managed to smile at the dark Male. But he didn't smile back.

"Has he eaten yet?"

The sound of Medan's voice made the blood in Farley's veins form ice. All around him the Males withdrew. How many were there now? Five, six?

"He still resists," said the dark Male.

"Farley? Resist?" The sound of Medan's movement filled the cavern. Her scent threw Farley's instinct for self-preservation in overdrive. He kicked, broken legs sliding in his own blood and body fluids.

Farley's view of Chrissy was replaced by a large golden eye. He jerked back but the shackles held him.

"The Little Gold who could."

If Farley didn't know better, he would say she sounded amused. But she'd have to have a sense of humor to be amused, and that was one thing Medan lacked.

Oh, and a conscience.

The Atlanta Queen's massive bronze head swung closer. Her nostrils flared and her hot breath raced over Farley's skin. She circled the alter, her scales sliding with each step, her wings rustling like fall leaves. Farley flinched with each and every stir of air.

"Farley..." She said his name like it was meant to be pronounced in Olde Tongue, *Fah-ruul-e-I.*

Farley forced himself to raise his head and look at the Atlanta Queen. She truly was beautiful.

"Tell me, Little Gold. Do you think Haley will save you? Or do you think she will leave you to become the *food* you were meant to be?" Medan turned her great head in his direction, her lips peeled back, flashing teeth as long as his hands.

"Haley won't come." Farley's insides screamed because he wanted her to come. He didn't want to die down here. Not at the hands of Medan or her Marked.

The Queen's long black tongue flicked out, the forks curled, testing the air. "I think she will come."

Farley shook his head. "They'll never grant her permission." No, the things Haley knew made her too big of a risk to be lost to the Hive.

"I think you underestimate her, Little Gold. She is predictable ... to a fault." Her head swung over to Chrissy. Farley had to give the girl credit, she didn't even flinch. "Are you displeased with the *food* I offer you?" Her tone went all sing song. "Is she not to your liking?" Medan moved around the Human, her massive form snaking with impossible grace. "Farley? Your Queen is speaking to you."

"I'm on the wagon..." Farley twisted against the iron shackles until his wrists ached.

"But she is willing." Medan held up a large taloned hand and made like Vanna White.

Pat, I'd like to buy a vowel please.

Farley shook his head. "Please, My Queen, I cannot take Human flesh and blood."

"But the meat is sweet, the blood rich." Medan turned her gaze on him. Farley couldn't look at her. The fear she bled was just too much. It made his balls want to burrow up into his stomach and his skin crawl away. Her tone darkened. "It never bothered you before."

Lots of things never bothered him before. But that was a long time ago, over a century.

"I seem to recall a Little Gold, so fierce and violent, his thirst for flesh the thing of legends." She moved closer and Farley jerked back.

Medan purred. "You instilled such fear in the hearts of the *Chetrah*."

"That was another time, another place; I don't eat Human flesh anymore. I gave it up."

"Because of her?" Medan's voice was completely calm, which meant her anger was rising.

"Yes, my Queen."

"To please her?"

Now that was a loaded question and Farley knew it. If he answered no, it would be a lie. If he answered yes, Medan was going to be pissed, because he was more interested in pleasing Haley than his Queen.

The Kin who gave him permission to keep breathing.

"Please..." Farley turned his head away and pressed his face into his arm. His skin was clammy against his lips.

"Look at me, Farley. Gaze upon your Queen with the admiration and fear you should have for her." His neck felt like it was rusted, but somehow Farley got his head to turn. His eyes opened too, which was a plus. "Good." Medan eased back and sat up on her haunches.

God of Man, she was huge.

The Queen put her front legs on either side of the Human. Her massive claws glistened in the low light. "Step forward, *Chetrah*." Chrissy didn't even hesitate. "Stop." She stopped at the edge of the table. Farley slid back as far as he could. He could smell her, a rich buttered chicken scent and the sweet undertone of chocolate.

Farley shivered, his body ached, and his *hunger* kicked the inside of his ribs.

Her name is Claire.

Her name is Claire.

Her name is Claire.

"Please, Medan..." Farley inched forward, even though he didn't want to. The shackles on his wrists released. He didn't know who opened them. He didn't look. He couldn't peel his eyes off the Human.

An ache shot through his jaws as his teeth punched through. The taste of his own blood filled his mouth and fed his *need,* making it stronger. Farley's metaphysical energy flared, responding to the prospect of *food,* knitting his broken bones, and closing wounds. A new ear unfolded from the side of his head as his preternatural-self sucked the last bit of his reserves, leaving him void. Starving.

Farley's vision slid away, turning the twilight of the cavern into daylight.

"I am here for you, My Lord." Chrissy smiled her beautiful smile.

Farley reached for her and she came to him "Your name is Claire."

"If that is what you wish, my name is Claire." Her lips touched his and he could taste her. "*Feed* from me, Your Greatness."

Farley wrapped one hand around the back of her neck and the other around her waist, and pulled himself up on his knees. Chrissy went with him, throwing her head back, offering him the softest part of her throat.

Farley wasn't going to be able to stop. His control was gone, his barriers were down. There was only one thing he could do and that was turn the need for *food* into sex. He'd learned very early in the hatching grounds how to survive. It wasn't very difficult because the lines between *food* and sex often crossed for Kin, and any other time they were so close together it was easy to mistake one for the other.

Farley turned with Chrissy in his arms and pinned her to the table. He thought of Claire, how sweet she smelled. How she laughed, how she called to him when...

He kissed her, plunging his tongue in her mouth, tasting her as a person. He touched her shoulder, ran a hand to her breast. He rolled a thumb over her nipple and she cried out.

Chrissy stared at him with surprise, but clearly wasn't put off by the prospect of what he was asking from her. She rolled her head back and forth, arching under him, as he dipped low and suckled a sharp pink point. Her scent changed. The buttery smell was gone, replaced by arousal.

"Claire…" Farley said it aloud. Hearing her name made it more real. "Claire..." He kissed her again and she reached for him. She stroked him and he moved between her legs. *Slow.* He needed to make this last. Every minute was more time for Chrissy to live. Maybe with any luck Farley would burn himself out. He'd be dead but at least the she would live.

Chrissy moaned, opened her legs wider, arched herself up to him. She glistened wet and pink. Farley hissed when she pressed herself against him. She grabbed his face and shoved her mouth to his, plunged her tongue between his teeth. He tried to stop her, but it was too late.

The sweet taste filled Farley's mouth, crawled along his palate, sank down into his gums, and even when he tried to spit he could only swallow. He looked down at Chrissy and she was smiling, a bit of crimson on her lip.

She giggled. "I think I cut my tongue on your teeth." Her hand touched his cheek. "Don't stop." She moved closer and nibbled his jaw. "I like this."

Farley felt his hunger rise like the climax of sex. And he was just as powerless to stop it. "Oh, Claire, I'm so sorry."

Chapter 11

Haley parked the car in front of the jewelry store and went inside. Like a lot of shops in the Gray Zone, the place was caught in a time warp. Somewhere between the fifties and sixties by the look of the tile floor and contrast of wood paneled walls. The poor lighting sucked handfuls of square footage, making the place seem smaller than it actually was.

And it was small.

A young couple stood off to Haley's right admiring several pieces inside an old wood display case. An older man at the other end tried on watches the salesman showed him.

Haley checked her watch. It was five o'clock. The sky had already turned a reddish gold bordering on copper. Sunset would be in the next half hour.

"Can I help you?" Haley looked up at the salesman. Like all Folk he had a perpetual teenage appearance.

She handed the shopkeeper Garrett's card. "I want something big, beautiful, and expensive. Surprise me."

His smile went Grand Canyon wide.

Haley left the car sitting in a parking space on the side of the building. Her ID and her cell stayed in the trunk. She slid the keys under the wheel well, leaving them on the tire. Taking a cab was too risky because someone might recognize her if they were asked about it later.

She walked up the dirty block toward the high stacked stone construct, known as the Wall, which enclosed the Atlanta Dens.

The Gray Zone, where the Dens were located, occupied a thirty mile strip of abandoned city and was a conglomeration of economy apartments, old factories, small businesses, and clubs. Each new decade had left its mark on the place, until it resembled a collage of ancient ruins and turn-of-the-century window shops. Change came slow to the Gray Zone. Progress had stopped and started at various points until entire decades had been misplaced in its growth.

Here poverty was thick, but pride was thicker. It showed in everything from sparkling cracked windows to swept broken sidewalks. There were very few cars on the street, but they were clean and un-vandalized.

And in spite of the nonhuman residents, people lived with their windows up and their doors open.

After all, there was only one rule in the Dens; leave what is not yours alone.

Or you might lose a hand.

Just one if you're lucky.

It was no secret that the city didn't waste a dime trying to keep any shine on the place.

Small shanty-town shacks, built from cardboard, tin, and scraps of wood sat flush against the Wall. On the inside, the sun was already too low for the light to make it over the stacked stone. Shadows were like ink. Streetlamps didn't exist here.

Haley headed east and into the night club district. Here the stone walls had been decorated with offensive neon lights. Medan's nightclub, the Pit, occupied almost the entire upper block.

Since the night was just starting to bloom, the place was still empty. Haley could hear guitars being strummed as speakers were tested. A set of double doors were propped open by a matching pair of bouncers dressed in black.

Haley walked past a group of teenagers, Human, dressed in fishnet and chains. They eyed her and made a few passing comments about her choice in wardrobe.

When she got to the door, one of the bouncers stopped her. "We don't open until seven. No walk-ins tonight. Kazy is playin'."

She'd heard of the band, one of several put together by Lesser-Breds, but she didn't own any of their CDs. Godsmack was more her taste.

"I'm not here for the music. I'm here to see Medan."

The bouncer laughed at her, but his buddy didn't; his buddy was Kin.

"Let her in." The Male's eyes went golden.

"Drey? You serious, man?"

Drey slid forward, his mouth open, his nose doing double time to suck in her scent. He grinned, wicked and wide. "She's Female."

"Duh." Bouncer Number One looked at his friend like he was the stupid one. He blinked a couple times then his face dropped. "You mean, Female," he said with a capital F. "No shit?" It was a Human thing to do.

He reached out to touch her, maybe flick a little bit of her hair, or poke her arm to see if she was real. He never made it. The Male caught his hand and flashed a mouth full of teeth.

"Whoa, dude, what's your problem?"

"She's Female," he said, like it should explain everything.

Drey bowed his head at Haley. When his friend didn't do the same, he twisted his wrist until he went to one knee.

Haley almost asked him to stop. But this was the Dens, not the outside world. She hurried inside, hoping with all hope that Farley was okay.

It wasn't hard to find the entrance. She'd seen enough crude maps of the place to know it was on the back wall. But being guarded by two Kin who were easily seven feet tall was practically a road sign. The Males did not acknowledge Haley, they simply stepped aside.

Haley headed down the uneven steps, wishing she hadn't worn heels. At least they were only two inchers. Still, heels and carved stone didn't agree.

The staircase wound downward like an enormous screw, and just when she thought it was never going to end it dumped her out into a tunnel. Down here the lights were few and far between. And where there was light, it was almost always candles.

At the base of the stairs, Haley listened. There were the sounds from above, water seeping out of the stone, the candle flames sizzling on their wax column, and then...

There! She heard it again. High pitched, panicked. Something screaming way off or way down.

Haley ran, but after she took a few turns, the cries died out completely and she lost her sense of direction. She turned, wondering which doorway she'd come through, but all of them looked alike. Holes in stone walls.

Her hearts thudded in her chest and she fought the claustrophobic panic of dark, deep holes and no idea where the hell she was going or how to get out.

"You're Haley." It was not a question. She turned to see the tall dark shape of a man. He was dressed in a leather panel kilt and a bronze chest plate. He looked like something out of *Gladiator*. He smelled Kin, but he didn't scent her. When he stepped into the light she saw the scars. Fresh pink things marring him from head to toe.

Half-breed. He was a Feeder. Haley looked away, trying not to imagine the damage he'd endured to get messed up that bad.

"I'm here to see Medan."

"She is expecting you in the parlor." Obviously, tall, dark, and badly bitten expected her to know where the parlor was. Whatever the hell the parlor was. Haley eyed all the doorways, thinking how they needed to seriously consider some directional cues. He pointed to the second passage from the left.

"Straight down?" Haley asked. The half-breed nodded. She took the opening and the steep downward tunnel that followed.

The parlor turned out to be a massive antechamber. Unlike the other rooms, which were bare of anything but more tunnels, the parlor was packed with comforts. Wall-to-wall fur rugs blanketed the cold stone. Large lounging pillows were pushed to either side and the ceiling had been covered with lengths of silk.

Silver and gold chains glittered and sparkled, running the full length of the room, like forgotten Christmas garland. But they were nothing compared to the assortment of bright colored vases, marble statues, and Egyptian sarcophagi. The collection had no rhyme or rhythm. Just pretty things, sitting or hanging next to other pretty things. A collage of priceless paintings and shiny baubles.

The Smithsonian had nothing on this place.

Haley stepped from the shadows and into the warm electric light mixed with more candles. In the distance, the darkness shifted and swelled forward. The light struck scales and golden fire erupted from Medan's eye sockets. The Atlanta Queen thundered and Haley felt her knees go weak.

Medan's chest expanded, and her wings rattled. She eased forward, her body somehow missing all the priceless treasures, moving like liquid and sounding like death.

"Haley..." She drew it out like it was meant to be pronounced--*Hae-lelee*. "You came." She didn't sound a bit surprised. "Farley and I were betting on whether or not you would. I see I won." She parted her lips, and a growl ticked from her throat. Heat boiled from Medan's skin as the deep rumble of her fire lung rattled everything in the room. Haley stared at her, every muscle in her body rigid.

But then, Medan's *RHage*, her preternatural power, was Fear, and she was merciless with it.

"Human life has left you without manners." Coils of steam eased out from between her teeth. Her eyes flashed. Haley willed her knees to bend. Grudgingly, they obeyed. When she was on the ground she bent her head forward. Medan purred.

"Much better." Medan's massive form pulled back and she curled in on herself, tucking up her limbs like a large cat. "You may stand."

Actually now that Haley was down here, she preferred to stay. But it was better not to make the request. Haley willed her knees to lift her up and somehow she made it. Medan was bigger than she remembered, massive, and three times as scary. Her head alone was the size of a pickup truck.

"Your Majesty." Haley gave herself a mental high-five for remembering the use of a proper title. "I have come as you requested." She waited, hoping that Medan would hurry up and get on with this. She wanted to get Farley and get out.

Medan's golden eyes slid half closed and she fell completely still, taking on a strange lack of realness which made her all but disappear right in front of Haley's eyes.

It reminded her of Niles.

Life trickled in, moving her lips and projecting her voice. "I have called you here because I am pleased with your work in the *Chetrah* world. So pleased that I would like to extend you a gift." Haley was sure this was some kind of trick, but she didn't have a choice. Not as long as Medan had Farley.

"What kind of gift?" Her throat tightened, strangling her words.

Medan extended a claw and motioned her forward. Haley obeyed. She didn't dare not to. "You are very special to me, Haley." The Queen shifted, sliding against the fur-covered floor. "And I know you appreciate every gift I have endowed to you." Her body curved surrounding Haley. "So it is only proper I extend to you the greatest of honors." She stopped. Her large head dipped low, until Haley was looking at her reflection in one large golden eye.

"I--I'm sorry. I don't understand." And Haley didn't. Medan had kicked her out of the Hive, out of the Dens. She had survived only because of the grace of Humans. She had succeeded because of her own will. She existed today because she chose to be something more. Medan had nothing to do with any of that.

"Haley..." Medan turned her head giving Haley her other eye. "Don't you see? I am the one who made you what you are."

"Your Majesty, Queen Medan...may I speak freely?" Haley's Kin instincts said not to do this, but her Human-endowed curiosity wouldn't be silenced.

The Queen sighed. "Amuse me."

God of Man, Haley hoped she wasn't going to regret this. This was a dangerous game, but the truth was Medan wasn't going to end this until she wanted it to.

Haley said, "You kicked me out of the Dens when I was still white-scaled."

"True," she purred.

"I don't know you."

"Few know me."

"If I owe anyone for what I am, I would think it would be the woman who raised me and the Humans who have accepted me." Haley stared at Medan; the dragon was not breathing.

Haley waited.

Medan blinked, slow. Her black tongue flicked, stroking the air. "Did you know Farley is the only Male I have never been able to read?" Haley's brain skipped with the change of topic. Medan swung her head back and receded into the shadows again, leaving Haley standing alone. "It is a queer thing ... Queer. I rather like that word. It can mean so many things. Different, unconventional, suspicious ... worthless." There was venom in her tone. Medan's fire lung ignited, pumping heat until the air around her wavered. "Look around you, Child. What do you see?" She swung her head. "I do not keep the worthless."

Haley trembled. Sweat clung to her hair and formed in the creases of her body. The heat became unbearable but complaining wasn't an option.

"Then why did you kick me out?" Haley didn't mean to say it aloud, but the words were out so there was no going back. "Why did you expel me from my own people?"

"Because you were a threat." It was a kind of truth Haley didn't expect. The Queen's anger banked and coolness of the cave closed in again.

"How?"

Medan flexed her claws like a cat, the ebony *chelae* at the end glistened. "There are those among us who would have killed you." The Queen dragon kicked out her hind legs and her body became languid against the fur rugs. "Unknown blood or not, you are Female. So I chose to give you life. It was my first of many gifts." She yawned, flashing a row of razor sharp teeth. "I have always watched you, you know. Not directly. But I always knew where you were, and what you were doing." She turned her great head and lowered it to Haley's height. "You see, the other Queens did not think you would survive in the Human world. I made sure you did. I knew what you could bring to me, to all Kin, was priceless. A Female, in the world of Man, *Impressed* with an understanding we have never been able to grasp."

Inside Haley began to ache, her breath shortened, and her stomach clenched. She stared at the Queen, not wanting to believe a word, but at the same time scenting the truth in her claims. Medan truly believed what she said.

"Now that Niles Fury faces death, I will have to protect you myself."

"Niles?" Haley blinked. "What does Niles have to do with anything?"

"Oh." Medan did a terrible job feigning surprise. "You did not know?"

You know damn well I didn't know. Haley didn't trust herself to speak, so she shook her head.

The Queen continued, "Yes, well, he does his job well, does he not? He followed you. He watched you. He killed for you."

Haley's body jerked like she'd been hit by a current.

Medan made a pleased sound, followed by a string of clicks and chirps. "Oh, Haley, you do not know how many have been sent for you." Her words drowned in false concern.

"Sent for me?"

"Yes. Did you think the other Queens would give up trying to kill you? I wanted you to live but they ... they conspired against you. Eventually they gave up, except for Nidia." Medan exhaled a dramatic sigh. "They sent Humans because that's what you trusted. So it wasn't like it took much effort to kill them. Not for Niles. But there were others."

Medan's long black *chelae* toyed with the nap of the fur. "Males, Marked, sent to erase him. He killed those as well. All to protect you..." Her blazing eyes came up and pegged Haley hard. She knew the Queen was a craftsman with her words. What she was hearing wasn't completely true. But there was no scent of a lie.

"Niles protected me?" Haley made it a direct question because it would require a direct answer.

Medan did not hesitate. "Yes."

The room began to spin and when her knees gave, Medan caught her. Haley pooled in her massive hands.

"Oh, Child, this is so much for you to bear." The sweetness in her tone was sickening. "You see why I have called you here. Niles will be dead in a matter of days and you will be all alone. There will be no one to keep the Queens at bay. No one strong enough. No one who makes them afraid." Medan's bronze body coiled around Haley, making her dizzy. She shut her eyes trying to shake the overwhelming vertigo. "It is now up to me to make you safe."

Make me dead, that's what she really means. That's what she really wants.

But the truth was, if the Queen wanted Haley dead, she could just kill her now. It wouldn't be that difficult. Medan stopped moving and Haley decided to risk opening her eyes again. Bronze scales surrounded her and one giant eye hovered inches from her face.

"Are you well, Child?"

Of course she wasn't.

"I don't know." Haley sat up, her head swimming. Medan poured her out and onto the floor. Haley amazed herself by remaining on her feet.

"So, you understand now? You understand how much I have favored you? How important you are to me? And now, I must give you one last gift. One that will keep the other Queens from you or they will risk my wrath..." Medan hissed, her body vibrating, her wings rattling. Haley stumbled back and the Queen calmed, going from monstrous to passive like a flick of a switch. The abrupt change was more frightening than the actual display.

"How?" Haley's voice cracked. "How do you plan on protecting me?" God of Man, was that a contradiction in words!

Medan's fierce eyes softened and her body went pooled against the fur covered floor. "I will make you my *Er-a-ma-tah*."

Haley's Olde Tongue was inadequate. She had no idea what the word meant.

Medan must have seen the confusion because she said, "My Enforcer."

Holy shit. That did not just come out of the Queen's mouth.

Haley did a piss poor job of hiding her shock and the Medan laughed.

"The greatest of gifts, is it not?" The Queen sounded all too proud of herself.

Haley had to be careful. As in don't-get-your-throat-torn-out careful. "I ... I don't know what to say..."

"But it is a worthy gift for such a Female as yourself ... to be the Queen's claw, to be the mouth from which my voice will speak.

Haley blinked several times, trying to organize her thoughts so she could figure out what all this really meant. Human-written books were very limited on this kind of knowledge. Knowledge which should have been *Impressed* on her as a hatchling.

What *was* clear, in most of the books, was that such bonds could never be broken except by death.

Of one or the other. Whoever's came first.

Haley had a feeling that Medan was betting on that "whoever" to be her.

Haley said, "Can I have some time to think about this?"

The Queen rumbled. Her anger surged and heat from her fire lung rolled through the room, stirring the silks hanging from the ceiling. Fine golden chains glittered in the light.

Haley fumbled with her thoughts. She still had to get Farley out of here alive. "Please, your Graciousness." She bowed. "I do not mean to offend. It's just that--" How the hell was Haley going to explain this to Garrett? Good grief, how the hell was she going to explain this to the Bureau? Plain and simple, she couldn't. There just wasn't any way. Becoming Medan's Enforcer would make Haley too much of a liability for the Center. She'd be stripped of her Agent status and fired. This couldn't work, not if she was going to remain in Human society. "Please, Medan, you have worked so hard to build the life that I have, so many gifts that I do not want to be ungrateful for."

"Now you are grateful?" The Queen's tone said she wasn't buying it.

A wave of palpable fear rolled over Haley, choking her. She curled forward, trembling under the weight of the *RHage*. Every muscle in her body jerked and her mind threatened to short out. Breathing became a luxury. Just when Haley thought it was going to crush her it stopped. The tide receded and left her gasping for breath.

After a long silence the crimson in Medan's eyes dimmed. The rhythmic rise and fall of her purr echoed off the walls. "Do not wait very long. Your enemies are everywhere. Even among the ranks of those you work with. You cannot trust the *chetrah*, Haley. They do not wish Kin anything but death." Haley watched the Queen as she curled tight. "Go with caution, Child."

Her lids slid closed and she became stone still.

"What about Farley?" Haley asked.

"He lives." An eye partially opened.

"Can I take him with me?"

"I keep my promises..." There was a "but" in there somewhere. Medan's scaly lips curled. "However, he may prefer to stay."

No. No, he wouldn't.

"What did you do to him?" The accusation was just the sort of thing which could start an entire new round of Fun with Words.

"I did nothing." What Medan meant was, "more than you want to know."

Haley took a breath. "Where? Where is he?"

Medan slid her eyes to one of the passageways on the right. "Through there, stay straight. The room is at the end." Her eyes came back to Haley. The anger behind them seethed.

Haley looked at the doorway. "Please, Medan, ust tell me." She tried to swallow but her mouth was too dry.

"I swear to you, Child, I have not harmed him. I *fed* him. That. Was. All." Her gaze burned with an unspoken challenge.

Haley knew very well Medan didn't bleed for Farley, and his rank on the dominance scale put him on the menu, not on the customer list. Haley couldn't stop herself from asking. "What did you *feed* him?"

The Queen rumbled and flicked her talons across the fur. "I find it interesting how some of us become addicted to Human flesh. Farley used to devastate entire villages to feed his cravings."

Haley shook her head. "No, no, no ... God of Man, Medan, what have you done?"

Yellow fire flared in her golden eyes. "God of Man?" she laughed. "There is no God, Haley. Not of Man and not of Kin. There are only Queens. We are the only Gods."

Haley kicked off her heels and tore down the long dark tunnel, falling once when she smashed her shoulder against a rocky protrusion. She told herself the copper smell in the air was the wet stone. It could have been. She wanted it to be.

Haley burst in the room, hit a pool of blood, slid and fell. Her head cracked against the floor and her ankle screamed in sharp jabs, making her forget all about the black stars bursting in front of her eyes.

"Farley?" She rolled to her side, her hand sliding in crimson wetness, little pieces of something soft stuck to her skin.

Flesh.

Human flesh.

Haley got to her feet, limping until her ankle knitted enough to support her. She blinked and stared into the heavy shadows of the poorly lit chamber. It was hard to understand what she was seeing. Farley was on the floor, surrounded by a mass of something moving. Males. Dozens of them. All pale with translucent iridescence. White-scales. Hatchlings

They licked and sucked against Farley's skin, leaving white trails through the red wherever their tongues passed.

"Get away from him!" None of them obeyed. They were burning up with Hunger, their eyes fixated on the only thing in the room smelling like *food.*

As Haley closed in, their pasty white forms shuddered and rippled. Half-formed faces turned to stare at her. Mouths filled with way too many teeth gaped and sucked her scent from the air. The mishmash of Human and Draconian features made them hideous, made them repulsive. These were her people. These were Kin. And still ... they were foreign, unknown creatures. Monsters.

A lean, low growl squeezed out of Haley's chest. She swung at the first one, flaying his back with her *chelae.* The smell of blood sent them all screeching. The high pitched clicks, low thrumming, and hungry growls became deafening. Inhuman teeth flashed in half-Human faces. Haley stumbled back as they sucked in their clutch mate and devoured him in a symphony of gnashing teeth.

How many of them were there? Haley couldn't tell, but it was too many. She waded through them, kicking the ones who wouldn't move. And every injured creature was overwhelmed. Piteous cries were short lived and quickly replaced by the sounds of tearing flesh and snapping bone.

Here in the nest there was no place for the weak.

She had to get Farley out of here.

Haley tossed another Male out of her way and fell over Farley, blocking him with her body.

"Farley, look at me! Look at me please!" He craned his head back, his eyes on the pools of red. Haley grabbed his head and made him meet her eyes. "Look at me!" The sweet scent of pain blossomed and he screamed. Haley looked down to see one of them working its jaws to the bone in his leg. She roared and kicked, cracking its skull and splattering green ichor all over the other half-changed bodies. Its clutch mates converged.

"Go! Get back!" Haley hissed and they withdrew, but not too far. Their hunger pumped through the air on metaphysical currents. She growled, as her own *need* swelled. Haley was horrified by the fierceness of it. She shook Farley. His golden eyes focused and his face crumbled.

"I didn't mean to." He looked down at himself, then around. "God of Man, what I have I done?"

Haley snarled at the white-scales as they inched closer, flashing fang and *chelae*. They made small mewling noises, asking to be *fed*. The asking wouldn't last long. Pretty soon their Hunger would win out. Haley would have to kill them, or let them eat. And there were too many to kill.

She watched as more of them scurried in from the tunnels.

Where the hell were they all coming from?

"Haley..." Farley wailed, clutching his stomach. "It hurts! Please, I need more, please..." Some were like this. Their hunger for Human flesh so powerful their bodies revolted when denied. But Farley had gone so long without it. Surely, it wouldn't be this strong, this fast.

The white-scales rattled wings and chattered teeth. Their soft, colorless bodies trembled as one living thing.

Hunger.

Feed.

The feelings were so powerful they were almost a voice. Haley felt her own teeth elongate and a heat burn through her skin. Images flashed through her mind, of sinking her teeth into Farley's neck and taking blood, then scoring his stomach to eat the soft parts inside. "Not now!" Dark blue scales fluttered along Haley's arms and neck. Her vision slid away into the bright contrast of crystalline colors her brain interpreted as distance and forms.

Haley pressed her face into Farley's neck and inhaled his scent, remembering who he was. "I have to get you out of here." She heard him sob.

His hand touched her cheek and trembled. "I can't."

"You can. I can get you out. I need you to stand up. They won't hurt you as long as I don't let them."

"No, I can't, Haley, I can't stop again. I can feel it. It never felt like this before."

And I want to rip your throat out. Haley forced herself to think of something else. Anything else. Her dead flowers in the clay pot by her door.

When she had control, she said, "It's the white-scales. You feel their Hunger. I feel it too."

"Not like this!" Farley smacked his head against the stone. "Please, just go. I won't be able to stop again. I don't want to hurt anyone."

"You won't. You're not a man-eater."

"Yes, I am!" Farley's eyes flickered with copper and red. "I am. I've killed thousands of Humans in my life. I'm no different than Niles."

Haley pressed her face to his cheek. "You quit. You stopped..." The cries of the hatchlings made her whimper.

HUNGER!

BLOOD AND MEAT!

FEED!

"Shut up!" She kicked at them when they got close. "Just shut up, all of you!"

"Haley, just go."

"I will not leave you!" Her anger rose like heat. The hatchlings squealed and pulled back, their instinct for self-preservation momentarily overriding their need for *food.* "That's right, you're pissing me off!" But as the last of them trickled in from below, their motives were clear. They were going to *feed.* While they wouldn't touch Haley because she was Female, Farley was fair game. He had no rank on the dominance scale and that made him Food.

On hands and knees, one of the white scales came closer. His perfect Human form lacked a finished look, giving his skin a shiny plastic texture. His green Draconian eyes rolled down at Farley. His mouth gaped open, and teeth, too long to fit in his head, folded out. They weren't going to wait much longer. Minutes. Seconds.

Haley looked at Farley. His gaze was on the white-scales, his face calm. The pain and shame of what he'd done glowed in his eyes.

It's them. He'll be okay if I can just get him out.

But looking at the white-scales, Haley wasn't sure how she was going to do that. She'd never had to fight her way through the nests as a hatchling. Females rarely did. But they still got to witness it. This was all so strange to her. So frightening.

It turned her insides to think she had once been just like this.

The *need* of the white-scales washed over Haley and she sank her claws into Farley's arms. He bucked under her and one of the white-scales latched onto his foot. His teeth clenched and his breath hissed out.

Hunger drove Haley forward. She opened her mouth, her eyes on the thready pulse in his neck.

Just a little to tide me over.

NO!

Haley screeched and slung her head, trying to shake free of the *need.* It wasn't the white-scales she had to worry about now. It was herself. She had to change his scent. Stamp a big "no-free-lunch" sign on his chest.

Haley felt ridiculous even thinking about it. Hell, she wasn't even sure how to do it. But she knew from seeing other Males who *Belonged,* they smelled like those who *owned* them. And right now it was her scent keeping the white-scales at bay. Every Human-made moral instilled in her screamed it was wrong. She didn't have the right. It was stealing from Farley. Taking his identity. But if she didn't, the white-scales would eat him alive.

She said, “Do you trust me?”

“You know I do.”

“I think, I think if I get my scent in you they’ll leave you alone.”

Farley’s wide frightened eyes burned. He touched the back of her head. “Do it.”

The *need* of the white-scales beat against Haley like an insistent drum and she wondered if she would be able to stop once she bit him. Farley seemed to know exactly what she was thinking.

“Please, Haley! If I’m going to die, I’d rather you do it.” Because the white-scales were going to kill him one piece at a time.

Haley stared at the smooth line of his muscular shoulder, feeling ashamed. “I don’t know what I’m doing, Farley.”

“I’ll walk you through it. I’ve seen it done.” Of course he would. Farley had walked her through a lot of firsts in her life. Haley nodded and leaned forward.

All around her the white-scales howled. Finally, she was going to *feed* them. Haley heard the deafening crunch and tasted blood. She didn’t remember biting Farley, but now that she had, she needed to get control.

“Bite deeper. To the bone.” Farley’s pained words broke over his shaky breath. He wound his hands tight in her hair and pushed down on the back of her head. Haley worried her bite into muscle. Her jaw popped and dislocated. Blood rushed down Haley’s throat and her primal need to *feed* exploded. She heard Farley shout her name. Her cognitive half begged him to fight back.

“Gland, palate, push!” His voice cracked and gurgled. “Haley...” Saying her name kicked something in her chest. She was supposed to be saving him, not killing him. “Now, please...”

By shaking her head like a dog, Haley tore the bite deeper.

“Bone, in the bone...Ahhh--” His clavicle shattered and she tasted marrow. Metaphysical energy erupted between them and Haley felt Farley’s preternatural self slide against hers. Around them, the air vibrated with the high pitched whirr of hundreds of white-scales. Underneath the sound was the hum of metaphysical energy, ringing like a tuning fork.

Farley’s scent spiked and changed, going from something that marked him as Food to something that marked him as *Belonging*. He groaned. His head rolled back and his hands became a vice on Haley's hip. She could taste his arousal as it bled out to the white-scales banking their hunger. His erection bit into her stomach and he undulated against her.

The hatchling bodies surged forward. Curious hands, claws, and tongues licked and touched them.

Haley snarled, her protective instincts going full throttle. She bit deeper, pushing more of her scent into the wound until it poured over. The white-scales circled, feeding from the metaphysical fire storm. She could feel Farley under her, wanting more than just the touch of her preternatural self. He wanted in her. *Needed* in her. And Haley wanted to give him everything.

Clicks and whistles reminded Haley where she was. In the belly of the beast. This binding hadn't been done in the privacy of a safe haven. It had been done in a small corner of hell.

Hatchlings rolled and rubbed against her like kittens in catnip. It was time to get out. Haley stood up and Farley curled at her feet, pawing her legs and thigh.

They were surrounded. The sea of bodies rolled and surged. There didn't seem to be a way through. White-scales rose up to touch Haley's hands, tug at her clothing, begging ... for what, she didn't know.

But one thing was clear: their Hunger was beginning to flicker. It wouldn't be long before it was rising.

Move, thought Haley. *I just need you to move.*

In a synchronized pulse, the crowd split.

Haley didn't know how or why, she just knew her time was running out. She picked Farley up and carried him through the ocean of hatchlings. The darkness of a tunnel never looked so good. When Haley turned a little she saw her. Medan. The Queen was on the other side of the chamber, wrapped in shadows.

How long had she been there?

Medan's golden eyes flickered with bits of crimson.

Haley could feel the Hunger, heavy in the air, like a fetid heat. But the hatchlings were still basking in the shared euphoria. Medan had been the source of the Hunger and insatiable *need.* The Queen raised her lip, flashing teeth, then disappeared into the darkness. A wave of white-scales followed.

Chapter 12

Haley had no idea where she was going. She stopped twice trying to get her bearings but it was useless. The Hive was an endless maze of turns and dead ends. She leaned against the wall and tried to catch her breath. Farley moaned in her arms and pressed his face to her neck.

The bite marks on his body had closed to ugly black and blue bruises, but they weren't healing any more than that. He was cold and starting to shiver.

How long had he been down there, healing wounds, only to have them reopened? Being eaten alive? Medan's cruelty truly had no end.

There would be time to worry about that later. Right now she had to get out before something else crawled out of darkness.

Haley hitched Farley higher, adjusting her hold. Human shapes just weren't meant for this kind of abuse and her muscles were starting to fatigue. At least the blood was almost dry so her grip wasn't slipping.

With a grunt Haley moved off the wall and entered another room. A quick scan told her she was alone, so she crossed the chamber, took the first hall, and hit a dead end.

God of Man, she was never getting out of this place.

Something moved, and Haley pushed herself into a fissure that made her walk-in closet look small. She willed Farley to not make any noise.

"You need to take the other tunnel on the right." Haley recognized the voice and the scent. She leaned forward out of the shadows. Electricity hadn't reached this part of the Hive. It was still being lit with man-sized candles mounted in rock crevices. But she could still see the faint outline of the half-breed in the shadows.

He pointed to the tunnel. "Once you're inside, take the second left. It will be hard to see. It's small, narrow and rarely used. It will take you above the parlor and the staircase. You'll come out in a storage closet, top side."

There was weariness in his eyes as he watched her ease past him.

Haley stopped at the mouth of the tunnel and looked back at him. "Why?" He was Medan's. He owed Haley nothing.

The half-breed smiled in a way that made her sad and said, "Because I dreamed of you."

She shook her head, not understanding.

He gave a shrug and slid into the shadows. "When you kill her, don't forget I helped you escape."

Kill her? As in Medan?

Her pulse stuttered. Clearly, he had her confused with someone else.

The sound of Haley's bare feet slapping the floor accompanied her breathing as she headed up the tunnel. In the darkness, she relied on her natural sight. The half-breed's directions were dead on. Carrying Farley made it difficult to squeeze between the rocks, but she managed. The passage ended suddenly against a wooden door. Haley pulled and it gave. The opposite side had shelves holding cleaners and supplies. Somehow the hidden doorway did not come as a surprise. It was just the kind of thing she expected to find in a place like this. A click sounded when she pulled it shut behind her.

Thin lines of light traced the other door in front of her. Escape was just a few feet away. All Haley had to do was open it. Panic seized her when a spider slapped her in the face. Haley staggered, kicking a bucket and knocking a mop handle into her head, making too much noise. No one had followed her, but she couldn't shake the fear that the monster was coming up the hall behind her.

And her name was Medan.

Haley felt for the doorknob, which was difficult with Farley in her arms. The sudden wash of light blinded her, but with it came liberation from the panic. The smell of sweat, cigarettes, old beer and fresh urine slapped Haley in the face. She blinked, clearing her natural sight.

As Haley stepped into the bathroom, someone whistled. It was followed by spontaneous clapping and lewd suggestions by the small crowd of Human men.

Stalls were on her left, urinals and sinks on the right.

Just my luck. The men's bathroom.

"Hey, baby, do you take requests?" The man standing at the urinal turned and offered himself. From behind, a hand flicked her hair and another brushed her ass.

Two bodies blocked the door. They looked like a matching set of book ends. Both were dressed in black with sagging pants weighed down by O-rings and chains. Their faces were competing with their wardrobe for the *Most Amount of Metal* award.

The one on the left motioned Haley forward. "Hey, if you're putting out, maybe some of us would be willing?" Blondie pulled up his shirt, flashing pink scars at the edge of his boxers. "Little blood can be a turn on. You like razors or just use your teeth?"

Haley looked down at Farley. Crimson dominated the green of his own blood. They thought he was a bleeder, someone who likes to *feed* Humans, pretending to be Kin.

His friend didn't look quite so sure. He stared at Farley, who hung limp in her arms. Haley could see the hamster wheel turning between his ears. She was carrying a man, which was something Human women didn't normally have the strength to do.

"You need some help with your friend there? We could always find something creative for him to do, too." Another man reached for Farley. Haley stepped away. Two more moved up from behind, blocking any retreat.

All of them stank from a mix of drugs and arousal.

Haley growled and the sound rattled the walls. "Get out of my way." She'd been taught to never hurt Humans, but if it came to them or Farley, she'd break that rule.

"Fuck me, look at her eyes." Unsure Friend backed away, clearly having second thoughts.

"Contacts, dude, they sell 'em round the corner." Tweedle Dumb put his hand on the waist band of his baggy pants and pushed them down. "C'mon, bitch, I can teach you a thing or two about playing the bleeding game." He produced a razor in his right hand.

Haley opened her mouth, popping her jaw and punching out her teeth. She hissed, and scales raced over her arms, neck, and face.

"Holy shit! You don't buy those at no fucking Pseudo shop!" Unsure took off out the door. Tweedle Dumb dropped his razor and scurried over the wall of the first stall. Haley swung her head around, letting them all get a real good look, and just like any Human with an ounce of survival instinct they scurried back.

Juicy cursing replaced bravado. *Cowards.*

Haley stalked to the door, kicked it open, and slammed into the pounding music of the club.

Out here the bodies were thick and mostly naked. Male Kin and Lesser-Breds mixed with Humans of both sexes. The scent of synthetic pheromone traded places with the bitterness of tobacco.

Bodies propelled by the music slammed into Haley. She had to use her shoulders like battering rams to move them out of the way so she could get to the exit. Farley ade little jerks and jumps as his body temperature continued to drop. At least the night air was mild for this time of year, and it wasn't raining.

The urgency to get Farley somewhere safe made the city block feel like a ten mile trek. Up ahead Haley saw Garrett's car, a dark shiny beacon under a dying street light.

The keys were where she'd left them. She opened the door and put Farley in the front. She took off her blazer and covered him, cranked the car, and turned on the heat full blast.

She didn't want to leave him, but she didn't have a choice. She needed her alibi. Three minutes later she was back in dry oven heat of the sedan.

The tires squealed against the asphalt as Haley pulled out into the desolate street. She glanced at the LED clock in the dash. It was eight thirty-eight. She'd made good time, considering.

A half-hour later Haley pulled into the parking lot of her apartment from the back side. Living in a building with mostly elderly people had its advantages. Most were in bed by eight. With any luck, no one would see her.

Haley got out and went around for Farley. When she had him in her arms she hit the automatic locks and carried him across the parking lot to the rear lobby. A keypad on the door kept nonresidents out. She keyed in her number. The light turned green and the locks released.

There was no elevator in the back, which was exactly why she took this route. It wasn't handicap friendly. And since more than half the residents used canes and walkers, they didn't put in much time on the stairs.

Haley climbed the steps. Her insides felt like they had ice floating in them. Pretty soon she'd be shivering. They needed heat and food. They'd burned up a lot trying to stay alive.

With a quick peek through the window in the door at the top of the stairs, she verified the hallway was clear. Sounds of way-too-loud TVs wafted out into the hallway as she headed to her apartment.

Standing at her door, Haley felt for her keys and realized she'd left everything in the car. She put Farley down long enough to tip the flower pot up and retrieve the spare from under it. He muttered something under his chattering teeth. His legs and arms danced as the tremors jumped up another notch.

Inside, Haley carried Farley into the bathroom where she put him in the tub and cranked on the shower. Thanks to the on-demand water heater under the sink it came out steaming. Farley raised a hand, like he was reaching for something she couldn't see, then rolled his head away, mewling. She didn't want to leave him, but they needed food.

Haley went back to the kitchen and threw open the freezer. She crammed what she could into the microwave and turned it on high. Chicken pot pies sat balanced on Hot-Pockets which were competing for room with three bowls of macaroni and cheese.

Processed food was a poor substitute for the flesh and blood of their own. But Haley was in no shape to feed Farley and he definitely couldn't tend to her. The food would help. If worse came to worst she'd just call Deshi.

While the frozen dinners turned in the microwave, Haley looked in the fridge and found two packages of hot dogs. Haley emptied both of them into a plastic pan and went to check on Farley.

The worst of the spasms had calmed under the hot water. He looked at her and smiled before closing his eyes. Now that the water had erased the blood, Haley could see the extent of his wounds. Unhealed bones in his legs bulged under his skin and pink scars marred his thighs and calves like a bad road map. The bites from the hatchlings were still open so that meant the scars were probably a lot older. Had they been doing that to him while Medan toyed with her?

Haley didn't want to think about the answer.

The microwave beeped, and Haley made herself go back to the kitchen. She threw the hot dogs in for two minutes. It was the longest two minutes she ever had to wait. When it was done, she piled the load in her arms and carried it to the bathroom. She knelt by the tub and pulled Farley closer to her. With a pot pie in one hand, she used her fingers to spoon it into his mouth.

He resisted and tried to spit it out.

"There is meat in here. Chicken. You like chicken." She pushed the food through his lips and onto his tongue.

"It's cooked." He grimaced and tried pulling back.

"Yeah, well, right now neither of us really needs to be eating anything cold. Think of it like coffee after an all-nighter at the bar." She pushed another scoop into his mouth. "C'mon, Farley. Work with me here."

His legs scissored and his arms flailed.

Haley abandoned the pot pie and went for the hot dogs. She bit off half for herself and chewed while she broke the other part into small pieces. Farley took that a little better.

"I can't *feed* you, Farley. You know I would. But I've got the chills too." As if to drive home the point, when she reached for another Ball Park, Haley's hands decided to do some break dancing. "Damn it." She shoved a hot dog in her mouth. Her body rebelled with a gag reflex, but she managed to keep it down.

"Haley?"

"I'm right here." She concentrated on keeping her hands steady so she could break off the hot dog into small pieces.

"What if I can't stop again?" Haley brought her gaze up. Farley's eyes were dark brown. She preferred the gold. They weren't so sad looking when they were gold.

"Don't be silly, you'll be fine." She tossed the pieces of hotdog into the pot pie, stirred it with her fingers and spooned it up. "Here, open wide."

"But what if I can't?"

Haley stared at him. The mush she'd made slid down her fingers. Not stopping just wasn't an option.

"Shut up and eat this." She pushed the glob between his lips. He grimaced. It took her rubbing his throat and holding his mouth shut for it to go down.

"Man, that's terrible!" Farley shook his head as she came at him with another bite. "No more, please." She forced him to take it. "Jesus Christ, how can you eat that shit?"

"It's not that bad." Haley held back another gag when she took a bite. "I've seen you put away half a dozen Big Macs. This can't possibly be as nasty as those things."

"It's the--" She shoveled in another scoop while Farley's mouth was open. "The sauce makes it edible." He coughed and sputtered but held it down. The improvement was a welcome sight.

Haley made Farley eat the last two Hot Pockets on his own, then stripped off her clothes and climbed under the water spray. Her temp wasn't dropping, but it also wasn't getting better. She curled up next to him, relishing the heat blasting against her skin.

They laid there, bodies pressed together, metaphysical currents exchanging back and forth. Haley couldn't help but stare at the web of flesh on Farley's shoulder *marking* him as hers. An ugly imperfection mucking up his otherwise flawless Human shell. It was obscene.

"I don't mind it." Farley's hand touched the back of her head and petted her soaking wet hair.

In a species burdened with vanity, she had a hard time believing that.

"It's different because this is a *mark*. It shows I *Belong*. It's a badge of honor."

She looked up at Farley. "How are you doing that?"

"What?"

"Reading my thoughts."

"I'm your Marked." He licked her cheek. "It's part of the job description. Knowing what you *need*." He licked the corners of her eyes. "Marks are supposed to take care of *To Whom They Belong*."

"But you're reading my thoughts."

He nodded and ran his tongue across her lips. "Only this close. Only when we touch like this. I couldn't hear you when you were in the kitchen." He nibbled her lip. "Open for me, Haley." She parted her lips and his tongue slipped inside.

Farley made a pleased sound like he just tasted something wonderful. The metaphysical lines between them hummed and Haley gasped. It never did that. Not before she fed him temporal fluid.

"That was before." Farley's words brushed her lips. "Now I *Belong* to you..." His tongue plunged into her mouth and his hands slid down her back, pressing her against him. Fingertips pushed between her shoulder blades and at the base of her spine, hitting both *ulysiss* glands at the same time. Haley couldn't contain the cry rising in her throat.

Farley caught it with his mouth, growling. "There's more than one way to make heat." He smiled, flashing fangs.

Haley put her hands on his cheeks and made him look at her. Part of her was terrified that what he was doing was because of the Marks, not because he wanted to. How could he want to be around her after Medan used him like that?

"Have I ever not wanted you? The Mark has nothing to do with how I feel." Farley licked her cheek. "Always have felt." Again. "Always will."

They had been sharing their bodies for decades. But something had changed.

Farley snarled and pushed her under him. "The only difference between now and then is this." He tilted his head to his shoulder. Haley's gaze went to the scar nestled against his collar bone. "You feel now what I've always felt."

"You don't regret it?" She kept her eyes on the scar. Farley had learned to enjoy Human ideals of individualism. Haley never treated him as a lesser. Outside the Dens he was safe to speak his mind. But she couldn't look, because looking at him might tell her something she didn't want to know.

"Oh, I have regrets." Her eyes moved against her will. Farley tasted her mouth. "I regret you didn't do it sooner." His hand slid down Haley's side. "I want to do this again, later, the right way." Fingers pushed into her lower back and a hand tightened on her thigh. Heat welled between her legs, hotter than the scalding water that pelted her skin. "But I can't wait and neither can you." Farley rubbed himself against her and hissed. "God of Man, Haley, I can feel your every *need*." He pushed her legs wider, hitched her upward and buried himself with one hard push. Haley was on fire, and he wasn't even moving yet.

Sex between them was always good. Nothing about Farley was spectacular or unique, but they fit together like puzzle pieces. A lot of the pleasure was just in the comfort, but now that he was *marked* every touch was magnified.

Farley shuddered and his breath blew against her skin on a pant.

"Christ, I don't know if I can do this."

Haley slid her hands down his back and dug her fingers into his hips, keeping him where he was. "Don't you dare stop!"

Farley laughed against her shoulder, but it was a desperate sound. He pulled back slowly and came forward again. It was like a thousand pleasure points pricked her skin. Farley's knee slipped against the bottom of the tub, and a cry escaped his lip. Even accidental movement was too much to bear. Haley arched her back, taking him deeper, forcing him to move. It felt so good. It was painful, but she couldn't let him quit.

"Roll me," Farley said.

"I'll hurt you." More like kill him. Haley felt like a hatchling with very little control. Any other time she might have risked it, but now she didn't trust herself. Her metaphysical energy was simply too wild.

Farley shook his head. "No, no you won't. I can do this if I'm in the *Rise*. You *need* this. I can feel it." His breath burst against her neck. "Please, Haley..."

This was why Males died for those who *marked* them. Self-preservation was abandoned at the door. Haley wasn't about to let him be that way. A mindless, willing Kin.

"Farley?" In spite of her body screaming for more, her voice was calm. He looked at her, brown eyes swimming in gold. She stroked his chin with her thumb. "Give me your mouth." He obeyed and she brushed his lips with her own. "Open for me." She petted his back until his muscles began to relax. "That's it..."

Farley growled. "If you just--" Haley cut him off by covering his mouth with hers. "Roll me."

"I can't do that and you know it. If I kill you, how are you going to live up to your promise to do this right the next time? Later, there will be more touching." Her words came out muffled against his mouth. "There will be more biting." She pulled him against her, using her legs. "Licking." Her voice trembled.

Farley ran his tongue across her cheek and slid to her ear. "Let's not forget..." His lips latched onto her lobe and pulled with a wet sucking sound. She laughed and he moved. The new metaphysical lines between them were like a cramped muscle that didn't want to move. But it had to. Even if it hurt.

It didn't take long for Farley to quicken his pace. Haley clung to him as he pushed into her. His hands gripped her hips and jacked her higher. The angle hit her deep, made her gasp, and he barked against her neck, trying to hold back until that moment right before release where she could Roll him without tearing his metaphysical energy apart.

Heat spread across his lower back and down his thighs. Haley could feel it through every inch of skin that touched her.

"Please, now, please." The muscles in his neck stood out and his grip tightened until it hurt. Haley's Female instincts reveled in the pain she caused him. She knew she could hold him there at that brink and never let him cross. He would fuck her until his hearts exploded if she wanted it.

The fight to reign in what Haley's instincts demanded of her was a familiar one. A strange sort of comfort.

But stronger than her primal urges was knowledge of what Farley felt. He would die for her. He would surrender anything she wanted. And what made her value that were the Human instilled concerns she'd *impressed* from her Mother.

Haley threw out her preternatural-self, heat flaring until water hissed. The metaphysical lines binding her body in Human form intertwined with the energy that was Farley's. She entered him and it was his turn to cry out. His body tensed against hers until his spine bowed. His teeth sank into her neck, a reflexive reaction, and she reached inside with those invisible lines, pulling at the core of what gave him life.

Farley thrust with desperation and the orgasm took them both. It wasn't over. She spun him down, drawing everything he was straight through her, into her, moving herself inside his mind, through his thoughts. He screamed, releasing his grip on her neck. His body spasmed, crushing her against the back of the tub while he kicked.

Farley collapsed against her, chest heaving. He'd be out for a while. It was the same way with Deshi. Even when they were both with her at the same time.

Haley hit the nozzle with her foot, cutting off the water. She lay there for a while holding his unconscious body, his weight a welcome and familiar comfort.

Oddly enough, everything felt perfect.

And for some messed up reason, that bothered the hell out of her.

When she pushed Farley over, he flopped like a broken doll. And that made her think of broken bones, scars, and bruises. She touched his shoulder and arm. The Roll had healed everything except for the *mark.* Too bad the Roll couldn't erase the fact those terrible things had ever happened.

Haley climbed out of the tub, grabbed a towel and dried off. She wrapped Farley up and carried him to her bed.

Heat was no longer a problem. Both of them burned, almost feverish. Another side effect of the Roll, being so focused. Haley put a pillow under his head and pulled the sheet over both of them. She adjusted her positioning so she had her head on his shoulder and their legs were intertwined. This way she could listen to him breathe, feel his hearts, smell his scent.

Her fingers danced along his neck and played with his hair, stroking the short red tufts. The ends were beginning to curl. He'd have to cut it again soon or risk looking like *Howdy Doody*.

That thought made her smile. He'd been okay with his curls until that show had gotten popular in the late forties.

Not to mention his obsession with zoot suits.

Haley laughed out loud. Farley's pinstripes, and his fedoras, had been the talk of the office back then.

Of course, in the twenties...

She stopped herself and stared at him.

A hundred years and she'd never known how he felt. How he really felt.

Love is a Human emotion.

Then what sent her into the Hive after him? What made her break a dozen or more Bureau rules, risking everything she'd worked for?

It was something and it was powerful. Haley could feel it burning in her chest, making her body ache. The strange thing was she didn't want it to stop. The end of it was a fate worse than death.

Chapter 13

Colonel Dobson stared at that monster of a Male Kin called Niles Fury.

To him, Kin didn't have names, they just called themselves something. Parents gave their children names. Kin chose theirs, or they were given to them by the Humans they terrorized.

Christ, that son-of-a-bitch was huge.

There weren't many things that scared Dobson, and he wasn't about to admit this thing scared him either, but it did do something. Like make his balls draw up into his stomach and his mouth go dry.

They'd lost an Alchemist moving the beast from the trauma room to the holding cell under the lab. Goddamned dragon moved too quick. One minute he'd been down and the next he was eating that bastard's throat out.

He should have been dead. The Male, not the Alchemist. The lab lackeys cracked his chest and restarted his hearts with the defibrillator.

Twice.

And yet here he was, thirty-five feet below, in a concrete cylinder forty feet across. At least three inches of woven steel acted as a net between the viewing chamber and the top of the cell. Separating the rooms were an additional eighteen inches of fortified polymer, capable of taking a direct hit from mortar fire.

The devil himself couldn't have gotten out.

And Dobson still didn't feel safe.

All the damn thing did was pace. Wall to wall, back and forth. Every muscle in his body rolling and surging. It moved, not like a Human being, but the thing it was. Liquid. Deadly.

Niles stopped and his head tilted up. Dobson frowned. If he had a way to poke out the fucker's eyes, he'd be blind. Damn things would probably grow back. The Kin pulled up his lip and flashed long teeth. Scales rippled across his chest and arms.

Those Alchemists were going to have to do something about that. Their *oisis* pins didn't seem to affect him like it did the others, not even the Queens. It confirmed Dobson's feelings about the thing below. It was destruction waiting to happen. That meant there was only one thing to do about that. Find out how to control it.

His cell rang and he checked the number.

Speaking of Devils, *she* was on line four.

Dobson let it ring because it would piss her off. He liked pissing her off. It was a thing of beauty. Right before it clicked to voice mail he answered. "And what do you want?"

Silence. He knew she was there. He could hear her breathing. Or more precisely the breathing of the thing she talked through.

Kinda hard to dial those little numbers with big nasty claws.

The imagery made him grin.

"I am disappointed in you, colonel. I arrange to have the package delivered to your feet and you are not there to accept it."

It was Dobson's turn to take his time in answering. He reached inside his inner pocket, pulled out one of his cheap stand-in cigars, and stuck it in his mouth. "Look, if we're going to work together on this, you've got to stop trying to run the show."

"Oh, but colonel, I do run the show." She laughed, and it was an abnormal sound. "You have Texas because of me. You have Niles Fury because of me. And you almost had her ... because of me."

Bitch. Dobson was going to enjoy watching the Queen die. Maybe he'd call her up and put it on speaker phone. Record it. Too bad there wasn't a way to TiVo the event. That's the kind of thing a man would like to sit down to at night when he's giving himself a little hand action.

He said, "Well, it didn't work out. Now what?"

"You can tell me 'thank you'."

Man, he hated these games. "May I ask for what?"

"You may ask."

Silence. *Shit. Goddamn it.* "Okay, what do I owe the thanks for?"

"You have another chance."

Okay, now he was getting pissed off. He turned away from the viewing window because the Male was giving him the creeps. "A chance for what?"

The Female's voice lowered with a hiss. It sounded weird coming out of a Human mouth, pushed by Human vocal cords. Even in bipedal shapes, Kin still had a range of pitch and tone that Humans couldn't duplicate. "Haley was in the Dens. I do believe that qualifies as extreme violations?"

An odd kind of giddiness built in Dobson's gut. "Tell me."

"Farley was ... how shall we put it ... detained? According to my sources, Haley was denied clearance."

Of course she would be denied clearance. The Bureau was not about to risk her going into the Dens and never coming out. Queen dragons were known for their ability to be very persuasive either by scaring you to death or fucking with your head.

"What else," Dobson asked, because sure as shit that wasn't all of it!

"I have a request." The tone in her voice made his bowels cramp. The bitch never made a request; she gave orders and delivered threats.

She was up to something.

He said, "Let me hear it and I'll think about it."

A growl licked over the receiver. This far away Dobson wasn't afraid of her. She needed him as much as he needed her. And that arrangement would change, as soon as the virus was airborne.

She said, "I need Niles Fury to stay alive."

"For what?" He'd already thought of that. But if he wanted to keep Niles Fury for himself, he was going to have to die on schedule at his execution. It was the only way to make him available for the things Dobson had planned. It was a dangerous plan, a reckless plan. Niles Fury was a loaded weapon. An out and out nuclear bomb with a short fuse. He looked down through the viewing window. Niles stared.

Statue-still and unblinking.

Dobson couldn't decide who was worse. The Queen or Niles.

Right now Niles Fury was closer so Dobson picked him. "Listen, I can't promise you how long I can keep him alive. He's dangerous and he's powerful."

"You cracked open his chest, lost at least three in your lab. You worked hard to bring him back to life. You can't possibly need him gone that bad."

"How the fuck do you know that?"

"Because I *own* part of him, colonel. Half of him *Belongs* to me. I know everything he knows, I know everything he sees. I am connected to him in ways you could not imagine."

Dobson pulled his cigar out of his mouth and shoved it back in his coat.

"What are you planning to do?" He was going to regret the question and he knew it.

"Use him, of course."

"For what?" Colonel Dobson leaned into the glass. Niles was still there. His bloody eyes were still fierce, his dark skin perfect, every muscle carved and placed exactly where it needed to be. The braid on the back of his head still reached to his lower back. But it was impossible to see him the same if *she* had him.

And yet it had possibilities.

"If you have so much control of him then why don't you make him cooperate?" Dobson said.

She laughed, a girlish sound that had no business coming out of something like her. "It doesn't quite work that way, colonel. I only have half, not the whole."

Dobson narrowed his eyes and stared hard at Niles Fury. The Kin raised his left hand and flipped him off. He frowned. "Enlighten me then."

"In due time, in due time." A growl chased her words. "However, If you fail this time..." This time? He never failed. His blood pressure jumped and the pulse in his neck tapped out a beat. "I will use him to kill her."

"Haley?"

"Who else?"

"I want her alive."

"Then don't fuck this up." The line went dead.

A hundred curses speared through Dobson's head and none of them were adequate enough. If the bitch made good on her word, he'd lose both of them.

And that was not about to happen.

Chapter 14

Farley opened his eyes to darkness and a digital clock. The little red numbers showed four forty-five. He could hear Haley breathing and feel her body pressed to his chest. In the glow of the street lamp from outside the window her naked outline was a series of highlights. She'd kicked off the sheet.

His vision slid to its natural state and he stared at her like he did most nights when he stayed in her apartment. Watching her was a beautiful thing. Here she was relaxed, her brow never furrowed; her mouth was full and pouting, partly open.

Through his dragon eyes, the color of her skin was lost, but he didn't have to see those kinds of details to know her alabaster tone would be flushed from the Roll. He could feel it, a gentle warmth radiating from her body that bit deep into the bone.

It felt nice.

Best of all, what he did back in the Hive seemed like a far away dream. All the horrible things he ever did were erased in these moments. It had been this way since the day her adoptive Mother brought him to *feed* her. If the poor woman had only known what Farley was capable of.

Looking small, weak, and harmless had its benefits. Especially when dealing with Humans.

Just like beauty and perfection did for others of his kind, Farley's slight frame and innocuous appearance lured in prey. Made them easy to kill.

He'd killed that girl in the Hive.

Killed her and ate her. You fell off the wagon, buddy. You dined on the forbidden.

Lush.

Murderer.

Farley laid his head on his arm and stared at Haley. Her full breasts rose and fell with short quick breaths. Her respirations were always high like this after the Roll.

Her right hand was curled against her chest, her left over her rib under her breast. She slept like that a lot. Slightly turned, her legs a little bent, her face towards him, no matter which side he was on.

When he feathered his fingertips across her stomach her breathing hitched, then resumed.

Like all Kin, she slept hard, her brain shutting down, making her vulnerable.

And that was a realization that could no longer be ignored.

Haley was in danger. Medan would see her dead if she could. And Farley was powerless to protect her. Nothing but Food.

No wonder Females surrounded themselves with so many Males.

Haley was going to need protection. Males to keep her safe. Farley's primal need to make that happen forced his teeth down and scales to flutter along his neck. He tried to get a cap on his temper, but he wasn't like Haley. Control tended to elude him. Like earlier, he'd really made a mess of things.

But there were ways to fix that.

Practice makes perfect.

Farley circled her nipple with his thumb and felt it perk. His fingers followed her curves, came to her hip, then across to her groin, just above her cleft, resting on the edge of soft downy hairs. His fingers brushed her mound. Most Females didn't bother with such details. Farley liked those kinds of things. A lot.

He kissed Haley's shoulder, then her arm. With cat-like grace he arched up and over her, holding himself above her body, then slid down. His tongue brushed her nipple and he took it in his mouth and sucked.

Haley made a desperate sound. Her arms opened and her legs scissored. Tiny little points peaked out from her open lips. Farley grinned and dipped his mouth to her navel, probed it with his tongue, and nibbled the edges.

He kept his eyes on her face. He liked watching her, because she was so expressive. She never held back a cry, she never swallowed his name. She would scream for him if he wanted it.

And he did.

He traced the edge of her hip, feeling the softness of her skin and shape. Haley had been *impressed* by a real Human woman and her curves were not the artificial kind gleamed from metaphysical perfection.

Farley liked that too.

With a gentle stroke between her legs, he made her moan and felt wetness against his fingertips. Her scent blossomed and his cock responded to her *need,* growing hard until the point of pain.

This time he was going to do things right.

Farley licked her taste from his fingers, giving his palate fair warning. He didn't want to freeze up this time, unable to move because he couldn't control himself.

Her leg moved when he pushed at her thigh. He was careful not to put too much weight on her. Haley was deep in sleep, but even that had its limits. With forced gentleness he brushed his lips across her thigh, to her pelvis, then moved across until those soft hairs of hers tickled his nose. He shuddered, so close to her his body demanded more.

All in good time.

He kissed her there, then slid his tongue into the fold of skin and tasted the sweetness. His hands tightened on the bedcover, twisting it into knots.

Above him Haley moaned, her legs opened, and ... oh, yes.

He pushed his tongue deep, his fangs brushing her most tender bits of skin; then he drew the soft bud of flesh between his lips and sucked. Farley repeated the process, tasting her and relishing how her skin burned. He forgot about watching her, too enthralled with what he was doing. When she arched her back, he grabbed her hips, tilted her upward, putting a leg on his shoulder. Haley's breathing became desperate and her cries were the rhythm he went by. Farley wanted to go slow, but he could feel how much she ached. With one final thrash she came for him, bucking in his grip as he continued, bringing the second orgasm right behind the first.

He looked up to see her watching, eyes swimming gold, a small smile curled at the corner of her lips. The tips of her fingers brushed his cheek and she said, "Feed from me."

Farley kissed her mound and slid his tongue to her inner thigh. He pulled his knees under him, angled himself so he could watch her face, her leg under his body, his cock rubbing against her calf. Touching her was almost enough to bring him. *Feeding* from her definitely would.

With one hand he held her thigh slightly out and with the other he teased the tender folds of flesh were wet with heat. He slid one finger inside her, then two, his thumb a little higher up rubbing. Haley rolled her head back and side to side.

"Feed from me." Her voice cracked and her breath shuddered out.

Farley worked her until her body tightened around his fingers. Eyes were half lidded, mouth open so she could pant. Haley's hands kneaded the flesh of her thighs, stomach, and breasts.

Her *need* burned in Farley greater than any hunger he'd ever felt. He put his cheek against her thigh and let the scent of her sex fill him. His teeth ached as they lengthened and sharpened, until too long and awkward for a Human mouth.

When her breathing began to deepen and was chased by a moan, Farley sank his teeth into her flesh. She came for him.

Blood filled his mouth so fast it almost choked him. He bucked, orgasming from the *feed.* He took from her what she offered, the deepest strongest source of her blood, smelling of sex and her Female scent.

When Farley released his grip, his chest and throat ached from pulling. Under his lips the wounds closed. He licked them clean, savoring every taste. He realized then why he had been able to stop eating Human flesh.

Insides humming, he rolled away and lay on his back, lower parts of him aching despite the release. Haley's face filled his view. She kissed him, sucked at his tongue, licked her own ichor from his chin and then moved over him. One leg on each side, her core against his body rubbing him, until he was mewling like a hatchling.

In spite of the foreplay, her body was tight. Only the wetness made taking him possible. This was just sex, a sharing of bodies, but it felt like so much more. The bonds of the Mark made Farley's metaphysical energy swell until every inch of skin was prickling and alive. His fingers dug into Haley's hips and he moved to meet her while at the same time pulling down. Haley's head fell back, her mouth opened, a deep thrum kicked in her chest. Farley echoed the sound.

He needed more of her; he wanted everything.

Farley pushed himself up until he could reach her lower back, and dug his fingers into the *ulysiss* gland under the skin. Heat bloomed and she cried out, falling forward, her rhythm broken, but not lost. With his lips he caught her mouth and in one twist moved her under him. Her hands found the tender spot between his shoulder and the one right above the swell of his ass.

He swallowed back the roar that rose in his throat, and buried the rest in the pillow beside her head. He fought the surge of pleasure that rode up his spine and brought a flash of golden scales down his back and across his legs and arms.

Somehow he moved. With one hand planted beside her head he held himself up, and with the other he pushed her right leg high. The angle stopped her from being able to reach him and sent her thrashing.

This was what he wanted.

Farley pushed himself deep, hitting places that were not meant to be reached and making her cry out his name until her voice was hoarse and the syllables became meaningless. He came hard, barking curses, then again when her body clenched around him with her own release. Farley collapsed, his face in her neck.

Both of them stayed there, unable to move, legs and arms a tangled mess. Farley felt her arms wrap around him and her cheek press against his ear.

She murmured something, but he didn't hear it. His mind was working on how to keep her safe. He'd never imagined his life empty of her, but now it was an obsession. Farley knew Haley didn't believe Kin could love.

It's a Human emotion, she always said.

But whatever this was, it was powerful. It was a feeling driven by something stronger than even instinct. It overrode everything when he embraced it: every rational thought, need for self-preservation, the hunger, sex.

He rolled to his side and brought her with him, held her tight, his nose pressed to her neck, immersing himself in her scent.

Protect her at all costs. There simply wasn't anything else to live for.

Chapter 15

Haley poured Farley another bowl of cereal. It was his fourth. And he wasn't using one of those dinky little single serving bowls either. It was a salad bowl. The kind that served six. He'd started with Raisin Bran and then moved to the remainder of her Cheerios. When there wasn't enough for a full bowl, he mixed in some Fruit Loops. Now it was just the Fruit Loops. The colored bits of puffed, sugary wheat had formed a mountain that barely managed to stay inside the edges.

Farley sat perched on one of her bar stools, with no shirt, wearing a pair of black skaters weighted down in chains. It was one of many pairs that had migrated into her closet over the years. Along with some old jeans, a few shirts--mostly tees, but there was one button-up he wore at meetings.

"You've got to do some grocery shopping," Farley said, between spoonfuls of neon O's.

"And tell me, please, when am I supposed to have time? I do well to stop in at Jerry's on the corner." She watched him chew and shovel. Farley never did have very good table manners. But watching him eat was still a thing of beauty. It was almost as good as a strip tease.

"Tell him to carry more meat." He picked up the bowl and slurped the colored milk. "Sausage, bacon ... you'd think he'd at least carry cheese." He belched loud enough to rattle the walls.

Show off.

Haley spooned in another mouthful of peanut butter. He was right. She really needed to go to a real grocery store and stock up. Any more incidents like last night and they'd be in some serious trouble.

It was not going to happen again, she decided. Only thing was, she didn't believe it. Medan had asked her to be her Enforcer. What had she called it in Olde Tongue? *Ar-a-ma? Er-a-tah? No, Er-a-ma-tah.* That was it. No matter how the word translated it would only lead to one thing--an early grave.

But if Medan was telling the truth about the other Queens wanting Haley dead?

Yeah, right. How probable was that scenario? If the Council of Queens wanted her dead, she'd be dead. Wouldn't she?

Unless Niles really had been...

When she looked up, Farley was staring at her. His eyes were dark, his face grim.

"Please tell me you didn't just hear all that?"

"I didn't." He put the bowl down, pulled his feet up onto the stool and leaned over the wet bar in her direction. "This far away, you fade in and out like a bad signal. But it was enough to know I need to hear the rest."

She shoved her spoon into her peanut butter and glared at him. "If the *mark* opened some sort of telepathic connection, why in the hell can't I hear your thoughts?"

"Medan can't even force her way into my head to hear what I'm thinking." He reached over and pulled her spoon out of the jar and made a show of removing the wad of peanut butter clinging to it. "You can feel my emotions though," he said, around a mouthful of Jif. "She can't even do that."

"When I'm touching you, sure." Haley got another spoon out of the strainer and joined him in cleaning out the jar. "I don't think I like the idea of you hearing what I think. I mean, how is that going to work at Christmas?" She was trying to be funny, but his expression was dark.

"If I can't hear you, I can't know your *needs*. Now what was that about Niles?"

Haley frowned, shoved too much in her mouth, and fought to get it down. "Medan claims he's been watching me, and keeping the other Queens from arranging any unfortunate accidents." She took another bite, this one smaller. Man, they just didn't make peanut butter in big enough jars any more. Better than nothing. At least it's the real thing. No half-the-fat-and-thirty-percent-less-sugar crap in her house.

Farley waved his spoon around, animating his thoughts. "And you believe her?"

"Of course not!" Haley stood up and went to the fridge--there was a little more than half a gallon of milk left. She got two glasses from the cabinet, filled them and handed one to Farley as she sat back down.

Cows. Who could have known their hundred-and-one uses?

"But she didn't lie?" He made it a question.

"No. Have you ever met a Queen who did?" Haley had a lot of experience trying to talk to them on the phone through their Links and Marks. She was the only one in the Bureau who would even try. It was a tiring game of word chess every time.

"Thankfully, the only Queen I've ever had the pleasure to run into is Medan." He took another long swig and erased the milkstache with the back of his hand. "She can lie though."

Haley wagged a finger at him. "No, she doesn't lie. She just tells you what she wants you to know. All Queens are like that." She took another sip. "You ask them something like ... oh ... I don't know ... are you involved in any illegal flesh trading, and they will laugh a little and tell you they have never taken any bit of flesh that was not given to them freely. What they don't tell you is that her Marks held down the poor SOB and flayed him for her." When Haley looked at him she put a hand to her mouth. "God of Man, Farley. I'm sorry ... I didn't think..."

He tilted his head and smiled. "Z'all's good."

"No, no, that was completely ... stupid."

"Haley..." Farley planted one hand on the counter and tipped her chin up with the other. "It happened. I can't change it and neither can you. It's no different than surviving a hatching. We still have to live in spite of it." He licked her chin and lips, then rubbed his cheek against hers. His breath smelled like peanut butter, milk, and under that, the scent she'd burned into his marrow.

"Now finish what you were saying about Medan not lying." With his eyes so close, the brown depths looked like chocolate pools.

"She didn't lie."

"She just told you what she wanted you to know?"

Haley nodded, "Yeah."

"And that's not lying?"

"Apparently not in her mind, or any Queen, for that matter." She pushed a lock of dark hair behind her ear. "They don't smell like a lie."

Farley sat back on the counter, picked up the jar, and scraped out the last bite. "So?"

"That's it. She gave me the bits and pieces of the story that were true."

"So that means Niles has been following you?"

"Probably. Most likely, yes."

"And keeping any would-be accidents from happening?"

She nodded and finished her glass of milk. Farley tipped his glass toward the wall behind her. "Are those Hostess Twinkies I hear calling to me?"

Twinkies? She hadn't bought Twinkies since...

Haley searched the shelf near the fridge and found them behind a loaf of green, fuzzy bread, two bags of stale cookies, and something that might have been potatoes.

"They're old," she said, looking at the date. "Like three, no, make that four years past their expiration." She peeked in the box; the damn thing was almost full too. What a shame.

"Give em' here." Farley waved for the box.

"They'll make you sick." Even the cellophane had yellowed. Come to think of it, the box didn't look all that great either. She shook it and a dead moth fell out the end. Haley stomped it. The little petrified body turned to dust. Another Human imprint she'd picked up--her adopted mother's fear of bugs. Pretty humiliating, really.

"Twinkies will outlive us all. Give em' here." Farley grabbed at the air.

"Good grief, you eat these and you'll have to have your stomach pumped. Probably even have bugs in them."

"Makes for more protein. Give-give-give!" She handed him the box just to shut him up. Farley growled as he used his sharp fangs to decimate the wrappers. When he took a bite, he swayed groaning. "God of Man, I love these things. They're like sex, only edible."

"I thought that was my brownies?" Haley sat back on her stool and watched him pour the box into his lap and proceed to open the little yellow cakes one by one and cram them whole into his mouth. "You really need to work on your eating skills. You'd get invited to more dinner parties with Deshi and me."

Farley crammed another one in his already packed cheeks. Little bits of cream clung to his lips. He picked it off and held it on the tips of his fingers until he made room. Little kissing noises filled the air as he sucked them clean.

"Ouf apies e oring..."

"What the hell did you just say?" She eyed one of the last Twinkies, and seriously considered snagging it, but there was another dead moth and it was inside the wrapper.

Farley washed away his chipmunk cheeks with a few swigs of milk. "I said..." He took another drink. "I said that those parties are boring." He opened the last one, picked the moth off, ate it, then chased it with the Twinkie. Haley made a face and Farley grinned, flashing yellow cake and white filling, stuck between lots of sharp and pointies.

Haley glanced at the clock. It was getting close to eight and she still had to do her hair, put on her shoes, and try to shoo Farley out of her kitchen.

"So why do you think he did it?" Farley asked.

"Who?" She was thinking about how she needed to clean out her pantry and restock it with things that were actually edible, in date and bug free.

"Niles Fury. Why do you think he even cared what happened to you? I mean, look at the guy. He's got a reputation for Nasty even among his own people." He gave nasty a capital N.

"No clue." She picked up the glasses, put them in the sink and tossed in the spoons. "He's not all that bad though. Not really." Farley stared at her. "Well, he's not ... not really. He's just ... feral." She tossed the empty peanut butter jar into the garbage and started gathering all of Farley's empty wrappers. This was why she wouldn't leave him alone in her house. He'd have it looking like the city dump in a matter of hours.

"I think we need to find out why."

Haley laughed. "Sure, I'll just run on down to the prison again, since that went so amazingly well last time."

"Naw? You think?" He hopped down off the counter as Haley went headed to her bathroom. Farley followed. "He lived over in the Dens, southwest end."

"Yeah, right." She saw the look in his face. "Seriously?"

Farley nodded. He picked up her brush and made her sit on the toilet lid while he worked it through her still damp curls. "It was in that old fort construct that the MARTA Station backs up to. Safest place you could hop a ride. He kept most of the riff-raff cleaned out."

It didn't take a metaphysical scientist to figure out what he was doing with them either.

Farley sat on the counter while she bent over and turned the dryer on her hair so it would fluff. He said, "I'm thinking I might check out his old apartment. He's only been in prison for few months. I doubt anyone would be brave enough to actually go in there just in case he got out." Farley held her brush up to his nose and sniffed it. Every once in a while he'd stick out his tongue and lick the hairs sticking out. Haley watched him for a moment, amused.

When she stood up, he handed her back the brush.

"You sure you'll be okay?" What she meant was, would he go and eat any pedestrians while he was out on his own?

"I'm okay, I think. If I start getting the DTs when I pass any old people meandering in the hall, I'll turn around and come back." He grinned at his own joke. Haley didn't. This was a serious matter. Flesh addiction was a real problem.

Human blood and flesh was a profitable legal business, if it employed the willing. Only problem was, while there were plenty of those who would do it for money, or even for free, if they died, their family had the right to sue. Hell, if they survived and didn't like the re-arrangement of their limbs, they could sue. Queens were fiscally responsible for the damages done by any Kin in her city.

Being held responsible for some Humans' stupidity was an expensive undertaking. After all, what Human in their right mind *likes* having bits of their body eaten, especially when they know it won't grow back? Eventually the damage is just too great and someone dies.

The litigious nature of Human society fueled the illegal trade. It was just easier to take someone and make them disappear. Hard to prove a murder if you don't have a body. Better yet, bring in people from foreign countries. Sometimes the export of flesh was done with the consent of a country looking to reduce its numbers. Sometimes, it was done without it. The flesh trade also helped competing crime families to get rid of their problems.

In the end, it all boiled down to the fact that Human blood and flesh was as addictive to some Kin as cold beer and scotch could be to some Humans. Unfortunately, they didn't have a Flesh-Eaters-Anonymous. Nope, it was just off with your head.

“I won’t lose control,” Farley said, his voice all serious.

“You weren’t so sure about that last night.”

“That was before.”

She rolled her eyes, checked her hair in the mirror, and looked at him. He was staring at her like she was something yummy to eat.

“I’ll be late.” She turned away, but he grabbed her hand and yanked her off her feet. His kiss hit her lips hard enough for their teeth to rake against each other. His tongue reached deep, prodding, probing, tasting, suggesting nefarious possibilities. They were both breathless when he let her go. Haley stumbled back and seriously considered calling in.

So he won’t have to go alone, she told herself.

Yeah ... riiight...

“I’ll be fine. Go to work. I’ll be in later. Tell Garrett I’m following up on those shipping manifests or something.” He waved a hand at her.

She didn’t want him to go back there. Terrible things happened in that place.

Farley touched the scar on his shoulder. “I’m yours. She knows the rules.”

Yeah, but it didn’t mean Medan wouldn’t just break them.

Chapter 16

Dobson wasn't asleep when the phone beside his bed rang. It was the same phone that he'd had when the Whore was alive. Same bed, too. Seemed a waste to ruin a perfectly good bed on her account. The ring was loud because the phone was old. One of those fifteen pound corded monstrosities that was colored like Human skin. Only God knew why.

He kept it because he liked the way it rang. No electronic beeping noises when a call came over his line. His phone sounded like it was ready to take names and kick ass.

Dobson reached over and picked up the receiver.

"This better be good. It's--" He looked at the clock. "Four-thirty in the morning."

"It's Reynolds, sir." Ah, Reynolds, a real soldier, that one. Someone he could rely on. A real asset to his random tissue sampling in the Gray Zone. Not like it was that hard to do. Give out free drugs, or just plain cheap ones, and Kin would come flocking to your door like flies on shit.

Although Dobson had to admit, he liked the man better before he'd done the whole Alchemist crossover thing. Now meeting his gaze was like staring a dead fish in the eyes.

"Talk to me, soldier." He called all his street men "soldier." Whether or not they'd actually served with him was a moot point. After all, they were serving with him now. In this war.

"We have a situation."

Those were four little words that Dobson did not want to hear. Not now, not later, and sure as fuck not coming out of the mouths of anyone working the Zone.

Dobson sat up and swung his feet over the side of his bed. "Tell me you did not get busted by the local pussy PD." He scratched himself, picked up the phone and carried it as far as the cord would reach, which got him right in firing distance of the toilet.

"No, sir." There was a long pause. "It's just..."

"Then what?" He shook himself dry, arranged his shorts and carried the phone back to the bed. When Reynolds didn't answer him he said,

"You'd better start talking, because you do not want me to find out from someone else."

"Yes, sir. I understand, sir. It's just that, there seems to be a problem with this batch of synth-H." They sold five specific varieties, synth-H, C, H2, E, and X. H gave the wyrms a heroine-type high.

"I'm listening, so keep talking."

"We injected it into the subjects, just like always, but something went wrong. Bad wrong. Nine of them died."

Dobson rubbed a hand over his short gray brush cut. Most of his hair had decided to retreat on him to the back of his skull. Didn't matter. Hair was overrated anyhow.

"You lost nine total, or nine that you kept?" To keep suspicions down, they only took samples from the few they invited to stay around. Giving them the preferred customer treatment. Once they were high as a kite they could do whatever. Take marrow, take blood, hell they could cut their God-damned cocks off and they wouldn't know. Fuckers could grow back an arm unless you used Alchemy.

When they woke up they'd just wander off. If any of them remembered getting collected, who were they going to tell? The cops? And if they did, who was going to believe them?

If there was anything more useless than a junkie, it was a Kin junkie.

"Nine out of the ten we kept. We think the last one's on his way out, too."

Dobson stood up, tried to pace, and pulled the phone off onto the floor. "What the fuck happened? Can you tell me that? Can you at least fucking tell me what the hell went wrong? It's synth-H, for fuck's sake. We've been selling that shit for the past seven years and it's never killed anyone. So either Kin have suddenly developed some sort of biological reaction to it, which we know I'd have a greater chance of shitting the Virgin Mary out of my ass than that happening, or something happened." He waited for Reynolds to answer him.

"Erica thought there might have been a cross contamination."

"A what?" Spit flecked his lips and it felt like there were thunderbolts shooting against the back of his skull. "Do not..." He dragged the phone base with him and sat back down on the bed. It made sad little ding-ding noises along the way. "Do not fuck with me. Get her on the phone. I want her to tell me herself that there has been a cross contamination in my lab." It could undo everything. If his virus got out, the Center for Disease Control could get their hands on a sample and it wouldn't take long to figure out what the virus was being designed for. And if anyone happened to compare it to his little Beijing speed bump there could be hell to pay.

His hell and his pay.

"I can't, sir, Erica's dead. One of our usuals walked in talking about getting stiffed on the deal we'd made with him a few days back. We'd just lost the last one and number ten wasn't looking so hot. She had a few vials from an old batch and thought if we ran both of them through him we could figure out what was different between them." Erica was smart that way. Brutal. "We let him shoot up to make sure it was good. When he went down, we strapped him in. He must have metabolized it faster than we expected, or maybe Erica gave him a smaller dose just to make sure the synth-H didn't kill him ... who knows? He went ballistic. Erica had just gotten done getting the control samples and went to stick him. He broke her neck."

"And you have this son of a bitch, right?"

Silence. It told Dobson exactly what he did not want to hear.

"Fuck. I pay you enough money to buy you all the booze, fast cars and fresh ass your dick could ever dream of, and you're telling me you can't kill a fucking strung out Kin." God, he wanted to kill something. Anything.

"Martin says he recognized him." *Hallelujah, it's fucking Christmas!* "He says they took him into the PD Monday, talked to that Kin Agent they have there. Made some deal with Bauer, so they let him out last night. He came here because he was looking for a score."

"Jesus Christ, you must be fucking retarded." Dobson could not believe what he was hearing. "Do you enjoy fucking me up the ass, Reynolds? Because you are seriously fucking me up the ass right now." He got up, sat down, and scrubbed the back of his skull for a few more rounds. "Looking for a score? You actually believed that the son of a bitch was just looking for a score? What the fuck do you think that cunt's job is, Reynolds? Obviously you don't know, don't care, or are too fucking stupid ... did they fry your brain along with your soul when you crossed over to the Dark Side?" This was proof positive that just because you were an Alchemist, it didn't make you a genius.

When Reynolds spoke there was ice in his tone. "With all due respect, sir, I worked Vice in Texas. We didn't put the wyrms on the pay roll. Whatever that Female does here, I wouldn't know about it except for what I hear from you and Martin."

"And what's Martin's excuse?"

"He wasn't here when it went down." Short and clipped.

"So, how did he know who the Kin was?"

"He dropped his wallet. Martin made a call, got the details. He told them the wyrm is wanted in connection with a deal gone bad. If he shows up, they'll hold him. We have the bodies, might as well put one or two to good use."

"Incinerate the others," Dobson said. This fuck up might actually work out to be a good thing. He needed an excuse to access the Center's GPS data base, her email or anything he could use as evidence that Haley Night had gone into the Dens against orders from upstairs. If Dobson played his cards right, he could own her scaly ass by Friday. Maybe sooner.

Chapter 17

An ambulance sitting in front of the CFKR was not what Haley would consider a good start to the day. She parked Garrett's sedan in the front, and went in the main entrance.

She passed a team of EMS workers in the lobby and waded into a group of cops, all of whom had their side arms drawn and were looking down the hall as if the devil himself was about to come stomping up the nap carpet.

"What's going on?" It seemed like a perfectly logical question until Taylor grabbed her arm and shoved her back towards the door.

"Get back! The last thing we need is another one of you down there!"

"What the hell?"

"Fuck you!" That from Manuel. She didn't know either of them very well because she only saw them when they walked suspects back and forth for questioning. One thing for sure, they were throwing off a whole lot of I-wanna-put-a-cap-in-your-ass.

The front doors burst open and two teams of Alchemists in full riot gear went storming down the hall. There was only one reason they called in an Alchemist team. Something had gone bad in the Tank.

Haley went down the other hall and took the service elevator in the back. She came out into a corridor clogged with Cops facing off with Alchemists. She slipped around the mass of blue and found more of them blocking the doorway to the Tank. They stared down the hall, faces grim.

"What's going on?"

Angry cop eyes gave her some up and down. "Get her out of here." That from the guy with the blond brush cut. Considering no one did any push and shove, it meant either they really didn't want her to go, or they were too scared to touch her.

Haley was betting on scared.

It was Jenna, the only detective in the bunch, who bothered to answer her. "Your junkie in there has Bauer, McKinney, and Jones holed up in an interrogation room with him."

"My junkie?" Haley looked around at all of them. "How the hell did I get pegged with this?"

"Was asking for you the minute his scaly ass came into the building." Haley didn't know him, but his name tag said Tomlin.

"A lot of Kin ask for me when they come in here. They know I'm the only one that won't shoot first and ask questions later." They bowed up on her, voices rising, and juicy curses spilling out of clenched teeth. "Why don't you get out of my way and let me go down there and see if I can't stop this before it gets any worse?."

"Too late." John Tate had been on the force for a while and was a few years short of retirement. He didn't show it, though. Except for a little gray around his temples, he looked like a rookie.

"Let me go in there."

John Tate glared. "What part of 'too late' do you not understand?"

Haley leaned into him. "Well, it looks to me like you have a choice. You can tell your comrades to get out of the way and let the Alchemists have at it, then go in and scrape up any pieces that might be left over, or you can let me go in and try to calm him down.

Jenna shook her head and her eyes went back through the door where the Alchemists were demanding entry. "He's been shooting up with something nasty, Haley. I don't think there's going to be much we can do but scrape up whatever's left."

"Let me try." Haley looked at them. "Damn it, what have you got to lose? You don't even know if any of them are still alive." They still didn't get out of the way, but when she went forward they didn't stop her.

Half way down the hallway, Haley slowed down from a jog to a cautious crawl. She tilted her head and listened with her dragon hearing. Hearts pounded, breathing came quick, and there was a small whimper ... Human Male.

A quick glance back up the hall told her the cops had stopped parrying for position with the Alchemists. They were all standing silent, just watching.

"Creyal?" Haley called. Silence was the only reply.

The first four doors were empty, pale fluorescents flickering. Haley scented the air and tasted Bauer's familiar scent. The other two she wasn't sure of, but one of them was a woman and she was pregnant.

"Creyal? The boys upstairs said you were looking for me."

Haley came to the edge of the door. It was the same one she'd interviewed him in. She peeked through the gap and caught sight of Bauer, sitting in a corner with his head down, arms on his knees. His eyes were closed, his face calm. He looked like a man that'd come to the realization he was going to die and the only thing left to do was wait. The right sleeve of his white button up was crimson, and bits of his flesh and muscle were flapping out of the hole.

"Creyal? Talk to me please?" She stole another look. The woman was on the floor, curled up beside the overturned table. When she saw Haley, she shook her head and her eyes moved to the wall out of Haley's line of sight. Her eyes told Haley terrible things were about to happen in that corner. Things that no one ever wanted to see.

"Creyal, I'm walking in alone. Please don't do anything that both of us will regret." Haley stepped inside and understood immediately why they were all freaked out. Creyal no longer looked Human. The partial shift left him with a scaled body, a human shaped torso, a massive Draconian head and hands that were nothing but black gleaming Ginsu knives.

The third cop lay crumpled and bloody at Creyal's feet, his side arm beside his mangled arm.

Creyal's head swung in her direction. Haley walked up to him, her hands out. He roared and little streams of dust trickled down from cracks in the ceiling. Both the woman cop and Bauer jumped.

"Shhh." Haley touched his muzzle, ran her fingers along his jaw and his cheek. Spiny points of horn protruded from the back of his skull.

He shuddered under her hand. His feather-like scales rustled. Creyal's silver eyes rolled in the direction of Bauer, then the woman.

"They're going to get up and go now, okay?" Creyal clicked and chirped, and his wings rattled. "I'm here now, you don't need them. Let them go, Creyal. I'm not asking you. I'm telling you." His eyes rolled back to her. The pupils contracted, turning into slits. Bits of orange blossomed, like drops of paint, in the depths of his irises.

"Bauer?" Haley didn't look at him, because she wanted to keep her attention on the feral.

"Yeah." He sounded weak.

"Do you think you can walk out of here?"

"I'll dance out if you like."

She smiled. "That's not necessary. Officer?"

"I can walk," McKinney said. "What about Jones?"

Haley pulled Creyal's head against her. His cheek slid from her hip to her shoulder. He repeated the gesture from the other side.

"What about Jones? Creyal? Will you let them pull him out of here?"

Creyal's taloned hand came down on the man, pinning him.

Two was better than zero. Haley said, "Jones is staying right now. You two get out." Bauer got up, staggered, but made it to the door. "Your turn, McKinney." The woman didn't move.

"McKinney!" Bauer's voice boomed and the woman got her legs going. Haley heard the door shut behind her, and then lock. Bauer was no dummy.

Creyal roared and lurched to the center of the room. His massive head smashed the door and his claws laid into the metal. He flashed his teeth at Haley and snapped at the air near her face. She didn't blink.

Creyal shuddered and thick streams of saliva dripped from his gaping mouth. His tail whipped and smashed against the table, splintering it. He sat back on his haunches, looking weak. The muscles in his thigh danced as he leaned against the wall.

Haley approached him again and leaned into him, putting her face against his neck. His scales fluttered and his scent rose. It wasn't right.

She petted him, a slow up and down from his elbow to his neck. "You need to shift back, Creyal. This far changed, they have every right to use deadly force. I'm here now. Let me help you. Talk to me."

Joints popped, scales fluttered and a moment later he was leaning against her, his knees failing. Haley helped him to the floor and sat with his face cradled against her neck. His vacant stare was dark against his way-too-pale skin. The track marks on his one arm seeped thin lines of green ichor. He wasn't healing, and that was a very bad sign.

Haley pushed his hair back out of his face. He'd lost the tie that he used to hold it back, along with every scrap of clothing, which was on the floor in useless shreds. Creyal stared at her with a sadness she didn't understand. Her thumb traced his brow. He caught her hand and brought her palm to his lips. His tongue rasped her skin.

"What happened?" It wasn't drugs doing this to him. Not even synth.

This was Alchemy, and it was evil. She knew there were powers that could kill Kin, but whatever this was had no individual scent she could detect. But there was a change in him. Creyal had acquired a sweet, sickly smell that reminded her of rotten things in the ground.

"I couldn't stay away." He lifted his arm. "I was just going to have a little taste. I figured I could find out more info if I did my usual. But they wouldn't let me leave." He curled against her. His arm slid over her shoulder, and he tucked his head under her chin. "Something was wrong. It wasn't the usual kind of set-up. Smelled funny. Then I saw them."

Haley stroked his head and back and thrummed in her chest. "Who did you see?"

"Dead Kin." Every bone in his Creyal's body pushed against his skin. He'd changed a lot since Monday. "He was there..."

"Who?"

"The cop on the floor." Creyal's breathing was shallow. "I'm so tired ... so tired."

From the hallway the sound of cop voices and the scent of Alchemist magic drifted in.

"I'm okay, so please don't come in here guns blazing," Haley said. "We're good. All's good."

The door jerked open, and the Alchemist filed in, their body shields facing her, cutting her off from the other half of the room. Pin guns came up. "He's not in any shape to hurt anyone now. You can put those down." She started to stand.

"Stay down, wyrm!" The voice was male, but she had no idea which one said it. All dressed up in their big, bad, black cookie cutter outfits they looked just alike.

Haley said, "Hey, guys, any cops out there that might be listening. Please don't leave me in here with the SWAT team from hell."

She was about to call out again when someone yelled, "Stand down." Bauer came through the door, his arm done up like King Tut, and looking in need of a serious drink.

"He's sick," Haley said, and they all tossed her angry glances. Bauer shook his head and looked at the crumpled cop on the floor. Someone felt for a pulse and then yelled for the EMTs. "Didn't you hear me? He's sick."

"No one gives a shit about the fucking lizard." That from one of the Alchemists.

"Bauer!" Haley said.

The detective looked at her, dark eyes flashing. "He's not my priority right now, Haley. As far as I'm concerned, they can take him out back and lop off his head."

"He's sick, Bauer. As in ill. We don't get diseases." No one was listening. "For Christ's sake, Bauer, that son-of-a-bitch on the floor did this to him."

The man turned on her and jabbed a finger in her face. "And with any luck he'll fucking die. He destroyed six lives today. Six good Human lives. None of us will be the same, and Jones probably won't get to see his kid's..." Bauer curled his hand into a fist, and made an obvious effort to step away.

Haley stared at him, feeling detached. He was pissed. They all were. She was Kin, so it was her fault, too. She accepted that. Fine. But that didn't change things. "You need to call the CDC, Bauer. Kin don't get sick, remember. That means whatever this is, it's deadly. Creyal saw other dead Kin. There could be more. If it can kill Kin, it has the potential to kill Humans, too. And that means everyone could wind up like this." The entire room came to a standstill.

Bauer pulled out his phone and dialed.

Chapter 18

It was on the bus that Farley got nervous and a thin sheen of sweat broke out across the back of his neck. Over the driver's seat was an advertisement that read "It's SMARTA to ride MARTA."

No, he would have been SMARTA to take a cab. Now he was stuck inside this rolling cookie jar, smelling people and waiting for the Hunger to show up like a bad penny.

After the longest fifteen minutes of his life.

When Farley could see the Wall he stood up and pulled the cord. A bell tolled and the bus slowed. He got off and headed across the street and down an alley. His combat boots thumped on the pavement and the chains on his skater pants jingled.

It was cold today, and his Godsmack shirt didn't offer very much protection.

Correction, Haley's Godsmack shirt.

It was black and matched the pants, so he'd borrowed it. She'd given him the stink eye when he'd pulled it out of her drawer, but it was either that or her pink flowered one, and he really didn't feel like getting the shit kicked out of him today.

Farley tucked his hands under his arms, and wished he'd kept a spare jacket at her place. Other than the few stray pieces of clothing, everything there was hers. But that was going to have to change, wasn't it?

Yes, it was.

It took a lot of will power to get himself out of that building and on the bus. And it wasn't because he was afraid of any cravings popping up. Leaving Haley alone was just a bad idea. Every metaphysical energy point in his body said so.

He passed under a causeway and trotted along the edge of the concrete spillway that funneled excess rain water into the creeks. This was a bad part of the Gray Zone and Farley knew it. Usually he stayed near the Pit, Casey's, or the line of restaurants where a lot of the shippers hung out. The truck yard on the north end was another reasonably safe place.

Farley stopped just under the old iron bridge connecting the two sides of the stacked stone fort. It wasn't really a fort, it just happened to look like one.

Inside, the building was scarred by a run-in with the Society for Neighborhood Improvement and bore a combination of 1960's olive tile crossed with a 1990's face lift. It only went as far as the foyer. When Farley stepped into the hall, he could see why. This place made his little hole in the wall look like the Ritz.

Honest to God moss was growing on the walls, and a small tree coming up through a crack in the floor had surpassed weed status and was heading into bush frontier. The stairs didn't look safe in spite of being made out of stone. There were great gaping holes in the railing, big enough to drive a car through.

Farley headed up the hallway, hoping he was in the right part of the building. He only knew Niles lived in the area because Kin avoided it.

Eight doors later, and after taking a stairwell into a flooded basement, Farley decided the only direction left was up. So far, he'd only found a family of rats and an old burned out sofa, circa 1970. The room it was in smelled like melting rubber.

Rock shifted on the steps where the mortar had crumbled and left the flagstone flopping like the sole of a blown out tennis shoe. The long hall at the top was nothing more than a stretch of rotten wood littered with trash and a few shriveled rat skeletons.

About half-way up, he had a pretty good idea which room was Niles'. It was the only one with a door. When he jiggled the knob it came open.

Damn thing didn't even squeak.

Farley looked inside.

A flashlight would have been a good idea. The room was dark because the windows had been covered, leaving nothing but a thin orange line where the sun could leak in.

His vision slid to its natural state and he scanned the room. A desk, a pallet on the floor, a big trunk, and what looked like a radio in the corner was a complete inventory of the three hundred square foot space. Farley stepped inside. The walls fluttered when he moved the door.

Like they were breathing.

What the hell?

Farley reached up and felt scraps of paper, dimpled with writing and held up with thumb tacks.

The little sheets were everywhere, floor to ceiling, ceiling to floor. They fluttered whenever he stirred the air. Farley went to the window, felt for the blanket that covered it, and yanked it down. He blinked and waited for the splotches of green and red to fade. When he could finally see, he became rooted to the spot.

Okay, this is weird.

Newspaper articles, hand written letters, old maps, and pages from calendars covered every inch of wall space. The different lettering and overall changes in style told him that the collection spanned decades. Farley had never imagined Niles to be the coupon-clipper-stalker type.

Then there were the photos--lots and lots of photos.

They were of Haley. Candid shots, taken from a distance. Walking into the CFKR, sitting in the park, parking lot of her building...

Hopefully, Haley wasn't going to be right about the Twinkies.

Farley plucked a newspaper clipping from its place on the wall. It was dated 1938. The article was brief, talking about the official establishment of the CFKR and how the city of Atlanta had set a new trend dealing with the ever-growing concern of Human and Kin existence. Haley was mentioned close to the end, where the current CFKR director felt she could be an asset to the establishment of good relations with the non-Human residents of the city. They were all like that. Either she was mentioned, pictured, or quoted.

On the desk Farley found a ledger with more names and places, then an article from about ten years ago. Haley wasn't mentioned in this one, but another Kin was. Farley stared at the photo.

Frozen in time, with wings half spread, and his blazing blue eyes turned like he was listening to something no one else could hear, was the epitome of Kin acceptance; Justice, the Great White.

Nothing about him was like other Kin. With his ivory scales and large blue eyes, Justice gave off a gentle unimposing presence. He had no ridges, no horns, no thorny protection or armor. While not all Kin could breathe fire, they usually had some sort of natural defense or offense--such as quills or venom--but Justice had nothing. To top it off, rumor had it he was mute. Defective.

But he did have something that the Human world wanted, badly enough that they accepted him to the point of not making him walk around in a Human skin.

Justice could read minds. Not the pick-a-card-any-card, either. The city used his ability to save billions in trials as well as innocent lives.

And while the Great White looked like a harmless Disney version of My Favorite Dragon, Farley wasn't fooled. Kin didn't get as old as him if they weren't powerful.

Not to mention dangerous.

Behind the article in the section marked "names and numbers", there was only one phone number, but no name. Farley took out his cell phone, and for shits and giggles punched in the number.

On the third ring, a very normal-sounding Human voice answered. "This is Gregory." There was even TV noise in the background.

What had he been expecting? Justice was mute. Feeling like an ass, Farley did the only thing he could. Apologize. "I'm sorry. I think I must have dialed the wrong number."

"Who are you trying to call?"

The man called himself Gregory.

Farley hung up without replying. His phone was a disposable, practically impossible to trace.

Gregory. Where had he seen that name before?

He looked around, then down at the magazine cutting. The caption under Justice's photo read: *The Great White resides in the beautiful city of Atlanta with his Human companion, Gregory...*

Shit.

Human companion, my ass. He was Justice's Link. Farley was willing to bet his piddly-ass paycheck on it. He stuffed the ledger in his boot and looked around for anything else that seemed important. He decided a little photo evidence was in order and snapped a couple pictures of the walls with his cell phone.

Weird.

Especially the astronomy maps. What were all those lines?

Either Niles was seriously wacked or he was seriously wacked.

Still, Farley couldn't shake Medan's claim he'd been protecting Haley. And why the hell would the Queens want Haley dead to begin with? Females were competitive, sure, but dead? Usually that only happened if you put two of them in the same room together.

Haley had no ties to territory. She wasn't in line for a throne. Hell, no one even knew who'd clutched her. She was the equivalent of a red-headed bastard stepchild.

Farley turned to leave, but a small separation in the wall above the desk caught his eyes. He stepped up to it and felt around inside. The smoothness of plastic brushed his fingertips, and he knew immediately what it was.

A notebook of the electronic kind.

Niles was not only a coupon clipper but a technology man. World's just full of surprises. Farley gave the room a final sweep and tucked the Sony Vaio under his arm.

Outside, the wind had picked up, and he shivered as he headed up the sidewalk. Farley crossed the road, but when he got to the causeway he kept going. The scent of Male Kin was on the wind and he didn't need the trouble. And considering the area, there could only be trouble.

Farley dropped his head and turned his chin. Three big Males were coming up the sidewalk wearing worn out jeans and no shirt or shoes.

He slid the notebook under his shirt. At little further and it became obvious that they weren't going to get bored with this.

Farley faced them and they flashed fang. When he didn't react they slunk lower, until their hands held them up and feet pushed them forward. Walking like beasts and not Humans. Their eyes glittered with gold and orange. Their mouths opened, breathing him in. Beside him now, curious fingers prodded his clothes and traced his boots. Clicking sounds rode up in their throats, and their tongues tasted him where they could find skin. The one on his right worked Farley's pants leg up to his thigh, chasing it with his teeth.

These Males were too young to be out of the Hive. But knowing Medan, she might have found them unworthy and forced them to the streets to survive or die.

Considering the part of town they were in, the latter was more likely.

Movement from the tunnel caught Farley's attention and another Male slid from the darkness, heading up the sidewalk. And he didn't move like a hatchling. Hell, he moved like something old, and filled to the rim with bravado. As he got closer, a hand came up and pushed the hood off his head. The face confirmed what Farley already scented.

"Darco." Farley didn't even attempt to cap the growl in his throat. The Male smiled, flashing sharps. Black hair fell over his shoulders in thick waves and framed his long face. Like Farley, Darco was too pretty to be handsome. But then, clutch mates often *impressed* on similar features.

His Brother smiled, in the sick little way that suggested he was thinking things that you just didn't want to know about.

"I thought it was you, Little Brother." He stepped between the taste-testers and put his face in Farley's, cobalt blue eyes searching. His thin lips tilted up and he sniffed the air around Farley's mouth. "You smell different."

Darco leaned in closer and scraped his tongue up Farley's cheek. "Taste different. What's under your shirt?" He flicked his finger and thumped the plastic shell of the laptop. "Mmm, sounds expensive." Darco lips brushed Farley's ear. He whispered, "Can I see it?"

Farley growled. "I think you know the answer to that."

His Brother laughed and rocked back on his heels. The Males were working on Darco now, smelling, tasting. He didn't even seem to notice.

Which was bullshit.

Knowing his little talent for influence, he was probably making them do it.

"What do you want?"

Darco practically glowed in the light of Farley's discomfort. He stroked Farley's cheek with a pale white hand. "To be honest, the rumor mill was buzzing about your untimely demise. So you can imagine my relief when I caught a whiff of you ambling up the sidewalk. What are you doing here? This isn't exactly your part of the Dens."

No, but it was his. This was the exact kind of locale Darco enjoyed. Desolate. Isolated. Made it harder to scream for help.

"Free country," Farley hissed.

Darco laughed, in the subtle way that said he wasn't really amused, just not quite ready to hurt you yet. But he was getting close. He licked Farley's scent from his fingers.

"Definitely different." His blue eyes narrowed and a curious expression came across his face. He grabbed Farley by the back of the neck and slammed his mouth against his hard enough to knock teeth.

Farley knew better than to fight. He let his Brother taste him, tongue sliding around the inside of his mouth, raking against his palate, molars, the back of his tongue, gagging him with the depths he probed.

He broke off the tasting as fast as he took it. Darco smacked his lips while he made a show of rolling Farley's flavor around in his mouth. His lips thinned and little flecks of gold starburst in his eyes.

"That Female you Roll with *marked* you." It wasn't a question but a bitter statement. "You?" He grabbed Farley's arms, yanked them open. The laptop hit the ground with a crunch. Darco bit his lip, doing a poor impersonation of regret, and shrugged. "Oops." He yanked Farley's shirt up and over his head wadded it up and tossed it aside.

Darco put a hand on Farley's shoulder and forced him to kneel. "Little Brother, I don't know what to say. There appears to be a Female's *mark* on your shoulder."

Farley couldn't resist. He rolled his eyes up. "Jealous?"

With a sickening crunch, Darco's *chelae* punched through Farley's shoulder. Lines of green ichor cut trails down his chest and back. Through it all, Darco's face was calm, his cobalt blue eyes blank. Farley knew the look. His Brother was reaching dangerous fast.

The world took a tilt, and before Farley could blink, his face was having an up close and personal with the rock wall and Darco's forearm was planted at the base of his skull.

"I should have eaten you like the rest of our siblings." Darco's tongue slid up close to his ear and sharp teeth pricked his earlobe. "But you gave such good head."

Farley hissed as Darco's hand closed on his groin, squeezing until he was sure something was going to pop. "The *mark* might change things with the other Males in the Dens, but I am your Brother. That *title* means I will always be your Dominant. Hmm..." Darco adjusted his grip. "I don't know, but this could turn out to be a lot of fun."

God of Man, he always knew how to deliver the most amount of pain in the least amount of time.

The Male's face came around his shoulder. "I wonder what she'd do if she found me fucking you in her bed? Do you think she'd acknowledge my place?"

"It doesn't work that way with her."

"She's Female..." Darco hissed. A little more pressure. Black flowers bloomed in Farley's vision.

"She's not like other Kin." His knees tried to buckle, but the pressure Darco applied to the back of his head kept him pinned to the wall.

"We'll just have to test that theory, won't we?"

Darco let him go and Farley collapsed. With the blood flow renewed, a new kind of pain exploded between his legs. He rolled to his side and tried to keep his eyes on his Brother. He was kicking the pieces of laptop scattered on the concrete.

The smile was back on Darco's face. He leaned against one of the three Males, practically using his shoulder like a chair.

Farley pushed himself up and made it into a sitting position.

"You know." Darco looked down at the Male and toyed with a lock of hair curled near his ear, "I'm so disappointed in you." His eyes flipped up, so bright they were practically glowing. "You and I had everything worked out..."

"You're not making any sense." But then most things that came out of Darco's mouth never made sense. When he did speak to Farley, it was usually random lines or a conglomeration of words that were irrelevant. And considering the things he was often doing to him when he did talk, it was just better not to listen.

"No, it's just that you don't remember." Darco stood up, looking bored, and kicked the laptop around. "At least, I hope that's the case and you haven't gone and changed the rules."

Rules? What rules? Farley pulled his knees under him, started to stand.

Nope, not yet.

With a hop, Darco landed on the plastic case, making it snap, crackle, pop. He smiled. "You wouldn't go and do a thing like that, would you?"

"Darco, I don't have a clue as to what you're talking about."

The Male's icy gaze rolled up. A lot of Kin avoided Darco when he looked at them like that.

The switch flipped and it was gone. His features calm, pleasant. Which was also bullshit. Nothing about Darco was pleasant. Ever.

"Why were you in Niles's apartment?" Farley flicked his gaze up before he could stop himself. "Yeah, you were definitely up to something, weren't you?" Darco's stare slid to the vacant section of building and then back to Farley. "Maybe looking for something?" He stepped on the laptop again and it gave a final crunch. By the sound of it, the screen had just bit the dust. "This maybe?" He bounced his weight, grinding it into the ground. "Start talking, Little Brother, or I'm going to do something to entertain myself."

"Why do you care?"

Damn it. One of these days I'm going to learn to keep my mouth shut.

Darco put a hand over his hearts. "Because you're my Little Brother! And when my Little Brother is wandering around in the worst part of the Dens--the day after he's supposed to be dead, need I remind you--I have a right to be concerned." He smiled. Farley didn't smile. He just leaned his head back against the wall and waited for the last bit of pain to stop.

Darco inched a closer, thumb hooked in the waistband of his pants swaying back and forth, swinging his feet, scuffing his shoes loudly against the concrete. His head was down, his eyes half lidded. It was his thinking look. As in, thinking of starting a new game of pain.

There was no sense in trying to lie. Darco would smell it. And even if Farley could pull it off with some creative fun with words, all Darco had to do was go up there and check the place out. Farley wished he'd brought a box of matches, a gallon of gasoline and just set fire to the place.

Farley said, "Niles Fury has a little side hobby involving Haley."

Darco fell very still. The light behind his eyes darkened. And when he spoke, there was an odd lilt to his voice that Farley couldn't quite place. "You talked with Niles?"

"No," Farley said. "Haley told me. She found out from Medan."

The three large Males mewled. Darco threw them a quick glance and they fell silent. He turned his attention back to Farley. "And why would Medan care?" He stood beside Farley's foot, his free hand stroking his stomach. Farley averted his eyes to the three Males. They were sitting close together, trying to stay warm. He felt sorry for them. They were young and too stupid to get in out of the cold.

Literally.

Knowing Darco, he'd keep them around for a while, but eventually they'd become *food.*

"They look uncomfortable," Farley said. "Why don't you let them go inside and get out of the weather?"

Darco swiveled at the hips, throwing another quick glance. "They look fine to me."

"If their body temps drop too much--"

Darco's tone became insidious. "Like I give a fuck." He knelt down and shoved his face in Farley's. "Now, tell me why Medan has interest in Niles and his hobbies?" There was that lilt again. "I can make you, you know."

He could try.

One hand came up and planted beside Farley's head. "Is that what you want? Do you want me to make you?" Darco grinned. His teeth were longer now. Sharper. "Tell me."

"The other Queens are gunning for Haley." Farley went ahead and spilled the rest, just so Darco would stay out of his head. "Niles has been keeping them off her back. I wanted to know why. I went to his apartment, found a bunch of articles, maps, stuff I couldn't even read, and the computer, which you just broke."

"You should have said something."

"You don't normally have this much to say to me." Darco threw back his head and laughed. It was a genuine sound. Surprisingly enough.

"Now I remember why I didn't eat your throat out! It's because you made me laugh." He bumped Farley's shoulder with his fist. "You always did know how to cheer me up."

Good. Fine. "Can I leave now?"

"On one condition."

Farley knew he was going to regret asking, but he did anyhow. "And what would that be?"

"I demand a tithe."

"Why?"

"You passed through my tunnel back there and didn't pay. Now I want payment."

Farley tried to read Darco's expression, but it was just too peaceful. Which could only mean terrible things.

"What do you want?"

"Hmm, what am I in the mood for?" Darco licked Farley's mouth. "There are so many possibilities..." He tasted him. "Let me think..." The second taste was harder. His teeth raked against Farley's. When he came up for air, his eyes were bleeding gold. "You always did have such a great mouth ... and taste, such incredible flavor."

"Your tithe?" Farley asked, teeth clenched.

"I'm thinking." Darco drew Farley up and away from the wall until their bodies were pressed together. Closer now, their lips brushed. Farley trembled. Not because he was cold, but because Darco was trying to influence him again.

"Stop it."

"Your resistance is amazing. How long do you think you can keep doing that?"

"Long enough. Now get out of my head."

"Then cooperate." His eyes narrowed, and a thin growl ticked out of his throat.

Farley leaned into the other Male, opened his mouth, and caught his bottom lip. Darco made a pleased sound and slid his hands down and around Farley's waist.

Heat kicked up and their metaphysical energies threw off waves like a desert sun. The young Males circled them, touching, licking. Farley wrapped his arms around Darco, pulling him tight, and tasted him hard, trying his damnedest to choke the SOB with his tongue.

The growl in Darco's chest became a purr. Farley hissed as his Brother moved his hands across his lower back and dug his fingers into the flesh. A yelp burst out of Farley's mouth when the Male hit the *ulysiss* gland under his skin hard. Farley came forward, his face landing against his Brother's neck, spasms hitting the backs of his legs and arms like lightening. *Chelae* punched into his muscles, holding him captive with a mix of pain and pleasure.

His body responded. He was helpless to stop it.

Darco rubbed against him. His mouth touched Farley's cheek, his neck. He tried not to scream when his Brother sank his teeth into his shoulder. And failed.

The bite was dangerously close to his arteries. If Farley moved, he would rip out his own throat. Powerless to fight him, he went down and under his Brother. With claws in his lower back, Farley could only kick while Darco sucked at the wound, worried it with his teeth, then drank by pulling the blood through the tears he made.

Too weak to stop him, Farley laid there, letting his Brother grind against him until he finished. He knew Darco wouldn't kill him. He got too much fun out of torturing him like this. Still, his primal instincts were in full-fledged panic. And the fear he put off was exactly what his Brother wanted.

When Darco's mouth popped free, Farley scurried out from under him. The three Males moved in, drawn by the smell of sex and blood.

"By the egg of the Female who bore us, you taste good." Darco rolled over on his back, and kicked up a leg. His hands slipped down the front of his pants. "I thought you tasted good before she *marked* you." He shut his eyes and smacked his lips. "If that's what she tastes like, no wonder you like fucking her." He grinned and rolled his shoulders against the ground like a cat in the thrall of catnip.

Farley checked the blood flow on his shoulder wound. It was only a bruise now.

"I'm going to have to look you up more often. Or maybe I'll just have to try the goods first hand?"

"She's not like that."

"You keep saying that, but what the hell does it mean? She's not like that. She's not like that..." Darco fluttered one hand mocking him. His other one was still down the front of his pants.

"It means it takes more than being a Dominant to get her to Roll you."

"No shit? Really? I mean, because it's obvious she marked you because of your placement on the Food Chain. You're nothing more than a meal and a good fuck." He laughed, then groaned, eyes fluttering up into his skull.

"I think you'd better stay in the Dens where you belong."

Darco was too busy with himself to reply. Farley watched him, strangely detached. He wasn't one to pass up an opportunity of sharing, but Darco scared him. Even if he was his Brother.

While Darco did what he did best, Farley busied himself with examining the laptop. The thing was ruined. He picked at the silver casing. Green plastic and capacitors peeked through the cracks.

Even Ken in IT couldn't fix this mess.

He glanced up at Darco. The Male had other things on his mind and was still ignoring him. While his Brother was occupied, Farley broke apart the rest of the case and pulled out the hard drive. He was putting the thing in his pocket when Darco let out a final groan.

The young Males hovered over him, mouths open, sniffing, begging. Darco wouldn't let them touch him, which was cruel in a way.

"God of Man, that was almost fun." Darco craned his head to the side. "Didn't you hear me, little Brother?"

"I heard you." Farley turned to walk away.

"Where are you going?" When Farley didn't answer Darco followed. "Now, now, I didn't give you permission to leave."

Farley kept walking. Darco, like the majority of Kin, wasn't licensed to be outside the Dens. He'd made too many unacceptable Human social mistakes. And Medan was tired of paying for it.

Darco's hand closed on Farley's arm and spun him around. "Well, well, well, someone is feeling their oats today."

"I paid your tithe. I'm leaving." He jerked himself out of Darco's grasp. As he took two steps back, he turned, expecting to be grabbed, bit, slammed into the ground, anything, but Darco didn't move.

Just keep going. A few more steps, then Farley stopped. It wasn't like Darco to let someone walk away. He knew the bastard was probably influencing him, wanting him to stop, to turn, so he did.

The Male smiled. "Go on, run home. But I am going to meet this Female."

"Stay away from her."

Darco's eyes widened. "What? She's a Female. She has a right to choose who she wants to mark."

"You will not go near her."

His Brother's eyes narrowed and his smile went all cockeyed. "Are you going to stop me?"

Anger propelled Farley forward until their noses almost touched. Scales flashed along his arms and chest. "You set one foot outside the Dens and you won't have to worry about the cops, because I will kill you myself."

The smile on the Male's face went wide. "Let's see you try."

And Farley knew he didn't stand a chance.

Shame made Farley turn away. Darco's laughter chased him out of the Dens.

Chapter 19

"I'm telling you, there's nothing there. You're fine." Dr. Joyce Meyer gave Haley a pat on the shoulder.

Haley rolled down her sleeve; the needle hole in her arm had already closed. Her green blood sample now sat in a field of red.

"Well, something's wrong with him. He's sick."

The doctor took another look into one of five microscopes set up on the table. Outside in the hall, the cops were getting restless. On the orders of the Chief Metaphysical biologist--Dr. Corbin with the CDC--they had quarantined anyone with possible exposure. The only one allowed out was Jones, who was critical, and even then they'd transported him directly into quarantine at Grady.

Dr. Meyer nodded. "I agree. Your friend in there is sick. With what, I don't know."

"For Christ's sake, the lizard is stoned." That from the officer by the door. The guy couldn't seem to resist throwing in his two cents. Every five minutes.

Meyer gave Haley that look. The one that said "got stupid?" One of the assistants came in with a tray filled with more test tubes. Names were written on the side to identify them.

"There's definitely a change in the cell cytology, but it's localized to the nucleus. His *ulysiss* enzymes are elevated, so that's where we'll start looking. I need my lab to do a proper analysis." Her thin finger tapped the screen on the laptop. "But the chemical compounds do not seem to be crossing the metaphysical line. Whatever is causing this isn't normal, but it doesn't seem to affect Humans."

Meyer pursed her lips. It was a look that suggested she had more to say.

Haley said, "What?"

"I get the feeling I've seen this before."

"You mean like déjà vu?"

The woman smiled. "Something like that. If you don't mind..." She typed something into the laptop. "I'd like to send this to a friend in North

Carolina. He has a lot of experience with some strange stuff. This," she waved her hand at the screen, "would be right up his alley." She looked at Haley from behind her bifocals.

Haley shook her head and shrugged. "Be my guest."

To the assistant, Meyer said, "You can tell them they're clear to go. Give each of them a card and tell them to report any rashes, fevers, or limbs that suddenly drop off." She stopped the young man before he went out the door. "That last part was a joke, you know that, right?"

He blinked. "Uh, sure." Meyer patted his arm and sent him on his way.

Outside, the lab tech delivered the news and a flurry of movement and voices filled the hallway.

Haley checked her watch; they'd been down here five hours.

"What about Creyal?"

"He's sick," Meyer said. "But you already knew that."

Haley got down off the table. "Will he be okay?" As in, was he going to live?

A deep furrow appeared between Dr. Meyer's eyes, accentuating her other wrinkles. "I really hate it when I get these pop quiz questions. I hate pop quizzes." She called out for her help and instructed them to start packing things up.

"Can you at least give me some percentages, a maybe, anything?"

Meyer put a hand on Haley's arm. "I'll have them take him to my clinic. I have the best the metaphysical medical field has to offer there. I also have three Lesser-Breds and a Kin who work for me. If nothing else, they can *feed* him, comfort him, and give him what he *needs*. And if he dies, he won't be alone." Her grip tightened, which Haley took to mean the dying part had a pretty good possibility of happening.

"Will you call me?"

Meyer nodded. "I'll do better than that. I'll keep you up to date about what I find. Who knows, this could shed a lot of light on new and exciting possibilities."

"New and exciting" weren't exactly the words Haley would have used to describe some Kin-killing super flu. It sure did give her a new respect for Humans. Just about everything could put them six feet under.

"Haley?" It was Jenna. She stepped into the room. "Bauer's asking for you."

"I thought he went to the hospital?"

Jenna shook her head. "Been sitting over in room four, hooked up to an IV. One of the EMTs stayed and stitched him up." Haley said her goodbyes to Dr. Meyer and followed Jenna out the door. The detective stopped a few feet shy of the other room and turned. "Look, I know we don't know each other real well, and I won't pretend to understand you people, but I appreciate you getting my friends out of there." She offered Haley her hand.

There were a lot of things Haley wanted to say, but decided not to. Humans only pretended like they wanted to hear what you were thinking. She shook the woman's hand, and went in the room.

Bauer sat in a chair with his bad arm propped on the table beside him. Bloody flowers bloomed on the bandage. His shirt was off and the little gold cross he wore was propped up on the collar of his undershirt, looking tired. There were deep worry lines cut across his forehead, a testament to his pain.

He spoke without opening his eyes, "Jones will live." That was Bauer, always worried about his brothers and sisters in blue.

Haley folded her arms and leaned against the door. "And you?"

"I haven't decided yet. He bit me. They gave me anti-venom. I think I should have taken my chances with the bite." His gray cracked lips curled.

"You should have come and got me, I could have taken care of that for you."

Bauer cracked an eye. "You know I can't do that."

Haley looked at the cross dangling around his neck and wondered how the hell something so small could be so powerful. "It's just a little blood."

Bauer grunted. "What did Meyer say about Creyal? I saw she let the officers go, so I guess it's safe to assume he isn't contagious."

"She doesn't know what it is. Meyer is sending the samples to a friend in North Carolina." Haley shifted her weight and the sound of her moving made Bauer flinch. Either he was still jumpy around her, or the anti-venom was messing with his senses. She hoped for the latter. "Can you tell me what happened?"

Bauer took a deep breath, then another. No doubt about it; there was nothing warm and fuzzy about the way her people looked in their true form. Getting attacked by Kin, even in partial change, could make you shit your shorts. He said, “Jones found Creyal’s wallet at a murder scene, called in and gave us the heads up in case he showed. McKinney walked him down. She told him it was standard protocol.” Which wasn’t exactly true. Humans never wound up waiting in the Tank to see an officer. “By the time I got down here, Creyal was climbing the wall like a shithouse rat.”

“How did you get bit?”

Bauer’s eyes came all the way open. “I got in between them. Jones was acting twitchy. I wanted him to leave, and I wanted Creyal to sit down and shut up.” His face tightened and he sucked in his breath.

“I can still help.”

Bauer shook his head and threw her a glare that said, “don’t ask again.” Haley let out a sigh. She didn’t understand Humans and their religion, but it was a powerful force. Like a Queen dragon. Only nicer. “So, then what?”

“Jones drew his gun.”

“Why?”

“I told you he was twitchy. I don’t know what was said or what Creyal did to him, but he was freaked. I’ve known Martin Jones for a long time. He’s a good cop, a sound cop. I’ve never seen him like that before.” Bauer shifted in his seat again and threw out a leg. “Why are you looking at me like that?”

“What makes you think Creyal did anything?”

“What else would make Jones act that way?”

Um, guilt, fear of losing his pension, going to jail. Haley kept that to herself. Instead she said, “Maybe he was the one doing the intimidating?”

“He’s Kin, how the hell would Jones intimidate him?”

“He’s Male, middle-ranked, a drug user, and under the thumb of the D.A. until he delivers on his promise to help.” Which was now out of the question. “And if Jones was dirty, all he had to do is put it out in the Dens that Creyal was snitching to the cops and he’d disappear.”

Bauer shook his head. “No way. Martin Jones is a good cop.”

“And Creyal isn’t a killer.” Haley looked at his bandaged arm. “You never said how you got bit.”

"Not sure, really. It all happened so fast." Detective Bauer scrubbed his eyes with his fingers. "One minute I was standing there, Creyal behind me, Jones out in front. The next thing I know, there's gunfire and Creyal is half changed with his jaws around my arm. I hit the ground, and Jones starts screaming ... Christ. Son of a bitch about ripped him in half."

There was a knock on the door jamb. Haley looked over and saw the EMT. She was small, with a boyish haircut. "I've got transport on the way. Dr. Meyer says we can move you now."

"'Bout time, this chair is making my ass numb." Bauer shifted again and winced.

The EMT looked genuinely apologetic. "Sorry, they had the front blocked up with CDC trucks. I had to get the Metaphysics and the Pathology Director to call into the hospital and reassure them this wasn't contagious. Last thing this city needs is a panic."

Bauer waved at her. "Yeah, still doesn't make these chairs any more comfortable."

The EMT pointed to the hallway. "I've got two more guys to load up in front of you, so give me about twenty minutes, okay?"

She disappeared back out the door. A mix of male and female cop voices drifted in. Haley reached over and shut the door, sending the room into silence. Thick doors have many applications. Keeping in a pissed off Kin is only one of them.

"Did Jones try to shoot you?" The look that Bauer gave her said it was something he'd already considered and chose not to think about.

"The man was terrified, Haley."

"That still doesn't answer my question."

"Jones is a good cop."

Haley crossed her arms and stared at him. "How many times are you going to say that?"

"Damn it, Haley, even if he did, what the hell was he going to do about McKinny? She was standing right there."

"Either he would shoot her or he'd just push her in the way when Creyal started biting and clawing, and let nature go to work." Yeah, he really didn't like those answers.

"I'm done talking about this."

"Why? Because Creyal was only a Kin?"

Bauer jabbed a finger at her. "Do not go playing the species card with me, Haley. You are not IAB, and I do not have to explain anything to you."

Haley dropped her eyes and poked at the concrete floor with the toe of her shoe. No carpet in here. It would just stain. This way, housekeeping could just come in with a bucket of bleach, hose the walls down, and let it slide down the drain in the floor.

Too bad life wasn't so easy to clean up.

An electronic beeping broke the silence. Haley checked the number on her phone. It was Farley. "I need to take this, do you mind?" Bauer waved a few fingers at her without looking up.

Haley put the phone to her ear. "Yeah?"

"You busy?"

"Not really, why?"

"Can you meet me in the showers?" He sounded frustrated.

Haley slipped out into the hall and headed back up the corridor. "What's up?"

"I can't come to your office like this."

"Like this" could mean just about anything. The top three on the list were naked, bloody, and naked. And the office help just never seemed appreciative of Farley's willingness to stroll bareback in public. For Kin, clothes were just decorative, or at the most, a public service. Any other time they got in the way.

"You okay?" She willed him to say yes. Because if he said no, it meant the blood wasn't his.

"'Zall good. Look, call Ken in IT. I need him to look at something."

"You want him to meet you in the shower?" She could practically hear him shrug over the phone.

"Quicker I get this to him the better."

"Anything else?"

"Bring me something to eat. Chocolate if you can get it, maybe some cheese?" There was a snack machine in the break room. Normally it stayed stocked with a variety of Keebler goodness.

"I'm on it." Haley hung up and headed upstairs. She made it to her office, raided her change jar, then took the booty to the break room and fed the snack machine like it was starving. She hit the buttons and waited for the machine to start dropping the food in the dispenser. With a quick flip of her phone and punch of numbers she called Ken and asked him to meet her in the showers.

Silence. Haley explained she wanted to meet him in the men's shower. When that didn't work, she just told him Farley had something computer related for him to tinker with.

"I'll be down in fifteen. I've got to get this mail server back up before the entire PD drags me out into the parking lot for a beat down."

Haley hung up and watched as the last of the cupcakes wound its way down the silver guide wire and fell in the opening below.

Two more snack crackers hit the bottom and she was out of quarters. Haley scanned the counter, then opened a cabinet, looking for something, anything to help get the load down stairs. She found a box with five packs of sugar left in it.

Footsteps came in behind her and the female chatter stopped. A familiar candy scent drifted to Haley's nose. Claire's friends wandered over to the coffee machine with their heads together and whispered.

"Don't forget, ladies, even in Human form my hearing is better than yours. And trust me, you don't want to know the details of my sex life." Their mouths hung open as they threw her a quick over-the-shoulder glance.

Haley piled the food stuffs into the box. It wasn't going to be big enough, but she had room in her pockets. At least her blazer had pockets. For some reason, fashion designers seemed to find it humorous to make ladies clothing with pocket flaps but no holes to put anything in. Haley had hers tailored so there were real pockets in every one.

Claire stepped closer and Haley said, "Is there something you need?"

"I want to know what happened with Farley." Claire's voice was barely a whisper, and she kept her head turned away from her friends, like they might read her lips. "Garrett wouldn't tell me anything. He just kept saying I misunderstood."

Haley did nothing to lower her voice. "He's fine. Stayed at my place last night. We watched movies, lots of movies."And she said movies in a way that suggested other things. When she looked at Claire, her eyes were blazing. Haley smiled, knowing it looked down right mean. "Seriously, Claire. I overreacted about that phone call. You know Farley, he's always playing jokes. Got me good that time. Don't worry..." She paused and stuffed the last packet of crackers in her pocket. "He made up for it later."

One of the women coughed, spewing coffee out her nose. Her friend gave her a weak pat on the back.

"Something was wrong!" Claire put her hand over her mouth, and inched a little closer. Her voice dropped back down to a whisper. "Something was wrong, I heard you. He's my boyfriend, I deserve to know." When Claire was angry like this her scent left a spicy flavor on the back of Haley's tongue.

Haley tucked the box under her arm. "I think now's a good time to just put the whole dating Farley thing on the backburner. He's fine. Everything's fine. You didn't hear what you thought you heard and that's that." She pushed past the woman and headed out the door.

"Wait a minute." Claire's princess shoes slapped the carpet as she ran to catch up. She never wore heels. In her two inchers Haley could look her in the eye, which was one of the reasons she liked her three inchers more.

Claire grabbed her arm. Haley froze. Her instinct told her to bite. Females were not touched without consent. Especially by other Females. But Claire was Human and she was just doing what Humans do.

Haley blinked to clear her vision, then looked at the woman. "Claire, I don't have time for this right now. I have to go take care of something."

Claire's eyes went to the box of food. "He's here, isn't he?" she whispered. "Farley's here and he needs food because something's happened." She shot a quick glance around the hall as if to make sure her companions weren't close enough to hear. No, they were still in the break room, but their heads kept peeking around the corner to catch a glimpse of the show.

A growl ticked out of Haley's throat. She turned and walked. Claire ran to catch up. "Stay out of this, Claire."

"I won't. You can't make me."

"Claire..." Anything she said was just going to make it worse. Haley punched the handle to the stairwell and started down the stairs. Claire paused at the top. Good, maybe she wouldn't follow.

She did. "Why are we going to the locker-room?"

"Figure it out."

Claire paused again when Haley headed into the men's side. "Wait, you can't go in there!" Sometimes Humans and their fear of naked did come in handy.

Haley headed through the locker room, passed two half-dressed cops, and walked into the shower area. The clicking of her heels brought heads out of the shower to catch a quick look. Someone whistled. Haley ignored it. Farley was in front of the only full length mirror, craning his neck around to look at his back. Dried ichor covered most of his top half.

"What happened?" Haley put the box on the counter.

Farley's eyes locked on the food and he confiscated the box. "You are a life saver." He ripped open packages and stuffed crackers in his mouth. Haley gave him a once over. There were nasty black bruises around his *ulysiss* point. He wasn't food deprived enough to not heal, so that meant the cuts had been deep. Really deep. As in touch your own kidneys.

"Who did this to you?"

"Darco." Farley stuffed a cupcake in his mouth. "Bastard. I hate him."

So did Haley. More than that, she hated the things he did to Farley. But he was his Brother, and those were the rules of the Dens. It still made her Human-instilled ethics spark like they were going to short out.

"Who's Darco?"

Haley winced. She was really hoping Claire wouldn't follow her in here. Haley glanced at Farley and said "sorry" with her eyes. Farley just kept eating.

"Did you hear me, who's ... OH, MY GOD! What happened to you? Is that *your* blood?" Claire started towards Farley. Haley blocked her.

"Not right now, Claire. Seriously, you need to go."

"But, he's hurt." Her bottom lip trembled. When Haley looked back at Farley, he shrugged. "Don't try and tell me he's fine. I can see for myself that he isn't."

"I'm fine," Farley dipped his head in the sink and took a drink of water. "I promise you, I'm okay."

"Are you going to press charges? You are, aren't you? You work for the CFKR, they'll arrest this Darco for doing this..."

"He's my Brother. It's no big deal."

"I don't care if he's your *brother*. You need to ... your back. Oh, my God!" Tears burst out of Claire's eyes and her nose glowed. Farley scrubbed his face with his hand and ate another cracker.

A naked officer walked by and tossed a look to both Haley and Claire. Claire covered her eyes; Haley didn't. Some Humans weren't as shy as society would like them to be.

Farley sighed and said, "Claire, I'm fine. Just a little rough sex is all."

Claire looked like she'd been slapped. Her blue eyes blinked way too fast. Haley groaned and put her face in her hand. Leave it to Farley. He just didn't have a clue when it came to Human taboos.

"I really need to get out of these clothes." Farley ate another cracker and looked down at himself. "I didn't want the ledger to get wet though, or the hard drive."

Haley said, "Hard drive? What happened to the rest of the computer?"

"Darco happened." Farley went back to examining his back. "Damn him. I really hate it--"

Claire's voice cut over him. "You had sex with your brother?" Haley tossed the woman a look. Her face was pale, her eyes too big. The tears had stopped. Somehow she didn't think that was a good thing.

Farley sighed. "I lost your Godsmack shirt."

"I'll get another one." Haley kept her eyes on Claire.

"Farley!" Claire's voice cracked. "You had sex with your Brother?"

He looked at her. "Well, actually I *fed* him, he did some dry humping, then shoved his hands down his--"

Claire screamed. It was an ugly brutal sound. "You sick, sick, bastard. Is there anyone you won't fuck! It's bad enough you're doing her." She pointed at Haley. "But your brother? Your brother!" Claire threw herself at the sink basin and puked.

Farley raised an eyebrow.

Haley inched toward Claire, started to touch her back, hesitated, then tossed all caution to the wind. Her narrow bony shoulders racked under Haley's palm as she made small circles. "It's okay, Claire."

"No, it isn't." She heaved again.

"Claire..."

"Don't talk to me."

"Claire, you're being unfair."

"I could..." She gagged. "I could handle you, I could. I really could. I could even handle the idea of things happening with other ... other..." The gag stole her words. After a long moment of dry heaving she turned on the water and splashed her face. "His brother?"

This was one of those taboos that made Humans go all funny. "Claire, the title Brother is reserved for Males who survive the hatching grounds together. It's a title and it doesn't have anything to do with being a sibling."

Claire shook her head, grabbed a few paper towels out of the dispenser, and blotted the water off her face. "I think I need to go sit down."

"No, you need to hear this." Haley stepped in her way. "This is what I have been trying to explain to you."

Claire started to yell. "You never--" She caught herself and looked around. Her small trembling hand went to her mouth again. "You never said anything about incest."

Haley looked up at Farley sitting on the counter eating the last package of cupcakes. "Tell her, please."

"He's my Dominant." Farley wiped his mouth on the back of his hand. "And because he's my clutch mate, I have to submit unless I *roll* him." With that kind of tone, he might as well be telling her the weather forecast. Claire stared at him, like she didn't know who he was.

"I don't understand." A new trail of tears cut down her cheeks. Farley looked away. Haley knew it bothered him to see her cry.

"Look." Farley slid off the counter. "If it helps, I don't like him. Never did. But I did what I had to do to survive. If I didn't let him Dominate me, he would have eaten me like the rest of my Brothers. He leaves me alone most of the time." Haley wasn't sure if it was his matter-of-fact attitude or what he said, but Claire shoved past her and ran back out of the shower room.

Farley shook his head.

Haley pushed a lock of hair from her eyes and said, "You really need to start thinking before you talk."

He untied his boots. "It's her problem."

"You sure you're okay?"

"Yeah, I'll live." He stopped and leaned against the wall. The last showerhead kicked off and the remaining Human occupant walked by wearing a towel. Water drips echoed in the silence. After a moment Farley dropped his head. "Some days I hate coming in here."

"You don't mean that." Haley stepped closer to him and put a hand on his neck.

"Yeah, I do. If I thought I could get a job somewhere else, I would." Haley shushed him and he caught her hand and brought it to his lips. "I mean it. The whole Human thing..." His tongue stroked her palm. "You just don't see it."

"I know it's hard for Kin to adapt, but we don't have a choice."

Farley flipped his eyes up at her; gold flecks swam in the brown. "It wasn't always this way."

"No, and Humans didn't always have jet fighters that could chase your ass down and blow you in half either. The sooner our people learn to accept that Humans aren't food anymore, the better off we will be. If anything they're our equals, and in some ways, our Dominant."

A distant hello echoed from the locker room.

"We're in here, Ken," Haley said.

"Hey, sorry, I got held up." Ken came around the corner. His hands flipped up and down as talked. "There was a problem with the POP server responding and--" His tennis shoes squeaked to a halt on the wet tile. "Did I interrupt something?" He jabbed a thumb over his shoulder. "Because if you need a minute, I can wait out there."

"We're good," Farley said. He unzipped a pocket in the side of his pants and fished out the hard drive. "Here, see if you can do something with this." While Ken stared at the drive, Farley kicked off his boot and pulled out the ledger. He handed it to Haley. The second boot joined the first by the wall.

"This is a Toshiba. This came out of a Vaio? What happened to the rest of it?" Ken asked.

"My Brother." Farley unbuttoned his pants.

"Oh." Ken's eyes went wide. "Oooh!" He nodded at the door. "Is that why Claire was throwing up in the hall?" His eyes went back and forth. Haley looked at Farley, who cut a grin. "What's so funny?" Ken asked.

Farley shook his head. "Just remembering why I like you so much."

"Well, you can like me, but that doesn't mean I'll *feed* you or ... you know. I don't go that way, even for Kin." He adjusted his glasses and examined the hard drive. Farley laughed. "Did I say something funny?" Ken gave Haley serious eyes.

"Yeah, you did in fact."

Ken shrugged. "I should be able to have this up and running. Provided of course there isn't any physical damage. What exactly happened to the rest of it?"

Farley peeled his pants off and tossed them with his boots. Then dropped his boxers. There were more black and blue marks below his waist. "Darco stepped on it, stomped on it, kicked it around, and proceeded to do his impersonation of Tigger." Ken winced. "I'm getting in the shower, either of you want to join me?" Farley held up his hand. "Just kidding, that was a joke."

Ken smiled, gave two har-hars, then shook the hard drive at him. "How fast do you want the data on this thing?"

"As soon as you can." Farley stepped into the first stall and steam billowed up as he cranked on the water. "Can one of you get me some clothes? I don't think the office help will be as accommodating."

"Thanks, Ken," Haley said. The man gave a nod and wandered away, turning the hard drive over in his hands, looking like someone had run over his puppy.

"Clothes?" Farley asked again.

"I'll find you some. I know I have sweats in my locker." Haley went across to the women's locker room and retrieved her sweat pants from her supply. She looked at the shirts she had, but all of them were a little too girly. And Farley didn't need any more culture clash. The PD kept quite a few standard black-Ts with the department's logo on the front. After all, she wasn't the only one that got bled on.

Haley found a few in the last cubbyhole next to a stack of white towels. She took one of each and went back into the showers. A moment later, Farley cut the water off and stepped out. He examined himself front and back. The bruises were fading, thanks to the food. Haley handed him the towel.

"Thanks." He brushed it over his body. "Did you look in the ledger?"

"Not yet." She held the clothes up. "Found you some clothes though." He took them and walked back to the sink.

Farley shook out the sweats and put them on. He frowned when he looked at the shirt. "Nothing says 'snitch' like a police department logo."

Haley shrugged. "It was either that or Power Puff girls, and I didn't think you needed the additional trauma."

He took it off, turned it inside out, and put it back on. "There. That's better than nothing, I guess." He picked up the ledger. "This phone number in the back." He showed it to her. "You'll never believe who it belongs to."

"Who?"

He pulled out the magazine clipping. Haley stared at it for a second. "Justice? As in, The Great White Justice?" As if there was another.

Farley grinned, looking pleased. "Yup, I called it. His Link answered."

Haley shook her head and glanced over the article. The whole Brother thing came back to her, and she couldn't help but wonder if this wasn't the clutch mate Niles had been talking about.

"How old is Justice?"

"Why?" Farley looked over her shoulder, like the answer to his question might be in the article.

"When Niles and I..." She growled. "When we had our run in, he mentioned something about a Brother."

"Really? 'Cause as far as I know Niles Fury was the only Kin to climb out of the nest alive."

She tapped the ledger. "At his age, how would we really know for sure he didn't have a Brother?"

"Why does it matter?"

"'Cause if Justice is Niles' Brother, maybe he'll have some idea why Niles was watching out for me, if he really..." Farley stared with wide haunted eyes. "What's wrong?"

"There were newspaper clippings on the walls in Niles' apartment. Some of them went back decades. There were maps too, and letters, and lots of photos."

"So?"

"The articles were about you. Either they mentioned your name, or it had a quote you said. And the pictures were of you, too."

Haley pressed her lips together and made a thinking sound. "I'll call upstairs and get a request for all the calls Niles made in the past six months and see if Justice's phone number is in them."

"Only one problem with that. I didn't see a phone in his apartment."

"Well, if he had a cell phone on him, it's either lost or in the ADF storage room."

Farley snapped his fingers. "What about pay phones? Can you get the records for those?"

Haley nodded. "Sure, I just need a general area to check for service, then call in the numbers assigned to the booths. But where the heck would he find a pay phone?"

"The Dens. The place is about thirty-five years behind the rest of the city on phone service, and I doubt Bell South is real worried about whether or not Kin can reach out and touch someone. I think there were at least two near Niles' place."

"I'll make a call in for those." She started to turn, but hesitated. "Hey, why haven't you been reading my thoughts?"

Farley shrugged. "Been trying really hard not to. Besides, after this afternoon I really don't want to be anywhere I might not be wanted." He ran a hand over his red brush cut a few times.

Haley put down the ledger and put hand on his chest. "Don't ever think you're unwanted." Warmth spread under her palm and was followed by the thrumming of Farley's purr.

Chapter 21

"All we know is Creyal is sick, but they don't know what's causing it." Haley took a sip from her glass, then stabbed at her shrimp and lobster sauce while Farley worked on his second helping of Mongolian beef.

House of Lin was their favorite place to eat. Not only was it all you could eat, it was all you could eat with your choice of rare or cooked. And Mr. Lin didn't mind serving Kin, which was nice. He even let them eat indoors.

Farley pilfered a bite from Haley's plate. "But it's not contagious to Humans?"

She shook her head. Unlike Farley, she swallowed before trying to talk. "Dr. Meyer doesn't think so. I got an email from her before we left and she said he's improving. Apparently the cocktail of antiviral drugs and donor blood is giving his system time to heal the damage. The virus doesn't stay around very long. It's like it self-destructs. 'Denature' is the word she used."

Farley held up his hand and flagged down the waitress. She was all smiles and nods when he requested a third plate.

"Next time we go out, let's hit the arena." He grinned at her while he slurped in a stray noodle.

"No thanks, I don't really enjoy chasing my food around before I eat it." Which was true. Besides, she had better things to do, and with all the raw meat just waiting in the grocery store, it seemed like a complete waste of time.

Farley flicked a hand at her "That's because you're domesticated. A house cat eating out of a food dish put down by the Humans. Here kitty, kitty, ki-ti-Ooowe!" She planted the toe of her shoe into his ankle. Farley yelped, "Man, those shoes of yours are deadly." He rubbed his ankle with one hand and shoved food into his mouth with the other.

Haley glared at him and said, "You're really rude sometimes."

"Well, it's true. You know it's true. Don't try and deny it. You're so Human sometimes you scare me."

She took her aggressions out on the helpless dead shrimp on her plate.

It wasn't her fault she had appreciation for Human morals, ethics, and hang ups.

Haley's phone rang.

Farley groaned. "If that's the Center, please don't answer it."

Haley checked her watch. It was almost nine o'clock. Surely no one would be calling her at this hour. She checked the number. "It's Deshi."

Farley snorted. "Probably waiting outside your door getting twitchy. Tell him I get top this time." The people at the next table stopped eating and stared. Haley gave them her best "sorry about that" smile.

She flipped open the phone and put it to her ear. "Hey, we're out eating. What's up?"

Silence.

Haley checked her signal. Four bars.

Can you hear me now? You damn well should.

She put the phone back to her ear. "Deshi?"

A breath shuddered over the receiver.

"Deshi ... what's wrong? Deshi?"

When Deshi spoke, his voice was strained, like he'd been giving his vocal cords a serious workout. "Haley ... I..." His breath blew out in great gasps. "It's Emily. Oh, God of Man, what have I done?" The wail that followed sent her scrambling. Farley threw three twenties on the table and they took off out the door and raced for the street.

"Deshi? Deshi? What happened?" But she knew what happened. The worst. The most horrible. Deshi had *raged* and Emily was dead.

The phone went silent. When she looked, the screen read disconnected. Haley called back, but it only rang.

I should have never let him leave that day. I should have made him stay. I should have given him no choice. All the should-haves tumbled relentlessly through her head.

Farley grabbed her arm. "It's not your fault."

She shook her head. It was. It was her fault. She'd let him leave. He was in no condition. It was only a matter of time before this happened. She was Female and it was her job to take care of him.

He leaned closer. "No, this is not your fault. Deshi was the stupid one. He made the choice."

Haley yanked away and waved for a cab. One pulled up and Haley climbed inside. Farley was right behind her.

The cabbie put a hand across the back seat, blocking Farley's entry. "No Kin. Good cab, no Kin." The cabbie pointed to Farley. His gaze flicked to the *nevus* on Farley's arms.

Haley pulled out a fifty from her inside pocket. "Drive." The cabbie licked his lips and held up two fingers. She pulled out another two twenties, and threw it at him. Farley climbed in and shut the door.

"No mess up my seats." He poked his finger at Farley, then patted the headrest. "New leather."

Farley flashed his fangs. "No talkie." He flapped his fingers at the man. "Drivie!"

Haley put her elbow in his ribs. Farley crossed his arms and looked out the window. She gave the driver another ten and told him the address.

Busy streets turned into quiet private neighborhoods where spacious homes with their rolling green lawns sat under towering oak trees. Ansley Park was the kind of place that screamed old money. All the houses in this part of town were unique. No doubt, they just didn't make neighborhoods like this anymore.

Deshi's place was at the bottom of a cul-de-sac, lit by iron lamps dropped right out of a Norman Rockwell painting. They went well with the park benches set deep in the rolling field of winter rye grass as dense as Berber carpet. Of all the houses in Ansley park, Deshi's, with its English-cottage-meets-Scottish-castle sort of feel, was easily the pick.

The cabbie stopped at the end of the driveway and turned in his seat. "I wait, yes?" He held out his hand looking for another bill.

Haley shook her head and got out. Farley followed.

The cabbie waved at them and patted the steering wheel. "I wait, no problem."

Farley raised his lips and hissed.

"I go, I go." The cabbie threw it in reverse and missed Deshi's mailbox by a hair. The front wheel clipped the curb as he cut the corner too close. Haley cut Farley a look and he shrugged.

"C'mon." She headed up the cobblestone walk. A small porch light was on in the alcove, but it made more shadows than it offered light. Haley knocked on the door, then rang the doorbell. No one answered.

"Deshi?"

"I'll check the back." Farley sank into the darkness.

Haley kept knocking. "Deshi, it's us. Open the door." The easiest thing to do would be to break a window. But if he had the alarm system on, the entire Atlanta PD would be here in five minutes. With the way things were going so far this week, they were apt to shoot first and ask questions later.

Haley heard footsteps and peeked through the side window. Farley came across the great room, his expression bleak. He undid the deadbolt and opened the door, and Haley knew immediately why his face was dark. The sweet coppery scent of blood was in the air.

She started to ask how he got in. Farley threw a thumb over his shoulder and said, "Window in the kitchen was open."

Haley scanned the room. Expensive art hung on the wall in the great room, which opened into the living area, where a flat screen as long as her Mustang sat on a shiny mahogany entertainment system. There was no way you'd find something like that at Wal-Mart.

Under the warm glow of lamp light the flawless wood floor gleamed, framing oriental rugs. The kitchen was equally perfect. All marble and stainless steel.

The sounds of appliances kicking on and off and the tick of the grandfather clock were the only noises. All houses have a natural state of business that one can associate with being lived in. Deshi's house just felt dead.

"Deshi?" Still nothing.

Farley pointed up.

They headed up the stairs, scenting the air. Farley swung his head back and forth moving like ... well, a dragon. On the third floor the smell was stronger, thicker, with a musky flavor underneath. Half-way down the hall, blood stains covered the wall along with smears of brown. Death is never pretty.

Sometimes people were just so scared they shit themselves.

An intermittent trail of crimson got darker as it neared the bedroom door that was slightly ajar. Arterial spray fanned across the front of the white-washed wood. Emotional terror written in slaps of red. A frantic sort of fight happened here. The kind where the prey knews it was going to die, but refused to quit struggling. Hoping for escape when there is none.

Haley and Farley looked at each other. This was bad. Really bad.

"Deshi?" Farley asked. There was a sound of movement inside the room.

"What's that smell?" Haley sniffed. For so much blood, there wasn't very much of that tale-tale buttered chicken smell of Humans. This blood smelled musky, like an old fur rug.

Farley stuck out his hand and pushed the door. It swung wide, revealing a collage of broken furniture, torn sheets, and gutted down pillows. Deshi was curled by the closed bathroom door, completely naked, and covered in tuffs of blond hair, blood, and feathers. His teeth were down, distorting his handsome face. The portable phone lay in his lap painted with a red hand print.

"Deshi?" As Haley moved closer, she kept saying his name with a gentle firmness. When she was a few feet away he raised his head to look at her. Haley's foot hit apart something that had once been alive under the snowfall of feathers. Emily was dead. Bits of her were on the floor and Haley was stepping on them. An ache started across her chest and seemed to have no end.

Deshi blinked once, twice, and his eyes widened as his face became Human again. He covered his face with his arms and howled the piteous keen he'd made earlier.

She'd failed him.

Farley touched Haley's arm and held something up to her. She had to wipe the tears out of her eyes so she could see.

The little blue strip, smeared with red, and its shiny bone shaped charm just wouldn't compute. Farley shook it and it jingled.

"It's a dog collar. That's the smell. This isn't Human blood, at least not all of it."

A dog. Thank you, God of Man. Another dog. Emily had been spared again.

"Deshi?" Haley knelt in front of The Jersey City Prince. Blood glued feathers to her hands when she touched his shoulder. "Where's Emily?"

He finally raised a hand and pointed at the bathroom door. Farley leaned down and picked up the larger Male. With a heavy boot he kicked aside some of the debris and eased them both down to the floor. When Farley had Deshi situated, Haley turned her attentions back to the door.

"Emily?" She rapped on the door and listened. "Emily? It's Haley Night. I was at your wedding, remember? I know you're in there." *Because I can hear your heart beating like a scared rabbit.* "I need you to open the door for me so I can make sure you're okay." If she was hurt bad enough for the ER, Deshi was still a dead Male. Kin who struck out violently against their Human spouses served an automatic five years in the ADF. A death penalty for just about any Kin.

She tried the door handle but it didn't move. Inside, there was a quick breath and a small sob. "Emily, please. Please let me help you."

"He killed my parents' dog!" Emily screeched. "He killed their golden retriever. He killed him!" Her sobbing drowned out the rest.

Yeah, thought Haley, *you have no idea how lucky you are*. "Emily, please let me in so I can make sure you're okay."

In a high pitched voice, bordering on hysterics, Emily screamed. "Just call the police! I want the police and I want an ambulance! He killed Max! He killed him and he ate him!"

Haley winced, her own teeth aching. So much blood, so much violence, the smell of prey. "Emily, I need you to calm down, okay?" *Please calm down because I don't want this to get any worse.*

And worse meant Deshi eating her.

"Calm down? Calm down! He ate the goddamned dog and you want me to calm down!"

"Emily, for God's sake, shut the hell up before you make him come after you again. You're screaming like a wounded animal and he's reacting to it."

Silence. There was a sniffle and the sound of someone blowing their nose.

Haley took a breath and checked on Farley. He was petting Deshi, whose handsome face was contorted in a mix of fear and horror. Poor Beautiful Deshi looked like he was trying to wake up from a nightmare.

Haley blew out a sigh and turned her attention back to the door. "Emily, are you hurt?"

"Yes, yes, I'm hurt. I've got blood all over me. My robe is ruined." Another sob.

"Is the blood yours or the dog's?"

"Who the fuck cares whose blood it is? It's all over me, for God's sake." She sounded like she was going to start wailing again. Which was *so* not a good idea. The last thing Haley needed was two Males going into *rage.*

"I'm fine," Farley said. "And no, this far away I can't hear your thoughts, but I saw that look on your face."

Yeah, well, Haley was glad he was so sure of himself, but Emily just had the special gift of irritation. There were quite a few times that Haley imagined drawing blood on the woman.

Obviously, asking nicely wasn't going to work. Surprise, surprise.

Haley said, "Look, I'm going to give you until the count of ten to open this door. If you don't, then I'm going to kick it in. Usually when I kick doors in I break a heel and these are my seventeen-hundred-dollar Ferragamos. I break a heel on your door, and I'm going to be pissed."

Silence.

Haley counted. She was on five when the door clicked. When she tried the handle it turned. Inside, Emily was crouched in the immense claw foot tub, her bloody white robe wrapped around her like a body shield. Her pretty face was blotched and red, her short blond hair a mass of tangles. Even in a state of disaster she was still gorgeous.

"Can I come in?" Either way Haley was going in, but she at least wanted to give Emily a chance to make the right choice.

Emily gave a quick nod, then brushed her manicured fingers under her eyes, sweeping away new tears. Haley shut the door behind her.

The woman flailed a hand in her direction. "Lock it, lock it, quick." Haley didn't bother to tell her that if Deshi wanted through that door, it might last all of five seconds. And only because it was solid wood, not the cheap kind found in modern houses.

Haley put the lid down on the toilet and sat. The woman made some small gasping noises and put a hand to her lips. Haley waited for her to get through another wave of crying.

"I can't believe ... I can't believe he killed Max." More tears were scraped away by her fingers, smudging blood and mascara. "He was such a good dog. A very good dog."

"Better the dog than you." Haley didn't really mean to say that out loud.

Emily stifled a sob and used the sleeve of her robe to clean off her face. "Why? Why did he do this? I thought he loved me. I can't believe he would hurt me like this." She pushed up the sleeve of her robe and showed Haley the black and blue marks on her arms. "Look what he did," she said, and followed up with one big choppy inhale that bounced her shoulders.

"Are you bleeding?" Because Haley sure could smell Human blood.

Emily pulled the collar of her robe aside. There was a bite mark, but given the devastation outside, it was minor. Then she showed Haley the cut on her thigh. That one might need stitches. Which meant, if Emily ran her yap, the Jersey City Prince would be in a concrete Tank by morning.

Think. Think. There had to be a way around this. Number one problem was Emily. Any scenario that involved her going to the doctor ended up with Deshi in the ADF and dead in a matter of months.

"Is the ambulance on its way?" Emily adjusted her robe. "I want to go to that private hospital just east of here. Don't let them take me to Grady."

"Emily, you can't go to the hospital."

"What do you mean? They'll take you to whichever one you want to go to. The insurance will cover it."

"If you go to the hospital, they will put Deshi in a hole and he will die."

"Well, I'll figure out how to manage. Everything will work out." More fidgeting. "My mother did just fine after my father died. I know how to take care of myself."

Haley pressed her palms into her eyes, willing the pain in her skull to stop. "Can you stop thinking about yourself for five minutes, and think about Deshi, for once in your selfish life!" In the absence of her yelling, the bathroom became painfully quiet. She looked at Emily. The woman was picking at the gold hairs on the robe in between playing with her hair.

"I'm sorry. I didn't mean to yell." But it sure did feel good. "You know, Deshi could die over this. Doesn't that bother you even a little?"

Emily smoothed out her robe. "I just bought this two weeks ago. They'll never get the blood out."

"He ate the Chihuahua, too."

Emily's eyes flicked up. They were almost as blue as Deshi's. "What did you say?"

"He ate the Chihuahua because it slept in the bed with you and had your scent on it. He just told you it ran out the door because he was afraid you'd never trust him enough to *bond*. But trust isn't it. You don't love him enough to care that he's hurting. Don't you get it, Emily?" Haley threw a hand at the door. "This is your fault! All of this. The Chihuahua, that mess out there, this other dog ... dead."

"Excuse me?"

Haley put a hand on the tub and leaned closer. "You heard what I said."

"My fault?"

"Yeah, your fault."

"How dare you! How dare you blame this on me!" She jabbed a finger at the door. "He did this. He ate the dog, he destroyed the room, he came after me! He's the monster! Not me! Him!"

"And how long did you think marital bliss was going to last if you kept turning down becoming his Link?"

Emily's expression closed and some of the flush was replaced by gray. "That has nothing to do--"

"It has everything to do with this. Everything. He's starving, Emily. He's tried to tell you that for two years. He's been begging you to help him, and you've done nothing but ignore him."

"Starving? We were having sex..." A blush bloomed over her cheeks.

"Food, sex, it's the same thing. And probably what pushed him over."

There was no making this go away, but the mess needed to be taken care of. "I know a cleaning crew that can keep their mouths shut." Because they had cleaned up some bloody messes at her apartment. Granted, the blood had been a different color. "Will you let me call them? They're good. Very discreet."

"I don't care! Whatever. Now I want to go to the hospital."

"Emily..."

Emily's eyes flew wide and her face contorted in rage. Just like a Kin shifting in its Human skin, the real Emily revealed herself. "Don't 'Emily' me! I don't give a fuck if they take him out back and put a bullet in his head. He's a monster. I hope they do. I hope they kill him and save me the suffering. I want him gone. I want him locked up. I want him dead! Now get on the goddamned phone and call me an ambulance!"

Haley stared at the woman, trying to figure out what the hell Deshi saw in her. She knew what Emily saw in Deshi, a cash cow. A way to become wealthy without breaking a nail. It was the only reason she'd married the Male, and everyone around saw it but him.

But being Human left Emily holding all the cards. No matter what her numbers were, her race always trumped the Kin. Deshi had attacked and tried to eat his wife, and that's all any jury or judge would ever know. No one would stand up and explain the connection of food and sex. No one would be able to convince a jury of Human beings how painful it is to slowly starve to death. How madness consumes Males who are deprived of the metaphysical current, the life force of all Kin.

Getting Emily to care about anyone but herself wasn't going to happen. If the woman had the capacity for empathy, Farley and Haley wouldn't be here in this house. Instead, they would be heading back to her apartment, stuffed on Chinese food, her scowling about something obnoxious he said.

But here she was, in a bathroom as big as her den, sitting on a toilet lid while Miss Congeniality worried about the stains in her robe.

Haley found herself hating Emily. Not just disliking her, but hating her and wishing she would just go away. "Fine, I'll call your ambulance." She pulled out her phone and flipped it open.

"Good, about time." Emily checked her reflection in the shiny silver tub faucet and fiddled with her hair.

"You realize if he dies, there will be no more money. And in the ADF, he will die."

Emily waved a hand at her. "Why would I be worried about that?"

"Because you won't keep this house, you won't keep any of the bank accounts, and everything he owns will revert back to his Mother, the Queen of Jersey City."

Emily blinked and looked around, like maybe someone was playing a joke on her. "What are you talking about?"

Haley watched, taking pleasure in her fear. "He isn't Human, remember? He's Kin and he's a Prince. His Mother gave him everything, and if he should die, it reverts back to her. She'll get everything, Emily, and you'll be right back in middle class where he found you." Haley put the phone to her ear.

"You don't know what you're talking about."

"Wanna bet? If they take you to the hospital, your wounds will have to be reported. Then they'll come here and arrest Deshi. By nine AM tomorrow, his bank accounts will be frozen, as well as any access to his wealth. Everything Deshi owns must be returned to his Mother. That's Kin law."

The operator came on and asked if she could hold. Haley said yes. Sometimes an over-burdened 911 could be a good thing.

"He's my husband! I'll fight it!"

"Yeah, you could do that. But what are you going to use to pay a lawyer, your looks?" With the way Emily kept fawning over herself it was a good possibility she'd try. "Deshi's Mother would keep you tied up in court until you are nothing but grave dust. Your life span is like an inconvenience to her." When she shot Haley a doubtful look, she added, "Trust me, that Female hates you enough to spend more money keeping you in the poor house than to give you a cent. Deshi cut out his *nevus* for you. That alone got you put on the naughty list."

Haley waited for the woman to say something, but she just kept rearranging her robe and blotting her eyes.

"Fine." The operator came back on and Haley said, "Yes, ma'am, I need to arrange an ambulance--"

"Wait!" Emily stood up and climbed out of the tub. "I changed my mind. I'm not that hurt. It's just bruises. That's all." She flashed her arms, stumbled to the sink.

Haley apologized to the operator and told her they'd changed their mind.

"What am I going to tell my parents?" Emily said.

"Same thing he told you. Tell them it ran away." Haley stood up, and a wave of metaphysical heat blossomed over her skin. Emily started for the door, but Haley held out an arm and stopped her.

"Farley's *feeding* him." The truth was better than a lie.

Emily shook her head, then stared at the door. "What do you mean?"

Haley sighed. Trying to keep things like this from Emily wasn't going to work anymore. They were running out of dogs to take the fall.

"Emily, has Deshi explained anything to you?"

She shook her head. "I know he wants me to bond with him, become a Link. I don't think that's necessary."

"What else has he told you?"

"I don't understand."

"Has he explained to you about *feeding?*"

Emily let out a nervous laugh. "Well, he eats enough for an army, if that's what you mean. He says it's his metabolism..." Her words puttered out. "That's not what you mean, is it?"

This was a bad time to start giving Emily a crash course, but it was better than letting her walk out that door right now. "Because we aren't physical, we have to take blood and flesh from each other or a Link to live. It *feeds* our metaphysical side, sates the *need.* Eating food can't do that."

"We? You ... you mean you're..." Emily pulled away, eyes wide. "You're like him?"

"Yeah. I'm like Deshi."

Emily fluttered her hands. "I want out!"

"No, you don't."

Emily reached for the door and undid the lock. Just as it came open Haley put her shoulder into it, pushing it shut. "Give them a few minutes. Trust me on this." God of Man, they smelled good. Haley swallowed and felt her teeth prick her tongue. Normally her control was better than this.

Emily clawed at the door and yanked on the handle. "I want out. Please, please..."

"You don't want to do that."

Emily lunged for Haley, clawing at her face and eyes, spitting and kicking. It was like trying to keep an angry cat out of her face. Haley moved off the door rather than fight her.

Fine. Have it your way.

Emily jerked open the bathroom door. Haley took her time following her out. No need to rush. When she caught up, Emily was smack dab in the middle of the room staring at Deshi, cradled in Farley's arms, his jaws locked on Farley's shoulder. Head to the side, Farley's eyes were glazed, and his mouth worked as he panted. A combination of feeding and sex sounds came out of them.

Haley promised to thank him later for at least keeping his pants on.

Deshi tore a mouth full of flesh and fell away. Long sharp *chelae* tipped each of his fingers and he used them to claw the decimated bed as well as himself. His cock jutted up between his legs and he was soaked with ejaculate.

Emily's eyes took on a shadowed look. The way she stared at Deshi made Haley nervous.

Haley said, "It's not what you think. He loves you. Very much. So much he has managed not to kill you ... twice." God of Man, she hated that word, but it was one Emily would understand. Or at least she hoped she would understand.

In a dead tone Emily asked, "How long has he been fucking him?"

Haley winced and turned away. Yeah, it was time to leave. That was *so* not a conversation she wanted to have.

"C'mon, Farley, let's go."

It was Emily's turn to get in the way. She jabbed a finger in Haley's face. "I want to know! How long has he been fucking him? Huh? He talks to him in his sleep!" Farley grabbed his shirt and pushed himself up off the floor, staggered a little, but made it across the room. Emily slapped at Haley when she tried to pass. Enough! Haley knocked Emily's hands away, grabbed her by the throat, and shoved her into the wall with a thud.

"Tell me!" Emily spit and kicked. "I want to know how long that bastard has been fucking my husband!" Haley slapped her just hard enough to let her know she didn't appreciate wearing her body fluids.

"Two years! And it isn't just him. We both are! Just so you know, when he's in me, it's your name he calls out. Farley tries to never touch him, because Deshi knows how homophobic you are. Because trying to tell you it isn't like that for us won't work! So he suffers! He hates it. He hates being with us. Our friend loathes what he has to do! But he did it because he didn't want something like this to happen." Tears burst out of Emily's eyes, but Haley wouldn't put her down.

"Let her go!" Deshi came up on Haley like a bull. At the door Farley snarled, teeth long, and sharp. Deshi flashed fangs right back, while frosted silver scales rose across his chest and shoulders. Emily screamed, flailing her arms and reaching for the Prince.

Deshi threw Haley to the side. She hit the door jamb hard enough to crack the wood. Pain screamed through her side as a rib punched through her lung. Farley roared and Haley stopped him with her good arm. At the same time, Emily threw herself into Deshi's arms, wailing and clinging to him, with acting that could have landed her in Hollywood.

It made Haley want to vomit.

Deshi's eyes flashed with bits of orange and red. "Get out of my house."

Haley rubbed her shoulder as the bones finished knitting. "Deshi, you need to make sure this doesn't happen again."

He snarled at her and Farley bristled right back.

"I said get out!"

Emily's face was barely visible behind his muscled arms. Deshi murmured against her hair and stroked her back.

Yeah, now that he was sated he could go all Human and pretend it never happened.

Haley glared at him. "Next time there may not be a dog to get in the way. Remember that, okay?"

Deshi shook his head. "I'm sorry I called you. I should have never called you."

"Yeah, well I'm not. Because maybe this will be her wake up call. Link with her, Deshi. Link with her, so you can get what you need, before you wind up down in a hole waiting to die."

Deshi shut his eyes, looking pained. "Just go, please. Just go."

He sounded so pitiful Haley had to fight the urge to try and hold him. He needed out of this place. Away from that woman. When he turned his back, Haley walked away.

Think about it later, she told herself. Right now this needed to disappear. Even pissed, Haley didn't want Deshi taking a fall.

On the way down the steps, she flipped open her phone and called the cleanup crew. "Manny, I have a job for you in Ansley. One first aid and a cleanup. Yeah, it's *special*." There were three types of clean ups: the usual, the special, and the deluxe. Only the last one meant Human body parts. "I'll triple your usual fee and give you a fat tip if you can get to it tonight. Yeah, you'll need a truck." Haley thought a second about all the heavy furniture. "Maybe two. Thanks, Manny, you're a gem." She shut the phone and headed out the front door.

"How can you let him get away with that?" Farley skipped up beside her.

"He's a Queen's Son."

"Fuck that, he put his hands on you! He pushed you! Christ, if he did that to any other Female, they'd eat his throat out!"

Haley turned on him. "Is that what you want? Do you want me to go up there and tear his throat out? Do you want me hurt him? Bleed him? Force him to submit?"

The heat coming off Farley's body from the *feed* leaked all over her, feeling like super-heated cobwebs. "If you don't, then he's going to wind up killing Emily. Then what?"

With a growl she yanked away.

The wadded up T-shirt went back and forth between Farley's hands. "You know I'm right. Admit it." His face was inches from hers. She could smell him. Sex and food. The bite on his shoulder was only a light bruise now, but the scent of blood was on his skin. "Admit that I'm right. I am. You know I am. I--"

Haley shoved him and he landed on his ass, hard. "All right! You're right. He's going to kill her. He's going to kill her, and then I'm going to have to watch him die." Haley threw her arms out and laughed. It was a bitter angry sound. "He's just one more among so many. What does it matter? Medan doesn't care! She'd never let him back into the Dens after what he did ... did to himself for ... HER! God of Man, he cut out his *nevus* for ... her!" The tears came in a sudden flood, bursting out of her eyes, and running in twin streams down her cheeks. She damned her adoptive Mother for being so weak, and now here she was crying. Instead of a dragon, she acted like an emotional Human female.

And Haley hated herself for it.

Arms closed around her, and she didn't fight them. The deep thrum of Farley's purr punched through her bones. Haley hid her face against his neck and soaked him with her tears. She gave up trying to stop. She just wasn't strong enough.

It took years, hours, or maybe minutes. Time was irrelevant. When the tears ran out she stayed next to him, finding comfort in his scent and the feel of him against her.

Finally she said, "I don't know what to do."

"Mark him, or find someone who will."

It seemed like such an easy answer. A very logical and practical one. But Haley couldn't do it. Her Humanness wouldn't let her.

"Taking Deshi away from Emily would kill him." That much Haley was sure of. Whatever power Emily had over him was real. She was Human, not Kin, not a Queen. And yet ... she commanded him.

Close to her ear Farley said, "And if you don't, she'll kill him." Truth is often a difficult pill to swallow.

Haley shut her eyes and wished for an answer. None came. No divine voice whispered through her head. Even God could not accept them.

Alone, we are utterly alone in this world.

"We have our people," Farley said. But Haley didn't think it was enough.

Light cut through the darkness of the cul-de-sac, courtesy of high beams on two oversized Dodge trucks. They were both white with the letter E on the door.

"That's Manny, with the crew." She wiped her face, sniffled, and made a sad attempt at straightening her blazer.

Manny got out of the truck. Dark skin, dark hair, short and wide, he looked every bit as South American as he sounded. A dark splatter of iridescent color covered most of the right side of his face, marking him for what he was, Lesser-Bred.

No matter who you were, if you made a mess doing something, he was the guy to call. Legal, illegal, he treated all his clients the same. Manny never heard or saw a thing. He just cleaned. "I took the liberty of calling you a car."

Well, at least someone had thought about how they were going to get back to her apartment.

"Just put it on my bill." Damn, did she sound as tired as she felt? Yeah, she realized, she did.

Manny shook his head. "On the house. This time." His crew walked past him saying nothing, carrying paint buckets, shovels, Shop-Vacs, water tanks, an EMT bag, and lots and lots of plastic.

"He ate the dog." Haley wasn't sure why she felt the need to explain. At least she managed not to tack on the "again."

Manny glanced up at the house, his expression blank, his dark eyes sharp. "We'll be out of here in a few hours." He left without saying anything else.

After a few minutes the muffled sound of vacuums running and heavy broken things being moved leeched out into the still night air.

Another set of headlights preceded a black Lexus down the drive. It was so new the paint looked wet. It fit right in among the fancy houses and long drives.

The car stopped and waited for them. Automatic locks clicked as Haley reached for the door.

Together they sat in the back. There was a pane of glass behind the driver as black as the windows. Haley didn't have to tell him the address. Manny would have made sure he knew.

The trip was too long and quiet. Farley sat against the far door looking out. Neither of them spoke, and when the car stopped in front of her apartment, they didn't get out.

After a while Haley said, "I want to be alone tonight. If you need a cab, I'll call you one and pay the fare."

He shook his head. "I'm good."

"You sure?"

"Yeah."

She put her hand on the handle but didn't open it. "I'm sorry." It just seemed like the thing to say.

Farley gave a small nod, opened the other door, and got out. Haley did the same.

The car pulled away when the doors shut. Farley walked away with his head down and his hands in his pockets. And Haley went inside.

Chapter 22

"Hello?" Haley didn't remember answering the phone, it was just suddenly at her ear.

"I'm sorry to call you so early," Dr. Meyer said. "But you need to hear this."

Haley looked at the clock. It was just past four. She pushed herself up on one elbow, then swung her feet over the side of the bed. "I'm listening."

"The virus. I sent a section of the gene-typing to that friend of mine in Charlotte. I wanted to make sure I was seeing what I thought I saw. This is incredible. Terrifying, but incredible."

"Wait ... wait ... you lost me at Charlotte. Start over." Haley stood up and headed into her kitchen. Walking was good. Walking required blood flow, and that meant she'd be more awake.

"The virus we got from Creyal--it's not new. I've seen it once before in some samples that were sent to me from Beijing."

Haley grabbed a stool and barely made it before her knees buckled. "Fa-Da?"

The mass Kin death had actually made the front page of the *Atlanta Constitution*. And stayed there for six months. At first, there had been panic over the prospect of some super flu that could actually affect Kin. Then they discovered the thing wasn't really a disease, but a manufactured biological weapon. The virus was nothing more than a delivery agent.

"Yes. Part of this protein chain is an exact match; there have been changes, additions. The sample we had was too degraded for the current technology. But I remember what I saw. It was a very unique protein sheath, crystalline almost. It used the reactive chemicals in the *ulysiss* gland as a conductor. The only reason more Kin didn't die is because of the genetic difference, and that it needed physical contact for transfer. The virus in Beijing was coded only for three, maybe four bloodlines, tops. And it was too unstable to be airborne. It stopped because it ran out of victims in the radius it occupied."

But *thousands* had died in Beijing. One of the densest Kin

populations in the world lived there.

Ran out of victims...

Haley clenched her eyes shut. Every Kin in the world mourned the loss of so many. It had affected them all, such a great loss of life.

"So what are you telling me?"

"This new virus ... it's been coded with *hundreds* of family lines. The delivery is what's so unique." Haley heard Meyers move around. "Male Kin have only one sex chromosome. Pleitropy of this one gene will affect certain genes within the Kin genome."

"I'm sorry, but I don't understand what you're talking about."

Meyer laughed. "I'm sorry. You're right. Most Humans don't even know how many chromosomes they have, let alone what they do. I don't know why I expected you to be any different. Forgive me."

"Considering you just said the nicest thing any Human has ever said to me, all is forgiven." Haley smiled.

"Pleitropy is when a single gene affects the expression of polygenetic traits. The Male sex chromosome is unique to each family and it has a very high rate of mutation. Only a small amount of genetic information stays the same each generation. All organisms have the potential to develop alleles to existing genes, but your people are constantly creating entirely new protein chains. This change seems to be especially responsive to certain pheromones and enzymatic processes."

"You're losing me again, doc."

"Okay, basically the genetic code of your species undergoes genetic changes with each generation. The Male sex chromosome acts like a key. This key affects the expression of the genes, by turning them on and off like a light switch. And because Males only have one sex chromosome, they can only get that key from their Queen. That's overly simplified, of course."

It was Haley's turn to laugh. "Simplified is good! I get lost when you start all that high end metaphysical-genetics. So what does all this have to do with the virus?"

"I'm getting to that. Bear with me just a moment more. This virus was originally built only using chromosomes from the Male. This new version in Creyal is based on *Female* Kin genetics. This changes everything. The protein sequences of the Female sex chromosome have unique properties that seem interchangeable with the Male sex chromosome. This means that a bio-toxin attached to this virus would be universal."

Haley buried her face in her hand. Atlanta did not need this. Not with a Queen like Medan in the Dens.

Meyer called her name for the third time.

"I'm here."

"You all right?"

"No, not really."

"I'm very sorry. If it helps, Creyal is improving by leaps and bounds. I'm having a hard time keeping him out of my meds though. He's not helping his recovery by shooting up on all my morphine."

"Is there anything else?"

"Just one. We know this virus was manufactured with a combination of metaphysical biology and Alchemy."

Well, now, that was like mixing Drano and gasoline and just as potentially toxic. Someone either had a lot of nerve or was just plain insane. Haley wasn't sure which was worse. "Have you contacted the Bureau?"

"Not yet." Meyer paused. Her next words came out slow, like she was trying to choose them with extreme care. "How much do you know about Fa-Da, Haley?"

"Other than a lot of my people died, not much. There wasn't a whole lot made available to the public." The newspapers just printed the same vague assumptions in every new article. Only thing that changed was the name of who wrote it.

The doctor made a thinking sound. "Haley, what I'm about to tell you is extremely confidential. Do you understand?"

Haley gave a snort. "Yeah, I understand what confidential means. It's just all the genetics speak that eludes me."

"No, when I mean confidential, I'm talking higher than I-O."

If it was higher than I-O, it could only mean she wasn't going to like what she heard. "Tell me."

"Years ago, I started my work with the private military sector in the Bureau. That's how I recognized this, Haley. I was one of the people that helped build it. I didn't know what I was building at the time. Dobson made sure we didn't talk to each other. He had individual labs working on different things, and then only one or two trusted metaphysical-geneticist assembled the final product." Meyer paused. "The Bureau never proved it, but they suspect Dobson actually sold the virus to the Beijing flesh traders to use as a weapon on rival dealers. He did it with the consent of the Chinese government. It was a test run. To see if it would work."

"If what would work?"

The doctor's breath rattled over the receiver. "Haley, I'm so sorry to have to tell you this. They wanted to commit genocide. They wanted to kill *all* Kin."

Haley put her hand on the receiver so she could hold it steady. "Dobson did this?"

"They never proved it."

"But ... but you said he used the Bureau labs. How..." Her throat squeezed tight and she had to force out her words. "How could they not know what he was doing?"

Meyer was quiet. When she spoke, her voice was very flat. "I asked myself the same question many times over the years."

"Did you find an answer?"

"The only one I could come up with is that they just didn't care."

Haley nodded, even though Meyer couldn't see it. "Thank you. Thank you for telling me."

"Haley?"

No more bad news please. I just can't keep starting my mornings like this. "Yeah?"

"Be careful."

"I will."

She hung up the cordless and Medan's warning echoed in her head.

Your enemies are everywhere. Even among the ranks of those you work with. You cannot trust the chetrah, Haley. They do not wish Kin anything but death.

Chapter 23

The parking lot outside the Center for Folk and Kin Relations was normal. There were no CDC trucks, no SWAT, just little Crayola colored Toyotas, Fords, Dodges, and a few company Impalas. The company cars only came in charcoal gray and black.

Even though the building was the same, the cars all familiar, it felt strange and foreign.

The cabbie cleared his throat. Haley took the hint and got out. She was even kind enough to give him a tip, which he seemed genuinely surprised about.

A cloud of melancholy hovered over the Human-employees. This was actually a normal aftermath after dealing with a really bad day. And yesterday easily qualified in the top five.

Haley went to her office and checked her email, read police reports, and answered requests from lawyers who wanted her advice on non-Human clients.

It was a normal day filled with the same social problems she dealt with every day. *Then why do I feel like something is wrong?*

Because there was.

Dobson had cooked up a virus to deliver a bio-toxin specifically to kill her people. And even though Haley wanted to believe that he did it without the Bureau's knowledge, she couldn't.

Haley made it through two neglected stacks of files when there was a knock at her door. She didn't even look up. "Come in."

The door opened and shut. The scent moving through the small room was unfamiliar.

"Ms. Night?"

Haley pushed the papers aside and gave the visitor her attention. A small-framed, middle aged black woman held out her hand to Haley. She was dressed in a nice pink skirt and matching blazer. Her shoes were simple, white, like her blouse. A small gold cross dangled just under the collar.

Even though Haley had never met the woman she knew this was

Bauer's wife.

Haley shook her hand. The woman introduced herself and Haley was right. Her first name was Brenda.

Mrs. Bauer looked around. "May I sit?" Haley nodded. The woman smoothed out her skirt then sat gently at the edge of the couch. "I went to Mass last night. I went to confession. I asked my priest for guidance. I asked God for answers. I've prayed. A lot of people don't believe in prayer anymore." Her eyes came up. "Is it true that Kin don't believe in God?"

Haley coughed and dug a candy out of her dish. While she stalled for time by unwrapping it, she tried to tick off all the things that this could be about. Mrs. Bauer was quiet while Haley popped one candy, then two into her mouth.

"Mrs. Bauer, I'm not sure I'm qualified to answer that question." Haley relaxed when the woman smiled. Her dark eyes held no anger, no animosity. It was a pleasant change.

"Will you try?"

Haley blinked, shuffled papers. She stopped and shook her head. "No, Kin have no God."

"Then what do you believe?" The total lack of condemnation in her tone made Haley look up.

"Kin believe in life. Survival at any sacrifice. Even if it means eating your own."

Her face fell a little, but she held onto her composure. No throwing up in the hall for Mrs. Bauer.

Haley said, "I'm sorry. But I'm not sure what this is about."

Mrs. Bauer picked at the hem of her skirt at her knee. Her face was a strange combination of fear and sadness. "Lamar and I have been married for almost twenty-five years. He's told me a lot about you."

Oh, boy. That could mean so many things.

At least you're not sleeping with him.

Haley tried to smile, but it felt lopsided and fake. "Hopefully, some of the things he's said are good." She played with a pen on her desk.

"He's never said anything bad."

But there were so many bad things Bauer could say about her. It would take all Haley's fingers and toes to count off the awkward situations he had walked in on. Especially in the Tank.

"Haley?" Mrs. Bauer opened the small purse she carried. Her hand dipped inside and came out with a large syringe complete with a capped needle. "I need your blood."

Haley shut her mouth. No need to look like a barn door. She stared at Brenda's hand for a very long time. "Can I ask why?" After all, Bauer had looked pretty good considering.

"Lamar has developed complications from the anti-venom he received."

Haley sagged. "What kind of complications?"

Brenda stared at the syringe and turned it over and over in her hand. Her grip was tight, like the little piece of plastic was her only life line. "They don't know, but Martin Jones is dead. That lady officer..."

"McKinney."

Mrs. Bauer nodded. "Yes, they lost her this morning. Her husband is keeping her on life support."

"For the baby."

The expression on Brenda's face said that she hadn't known, but understood. "The doctors stabilized Lamar yesterday around eight. They had hoped he would improve. But in his weakened state the anti-venom is doing more harm than good. I was told that Female Kin blood could possibly save him." Hope flavored her words.

"I offered yesterday."

"I know. He told me."

Haley stared at the syringe in Mrs. Bauer's hands. "It's a sin. Your religion specifically prohibits the mixing of Human and Kin blood."

"We all sin, Haley. Eventually we all sin. But that's the great thing about God. He forgives no matter how terrible the sin is."

Haley shook her head. This was against everything Bauer believed in.

"Please." When Mrs. Bauer held out the syringe, her hand shook. "Please, Haley, don't let him die."

Of course Haley wouldn't let him die. But she'd worked with the man for years. She knew how he felt. She knew how devoted he was. In his mind, Kin were damned. Soulless. Non-Human. And while he treated her people with respect, he was also firm in his dedication to his God. And his God had no room for anything Kin. He tolerated her people because there was no saving them. And maybe he was right. Maybe that's why Kin didn't age, because for them there was nothing after life.

"I can't believe he would agree to this." As soon as the words left her lips she knew. Bauer hadn't agreed. "I can't. I can't do that to him. He'll never forgive me. He'll never forgive you."

"I don't care. He can hate me. But he'll be alive. You said you believed in life."

Haley shook her head and asked, "Isn't there anything..." The way Brenda's eyes burned said it all. This was it. Her only choice and she was willing to take it even if it damned her soul and damned Bauer's.

Life at any cost.

Haley took the syringe. Even though her insides were Jell-O, her hand was steady. "Don't let them spin it down. If the doctors spin it, you'll lose a lot of the healing properties." She clenched a fist. It would be better to take it from her neck, or better yet her inner thigh. The metaphysical properties of Kin blood were different depending on the location. It had been almost twenty-four hours and Bauer would need all the help he could get.

"What's wrong?" Brenda asked.

"Our blood... where it's drawn from affects the metaphysics. The wrist is the weakest point."

"Where's the strongest?"

Haley looked at her, then put a hand on her lap. "The inside of the thigh."

Her voice shook when she said, "Do it, please."

"Lock the door. Last thing I need is someone walking in on me."

There was no need to traumatize the woman further, so when Haley stood, she turned away. She pulled up her skirt until it bunched around her waist and put a foot on her desk. Just a little stick, a little blood, no big deal. But her Human-instilled ethics froze her hand. Bauer would not want this. He would rather die than choose this. Her Kin instincts said, *shut up. No one wants to die. Ever.*

"Haley?"

"I'm just looking for a good vein."

Wrong. You're looking for an excuse because Bauer deserves to have a choice. He also deserves to live into old age, not be robbed of what few years his short life had left.

Haley uncapped the needle with every intent on just stabbing the thing in her leg, but her hands wouldn't listen. Fucking Human *Impressions.* If she was a real Female, something as ridiculous as conscience would never get in the way.

"I'll do it." Brenda was right beside her. "This way you won't have to live with it."

"It's not me I'm worried about. You can never tell him."

A small smile touched Brenda's lips. "I never intended on telling him. If he doesn't know, it can't be his sin. I will bear it. I will pay for it." Brenda pushed gently at Haley's hands, and she let go of the syringe. "Where?"

Haley took a breath, and put her fingertip at the junction of her leg and torso. "Go deep and you can't miss the vein."

The needle went in with a sting, but felt nothing like teeth. Brenda's eyes widened and her lips pressed into a thin line. "It's darker than I imagined."

"Because of where you're drawing it from."

When the syringe was full, Mrs. Bauer stared at the plastic tube, her face drawn tight.

Like she's swallowed something bitter. Haley put her leg down and straightened her skirt. "You all right?"

"Just thinking ... how do I…?" She laughed, and it wasn't a happy sound. "I'm not even sure how to do this."

"Put it in a vein if you can."

"They have an IV in him." Her eyes came up. "Will it matter if it's diluted by intravenous fluids?"

"No."

"How much?"

Haley looked at the syringe clutched in the woman's hand. "All of it. If you don't see improvement, we can give him more. But I think..."

"This either works or it's too late." The finality of Mrs. Bauer's statement hit home. "It will work." She picked up her purse from the couch and tucked the syringe inside. It barely fit. Mrs. Bauer stood there for several heartbeats, her knuckles bleached by her death grip on the handbag. "I have to know..."

“What?”

Her eyes clenched shut, then snapped back open. “Will this ... will this change him ... I mean ... will he...” She couldn’t say the words. But Haley had a pretty good idea what she was afraid of. Mrs. Bauer didn’t want to lose her husband to the wyrms. She would do this only if he wouldn’t forsake her and go to them, consumed with their *needs.*

How easy it would have been to tell her yes, just so Bauer could have what he would want.

“No,” Haley said. “Bonding is more complicated than that. There are ... certain processes.”

Brenda’s shoulders eased and she nodded. “I need to go.”

“Please don’t get caught.” Not only are there religious violations taking place, but legal ones, too.

“Thank you.” Mrs. Bauer left Haley burning up with a horrible feeling inside her chest.

When she examined it, she discovered the feeling was guilt.

Chapter 24

Colonel Dobson felt like a man who'd just won the lottery only to discover his bitch of a dog had eaten the ticket.

"Did you hear me, colonel?" asked the Human mouthpiece for the Queen.

Fuck yes, he heard her. He just didn't like what she was saying. "I have it under control." It was getting harder and harder to cap his temper with this she-devil. Especially when she laughed at him. Which she was doing a lot of lately.

"Oh, colonel, colonel, colonel, you do amuse me so." Her voice dropped fifty degrees with a suddenness that Dobson was getting used to. "But I am done being amused."

"I have everything in order. I'm just waiting for my request to be granted. By this time tomorrow, I will own her. There's no need to make things more treacherous than they already are." The last thing he needed was a full blown Kin battle in the middle of the city. That would only slow down his plans. Something he just couldn't afford, thanks to Jones.

The bastard.

Jones had sold out. In a very, very big way. Two-point-eight-million sat in an off shore bank account in his daughter's name.

Germans, Japs, Russians, they hadn't nailed down who it was yet. But sure as shit, Jones had been working both sides for quite some time. This time something had gone wrong. Maybe he'd gotten the vials mixed up. Maybe he'd accidently broken the thing and contaminated the product. Who the hell knew or cared. 'Cause the virus was out. Now, it was only a matter of time before someone from the CDC identified it.

Yeah, that was going to be a helluva nut buster.

Dobson was now left scrambling to clean up the mess left behind. Jones and McKinney had died like they were supposed to, but that stupid Negro had been one of those lucky ones. Not many people survived that much air in a line.

Some kind of luck.

"I've heard some interesting reports about your recent activities."

Dobson fell still and tried with everything he had to not let his breathing change, 'cause she'd hear it. The bitch heard everything. "What kind of reports?"

"That your virus is working. That you have successfully killed as many as two dozen useless Males." There wasn't a drop of anger in her voice. Which confused Dobson, because it had been her city where they died, they had been her Males. Or at least the ones that lived in her Dens. He expected anger, venom, not ... praise?

The colonel steadied himself. This had to be some sort of trick. Some play of words. "I'm glad you approve."

"As you should be." A deep hiss came over the receiver. "But my pleasure changes nothing. Tomorrow she dies. I would suggest you stay out of the way."

Two could play it this way.

"I understand." Dobson smiled, then downright grinned. The tangible discomfort radiating from the silence practically gave him a hard on.

A growl echoed over the line. "I do not play games, colonel. Do not get in my way. Killing you will not bring me sorrow."

"I feel the same way about you, Your Majesty." She laughed and so did Dobson. "I just have one request." Abrupt silence, then a slow intake of air. Dobson could almost see her in his mind, thinking, carefully picking her next words ... moving her rooks carefully across the board.

"Speak."

"I want minimal damage. The city cannot afford the kind of devastation that your pet can cause."

"Pet?" The Queen sighed. "Oh, he is much more than a pet. I command Niles. He will do anything for me."

"Good, then it shouldn't be a problem doing this away from the Bureau." With this recent wrench, he couldn't afford losing an hour's worth of work.

"Should I send Haley an invitation to meet me out in the countryside? Or perhaps you will consider delivering her to my doorstep?" Anger trickled into her words, distorting the pitch and tone.

"Listen. You want her dead? Fine. But if you bring the attack into this part of the city, you will jeopardize everything I have worked on. This means your enemies will still be alive and there will be other Queens to remain your rivals. I cannot afford the loss of a single scrap of genetic information. If Niles starts taking out buildings, he could easily involve any number of my satellite labs, not to mention the fires will bring the entire place to a standstill for weeks. And I do not have weeks."

It was far more information than he wanted her to know, but it was the only way he knew to convey just how much was at stake for both of them.

Twelve hours. Twelve hours and Haley would be underground, pumped up with his virus, her blood being spun down into serum to be released as an aerosol. By the time the wyrm Queen figured out the truth, she'd be dying herself. Or better yet, dead.

Because she *would* figure it out. She always did.

"Did you have a particular spot in mind, colonel?" Her tone was a kind of calm that promised terrible things.

"You pick the location. I just need it to be at least three miles outside the Bureau's offices."

The Queen sighed, and the Human mouth she spoke through clicked its tongue. "I must admit, I am skeptical of your sudden amicable nature. It is ... unlike you."

Just like a woman. You can't make them happy when you disagree, and they don't trust you when you follow. The Whore was the same way. Dobson just chalked it up to not having the right equipment.

"And if I argued with you, would you change your mind?"

She laughed. "Of course not."

"Then why should I bother? To tell you the truth, I don't have the fucking time. Every minute I stand here flapping jaws with that Human puppet you use is time I could be getting what I need done. Now, if you don't mind, pick a goddamned spot so I can arrange to get her there."

A low growl licked over the phone and Dobson fully expected the Queen to throw a dragon-sized tantrum. Instead she said, "Will Gresham Park suit your requirements?"

Dobson took a minute to think. The distance was good. The team could respond in no time. And by the time the Queen figured out Haley wasn't dead...

"That will work."

"Good."

"What time?"

"Two. Do not be late." He started to hang up, but her voice held him. "Oh, and Dobson ... if I find out this is some sort of trick, I will use Niles to take the Fury from you. Even if it means ripping him out of the ground."

Chapter 25

Farley headed into the Resources office. They'd texted him about the phone records request Haley put in for him.

"There you are!" Judy Grimm flapped a handful of papers at him from the other side of her desk. "The ink on these is getting cold. I was starting to think you weren't coming."

No, I just didn't sleep worth a shit. For once.

Nope, he'd just laid there on his broken down mattress counting the cracks in the ceiling thinking about Deshi, one word taking precedence. Fool. An absolute fool.

That and fuck-tard.

And his chest still ached for him, because his friend was making a terrible choice.

"Hey, you okay?" Judy worked the piece of gum in her mouth like her life depended on it. Her eyes flicked up and down over Farley's body, but there was absolutely no desire in them, just concern. Not that Farley hadn't tried stirring those feelings, but Judy said she was gay.

As in female to female, not the happy kind of gay.

Lesbian, she told him.

Yeah, whatever that was supposed to mean. Humans and their carnal boundaries escaped him.

He took the papers and scanned them. Over one hundred phone calls had been made from the pay phone closest to Niles' apartment in the past month alone.

Whoa, now this was interesting.

Every seven days or so Justice's number popped up, usually on Tuesday, sometimes Thursday. Farley flipped the papers, going back six months. The pattern was the same. A lot of people used this phone, but the likelihood of this many people from the Dens giving the Great White a ringy-dingy just wasn't happening.

That was about as likely as ... well, Judy going out with him.

She smiled and craned her head like she might be able to catch a glimpse over his shoulder. "Did you find what you need?" Damn, she was cute. Same height as Haley, with long dark hair she kept braided in the back. She was tawny like Farley, her small tight breasts almost invisible.

They could easily wear each other's clothes. Both of them preferred black skaters with chains, and T-shirts. Today, hers was Seether, his was Disturbed.

"You're looking at me like that again." Judy reached out and tweaked his ear.

Farley winced. "Sorry, just admiring your shirt."

She looked down and gave the hem a tug. "I got it at their concert. Hey, are you going to get tickets to the Battle of the Bands in December? I hear all the wyrm-based ones are going to be there."

Farley shrugged.

"What's eating at you? You're usually way more talkative than this. You've been here," she checked her watch, "five minutes and haven't asked me out once. Normally you're working on your sixth try by now. You sick?"

"Kin don't get sick." Then he thought about Creyal and added, "Normally."

"Well, something's wrong." She popped her gum in rapid succession, then froze. Judy's eyes widened a little. "You didn't break up with Claire, did you? 'Cause if she's available, I'm so after that piece of."

"She's not gay."

"Well, me not being straight doesn't stop you now, does it?" She grinned. "Hey, half the fun is making the attempt."

"No, I didn't break up with Claire." At least not that he was aware of. But then, after the locker room incident...

"You don't look too sure about that." Judy put a hand on his arm. "You wanna talk about it? We can go get beers after work."

"Naw, z'all good. Just some relationship difficulties is all." Well, he was sure *something* was being difficult, but it didn't have anything to do with Claire. "I gotta split. Haley will want to see these." He stalled and gave Judy a cockeyed smile. "If I was having heartbreak ails, could you find it in that heart of yours to *ease* me?" Farley breathed in her scent when she leaned close. Her cheek nearly brushed his. Warm air stirred against his ear, making his temp kick up. This close and he could see bits of green in her gray eyes. Judy had great lashes.

Man, he wanted to put his lips on hers, run his tongue across her skin.

"Still gay," she whispered.

He sighed. "Your loss."

"You keep telling me that." She went back to her desk. "Oh, an F.Y.I. for ya." He leaned back over her desk and she tapped the computer screen. "I'm not sure what it means exactly, but I saw an internal investigation request come over the system. It had your partner's name on it."

Farley raised an eyebrow. "What did it say?"

Judy shrugged. "Don't know. Couldn't see it. Usually, any kind of I.N.I. requests go through Resources because we have to file them with the individual's personnel report, as well as alert their legal defense. Everything has to go through the lawyers first. Annoying, if you ask me."

"And this didn't come through here?"

"Nope, it went right upstairs."

"Which means what?"

She switched the screen and pointed to a number at the end of a name. "See this? This is Agent Gills. He had one pulled on him because of a missing file on a case. The S here at the end means it's a standard double check. He probably has the damn thing stuffed in his trunk again. Anyways, your partner--" she clicked back to the other screen. "There is an M at the end and then a one." Judy pulled at her bottom lip as her eyebrows clenched.

"And you don't know what that means?"

"I've never seen it before. So I looked it up." Judy patted the large white binder on her desk. "It's a Military code. Someone in the Bureau's Military section has called an investigation on her. And that number one..." She looked back at the screen. "That one means it can only be the Head of Operations for that section. You know who that is, right?"

Farley's legs shot him down the hall and drove him up the stairs two at a time.

Dobson had requested an I.N.I. It didn't mean he would get it, but the fact he'd bypassed Resources was a good sign the S.O.B. had something up his sleeve. Farley hated Dobson. That jerk was the reason he'd lost his Agent status and almost wound up in the ADF doing a six month stint. He would have never survived the *need* that long. That kind of fortitude just wasn't possible for Food.

As he took the corner, his shoulder smashed into someone and sent them spinning. They cursed, and Farley shouted an apology, but he didn't have time to slow down. One right and a left and he skidded to a halt in front of Garrett's office. If the guy didn't know, he needed to. And if he did know, Farley wanted something done about it.

Garrett was on the phone. He looked up but didn't motion him in. Farley bounced on his toes, waited, and waited some more. Garrett kept an open door policy. As in, "my door is open and you just stand there 'til I tell you to come in."

Which was going to take forever.

Fuck.

Farley walked up to the man's desk. During a pause in his conversation Garrett turned his chair away.

Farley shuffled, he shifted, he picked at the corner of the desk. Fifty years later, Mr. Chatter-Box-Garrett finally hung up the phone. He was the only man Farley knew that could have a twenty minute phone conversation and say all of two sentences.

Those storm gray eyes pegged Farley where he stood. "I know I didn't just see you walk into my office and stand here at my desk without invitation." Garrett stood up and the term brick shithouse came to Farley's mind.

"Dobson called an I.N.I. on Haley and I want to know what for."

Garrett's eyes widened. If he didn't know, it most likely meant this was bad. Really bad.

"When?"

"A few hours ago, I think."

Farley did not like the look on the man's face at all. "You can do something about this, right?"

"If you're asking me if I can override it, the answer is no."

"Why the hell would Dobson have grounds to call for an I.N.I. on Haley? She's no military threat. It's not like she's been rubbing shoulders with Medan or something..."

No, but she did go into the Dens. *Shit.*

Garrett's stare was stone cold and Farley knew. "She didn't have clearance?" An angry growl ripped out of his chest.

"If you're going to start that crap, go close my door. We don't need the entire office seeing it or hearing it."

Farley clenched his fists and eyes shut. He willed himself back in order. Everything listened except his vision.

Garrett cleared his throat. "I don't have any idea why Haley would be denied clearance for anything. As far as I know the only place she's been is here, home, and any and all approved locations. Last Tuesday, she took my car to pick an anniversary gift for my wife." The man's eyes flashed. "She loved it, by the way. She plans on wearing it out next month when the Center has its annual dinner."

"Garrett..."

"I know exactly where she was the entire three and a half hours. I followed protocol and had her use one of our cars. My car, to be exact. The GPS device has her logged exactly where she was supposed to be for the entire time it took that piece to be finished."

Silence fell and Farley folded and unfolded the phone records in his hand. His eyes never left Garrett's face and Garrett never looked away. "Then why would Dobson have grounds to call an I.N.I. on her?"

"We don't know that he does."

Farley didn't think the man really believed his own words. He was just hoping. And hoping wasn't good enough. "And if you're wrong?"

"We'll get through it."

Farley bared his fangs. The only reason he didn't get into the man's face was because he couldn't reach him. Standing on the desk just sort of ruined the effect.

"You should have told her no."

Garrett closed the distance for him. "I think you need to back away from my desk before you're kissing the sidewalk outside this building." It killed Farley, but he stepped back. He hated knowing even though he could break Garrett in half, the man was still his Dominant. In Human society, they called it being "boss." Unfortunately, the person in charge wasn't decided by strength and speed.

Farley paced, crushing the papers he carried. He had to burn his anger off somehow and moving was the only way. 'Cause biting and clawing was out of the question.

Garrett said, "I promise you, I will take care of this."

"How?" A growl chased his question.

Garrett's mouth made a slash.

"You don't know, do you?" Farley kept himself rooted to the spot even though his legs wanted to tap dance all over the desk.

"No. Not yet. But let me handle it."

"I'm telling Haley."

"You do that." Garrett sat down at his desk. "Now, if you'll excuse, me, I have some phone calls to make."

Chapter 26

Haley waited on hold as the History Department secretary transferred her call over to Orin's office.

"Ancient Histories, Orin speaking." Damn, he sounded so Human. Even Haley couldn't tell over the phone. Not a lick of Olde Tongue accent in his words. And he did speak it. All five dialects.

"Orin, it's me."

"Haley, just the Kin I wanted to talk to. How's life treating you, my friend?"

"Good, pretty good. I take it you got somewhere with that ledger I sent you?

He laughed. "You could say that. Niles Fury, huh? I never would have guessed his hobby to be along the lines of sky-watching. A Kin like that? If word were to get out, it would tarnish his grisly reputation with his brethren."

"He watched stars?"

"Apparently, he did. Those first set of dates in the book correspond with hatching records in the International Clutch Database. The second set matches up to astrological events. Specifically the dates and times of star deaths."

"What?"

"It looks like Niles was trying to match up the hatching dates of Queens with star births and deaths."

"And next you're going to tell me this means something special." Haley had been hoping for something concrete, not the wild goose chase of a mad-man.

"Actually it doesn't. There are billions and billions of stars in the galaxy, and because of their distance, by the time we see them, many of them don't even exist anymore."

"Then how could he know when a star died?"

"Well, that's the thing, he really couldn't. There isn't a dragon in the history of our people who has lived as long as the stars. In the grand scheme of things, we aren't really as immortal as we think." He laughed.

"Don't tell Medan I said that, of course."

Of course she wouldn't. Not "I-am-the-only-god" Medan. Nope, Haley liked her arms and legs firmly attached, thank you.

"Mum's the word." She reached for a candy. "If the dates of star deaths can't be determined, then how do you know that's what he was cataloging?"

"Now, now, I never said they couldn't be determined."

"So his dates were on mark?"

"Yeah, they actually are." Orin sounded impressed. Really impressed.

"How?"

"Because just like Kin, stars give off a metaphysical signal."

"And what? He had a metaphysical telescope in his pocket or something?"

Orin laughed again. "You've been hanging around Farley too long, he's made you snarky."

"Snarky?"

"Yeah, that's my new word of the month. I give myself a Hershey Kiss every time I get to use it."

"Orin, you seriously need a hobby." Haley sat back in her chair and glanced up at the clock. Hopefully everything had gone okay with Bauer. She was already going to one funeral this month. Why Humans had them, she couldn't understand. Dead was dead. Everyone getting dressed to go stand over a metal box and cry just seemed like punishment for the living.

Orin said, "It's called an EMR."

"What is?"

"The telescope they use today to listen for metaphysical signals. It stands for Earth's Metaphysical Radiation."

"You know, I don't know what it is about you people and your fancy professional titles, but you're the second person today to assume I have any expertise in the area of science outside basic Kin physiology."

"Well, I'm by no means an expert, so don't ask me to explain all the metaphysical science behind it. I only know what I've read. Which is metaphysical energy doesn't have to travel through space like light or sound. That's how they've looked at and listened to stars for decades. Our planet also gives off a metaphysical signal. By tapping into the waves produced by the Earth, they can quote-unquote *hear* the stars as they are born, and as they die. It does have its limits. Seems only certain stars transmit on the Earth's signal. They're working on a way to try and go beyond the limitation now."

"So did he buy one off eBay or what?"

"Of course not. They're still experimental and extremely expensive."

Haley stared at the phone a second before putting it back to her ear. "Orin, I was joking."

He coughed. "I knew that."

She wondered if he still blushed. And if he did, he just had to be glowing.

Orin said, "Anyhow, I called one of the professors over in the Astrophysics Department, had a chat with him about some of these dates. I can only confirm the last fifty or so, but they're right on."

"Why only fifty?"

"It's only been in operation for about three years."

"Then how did he get all those dates--centuries worth?"

"Honestly? I think he might have been able to hear them."

Haley stood up. She couldn't go very far, the damn phone was one of those tethered models. "Heard them? Stars?"

"It's not as crazy as it sounds. Telepathy in Kin isn't all that uncommon. Sometimes we're born with certain types. And look at the Link bonds that create metaphysical ties with a Human host, even what Queens can do to other Kin. There are some obscure documents where all sorts of abilities are referenced."

"And do any of those same documents reference other popular Kin fairy tales?"

Orin chuckled. "You know, the Human Bible has a lot of unbelievable references in it, too."

"When did you convert?" Haley sat on the edge of her desk and picked out the last green candy. "This I've got to hear."

"You know what I mean. Sometimes an ancient people can only describe things as they understand it. And if anyone qualifies as an ancient people, I think we do."

"Touché." She bit down and the candy went out with a loud crunch. "So what do dying stars and Queens have to do with each other?"

"Well, that's where you get into all those fairy tales you don't care for. Olde Lore says the power of Queens is dictated by the stars. Her life, her strength, everything is written into the heavens. That if a Female Kin is born at the moment a star dies, then she gains the power it releases. It's called *oobura*, and basically it translates into 'the taking of power.' Like *feeding*. Because of the Male to Female ratio in our species, plus the star qualifications, it's a fairly rare occurrence. But Niles appears to have dates going back as far as three thousand years."

"Please tell me you don't believe that kind of tripe."

"Of course not. Metaphysical biology and astro-metaphysics are two completely different creatures. There are some similar sciences between them, but they are as different as night and day. To expect one to predict the other." Orin made a disbelieving sound. "But what I believe, and you believe, is completely irrelevant. Niles believed this, or at least seemed to. And if he believed it, then there are others who will, too. Others like the Queens."

"That's 'cause they're Hive bound and stuck in their ways." She winced.

"Don't worry, I won't tell if you don't."

"Thanks, I appreciate that."

"Haley?"

"Yeah?" She dug in the jar of candy hoping to find one last green survivor.

"Your name is in this ledger. You know that, right?"

"Yup, I saw it a few times." She didn't find one so she settled on a yellow. "Please don't tell me I'm destined to become a Queen holed up in the ground for eternity?"

"No."

She gave an exaggerated sigh. "Good, 'cause there is no way I'm giving up my shoes or my panty collection."

Orin was quiet. Haley ate another piece of candy. "You still there?"

"I'm here. Haley, I don't know quite how to tell you this because it sounds ridiculous."

"And the whole Queen stardust thing doesn't? C'mon, spit it out."

"There is no way to verify the accuracy of the date beside your name, but I did some checking. A star didn't die on the day you were born." Well, Haley wasn't going to cry about it, that's for sure. "The date that appears by your name seems to correlate with global events that were believed to have been a catalyst by the passing of an interstellar storm."

"Are you going all *Star Trek* on me? 'Cause I really hate the whole 'use the force' bit, and that green guy, Yoda, he creeps me out."

"That's *Star Wars*, not *Star Trek*."

"Oh, yeah. *Star Trek* has the pointy eared dude."

"Haley, this isn't a joke."

"Sure it is. Niles followed me around because of some Olde Lore that has absolutely no basis in the real world. And apparently a bunch of Queens hate my guts because of this same hand-me-down tall tale."

"You're angry." He sounded surprised. Haley cracked another piece of candy in his ear.

"You bet. I'm getting strong-armed by Medan because of some stupid *Star Wars* versus Captain Kirk and his merry men story that is so ridiculous you'd have to be brain dead to even consider it."

Orin's sigh rattled the receiver. "Haley, I remember the night skies the day you were born. It was terrifying. Beautiful, but terrifying. Everything on the planet with a metaphysical binding felt it. Many of us thought we were going to die."

Curious, she asked, "What happened?"

"We don't know for sure, because we only have x-rays to study the ripples that are still millions of light years from our planet. Apparently, there was some sort of cataclysmic event that left a void in space. And if Niles could hear stars dying, then the day of your birth he was probably deafened by them. The event was biblical, but we won't see the changes in our sky for millions of years. It's the metaphysical pulse it created that caused so much upheaval. Theoretically, even the frequency of the Earth would have been supercharged. You're pretty young, but there are several of us who remember the strange heavenly events. Fire falling from the sky, night becoming day, electrical storms. It was seen all over the world."

"Wow, you really know how to make a girl feel special." She was trying to be funny, but Orin didn't laugh.

"Just be careful. Queens have killed for less."

He was right, which didn't make her feel better.

Farley came through the door with a wad of papers in his hand, eyes swimming with bits of gold and the anxiety coming off in sour waves.

"Hey, Orin, I gotta go. Farley's here with something important." She hung up. "What the heck got under your skin?" He handed her the papers and she scanned them. "One phone call a week it looks like. This is great, but--" Farley went to her door, closed it, and turned the lock. "You okay?"

"I'm okay." He kept staring at the floor.

"Well, something's wrong."

"I think we should leave."

"Leave?" When he looked at her, she realized what "leave" meant. "Farley?"

"Dobson has called an I.N.I. on you. And that can't be a good thing." His hands clenched and unclenched. "We should just leave. Get out of the country; go somewhere, anywhere but here."

"I'm not afraid of Colonel Dobson."

"You should be. Trust me. He's dangerous. He hates us." Farley took her wrist and pressed his thumb against her pulse. "Please..."

"I'm not going to leave my job because of some species extremist."

"I think he knows you went into the Dens. I know you didn't have permission."

She looked away. Yeah, there was that.

"We really need to go." He gave her hand a tug.

"I should talk to Garrett."

"I already did."

"And?"

Farley let out his breath slow. "He said he'll take care of it."

Haley frowned at him. "Garrett will do what he says."

"I think he will do what he thinks he can."

She shook her head. "If Dobson knows, that's all the more reason I have to stay." Farley paled, and his hand tightened on her wrist. "If I go, then Garrett will have to take the blame. Forget the fact that he would lose his job. He'd wind up in jail. And I'm not talking about the local pokey either. Federal prison. Hard time for a long time. I have faith in Garrett. He'll get this taken care of. He's a good man, a trustworthy person and he'll make this okay." Haley picked up the papers Farley had given her and shuffled them. "I am not a coward."

"I didn't say that."

"No. But if I ran, I would have no chance at a defense. Besides, what about Deshi? I can't leave him."

"He already made his choice." Farley's voice was cold.

"Trust me, the worst we can do is run." Haley picked up the phone and dialed.

"Who are you calling?"

She waved the papers at him. "I'm calling Justice. I need to find out what he knows about Niles." And if Dobson was going to pull an I.N.I. on her, there was no time like the present.

"Hello, this is Gregory." The voice was Human and very ordinary.

"Yes, sir. My name is Haley Night. I'm an Agent with the CFKR. I'd like to speak to Justice, if he's available." The man on the end of the line went quiet. Only the sound of his breathing told Haley that the phone hadn't gone dead. "Hello?"

The breathing deepened and the rhythm changed. When the man spoke again it was still the same generic Human sound, but the inflection and annunciation had altered.

"This is Justice."

It wasn't the first time Haley had heard the words of Kin come through the mouth of a Human Link. But it was still weird

Haley cleared her throat. "Justice, I need to speak with you about a Kin named Niles Fury."

"I see."

"I did a records search on the pay phone outside his apartment and it appears he's been calling you for the past--" She glanced at the papers. "Well, for at least five years."

Haley prepared for an argument, evasion, even an excuse. But after a moment of quiet, Justice said, "I will meet with you. We will talk."

Not one to look a gift horse in the mouth, she asked, "Where?"

"In my home." No hesitation, calm, gentle ... matter-of-fact.

"I'm not sure that would be appropriate, considering the questions I'm going to have to ask you."

A soft chuckle sounded over the line. "All will be well. Do you know the address?"

Of course she did. Who on earth could miss the place? It was Donald Trump meets Fort Knox. You'd have to be blind not to notice the building, let alone those giant walls.

"I can find it."

"Good. Then we will meet. Will an hour give you enough time?"

"I'll be there in half."

That laugh again. Smooth and thick, like warm fur. "Very well, Haley Night, very well." The line went dead, and she stared at the phone for a few seconds before hanging up.

"Well?" Farley asked.

Damn, she'd forgotten he was even there. "He said he'll meet with me."

"Just like that? Are you going alone?"

"Are you asking to come with me?"

He smiled a little. It loosened the tightness in his eyes. "Yeah, I'd like to use the time in the cab to try and talk some sense into you."

Chapter 27

It took them twenty minutes, plus a five minute argument with the cabbie who didn't want Farley riding in his cab. Haley threatened to have Immigration investigate his status. He shut up after that.

An iron gate met them at the entrance, guarded by two men with earpieces, Oakleys, and matching suits.

"Jesus, I wonder if he's going to require we call him Mr. President."

Haley drove her elbow in Farley's rib.

She said, "We're here to see Justice."

One of them said something into his wrist. A second later the iron gates shuddered open. The men stepped out of the way.

Haley went in, but when Farley tried to follow, a hand came out. He flicked his eyes up to the Human and growled. "I suggest you move that if you want to keep it attached."

"He's with me." Haley grabbed his hand.

Suit-on-the-right replied, "Justice says only you." He dipped his head at Farley. "He can wait here." He made it sound like it was some sort of privilege.

Farley said, "I'm not a fucking dog."

Some "Arf-arf" sound effects came from Suit-on-the-left

Farley flashed his teeth and growled. Haley caught him by the shoulder with her one hand and held his neck with the other. The two Suits drew guns from somewhere inside their jackets and held them like men who killed on a regular basis. Haley pressed her face into Farley's neck. "When's the last time you ate?"

"I should ask the same of you." He looked at her. Sharp pointed fangs distorted his upper lip.

"We'll go eat then. I'll just come back tomorrow."

He shook his head, blinked, and his eyes darkened to brown. "No, go. I'll be fine." *He doesn't mean it*. "Yes, I do."

"Stop that."

"I can't." Farley put a hand on her cheek. "Go. I'll wait here. I'll behave." He stepped away, and went to sit on the curb.

Suit One and Suit Two put their weapons back and resumed their post.

Another pair of guards stood at the main entrance and a third one inside the foyer. Haley didn't have a problem figuring out which way to go. A single hallway led to a single elevator. She stepped into the lift. There were no buttons to push. The door closed and the metal box slid upward through the layers of concrete. No ding marked her arrival. It stopped and the doors opened into a magnificent room worthy of an *Atlanta Living* cover. But it was the Kin standing near the floor to ceiling glass windows who stole Haley's breath.

Colored like ivory, the afternoon sun shattered across the textured surface of Justice's scales, making him glow like a million stars condensed into a single shape.

His head turned. It was all curves and planes. No ridges, horns, or armor disrupted the shape. His luminous blue eyes pulsed with light.

Haley struggled to keep her hearts in her chest. It wasn't fear she felt, but an incredible presence. It rubbed along the inside of her skull, warm and seductive.

Would you like to sit or do you prefer to stand?

The voice breathed through her mind. She put a hand to her temple and stepped back.

Do not fear me, Haley Night. I will not harm you. I could never harm you.

The strange thing was, she believed him. Trusted him. Justice moved one graceful step in front of the other, body sliding across the space like something liquid.

Silent. Even as large as he was, he made absolutely no sound.

"I think I'll stand." She hoped her knees would support her.

Up close Justice was overwhelming. Almost as big as Medan. Were the rumors true about him being mute?

A vow of silence, actually. He dipped his head.

"You invade minds, too?"

Sometimes it is unavoidable.

The scales along his neck and side raised, then settled with a slight flutter.

May I greet you? God of Man, his voice. It wasn't a powerful sound that demanded respect or declared power; it was almost tangible. It moved through Haley's mind, putting her at ease, even as a hundred questions bounced around inside her skull.

There will be plenty of time for answers. Please, allow this old Kin to be touched.

His head lowered, his expression humble. Haley held out her hand and his lips parted. His pink tongue slid out between his small, sharp teeth. The forked ends touched her fingers, wrapped around her wrist, and slid up her arm. He thrummed as he tasted her, and she couldn't stop the heat spreading across her skin.

With her other hand she touched his muzzle, then his jaw, caressed the length, stopped at his cheek, and laid her palm flat. Justice scented her, drawing her taste across his palate.

It has been far too long since I have touched one of my own.

"How long?"

Justice didn't answer, only walked back to the window, body surging, muscles rippling. Watching him was hypnotic.

You should not make your Marked wait for you too long. He hungers.

The Great White looked out the window and his sky blue eyes held palpable longing. His breathing slowed until he became still and he took on the appearance of something not real.

"Why was Niles calling?"

He blinked. Once.

I owed him a debt. So, we came to an agreement.

"What kind of agreement?"

Justice's chest expanded and life brimmed over, animating him from head to toe. He opened his wings and sat back on his haunches, tucking his slightly smaller front legs near his chest. Then it was gone. Whatever made him real flickered out, and he became still again. Silence.

"Justice?"

To watch over you.

As Haley approached, his head dropped, and she had to stop before running into his muzzle.

"Why?"

Because of what you are.

"What am I?"

Silence.

"What is it you think I am, Justice? What is it Niles thinks I am?"

I cannot answer that question yet.

"Yeah, and why not?" Anger licked her tone.

You are not ready.

Haley glared at him. She wanted to be angry. She wanted to yell. But his voice snuffed it out. She caught herself reaching to touch him and froze. He stared down at her, and all she could think was how nice it would be to drown in his eyes.

You must trust me, Haley Night. I do not wish you harm.

She did trust him. Damn it. And all she wanted to do was be suspicious.

"Justice, are you Niles' Brother?"

A deep, dark calm filled her head. It was more real than anything her ears could hear. When he spoke, the presence of his voice was a physical relief.

There was only one egg in his clutch.

She frowned. That wasn't the answer she wanted to hear. For a moment she wondered if she could make him tell her.

He tilted his head, and even though nothing about his expression changed, Haley had the distinct feeling he was amused.

"Please, if you know anything, tell me."

When I was young, the Humans I lived among thought knowing was the answer. So they brought me gifts, and I would answer their questions. In their greed for knowledge they sacrificed their food and land. When there was nothing left for me to eat, they presented their sons and daughters.

In the end, they destroyed everything they were for what they thought they had to have. And even with all the answers to their questions, they were left barren.

"So you think knowledge is bad or evil?"

Of course not. However, knowing what you are not ready to understand can be a destructive force.

"Can you at least tell me who Niles was protecting me from?"

All the Queens fear what you represent. But it is Nidia who wishes to have your head.

Nidia? The Queen of North Carolina? Unlike most states, North Carolina only had one Queen because she had eaten the others.

Justice rumbled deep in his chest. *She has allies among your Bureau. Men who want absolute power. She manipulates them.*

"Them?"

He didn't reply.

Haley blew out her breath. This was almost as frustrating as trying to get an answer out of a Queen. At least Justice didn't take pleasure in stirring fear. Could he do such a thing as a Male? He was Ancient, that much she knew, and it seemed like the Ancient Ones didn't follow the rules.

"Okay." She flopped her arms in a sloppy shrug. "I guess that's all the questions I have." She waited for him to say something. He didn't. "I'll see myself out then." Haley turned and headed back toward the elevator, her high heels cracking the silence. Just as she got to the edge she felt The Great White's thoughts roll into her head.

When you need me, I will help you.

So far he'd been about as helpful as a paper cut. Haley stepped into the elevator and the doors slid shut.

Chapter 28

Farley glanced over his shoulder at the Suit One and Suit Two, feeling like a third wheel. But then this is the way it always was. Haley was Human enough for the world, he wasn't.

A growl ticked in his throat and he found himself wondering what Suit One and Suit Two would taste like.

Let's not go there, buddy. Okay?

A buzz lit up in his pocket and he retrieved his cell phone. The number was from the Center.

He put it to his ear. "Hello?"

Ken sputtered in his ear. "Sorry about that, I'm having to eat and tech." There was a slurping sound, then he said, "Don't mean to eat in your ear, but upstairs is on my ass about a hack attempt on one of the outside systems."

"You get my hard drive worked out?"

"Oh, better!" A crunch, then a muffled reply.

"Ken, I can't understand you when you're talking around a mouth full of whatever." Not to mention it made it hard to concentrate on the conversation. Farley shifted in his skaters.

"Sorry ... I not only got the hard drive cracked, I found out something interesting about that email Haley received." Movement rustled over the phone. "The hard drive first. There was information on it. Lots of stuff. Mostly JPEGs ... scanned articles out of newspapers and magazines. It looks to me like Haley has a stalker."

"Yeah, that much I already figured out. Niles' apartment walls were pretty detailed."

Ken whistled.

"Anything else?"

"Yeah, well, see if you can top this. There's a text file on here that reads like the Book of Revelation."

"Which means?"

"Doomsday, my man, doomsday. It's some scary stuff. Very Biblical sounding. Well, the part of it I can read anyways. Most of it's in your language. I've tried to run it through a translator, but it didn't work too well. I think I understood it better in Olde Tongue." He laughed and chewed in Farley's ear again. The sound made his hunger kick.

"Does it actually say anything useful?" Farley wished for anything that would actually amount to something.

"No, man. That's about it. Oh, there's a word that I did get a hit on from the translator. *Augury*. I had to look it up. Means *Omen*. Does that help any?"

Farley's insides went cold.

Augury.

God of Man, is that what the Queens thought Haley was?

He glanced over his shoulder and up at the glass wall several stories up. Someone was watching. He could feel it like a hand on his back.

"You there, man?" Ken's voice was tinny and distant.

Farley peeled his tongue off the roof of his mouth and swallowed. "I'm here."

"Do you want to hear about the email or no?"

"I'm listening."

"That IP did come from the D.A.'s office, as you already know. But I decided to do a little more poking around with the headers and then with the email. See, I've been on the D.A.'s staff for a while now, about their really poor lack of upkeep on their servers. At least once a week I get embedded code on emails sent from them."

"You mean like a virus?"

"No, not quite that malicious. More along the lines of malware or something stupid like that. Harmless really. Mostly just irritating. I run a tight server; I don't appreciate picking up bed bugs."

"So is that good or bad?" Farley's computer skills were barely above average. He didn't even have an email account.

"Both. You see, a lot of the office help over there thinks it's cute to use stationary, those little HTML tidbits that turn the background of an email pink or some stupid shit. I've got our system set up to shred that kind of crap before it gets sent out to anyone in our office. When I went digging around on that resource code again, I was able to back-track the thing and restore it to what it originally looked like."

"It didn't happen to have a name, address, and letter of confession, did it?"

Ken gave a snort. "Not quite, but almost."

"You know who sent it."

"Yup. See, this is why I don't want this crap on my machines. It's harmless except for the little bits of data it copies and sends back out. Well, when I looked at the info it gleaned, I could see that the email was sent from the office of the D.A., but it was done remotely from inside the office. His secretary, June Dowery. She's the one who sent it."

"But why?"

There was a rustle, like Ken shrugged. "You got me."

"Can you do something for me?" Ken gave a muffled affirmative. "Would it be possible to hack into their phone system? Check any outgoing calls? I've got one specific number for you."

"Hold on, let me get a pen." Farley gave him the number. "You think she may have called this person?"

"Don't know." *But I sure don't trust the S.O.B.* "Check it for me, please."

"Give me a few hours. I'll see what I can find."

"Oh, and Ken?"

"Yeah?" His drink rattled again.

"Just so you know, eating in my ear is a real turn on."

"Maybe I'll start charging you for our phone time then. Later, man."

Farley narrowed his eyes on the windows of the building, but could see nothing but the bright blue sky reflected back. Yeah, Justice was watching all right. There was a reason why that secretary sent the email. Maybe she didn't even know she had. If Justice could read the darkest secrets of Human criminals for the courts, Farley couldn't help wondering what else he could do.

Chapter 30

Haley came out of the building hearts racing. The panicked feeling wasn't there until she hit the bottom floor, but now it consumed her.

She came down the walkway and towards the gate with a wave of anxiety nipping at her heels. Farley stood and Haley threw her arms around him.

"What's wrong? What happened? Did Justice do something to you? What did he do? Haley?"

She couldn't speak. And even if her voice hadn't gone on a sudden hiatus, she still didn't know what to say.

Farley growled. "Please talk to me." He stroked her head, nuzzled her cheek, licked at the corners of her eyes. "Tell me what happened. You're shaking."

"I don't know."

"Something happened! What did he say?"

She made a sound, something crossed between a sob and a laugh. The wave of anxiety receded. "Nothing. He said a whole lot of nothing." Her grip loosened.

"Then why are you upset?"

Haley shook her head. "I just..." Now she felt silly.

"You're not being silly. Something upset you."

"I'm just hungry. All the stress is getting to me." She shook her head. "Niles spent years protecting me and Justice won't tell me why."

Farley tugged her hand. "C'mon. I know a place about a block from here. We'll eat and then worry about the whys."

Haley let him lead her down the sidewalk.

Under a ruby red umbrella, Haley dove into her second hamburger while Farley finished his third. It was warm, so they decided to sit outside on the patio of the Street Corner Café.

Not that they had a choice. The sign on the door said "No Kin inside." But at least they didn't have a problem serving them out of the small sliding window.

With food in her stomach, Haley felt better and even more ridiculous about her panic attack. A lot had happened this week. She chalked it up to stress. Did other Females get like this? Probably just another annoying Human frailty to add to the list.

Farley crammed his face into the edge of a hamburger the size of a small dinner platter. The menu had three sizes: small, large, and OMG That's Huge. It was called the Hugo, for short.

"I love these things. I can eat six on a good day." Farley threw his head back and crammed in a handful of French fries. They poked out of his lips as chewed. Haley sighed. He really needed to work on his manners.

As they ate, a few more people wandered up and took up at surrounding tables to enjoy the mild weather of a late Georgia September. Haley glanced over at some women watching them from the window. They had their heads together and were laughing. The expression on their faces said they found Farley and her extremely amusing.

Haley looked away and pushed the rest of her hamburger back.

"You full?" It came out more like "mu muul." Farley finished off his second root beer and belched. One of the construction workers sitting nearby yelled out a congratulations.

The little red basket with half Haley's hamburger slid back into her line of sight.

"Finish it," Farley said.

"I'm full." Well, she was, sort of.

Farley eyed her. "No, you're not."

Haley pushed it back towards him. "Yes, I am."

"Eat." Farley flicked a finger at her food. "I like watching you eat. No one's going to deprive me of that. Sure as hell not them." He threw a thumb over his shoulder at the girls in the window, then stuffed the last of the Hugo into his mouth.

Haley glanced back through the glass and regretted it instantly. The young women had teamed up with a few boys wearing lettered jackets. There was a whole group to point and laugh now.

Farley kept staring so she picked up a French fry and bit the end off.

"So, Justice didn't say anything about why Niles was calling him?"

"Huh?" Haley peeled her eyes from the window. Oh yeah, that's why they were here. To eat ... and ... talk. She ate another fry. "Um, no. He just said that he owed Niles a debt."

Farley arched an eyebrow and picked up his fourth burger.

Haley picked up two French fries, then a third.

"Did he say what kind of debt he owed?" Farley emptied half the ketchup bottle onto the wax paper in the bottom of his basket, stirred in his fries, then picked up the bottle of hot peppers and dumped it all on top. Haley watched and so did everyone else on the veranda. Farley used the mustard to make a series of tic-tac-toe lines, then poured in the A-1. He pointed to the tomato and lettuce Haley had removed from her burger. When she shook her head, he added that, too. At the top of his food pile, he poured salt until a snow cap formed.

Even the woman at the service window brought her friend over to stare.

"You are *not* going to eat that." Haley flicked him a look.

"Sure I am." Farley jabbed his fingers in, spooned up a heap, and shoveled it into his mouth. He chewed and swallowed. "God of Man, if I only had some Twinkies. It would be perfect." Farley took another bite.

"Can you at least use a fork?" Haley grimaced.

He shook his head and showed her his fingers. "Tastes better au' du natural."

For whatever reason, a thought struck her. "Did Ken ever call you about that hard drive?"

Farley nodded and some of the enthusiasm seemed to leak out of his appetite.

"What did he say?"

He shrugged. "Not much. Hey, you want ice cream? They have great sundaes with all the trimmings."

"Farley ... what did Ken say?"

"He said he found out who sent the email. Yeah, there is this..." He flipped his hand like he was erasing a chalkboard. "Never mind. All you need to know is that he did his tech-geek stuff and figured out who sent it."

"Who?"

"Some lady name June; she's the D.A.'s secretary."

Haley's mouth dropped. "What? Why? Why would she do that? She would know they canceled any further interviews with Niles."

Farley made an indecisive sound around a cheek-bursting wad of French fries and hot peppers. He chased it down with some root beer. “I don’t know, but I asked Ken to hack into their phone lines and see if Justice’s number came up there, too.” He went back to chewing and swallowing.

“Why would you think Justice would call her?”

He took a sip of root beer. “Um, ‘cause he called Niles ... and...” He looked back at his plate. It was just about empty. “I don’t like him.”

“Justice?”

“Yeah, I don’t like him. I don’t trust him.”

“You’ve never met him.”

He looked at her and shook his head. “No, but I didn’t have to. He wouldn’t let me go in with you, and you came out of there practically terrified ... for Christ’s sake, he dicks around with Human minds and sends them home with Swiss cheese for brains.”

Haley cocked a smile at Farley and pointed a French fry at him. “Farley, I do believe you’re jealous.”

Chapter 31

"Am not," Farley said for about the hundredth time. Haley was still ignoring him. The cabbie let them out in front of the Center, and thanked them for their business.

Haley headed up the sidewalk and Farley walked backwards, trying to get her attention.

"I'm not jealous."

She threw him a glare, yanked open the door and went inside.

Farley bounced on his toes. "Am not!"

Garrett's voice cut across the room like a knife. "I need both of you downstairs!" Haley glanced at Farley, then her boss. When Garrett turned they followed.

After Garrett shut the door to the conference room, his hard gray eyes gave them both the once over. "Did something happen that night with Medan?"

Haley pressed her lips together, trying to think. A lot of things happened. "Like what, sir?"

"As in, something. Anything. If so, I need to know now. Right now." He stabbed a finger at the floor. "Because when we walk through that door, I cannot help you any longer."

Haley shuffled her feet, dropped her head. A real Female would never be so submissive.

"Sometime today."

"I *marked* Farley."

Garrett's eyes flinched then slid to Farley. "*Marked*. As in, what, exactly?"

"As in *marked*. I made him *Mine*. Farley *Belongs* to me now."

"What else?"

She shook her head. "Nothing."

"I don't believe you."

"Nothing else happened." She met his steely gaze.

"You didn't make any *contracts* with Medan?" He said "contracts" like it was a dirty word.

"Contracts?" She tried to think. "She wanted me to become her Enforcer." Maybe that was it.

"And?"

"I told her I needed a few days, but I have no intentions of doing it."

He glared. "Anything else? And I mean *anything*."

Haley swallowed. "Garrett? Who's in that conference room?"

"Eight board members, five Alchemists, and Colonel Dobson."

A growl leaked out of Farley's throat.

Garrett shot him a look. "If you don't can that shit, I will personally see your ass hauled into the Tank until you cool off. I've sent for a Center Rep. Until she gets here, you will say nothing. Nothing. Am I clear?" His jaw twitched and the gray mustache trembled.

Haley nodded. Garrett looked at Farley, who dropped his eyes.

"There's one more thing." By the tone of Farley's voice she knew exactly what he was going to say. Haley tried desperately to tell him no with her eyes, but he wouldn't look at her. "I ate a MKFK member."

Garrett didn't move, but his cheeks grayed.

Haley said, "It wasn't his fault. Medan ... Medan made him."

Garrett's Adam's apple worked like he'd just swallowed something foul.

"I'll just make this easy for you, okay?" Farley reached into his wallet and pulled out his CFKR ID. "Here, take it. I'll quit."

"Farley!" Haley reached for him, but he stepped away. "It wasn't your fault."

He nodded towards the Conference room. "Yeah, but they don't care about that. Do they?"

"Please, Garrett, he had no choice."

Her boss stayed silent and reached down, taking the ID. Farley's eyes widened, like he didn't really expect the man to do it, but when it was done, his stare went hard.

She caught Farley by the wrist and stepped up to him. "Don't. Don't do this. Don't leave."

"It's not my choice." His lips brushed her ear. "Let's just go." She looked at him and glared at Garrett over her shoulder. "Let's just get out of here. Leave. We don't need Humans. We're Kin."

"You don't mean that." But he did mean it. God of Man, he meant every word.

"Let's go, Haley." Garrett slipped the ID into his jacket pocket. Farley's grip tightened on her wrist, and his thumb rubbed her pulse. "We have a room full of board members trying to decide if you should keep your job." She looked back at Farley. His eyes were dark. Possessive. "Haley!" Garrett barked.

She pulled from Farley's grasp and he whirled, storming back up the hallway. The door slammed shut hard enough to crack the drywall. Haley wanted to go after him. She could feel his pain like an audible cry, then it was gone.

Even though every Draconian part of Haley demanded she tend to her Marked, she followed Garrett.

Chapter 32

Rage tasted bitter in the back of Farley's throat. He cleared the steps, taking two, then three at a time. It made his muscles scream and he relished the pain.

Fucking Humans.

His lithe legs ate up the long hallway. The skaters he wore rattled and swished, a chorus to his angry breathing. He hit the next door with both fists, punching it open. The small glass window in the top burst.

"Farley!"

Farley turned and flashed fang. Claire's hands came up as she recoiled.

She did manage not to scream.

Kudos for her.

Claire said, "What's wrong?"

Farley scented her, her fear, her concern, her ... pity. With a snarl he took a turn, going anywhere just to get away. A Human giving him pity. How pathetic was that?

"Farley, please wait ... wait."

He grabbed a door. It looked just like all the others and it had to go somewhere. Somewhere away from here. Away from these ... these ... *chetrah*.

Farley wound up in the dark. His natural sight slid in, revealing four walls and lots of block shapes. There had to be a way out somewhere. The lights clicked on and he hissed as his retinas lit up like the sun.

"Son of a bitch!" Farley pressed his fingers into his sockets. His hip hit something hard and he almost fell. Small hands grabbed him and he slapped them away. "Leave me alone!"

"What happened? Please, tell me what happened!"

"I said get the fuck away from me!" His sight came back, followed by a sharp pain in the back of his skull. He wanted to pace, needed to pace, but there were boxes and old copiers and bits of computer everywhere.

Claire stood by the door, her small shoulders hunched and her eyes very large. Farley turned round and round looking for somewhere, anywhere he could go.

But he was trapped. Just like life. Farley gave up and stood in the center, his shoulders rising and falling with each desperate breath.

"Is it your Brother again?" Claire hiccupped.

Compared to this big Brother is a cake walk.

What did just happen down there?

Oh, yeah. Now he remembered. Haley chose to face a room full of Humans who wanted her ass on a silver platter, rather than leave with him to stay safe. And the cherry on top? He'd just lost his job. Funny, he never thought that would bother him, but it did. In fact, it just chewed up all his soft parts and spit them right back out.

Farley flicked his eyes up at Claire. The fear she put out was intoxicating. Absolutely sweet. Dark chocolate for the senses.

"Farley, tell me what happened, please."

"I got fired."

"I'm sure it will be okay." She came forward and petted his arm. Farley's nerve endings fired up like tiny blow torches.

"No, it won't ... Haley..." She was going in there alone because he was powerless to protect her.

Claire moved closer. She said something but it didn't make sense. Farley was absorbed by the way she moved, felt ...smelled. Claire smelled like *food.*

Farley's body went forward, leaving his brain ten steps behind. By the time his cognitive thought caught up to what the rest of him was doing, he had Claire by the waist, her ass propped up on an old copier, and his pants undone. One hand was under her shirt rolling her nipple, the other stroking the wetness blossoming between her legs while her panties slid down her right ankle. Farley didn't remember getting there, but here he was. He leaned into her, his forehead on her sternum, the sound of her breathing in his ears. It felt good. This taking, this bit of Dominance. Farley sucked the taste of her from his fingers and growled. When he looked at her she whispered for him to do things to her, to love her.

He growled. If he wanted to, he could kill her. Claire was weaker, helpless. She was nothing more than Food and sex.

Just like me.

"Farley..." His name came out on a desperate gasp as Claire rocked against him. Begging for him, wanting him. The small helpless sounds she made kicked him in the ribs, then the groin.

Claire reached for Farley's cock, but he grabbed her wrists and pushed them out and away. Like a Dominant, he didn't want her to touch him.

"I'm in control."

Claire seemed to like that idea. A lot. She dropped her head back and raised her hips to him, but he held her back.

"Don't you want me?" She looked on the verge of tears.

Thing is, Farley didn't want her to want him. God of Man, help him, he just wanted to take out his rage. He snarled, yanked Claire off the top of the copier, and slung her like a rag doll into an old office chair. She stumbled and threw out her hands to catch herself, leaving her on knees, face first in the old leather. Farley grabbed her around the waist, popped up her hips and kicked her legs apart. When he yanked her by the hair she called to him, begging.

In one hard stroke he entered. Claire's breath exploded over and over in deep pants as he wasted no time in moving.

Farley wanted to show himself, prove he was as Male as any other, these Humans and their stupid social rules. Farley fucked her until the sweat rolled off her back, turned her pink blouse dark and matted her blonde locks to her face. All the while Claire said stupid things like how much she loved him. It only made him angrier, more determined to take something, anything she had to offer.

When he came it was violent and painful and he embraced it.

Farley sank his teeth into his forearm to keep from burying them into her back. When that wasn't enough, he scored his stomach until the ichor ran in streams down his legs. And he still needed to hurt.

Anger pushed Farley to his knees and he crumbled, wishing for his rage to go away. He hated his lack of control almost as much as his lack of strength. He was weak. He'd lived through his hatching because he was willing to fuck anything Dominant, and he'd survived life because he preyed on the weak. Haley made him hers, not because she wanted him, not because he was worthy, but because she had to save him. Because he couldn't save himself.

And the only reason she pitied him was because of her Human-instilled ethics. Her first *Impressions*.

The acknowledgment of his own worthlessness made Farley shake until he thought he was going to burst from his Human skin.

"Farley ... Farley..." Claire put her arms around him, stroked his head. He loved her scent, her taste. He wanted more of her, but she wasn't Kin and he wasn't strong enough for his own kind; he was only good enough for *food*.

Something that sounded like a sob escaped his lips. "Haley." Just saying her name hurt.

"What did she do to you? Farley, I've never seen you like this. What did Haley do?"

It wasn't Haley, it was him. But how did he explain that to Humans, who thought everything deserved to be saved? That the weak should live?

Farley tried to stand, stumbled, found his shirt. When had that come off? He fumbled with his pants. Disgusted by his behavior, he stumbled back. "I'm sorry...I shouldn't have..." He shook his head, tried to turn, and clipped his hip into an old desk. Claire grabbed his arm and he pulled away from her. He had to get out. Where the hell was the door?

Claire's small hands dug into his arm like claws. "Come live with me. Let me take care of you. You won't ever have to go back to the Dens. You won't ever have to go back to her! Stay with me."

For a split second the thought glimmered; living off Claire's blood and her flesh, making her his, taking her as a Link. Hands on her hips, Farley stepped on his shirt as he pressed her against a wall of boxes. She moaned under his touch, stroked his shoulders. Claire's fingers lingered on the scar. Touching it sent a bolt of heat down his spine.

She studied the marred flesh. "Why didn't that heal?" Claire prodded the ridges of the bite. "Who did this to you? Why hasn't it healed?"

He looked at the *mark* on his shoulder. Her fingers brushed the skin and his metaphysical energy responded, searching, reaching, but it found nothing in Claire.

And it never would.

"I *Belong*." Saying it made him feel numb. Farley moved her hand off the *mark* and stepped away.

"*Belong?* What do you mean, *Belong*?"

Keeping Claire was a pipe dream. He was Food and they couldn't

Link. "I have to go." Farley zipped up his pants and snatched up his shirt. Claire called to him when he went out the door.

Chapter 33

Haley did her best to meet the gaze of each Human in the conference room, except for the Alchemists. Meeting their gaze was like trying to outstare a dead fish.

Very scary dead fish.

At the head of the table Colonel Dobson leaned back in his chair. He looked all the world like the cat that ate the canary … and was now back for the parakeet.

"Sit." Dobson motioned to the chair closest to her.

She did.

"Do you understand why you've been called in here?"

Garrett said, "I've called her a Center Rep. I think it would be best to wait until she gets here before we start."

Dobson steepled his fingers. "That may be a while, Pip. I took the liberty of telling the Rep office we wouldn't need their services."

"You have no authority!"

"But we do." That from one of the board members. Her hair was silver, her eyes shrewd. "The Center is not obligated to waste resources for her defense."

"All CFKR employees are guaranteed protection from misguided prosecution from the disciplinary board."

"Actually..." Dobson flicked something from the sleeve of his uniform. "Haley isn't. She's Kin. She isn't entitled to any rights. She's here because she's a novelty."

Garrett leaned on the table. "I did not bring her in here for you to crucify. This was supposed to be a general inquiry. Not a full-fledged prosecutorial procedure. She came in good faith. I will not let you abuse it."

"What about her partner, the Male Kin she works with? Why isn't he here?"

Haley felt too dizzy to try and figure out which one of the board members spoke.

"I let him go. He is no longer a part of this Center."

A wave of murmurs and unhappy comments crashed into Haley. When she looked up, Dobson was glaring at her.

The man in the electric blue tie said, "Since the Male has refused to attend, we'll just have to have him arrested."

"He was terminated before this meeting; therefore, he is out of jurisdiction."

One of the women barked a laugh. "And you don't think we can still have him arrested? Not only could he stand accused of crimes against Humanity, his behavior put the CFKR at risk. There's no telling how long he has been leaking information to the Queen of Atlanta. Not to mention, there are at least a half-dozen Federal Bureau of Non-Human Affairs charges he could be brought up on. And if the reports we're hearing are true, he'll stand trial for murder."

Garrett voiced a protest and they all started in at once, the accusations flying so fast it made Haley's head swim.

"Stop! Okay, just stop!" Haley stood up and the room came to an uneasy quiet. This was nothing more than a dog and pony show, and she wasn't about to give them the pleasure of a performance. "The fact that Farley isn't here has nothing to do with anything. All of you know damn well he's been loyal to this Center. So just leave him out of this. You brought me here because you want something." She looked at Dobson. His expression hadn't changed. "Specifically, *he* wants something. So what do you want, Dobson? Just spit it out!"

The colonel tapped his upper lip with a callused finger. Either he hadn't expected her to be so blunt, or he had counted on it. Haley couldn't tell. When he spoke, his voice revealed nothing of his feelings. "I'm going to ask you a few questions. If I find out that you violated protocol, then I'm going to have you arrested for conspiracy, crimes against Humanity, maybe even espionage. You will be tried and you will be found guilty. And because I know you didn't do it alone, anyone who helped you will spend a good thirty or more years in Federal prison." His eyes slipped to Garrett. "And as you know, Humans don't live forever like Kin." Yeah, thirty years would be Garrett's whole life. The lead in Haley's chest dragged her back to her seat.

Dobson waved a hand at the five uniformed Alchemists. "They're here to make sure you tell the truth. And if you don't answer my questions truthfully, I'll add perjury." He leaned forward eyes flashing, a small hard smile on his lips. "And trust me, you do not want to answer my questions. In fact, you want to avoid them at all costs."

Haley stared at the table, wishing for a crack in the earth to swallow all of them. "What do you want?" Somehow her voice remained steady.

"I want you here in the morning. At that time you will report upstairs. I will debrief you and you will be transferred to a different facility. You will be moved out of your apartment and into an onsite barracks."

It all sounded so simple. And she knew it wasn't. "So, you're basically telling me that I'm going to prison."

Dobson's eyes hardened. "If you want to experience what real prison is like, I can arrange it. Here you will be able to have contact with your own. Controlled contact, but contact. This will be a country club in comparison."

"Fine." She stood up, and Garrett stepped in front of her.

"You don't have to do this."

"I won't hang you out to dry, Garrett. I won't run."

"I'm afraid that's what he's counting on, Haley." His jaw tightened. Next to her ear he said, "Listen to me, fight this. Buy some time for me. I'm in contact with some people, *our* people. I'm working on this, but I need a few days." She knew he was competent, and if anything could be done he would make it happen. But if he failed, it was more than her. It was him, and it was Farley. They'd all face punishment because she didn't make things easy for Dobson.

"I'm sorry." Haley stepped around Garrett and looked at Dobson. She nodded once. "I'll be here."

Chapter 34

Haley stared at her desk for a very long time. It was an old wooden piece she'd been assigned way back in the twenties. As the office modernized, she'd kept it and now it was a beautiful antique in a building full of plastic dipped pressboard on chrome legs.

Odd thing, other than the desk, there wasn't much else she felt attached to. Not even the photos on her walls of annual luncheons, awards for community service, thank you notes from eleven different mayors over forty some odd years. The only thing in the office she wanted to take with her was Farley, and he'd walked out.

Good thing, too. It would have been a mess with him there.

Haley decided to walk home. She needed the time to think. Plus it helped her burn off her anger. Half a block from work, she dialed Farley's cell. At least the thing was his and not the Center's. Hopefully he hadn't run out of minutes.

It rang until it clicked over to voice mail. She hung up and dialed again. On the third try he answered.

"Farley?"

"Yeah." God of Man, he sounded rough. Like he'd been drinking, smoking, and beating the hell out of himself.

"Are you okay?" He was quiet so long she checked her signal. "Farley?"

"Haley, I know why Jane in the D.A.'s office sent you the email." Were those sirens in the background?

"Where are you?"

"At the Morris and Law House intersection."

"Why do I hear sirens? What's going on?"

"There was an accident." But there was usually an accident at that intersection and a yearly fatality. The city had reworked the corner four times, but it never seemed to change things. It was just a busy road with too many lanes for the area and too many people coming in and out of the complex.

"Are you hurt?"

“No, no, I’m fine. I just ... Haley ... I’m scared for you.”

“I’m okay.” She thought about Dobson. “At least right now I’m okay.”

The blare of a fire truck sounded off, drowning out the sirens.

“Farley?”

“Still here.”

“You were going to tell me about Jane?” She walked faster, but instead of taking a right at the end of the block towards her apartment, she turned a left, and headed towards Morrison.

“A Prius pulled out in front of a garbage truck. I don’t know if the brakes went out on the thing or what. But it didn’t even stop, it just dragged the car. It’s a mess.”

“Was anyone hurt?”

“You can say that. It was Jane in the car, Haley. She’s dead.”

Haley stopped.

“I went to help. I got the door open. That’s when I saw it. She’s *marked,* Haley. She’s *marked* by Nidia.”

Haley rounded the corner and a barrage of blue, red, and white emergency lights turned the afternoon into some sort of retro dance scene. Only no one was playing any music.

The crack and hiss of radios joined the shouts and high pitched whine of metal cutting metal. At least five cars were involved, and there were people everywhere, sitting on curbs, talking to EMS and Firefighters. The main event looked more like the remnants of a crushed and mutilated soda can than it did a car.

Haley spotted Farley sitting on the curb, watching everything. “Hey.”

White points protruded from under his upper lip.

“You okay?” She stared at his mouth and he nodded.

“It’s the blood.” Farley shifted his legs and reached into his pocket, removing a PDA. “I took this from her purse.” He handed it to her. “Look under D.”

She did and froze. Dobson’s name was there and the last call that had been made to him was this morning. Haley checked for more calls. There were several.

“Justice said it was Nidia and not Medan.” She looked down at Farley. He had his arms folded over his knees and his head was down.

"What's wrong?" She sat down beside him and stroked his arm.

He took one breath, then two.

"I can't protect you." Farley's eyes clenched shut and he looked away from her.

"Protect me?" She put the PDA in her pocket so she could reach for him. He was stiff under her embrace, like he didn't want to be held, but pulling away wasn't an option. "Farley, we've been friends for a very long time. Why would you need to protect me?"

"I'm your Marked. Your First Marked. It's my job. You took me as your First, when you should have taken someone strong. Someone like Niles..."

"Where the hell did all this come from?" She tried to get him to look at her, but he wouldn't. "I don't understand."

"Exactly." He stared at the car wreck. Two neon yellow colored HERO trucks pulled up alongside a small collection of cars that had blown out tires on all the debris. "You're too Human sometimes, you know?"

Haley sighed. "I know. Sometimes I feel like I'm being pulled apart. I don't know where I belong." She touched his head and fondled his red curls. It had been so pretty when he wore it long. "That's why you're so important. You help keep me grounded. You accept me..." A small unhappy laugh fell out of her mouth. "Well, most of the time you accept me."

"Why did you Mark me, Haley?"

She tried to smile, but it didn't work. "Because not doing it wasn't an option. I couldn't leave you, I ... couldn't."

"A smart Female would've."

"I'm not that smart, I guess." She petted his hair some more and tried to imagine her life without him. It didn't work. It hurt too much.

"You need to take the PDA to Ken. He can download the info. There might be more on there, who knows? If Nidia is working with Dobson... What's wrong?"

She shook her head. "I can't ask Ken for anything. I'm being moved."

"Where? And on who's order?"

"Dobson." Just saying his name made her feel sick. "I don't get it. Why would Nidia help him kill Kin?"

Farley shook his head and ran a hand over his brush cut. "Nidia is ruthless. A virus would be an easy way to get rid of all her rivals. Hell, she wouldn't even have to leave the Hive to do it."

"Yeah, but it would kill her, too." Nidia and Dobson working together? God of Man, could it get any worse?

"From what I've heard about her, she's arrogant enough to think it won't, and resourceful enough to have a back-up. Medan would never admit it, but rumor has it Nidia scares her." That made Haley raise her eyebrows. "Like I said, not that she'd ever admit it."

Haley stood up and held out her hand to Farley. After a short pause he took it. "C'mon. Let's go home. I'll call Garrett. I don't know if he can do anything or not, but maybe the PDA will be enough to put Dobson under a rock."

For a while anyways

Chapter 35

Haley had the cabbie stop at the street corner instead of pulling into the parking lot because all the lights were on in her apartment.

A shadow passed in front of the curtains. "Whoever it is, they aren't very professional." Which meant they weren't Dobson's. And if Nidia was as ruthless as Farley claimed, then she wouldn't settle for anyone but the best.

On the back of an angry growl Farley said a name, "Darco."

The cab door flew open and Farley took off across the parking lot. Haley tossed a twenty at the cabbie and ran after him.

"Wait, Farley! Wait!" But Farley was too busy snarling like a rabid animal and weaving through the parked cars. He slid across the hood of a red sedan, hit the ground, and took another shortcut by leaping onto the bumper of an Escalade, going over the top before he hit the asphalt again.

There was a split second of hope at the entrance because he didn't have a key card, but then an old couple pushed open the door from the inside and he blazed past them.

"Damn it, Farley!"

As Haley started up the steps, the stairwell door crashed against concrete. She got to the hall just in time to see Farley cut down to a jog. He stopped a few feet from her door and pressed himself to the wall. She approached and he motioned for her to stop. When she didn't, he went in.

The scent wasn't Darco's, but it was familiar and there was an odd burnt plastic smell to go along with it. Farley crouched by the bedroom door and held up what looked to be the remains of a hospital gown to his nose.

In the bathroom the shower was running.

Okay, now she was getting pissed. Not only had someone broken into her house and had it smelling like burning milk jugs, but they were taking a shower. Haley marched past Farley and yanked open the door. Among all the white with peach highlights, a lean figure stood under the shower, rinsing the soap from his long black hair.

"Creyal?" He glanced at her from over his shoulder. "What the hell are you doing in my apartment? And how the hell did you *find* my apartment?"

At her back, Farley snarled.

Creyal took his time rinsing off. After he turned off the water, he snagged a towel off the rack before Haley could stop him.

Those were her good towels, the kind that were meant to give a bathroom color, not the kind meant to be used.

Haley was sure all the turning and stretching he did was to show off every piercing and ink mark he wore.

Haley folded her arms and glared. "If you're through desecrating my bathroom, I'd appreciate it if you'd get out."

Creyal's lavender gaze rolled over her. "I came here because I didn't know where else to go."

"And how did you find *here*?"

"I did a redial on the phone number Dr. Meyer used to call you this morning. When I got the number, I did a reverse look up for the address on her computer." He shrugged like it was no big deal. "I didn't plan to come without calling first, but I wasn't given much choice." He dropped the towel and walked past her into the bedroom and opened her closet.

"What the hell are you doing?" She slammed the door shut, almost catching his fingers. "You come into my apartment, you get in my shower, and now you're digging through my closets?"

Creyal leaned in close and thrummed.

"If you prefer me like this, I will be most happy to oblige." He raised his hand to touch her and Farley lunged. Haley threw her shoulder into him and pinned him against the wall. Creyal stepped back, eyes dancing.

"Farley!" Haley held him, but only barely.

"Looks like I'm not the only one who's been having a bad day."

The feral went back to the closet. Farley's eyes flashed orange and red as he watched the other Male pick through her things.

"What do you want, Creyal? And why are you out of the clinic?"

"The clinic's gone." Creyal plucked Farley's black dress shirt from the closet. He insisted on keeping his nice clothes at her apartment because of the rats in his.

Creyal slipped it off the hanger and put it on. He moved over to her drawers. Farley's glare tracked him across the room.

Haley said, "What do you mean, the clinic's gone?"

Creyal opened the first drawer and pulled out a thong. A crooked smile cut across his face. He dropped it on the floor and continued pulling out one pair after the other. "Have enough?"

"I like lots of underwear."

"I'll say..." He picked up a lacy red pair.

"Don't you dare, Creyal." He slid his lavender eyes over to her, then Farley, and promptly made a show of scenting it. Farley let loose with an angry screech.

"Damn it, Creyal!" He went to the next one and pulled out her bras, dropping them on the floor. "Third drawer down. There are pants in there." She looked at Farley. "Can you please just calm down?"

"He knows the rules," Farley hissed. "If you won't make him abide by them, I will."

"This isn't the Dens!" Haley grabbed his cheek and made him look at her. "This is my home. The only rules here are mine!"

From over by the dresser Creyal said, "These jeans are a little long in the leg to belong to shorty there. Does he know you're, how do the *chetrah* put it, stepping out on him?"

"They belong to another Male, Deshi. He's a friend."

Creyal's breath brushed her cheek. "You sure do have a lot of *friends*." He puckered his lips and kissed the air in front of Farley's face. Which, of course, sent him into another tirade. "Will you quit aggravating him?"

"Why not? Food is fun to play with before you eat it." Creyal plopped down on her bed and lay back, twirling her red panties from the end of his finger. "I call dark meat."

Farley lunged, twisting and turning, his body bending at impossible angles in an attempt to escape Haley's grip.

"Damn it, look at me!" He wouldn't. His eyes were on Creyal. All of a sudden, the only thing Haley had in her hand was a piece of his shirt and his arm. The rest of him was going right for the other Male.

Desperate to keep them apart, Haley swung him into the dresser. Farley bounced off and hit the floor. She threw herself on top of him, planted her knees on either side of his hips, and locked her hands on his wrists.

"Listen to me--"

"Let me up so I can kill him!"

"You're not ruining my carpets!" Farley bowed, almost throwing her off. "Stop it, Farley."

"Or what? What are you going to do, Haley? This isn't the Dens, remember? You aren't a proper Female; you may not care if he disrespects you, but I care! I will not let him treat you like you're Human!" He bucked her off. Farley was almost too fast. But by some miracle, Haley managed to snag his ankle. His hand shot out towards Creyal, but the Male pulled his leg out of reach.

And damn him, if he didn't wiggle his toes.

"If I had known this was going to be so entertaining, I would have brought snack food." His lavender eyes landed on Farley, who was doing a pretty good impersonation of the Tasmanian devil. If Haley hadn't been so scared for him, she might have been impressed. "'Course as small as you are, being the main course is out of the question."

Haley got her arm around Farley's neck and pinned him against her chest. Farley continued to thrash and her Female instincts flared in response. This was her Male, her *disobedient* Male, and she had to get him under control. Going on instinct she sank her teeth into the *mark* and struck bone.

Farley keened. The barriers he'd thrown up to close her out crashed, and she could feel him: every emotion, every ounce of anger, every fear, the sense of abandonment. A sob jerked her shoulders and tears rolled down her cheeks. No wonder he was out of control. She tasted herself in his blood and the metaphysical ties that bound them hummed.

Haley pulled, drank him, and took from him all his *rage*. Farley sagged against her, languid.

After a moment she released her bite, and rocked him, petting him up and down. "I'm so sorry. I didn't understand."

"I know." His breath blew against her skin. "You can't help it."

Movement made Haley look up. Creyal was on the floor now. He crawled closer.

"Stay right there."

"You said you didn't have any Marks."

"He's my First and it's sort of a new arrangement." The Male reached out and Haley growled at him.

His lavender gaze pleaded with her. "I just want to ... touch. Please ... please..."

"Get out."

Creyal dropped his eyes along with his hand. "And go where? The Clinic was burned to the ground by a bunch of EFM people. Dr. Meyer was going to help me get a place. If I go back to the Dens, the people who tried to kill me will find me."

"Was anyone hurt in the fire?"

Creyal shrugged and sat back against the bed. "I don't know, I was ... sort of out of it."

"Stoned." Haley made it a statement because she knew damn well there would be no reason for pain meds.

Creyal rolled his eyes. "Yeah, I was chemically impaired."

"I thought you were going to quit."

"Didn't work out for me." His hand inched forward and just when he was going to touch her shoe, she pulled away. A deep frown pulled at his mouth.

Farley sat up, rubbing his face, and looked at Creyal. "Fuck, you're still here?"

"Seems *To Whom you Belong* isn't very good at controlling you." Creyal leaned back and propped his head on his hand. "And I know it's not because of your strength or age, so what is it?" His gaze slid to Haley. "Or maybe you're just really bad at being Kin?"

"I've been called worse." She stood up and helped Farley to his feet. "C'mon, I've got OJ in the kitchen, and I'll call for pizza."

"You're leaving?" The feral looked up at her and he stroked his stomach with a wide hand. "I don't please you?"

"Creyal! Out!" Haley pointed to the door. "Get out of my house now!"

Creyal grinned, showing fangs. "I remember how you held me in the basement of the PD. You really don't want me to leave. You're just like any Human woman. You want me and you know it." His hand went down and he stroked his denim covered erection.

"You know what? You're really starting to get on my nerves."

"You said I was worthy." Creyal rolled over and came up on his knees. His head swung from side to side and he thrummed. "You said I was a beautiful Male and any Female would be proud to *own* me. I want to be *owned*." He reached for her, but she backed away. Creyal's face fell and his hand trembled. "Please... Let me touch you."

"Get out, Creyal!"

"You *marked* him, why not me? He's nothing but Food."

"Get out now!"

In a blur of speed, Creyal shot right for her. He seized her by the shoulders and pinned her against the wall.

"What kind of Female are you? What Female is weak ... submissive, and stinking of *chetrah* sweat?" His elongated teeth grazed her neck, leaving small nicks in her skin. Haley had the urge to tear out his throat.

Yeah, like that was going to make her day go better.

Creyal opened his mouth and stroked her neck with his tongue. "The little Male can watch. I'm used to an audience."

Haley growled. "This is your last chance, Creyal."

"To what?" He undulated against her. "If you were anything like a real Female you wouldn't be standing here, too afraid to stop me."

"I'm not afraid. You're just too stoned to scent the difference between fear and pissed off."

He laughed. "I think I like this. You're almost as easy as Food."

Haley hit him. One knee into the stomach, then her palm cracked him in the nose. He went backwards and she followed him down. Her teeth punched through his windpipe, esophagus, grazed his spine. She pinned his arms, holding him immobile. The Male kicked once, then twice before falling still.

Haley felt him swallow, gag, and struggle for air. She gave him a minute to think about death, then unlocked her jaws and climbed off.

Creyal lay there trying to breathe and bleeding all over the carpet.

Looks like another job for Manny. Two cleanups in a week. It was a record, even for her.

"When you can stand, I want you out. Next time I won't stop." Haley paused at the doorway. "And one more thing. You have my *chetrah* Mother to thank for me not ripping out your throat. She taught me kindness above cruelty."

When Haley walked past Farley, he smiled.

Chapter 36

Thirty minutes later, Haley paid the pizza guy, tipped him, and carried four boxes of Pizza Hut's best to the counter. Farley was perched on the bar stool, angled so he could see into the bedroom.

She put the boxes on the counter. "Is he still on the floor?"

Farley nodded, seized one of the boxes and popped the top. "Mmm--anchovies, my favorite." He ate while keeping his eyes in the other room.

Haley checked the clock. She'd called Garrett five minutes after the order and he still hadn't called back. Which meant he was busy. Hopefully he was busy with whatever he needed to do to get Dobson's order tossed out. The idea of showing up in the morning left a heavy, sick weight in her stomach.

"He's up," Farley announced.

Creyal appeared in the doorway, head down and rubbing his bruised throat. He moved across the living room and towards the door. Now that all the swagger and bravado was gone, he was awkward. He paused a few feet from Haley and gave a small, timid apology before heading for the door.

Haley sighed. "Wait." Creyal flinched. "Eat first, and then you can go." He stayed where he was. With all his hair in his face, she couldn't see his eyes. "Creyal, you need to eat. You look like a centerfold piece for *Vegan National*. I mean, unless that's the look you're going for."

His head turned in her direction "Why?"

"Because you're not taking care of yourself. Besides, you're already wearing Deshi's pants and Farley's shirt. You might as well eat a little pizza." She shrugged. "Completes the whole home invasion package." His shoulders fell and he opened the door. Haley hopped off the bar stool to stop him. "Wait. I was kidding. You know, funny ha-ha? Creyal, please. Sit down and eat." He let go of the knob and she bumped it shut with her hip. "It's all right."

Haley pushed him onto a stool and moved a box of pizza under his nose. He still didn't move. When she looked at Farley he was stock still, a piece of Italian genius in one hand, his eyes frozen on Creyal, watching him.

"How come you never act this way around Deshi?"

Farley took a tentative bite of his pizza slice. "Deshi's never been disrespectful. Him," he pointed, "he's done nothing but dish out disrespect." Creyal still wasn't eating.

"Damn it." Haley stood up and pushed his hair back out of the way. Maybe if he could actually see it, he'd eat. She checked the glass jar on the bar that collected every paper clip to forgotten pen that came out of her pocket at the end of the day, and found a rubber band. Haley pulled his hair back, and slid the rubber band in place. It wasn't perfect, a few stray hairs hung out across his eyes. "Eat." Now he was staring at her. "Oh for Christ's sake, what now?" She glanced at Farley, who shrugged.

Creyal said, "Females do not tend to Males that are not theirs."

Haley let out a groan. "Can you please stop? This isn't the Dens. I didn't grow up in the Dens. I don't use the same rule book as other Kin, so you might as well get used to it. Now eat. It's getting cold."

The phone rang and she almost knocked the pizza to the floor diving for it.

"Hello?" *Please be Garrett.*

It was.

"Haley, are you watching the news?"

"No, why?" She looked around for the remote and saw it on the arm of the sofa. "What channel?" She turned on the flat screen.

"Doesn't matter, it's on all of them."

It took a minute for her to realize what she was seeing. Fire, lots of fire. "What's going on?"

"Dr. Meyer's clinic was fire bombed. They say that the Earth For Humans group is claiming responsibility, but I've got a couple of eyes on the scene. That's not your typical truck and fertilizer combo. Whoever did that knew what they are doing." Haley glanced over at Creyal, who was huddled over the pizza, tentatively picking at it, like he was scared he'd mess it up.

"Is Dr. Meyer okay? And her staff?"

"She's alive."

Haley learned a long time ago, that for Humans, being alive can be worse than being dead. "How bad?"

"She's burned over fifty percent of her body. At her age, she's in bad shape. But someone pulled her out of the fire and whoever it was wasn't Human. Witnesses claim he got her to the parking lot and went in for the others. They don't think all of them will make it. A few are worse off than Dr. Meyer. There are at least eight patients unaccounted for, including Creyal. So, he may be dead."

"Creyal's fine, sir."

Garrett was silent for a second or two. "You say that like he's sitting in front of you or something."

"Actually, he is. I came home and found him in my apartment."

"Haley, all the evidence that Dr. Meyer collected was in that building. I think Dobson may have arranged for it to be leveled. And I'm sure he meant for Creyal to die."

She sighed. "We have another problem. June Dowery sent the email for me to do the interview with Niles."

"June was killed this afternoon pulling out of the D.A. office parking lot."

"I know, Farley saw it happen. He went to help. Garrett, June was a Link."

Her boss made an unhappy sound. "As in a Human Link to a dragon?"

Was there any other kind? "Yeah, specifically the Queen of North Carolina, Nidia."

"And why do I have a feeling this isn't all the bad news you have for me?"

"Farley stole her PDA. It has Dobson's number in it and a list of calls. They've been talking back and forth on a regular basis, and I doubt it's been conversations about the weather."

"Damn it." Something shuffled in the background. It sounded like Garrett was throwing things around on his desk. "How did she get into the D.A.'s office?"

"It might have been a recent bonding."

"You don't sound too convinced of that."

"No, I'm not. I'm no expert, mind you. There's a lot about my people that I don't understand. Especially the Females." Marking Farley had shown her there was a lot about the metaphysical bonding that couldn't be gleaned from books. "Garrett?"

"Yeah, Haley."

Haley shut her eyes and sank to the sofa. "He's going to kill me, isn't he?" She waited for Garrett to say something, anything. The continued quiet the worst kind of confirmation she could have gotten.

When he finally broke the silence, he said, "You need to consider disappearing."

She laughed. "Garrett, I can't run. If I do, you wind up in the pen."

"Don't worry about me. I've been in worse places. Look, I know a guy who does private charters. He owes me a favor. I can arrange for you to get out of the country."

"And go where? I'm Female. I was kicked out of the Dens. I'm from unknown blood. That means no Queen will have me. I may have a lot of pull with the Males of my people, but to the other Females I'm just high ranking Food. The safest place I can be is in Atlanta. Medan wants me as her Enforcer, and until she is pissed enough to have me killed, it's unlikely the others will get too close."

"If you're her Enforcer, the other Queens won't touch you?"

Haley thought about that. "It's a bond. I don't know a lot about it. I've never met an Enforcer. What I do know is to attack any one bonded to a Queen is considered a direct attack on the Queen they speak for."

"Would Dobson be able to get to you?"

"I don't think Dobson follows the rules of the Dens, but Medan may take it as a personal insult and go after him."

More shuffling echoed over the receiver. "Haley, if you won't leave the country, then do what you need to do to survive."

"Garrett, sir, if I become her Enforcer, I may compromise the CFKR, the Bureau, and every case I've ever worked on dealing with illegal trades. I don't know how much control she will have over me. I don't know if I will be able to keep secrets from her."

"You marked Farley, right?"

"Yes."

"Do you control him?"

Haley glanced over. Farley was talking to Creyal in a low voice. How much control did she have over him? Something had gone wrong this afternoon. Biting him had stopped it, but she had no idea why his behavior even happened in the first place.

"Garrett, that's knowledge Females are *imprinted* with by a Queen. I had a Human adoptive Mother. I *imprinted* on her. So to tell you the truth, I don't have a clue."

"Haley..." His sigh belonged to a defeated man. "Do what you have to do to protect yourself. I'll worry about the back lash."

"But--"

"No. No excuses. Do it. If the Bureau won't protect you from Dobson, then they don't deserve your loyalty." His words surprised her and at the same time made her realize the depth of his concern. His friendship.

"I'll think about it." It was the best she could give him. Sad thing was, it seemed like the only choice she was left with.

"One more thing. I need you to get that PDA to Ken."

"I can drop it off on my way to the Dens."

"Do it."

"You still trust him?"

"Ken?"

"You don't think Dobson has gotten to him?"

"Is there a reason why I should suspect he has?"

"No, it just seems like the colonel has his claws in every branch of everything I once believed in."

Garrett barked a laugh. "You have no idea, Haley. You have no idea."

After a little more talk about Dr. Meyer and the loss of evidence, Haley hung up and went to sit back down at the wet bar beside Farley.

He said, "Dobson torched the clinic, didn't he?"

Haley nodded. "Yeah, that's what Garrett thinks. He wants me to take the PDA to Ken. He says we can trust him. I figure we'd drop it off on the way to the Dens."

Farley gave her sad eyes.

"It's my only choice." She tried to muster a smile, one that would say don't worry, but she couldn't get her lips to make the lift off. Then her voice had to go and do something stupid, like crack. "I don't know what else to do."

Every instinct told her that going to Medan was as dangerous as Dobson.

Farley pulled her face into his neck. The strength of his hold was crushing. Haley welcomed it. Maybe if he held her tight enough, her world wouldn't fall apart.

"I want to go with you." Haley started to shake her head. "Don't tell me no. Please." Yeah, and what would she do if Medan decided he would be a fun accessory to play with again? "Please." Farley trembled and Haley could smell his desperation.

He needs this, because going without him will confirm all his fears. That he was weak, without worth, and helpless to protect her.

Hell, she was helpless to protect herself.

"Okay. Just promise me one thing." Haley made him look at her. She wanted to tell him to run if things went bad, hide, leave, save himself. All the things you're supposed to tell the person you care about, when something dangerous is coming to snuff you out.

Instead, Haley told him what she was really afraid of. "Don't let me forget who I am. Please, Farley, I don't want to become her puppet."

He smiled. "It'll never happen."

She could only hope he was right.

Chapter 37

Above the cab, the street lights dwindled in numbers until there was nothing but night. They passed through the dirty, trash-covered streets of the Zone, leaving Human society and all its garbage behind.

A block inside the Wall, offensive neon lights butchered the darkness and crowds of people gathered. For all its proximity to the Hive, the Pit was one of the safest clubs on the strip, which why everyone from business men to college kids shed their moral skins and flocked here.

The cabbie stopped behind a line of cars waiting to pull up to the door. Haley paid him and got out. Farley and Creyal followed.

"C'mon."

Haley grabbed Farley's hand and headed toward the doors. Moving through the wall of people was like trying to move through quick drying concrete. Farley snapped off a few creative curses when he got an elbow to the side of the head.

Haley recognized the Kin bouncer and pushed to get closer. "Hey!" His eyes widened and fell where she touched him on the arm. "Can you get us in? We're here to see Medan."

He turned her hand over and pressed his face in her palm. "For you? Absolutely."

Farley stepped up beside her and the bouncer flicked his golden eyes in his direction.

"He's with me," Haley said. The Male's eyes went up and over her head. She caught sight of Creyal in her periphery. "Him too."

Inside, the mass of people and flashing lights was stifling. When Haley looked back at Farley his eyes were bright gold, his teeth extended.

"Are you okay?"

He waved a hand in front of his face. "It's the pheromone. Shit gets more real every new batch they make." Haley glanced at Creyal. His eyes were all silver but he hadn't popped any teeth.

"The entrance is in the back." She pointed to the rear of the club, just in case her words had been stomped out by the noise. Considering she couldn't hear herself think, that was pretty much a sure thing.

They moved, but it was a losing battle. Too many people were packed in the place. Obviously, Medan wasn't worried about violating any kind of occupational codes.

As they made their way past a string of tables, Haley did a double take. Three women, in various stages of undress, were climbing all over a Male sitting in the booth. She looked away only to see two Males hovering over a Lesser-Bred on the other side. The sounds of sex and feeding rivaled the guitar riffs.

Creyal moved up and blocked her view. "If you're going to get down there tonight, you need to start moving." He threw a worried glance over his shoulder. "They smell you."

Males closed in, their mouths opened, their throats working as they drank down her scent. Deep thrums, whirrs, and clicks were carried on the waves of music. Haley went backwards and bumped into Creyal.

"What do they want?" At least she didn't sound as panicked as she felt.

"You." Creyal leaned in close. Farley growled. "What are you going to do, Snack Cake? Take on all of them?"

Closer now, they reached for her. Some had blood on their faces, some smelled of sex.

"What the hell's wrong with them?" She tossed Creyal a desperate look.

"They're drunk on the pheromone." It came out slurred.

"Why aren't you?"

Creyal lifted his arm and thumped the crook. "Still stoned. Trust me, I'm getting there." His wide hand pushed apart his shirt and stroked his stomach. "Mmm—" He grinned. "This is almost as good as H."

Male Kin filled the floor at her feet. Crawling over each other, reaching for her, stroking her legs, touching her skirt. This wasn't what Haley had expected. She had no idea what to do or how to control them. Nothing like this happened in the Tank. Hell, this many Males in one place didn't happen outside the Wall. The cold panic of fear boiled under her skin. The Males hissed.

"Fuck, stop that!" Creyal grabbed her shoulder. "What the hell's wrong with you? You're starting to smell like Food."

"Well, I'm sorry, but this isn't exactly what I expected. Hell, I've never even read about anything like this." She clung to Farley, trying to keep him with her and not let him be carried away by the Males. "Why aren't they going after the Human women like this?"

"Christ, you really are domesticated. You're Female, your scent is unmistakable."

Before Haley could snap off a reply, a tongue hit her calf, another on the back of her knee. Then hands, dozens of hands, inched up legs until fingertips brushed the underside of her ass.

Haley didn't have the sexual inhibitions that Human women did. More than once she'd had a Male suck the back of her thigh in the Tank. The behavior was a sign of respect, even affection. But this? So many bodies, so many Males, were overwhelming. These weren't white-scales, but fully mature Males, strong in mind and body. And sex in public was not an option.

So much for not having inhibitions.

One, okay, I have one.

"Farley!" His gaze came up, but he couldn't seem to focus. "Farley." He pulled at her blouse, freeing it from her skirt, and slipped his hands up and grabbed her bra. Haley growled and shook him hard enough to snap his head back.

"*Need...*" Farley lurched forward and she went backwards. Creyal caught her and became the only thing keeping her from hitting the floor and being smothered.

The music screamed from speakers above, and the color of the strobes changed, going from white and yellow to blue and red. Haley struggled to stand as another wave of bodies rushed forward. With one arm she held onto to Farley and the other she clung to the feral.

"God of Man, Creyal, please don't let me fall!" She'd never be able to control the panic if she hit the floor. Somehow they wound up in an alcove between the booths and wall. It didn't stop the Males. They just climbed higher.

"What do I do?" She looked over her shoulder at Creyal. "Please. I don't know what to do."

"You're the Female."

Farley caught her mouth and his tongue thrust deep. The taste of him on her palate brought a moan out of her throat. The wave of Males rumbled and whirred. Behind her, heat blossomed across Creyal's chest.

Farley whispered something near her ear, but she couldn't understand him. He tried again.

"Ah, fuck, Haley, you've got to do something." Haley felt Creyal's erection press against her back. He laughed; it was a sound that bordered on madness. One of her shoes was pulled off. Lips closed around her toes, sucking.

Farley pushed himself closer. "Roll..." His mouth touched hers. "Roll me, Haley." He sucked on her bottom lip, licked her chin, her cheek, and nipped her ear.

"Now? I can't Roll you here." He pulled her legs up around his waist and moved between them.

"Roll me." The request came from a Male pressed to her hip. His hands worked the skin of her leg. "Roll me," said another. "Roll me." The plea became a chant echoed by all of them.

Creyal laughed again. "Oh, that sounds like a brilliant idea!" He shuddered and slid part way down the wall.

"Creyal!" Haley tried to kick but Farley had both of her legs. Someone bit her on the ass. Mouths and tongues licked and sucked the backs of her thighs.

"Haley..." Farley pulled at her panties, ripping them. "This is the Dens. Roll us so we can *feed*. We can't stop." He pushed himself against her, the bulge in his pants rubbing against her core. She gasped.

Farley parted her shirt and pushed up her bra. His mouth latched onto her nipple and Haley couldn't stop her body's response. Her metaphysical energy flared. Behind her, Creyal moaned. She felt him fumbling with his clothes. All around her the Males responded, losing their clothing, rubbing against each other.

Rolling them would *feed* them, control them. Only problem was she'd never done it without using sex to push the metaphysical energy. Like Rage for some Females, sex pushed her preternatural self out of her metaphysically carved shell. Rage was something most Females had in spades, but Haley's Human *impressions* left her without those aggressive tendencies.

But reality was closing in fast. If she didn't do something soon they were going to pin her to the floor, and a fight for her attention was going to start. And anyone who was Food would be the first to go.

Farley growled and tried to keep his position. Haley pulled him against her. He was what she knew, who she... She refused to even think about the L word. Her mouth met his and he bowed against her.

"Unbutton your pants."

"No sex in public. You always said--"

"Farley, I don't think we've got much choice at this point. Creyal, I need you..." Good grief, it wasn't like things could get any more compromising. "Between my shoulders." He blinked and seemed to find her in the haze of drunkenness. "Put your hands under my shirt, I need your help. I can't just Roll them without..." Sex, she was trying to say sex. "I don't know how." She didn't have to ask twice. He stripped off her blazer and pushed her shirt up until her skin pressed against his and his purr echoed through her body. His fingers pushed against her lower *ulysiss* and Haley arched into the sensation. The heat blooming across her skin was unbearable.

Haley yanked at the hem of Farley's skaters, but he shook his head.

"What the hell is wrong with you?" Creyal kicked Farley in the shin. "If you don't fuck her, I will!" The threat brought Farley's head up. His eyes went gold then bronze. A deep growl licked out of his throat. "Do it, Snack Cake, because the Dominants are inching their way over here, and I really don't want to be at the bottom of the slaughter pile."

A small group of Males wearing Medan's *mark* made their way through the mass of thrashing Human bodies. They were tall, massive, and feral looking. And there was no doubt in her mind, when they arrived, Males would die.

Farley's lips touched her ear. "Roll us. Just Roll all of us."

"I don't know how ... not without everything else..." Just another *impression* she'd been left without. It wasn't fair, to be Female and helpless like this; unable to protect herself, unable to protect what was hers. She pulled Farley closer and buried her face against his. There was no way he was going to survive this. They'd take him from her if she didn't stop them.

"Ah, bloody hell!" Creyal jerked Haley back, flipped her, and slammed her cheek against the wall, putting his hands on her without permission, taking her away from *To Whom She Owned*. "Fucking domesticated Female."

Farley barked a cry as he was swept away. True Rage hit Haley and her metaphysical energy surged. Powered by anger and violence, the Roll had never felt like this before.

Haley's preternatural self steamrolled over their bodies, and they went down, writhing in a mix of pleasure and pain. She knew she could hold them there, gleaning and plucking what she wanted, and she knew she could kill them. All Haley had to do was rip out their life force, consume them, and they would cease to exist. They called to her as one. Bodies arching, writhing, begging for more. With an internal twist, she let them go and fed their metaphysical force with her own.

Under it all, deep in the belly of the Hive, Haley felt the Queen stir.

Chapter 38

When Haley opened her eyes she felt strangely alert. Like every nerve ending on her body had been given a double shot of espresso. The wall of bronze in her vision moved and was replaced by a golden eye.

"I took the liberty of bringing your Marked. I also brought the other Male, but if you do not want him, I will feed him to my hatchlings." Medan moved away, leaving her shivering in the cold of the cave.

Once again Haley was in the parlor, surrounded by piles of priceless things. Of course there couldn't be anything practical, like a clean shirt and a skirt. No, Medan had to have things like rubies, gold, and--Haley squinted--was that a Monet? Probably.

Creyal was on the furs next to Farley, bent at an odd angle, like he'd been tossed there to land wherever.

Medan curled in on herself, her golden eyes flashing. "Is there a reason for your visit? Or perhaps you simply pined for my company?" Her fire lung rumbled.

Haley had the inescapable feeling that Medan not only knew she'd be back, but when she'd be back. And considering she'd never had any plans of returning to this place...

The realization curdled in her stomach like rotten meat.

But no matter what she felt, hell, what she *knew*, the facts were still the same. She needed Medan right now. Needed her protection, or Dobson was going to win. Haley fumbled with her ruined clothes. No amount of tucking or tugging was going to make them look better.

She sighed and said, "I think you know."

"Nidia is a fool. She conspires with the *chetrah*, thinking that they will not betray her."

"Why does she want me dead?"

"Did Justice not explain these things to you?" Haley's eyes widened and Medan laughed. "Nothing happens in this city without my knowledge or consent, Child. I allow for a certain amount of freedom for all Kin. I feed them. I house them in the Dens. They want for nothing."

And everything, thought Haley.

Medan sighed and it sounded as sincere as canned applause. "I do believe Nidia is going soft in the mind. She imagines a death for Queens that will come in the form of a Female. An Augury. Certain signs mark her arrival. Certain gifts will be bestowed upon her. And when she reaches her peak of power, she will wipe out all her enemies and lay claim to the earth." Medan's growl thundered throughout the cavern. "Very biblical, is it not?"

"Why me?"

"Why not?" Tendrils of steam billowed from the darkness and the temperature shot up twenty degrees. "You are an opportunity. Nothing more." The light dimmed in her eyes.

An opportunity? Is that what I am? A chance for some deranged Queen to take out her frustrations? For the first time in her life Haley didn't long for the Dens. She wanted away from it all, to be secure back in Human society, where there were rules and logic. Here ... here it was madness.

Now she had no choice but to embrace it, because she wasn't strong enough to defend herself, especially if Nidia could manipulate the people in her world.

"What about you?" Haley asked. "Do you believe I'm some servant of Death?'

"No. I think you are nothing more than a bastard daughter. One any other Queen would have killed."

"Why didn't you?"

"Because I saw an opportunity."

"What's that supposed to mean?"

"We take their Human shapes so that they are easy to hunt and so we can survive with fewer resources. We make ourselves beautiful so that they will come to us, worship us, *feed* us. We offer them sex, immortality and power, and they eat it and they hunger for more. And yet our strengths still dwindle. We no longer rule the skies; we can no longer hunt as we please. We hide and hope we don't break their rules or offend their ways, because if we do then they take *our* lives.

"You are a weapon of accidental design against the Humans who want to destroy us. You, Haley Night, *Impressed* by Humans, weakened by their ways, are our only hope to survive. I chose to send you into the world for one purpose, to be more like them, to imprint a deeper understanding of the *chetrah*, to be able to walk among them as one of their own, a spy of spies. That is why I did not kill you from the egg. That is why I have worked so hard to keep you alive. You offer us what we can never have. A means to know our enemy. A means to live at all costs."

The Queen's words settled into Haley's bones. "How long have you known about Dobson and Nidia?"

"I knew something was being planned. Colonel Dobson is the Deviant Neustrass. His hate infects him, his disease is shame." Medan moved forward. The shadows drew back from her muzzle and head. Beautiful, thought Haley. In all her fearsomeness, the Queen was beautiful.

In the corner, the two Males stirred.

Medan glided across the room, her massive form weaving through the narrow path between the priceless artifacts. Her limbs and wings missed them by feet, inches, hairs, disturbing nothing.

"I was impressed with your display in the Club." Her head thrust forward like a snake, deciding on whether or not to strike. "You should be careful here at night, when the pheromones are thick. The Males cannot control their *needs*." Another thrust of the head. Haley backed up and put herself between Medan and the two Males who were just beginning to rouse.

"Please, Medan." *Don't kill. Please don't kill them.*

Haley kept her pleas to herself. Medan was apt to snuff them out just because she begged.

Medan gave her an amused look. "Dear Child, you would be better to just end their lives now. Fuck them if you like, but kill them, because they are too weak to hold a *RHage*." Haley didn't understand, and it must have shown on her face. Medan hissed and rolled her head to the side. "Of course, those are things you could not know about. Or have. Yet." Her tongue flicked out, tasting the air. "Tend to your Males, then we shall talk. You have something you want from me and I ... have something to show you." The Queen moved over her, beyond her, her massive body slipping with ethereal grace. "When you are done, meet me in the ante-chamber. It would be a shame to stain the furs." Blackness absorbed her as she slipped into the corridor.

When Haley couldn't hear Medan anymore she went to Farley and

Creyal.

"What happened?" Farley sat up.

"I don't know." Haley pulled him to his feet, then offered Creyal a hand.

"Shit, this is the Hive!" Creyal pushed himself flush with the wall.

"Calm down." She knelt beside him.

"I didn't crawl out of this place just to wind up back down here." Creyal clenched his eyes shut and a sheen of sweat popped up across his upper lip. "I need a score. I need three scores. Be a doll and get me something. An A-bomb would be nice, or some Horse." He shook so hard his piercings flickered in the light.

"Listen to me." Haley put a hand on his cheek. He felt cold. His core temp should have been soaring after the Roll, but it was dropping. "Creyal..." She pulled his chin up and his eyes popped open. "I need you to stay focused. I can't have you smelling like Food. Now please. Get up and walk with me. I can't leave you here. There's no telling what will crawl out of these tunnels." He blinked several times, like he was having a hard time focusing.

Creyal shook his head. "No ... no way."

Farley yanked the feral up. "Listen, asshole, for once in your life, think of someone other than yourself. She needs us to go with her. Talking with Medan isn't exactly a cake walk." Creyal shoved him back. His eyes darted around the room.

"No, you go with her. You *Belong* to her, not me. I owe her nothing."

"She kept both of us from becoming *food* up there. You owe her."

Scales flashed across the feral's neck and his eyes flared silver. "I don't owe anybody shit. Not a Snack Cake like you and not her. The way I see it, what happened up there wouldn't have happened if she wasn't so fucking domesticated." A sharp hard laugh burst out of his lips. "There is no way in hell I'm facing off with that Queen. Not now, not ever. Now excuse me, I'm getting out of this hell hole. I'd much rather be upstairs banging some Human ass than getting eaten." He knocked Farley out of his way.

Creyal glance back and forth between the two tunnels at the front of the room. When he took the correct one, Haley had to assume he knew his way out.

Farley growled. "I hope the asshole gets lost."

"He was born down here. Surely, if he remembers anything in that drug fried brain of his, it's where the exit is located." She tugged at her tattered clothes. "C'mon. The last thing we need to do is keep Medan waiting."

Haley headed down the tunnel, which took a steep drop into a well-lit room. Here the floor was a smooth, seamless mass of marble. The pale gray and white was a startling contrast to the otherwise dark pyrite flecked walls. In the center sat Medan, drawn up to her full height, her wings partly open. The flickering candle light illuminated every inch of muscle, every scale, and every spiraled length of horn. It was a carefully staged, imposing picture that succeeded in showing exactly what she was: power, violence, and fear, in the form of a Queen dragon.

Farley's grip tightened on Haley's hand.

"I was beginning to think you had lost your way, Child. You are short one Male. Does that mean you have dispatched him?"

You know damn well I didn't. "No, your Majesty. Creyal..." Haley didn't want to tell her Creyal ran. She tried to think of a way to word things. "I sent Creyal away. He's too weak for this." It didn't smell like a lie, but it didn't exactly feel like the truth.

Medan thrummed. "You protect him. I find that ... quaint. But I do not like to be lied to. I will forgive you ... this once." Her head thrust forward, too fast to see, and stopped an inch from Haley's face. "But do not lie to me again. Ever. You will never be cunning enough to deceive me." Haley shut her eyes and willed her stomach to be calm. Farley pressed himself to her back. The feeling of him against her stilled the rising fear. When she opened her eyes, Medan was watching them with a strange expression.

The Queen tossed Haley a coy look as she moved away. "Tell me, Child, how does it make you feel to know that the *chetrah* you work so closely with hate you? Betray you?" Her golden eyes flashed and turned red.

"It hurts. It makes me angry."

"Do you feel they should be punished?" A double-edged question if there ever was one. Haley had to take a few seconds to come up with an answer.

"If you mean by the Human courts, yes, but not by us." There. That seemed safe enough.

Medan blinked once, then twice. “I have something to show you, Haley. Something for you to take to your *chetrah* boss and his people.”

The Queen made a motion, and from a small doorway, two large Human shaped Males came forward with a body hanging between them. Haley recognized him immediately.

“John Tate,” Farley said near her ear.

John Tate had been stripped down to his boxers. Duct tape wrapped around his mouth. He fought the Males who carried him. It reminded Haley of how a fly looked stuck between a screen and glass. And just like an insect, no matter how hard John Tate flapped, he just wasn’t going anywhere.

As the Males brought John Tate all the way into the light, Haley saw the mark on his shoulder.

They dropped him in the floor at Medan’s feet.

Medan said, “He is one of Nidia’s.”

John Tate pawed at the tape until he got his fingers underneath. He ripped it off, leaving bits of glue stuck to his skin and bits of skin stuck to the tape. He stumbled to his feet and tried to run. Medan blocked his way, moving too fast for anything Human to see. Her wings rattled, filling the room with the sound of a thousand rattlesnakes.

“Fuck ... shit...” John Tate stumbled and fell on his ass. “Haley, help me.” His eyes darted over to her. “You know me. You’ve known me for years.” He crawled a few feet towards her, but Haley couldn’t stop staring at the scar on his shoulder.

“How come I didn’t know? How come I never smelled it?”

“He is not her Link. He is only a servant, a companion, a ... pet.” Medan snapped her teeth and John Tate screamed. “It’s why he stays strong and does not age as quickly as other *chetrah*. But he does not *feed* her. The *mark* was made by one of her Males and they have not stained him with their scent.”

And Haley had always thought he just had good genes. “John, why...”

“I’ve g-got four k-kids.” Muscular earthquakes racked his body. “I needed the money. She offered, I couldn’t say no.” Tears burst out of his eyes and a string of snot coated his upper lip. “Do you have any idea how hard it is to raise four kids on a cop’s salary?” Medan huffed a breath across his skin and John Tate bolted. She stopped him with a foot and pinned him flat.

The Queen's tongue slid up his neck and across his cheek. John Tate screamed, whipping his head back and forth, trying to keep the forked ends from sliding across his mouth and eyes.

"Oh-God-Oh-God-Oh-God!"

Medan laughed. "Down here, your God can not hear you."

She released him and he tried to get away. Sliding in his own urine, he fell hard. A normal Human would have broken something. But John just had the wind knocked out of his lungs. He curled into a ball on the floor and tried to hide himself under his arms.

John Tate began to pray. "Hail Mary, full of grace, the Lord is with thee. Blessed art thou among women..." Medan roared and John keened like a wounded animal.

Medan pinned the cop again. She raised her head and Haley caught the pleased gleam in her eyes. "Look at him, Child." She obeyed, because not doing it wasn't an option. "He has betrayed you. He has given your enemies a way to bring you harm."

"I didn't have a choice!" Tate shook his head. "She would have killed me. June came to me. That's how I got involved. June came to me and she offered me money. I'm sorry I took it. I took it ... oh God, help me."

"Fuck you, Tate," Farley snapped. The sound of his anger brought Haley's head around.

"Farley..."

"No, he hung your ass out to dry. No telling what he's told that bitch. What did you tell her, Tate? Huh, what did you tell Nidia about Haley? And Dobson, were you doing him too, or just the Queen of North Carolina? If I'd known, I would have ripped your throat myself."

Tate's face became a portrait of Human horror. "No, Farley. You don't ... No ... I never, I never ... I just told her small things. Insignificant things..."

Farley growled, flashing teeth. "You know what, Tate, I hope your God does exist, because that means you're going to Hell. Unforgivable sin, isn't it? To make a pact with the Beast?"

Medan blinked and inclined her head. "Your little Marked understands. What about you, Child? Do you hate him enough to kill him?"

Haley looked at Farley, then Medan. "No." God of Man help her, she only felt pity for him. "I'm angry, yes. But kill him? No."

The Queen rumbled and moved her head closer. Her golden eyes swirled and pulsed with an inner fire. "You have so much to learn, Child. So much to learn." She turned back to John Tate.

His hands looked so small pushing against her massive claws, trying to move them. "Please ... Medan ... please ... Haley, help me." His legs kicked but he was getting nowhere. His entire body rattled under the weight of the Queen's *RHage*.

John choked, turned his head and vomited, retching so hard that bright red blood was swirled in the yellow bile. He coughed, snorted and vomited again. All the while, Medan watched with a kind of patience that Haley would have never dreamed she possessed.

"Please don't kill me," John whispered. "Please, I'll do whatever you want. Please don't ... my daughter's going to have her first baby in a week. My family, I want to see my family again..."

Medan purred. "This is not your Human society, *chetrah*. Here, there is only one way for enemies to pay their debt, and that is with their life. And your life, however pitiful it may be, will simply have to do." Under her claw John prayed again.

"Medan..." Haley choked back a sob. "My Queen... When the D.A. sees the mark on him, they will prosecute him to the fullest extent of the law. He'll go to prison. He'll go to prison and they won't ever let him out for what he did."

"You do not want me to kill him." It wasn't a question. Medan applied a little pressure to her captive, pushing the air out of his lungs until he was gasping. Haley clenched her fists. "You feel pity for him. You cherish his life despite his hate of yours?"

"Yes."

Medan dipped her head. "I see." She flicked her gaze up at Haley. "It would please you if I gave him his life?"

She shut her eyes for a second and willed her words to form against the Fear Medan radiated. "Yes."

"It would ... ease you."

"Yes, your Majesty. Yes."

Medan gave a snort. “Then I will not kill him.” Haley’s eyes snapped open. Medan lifted her foot. John Tate was still too occupied with catching his breath to run.

Haley started to tell her thank you, but the Queen caught her gaze and held it. Right then and there, she knew something terrible was coming. Something unstoppable.

“No, I will not kill him. I will just break him instead.” Medan tilted her massive head and a thin line of gold dripped from her temple, clung to her cheek, then splattered against John Tate’s face. He tried wiping it away from his mouth, but it was too late.

John Tate kicked and rolled, mouth working like a fish. His eyes glazed and he clawed at his neck, chest, and then groin.

“Ah ... yes. This will be much more fun.” Medan thrummed as she scraped the temporal fluid from the side of her face and held her razor sharp claw out to John. His hands latched onto her toe and his mouth on her talon. He sucked, he licked, slicing open his lips and tongue. Red blood mixed with the gold.

“Jesus...” Farley turned his head. Haley didn’t. Haley made herself watch. She’d brought this on the man.

When his chest was covered in scarlet and his lips so mutilated they hung from his jaw, Medan poured more on him. It slapped him in the face and rained down on his hands. John smeared it over his skin. The grin on his face was made more gruesome by the damage to his lips. He licked at his arms and bit his own hands until he was chewing mouthfuls of flesh, all the while making small mewling noises.

“Ore...” He held his hands up to the Queen and she gazed at him like he was something precious. “Ease, Ore...”

“Pray to me, John. Pray to me, and maybe I will give you what you want.”

“Medan, please, no--” Haley slapped her hand over her mouth too late. The Queen narrowed her eyes and steam rolled from between her lips.

With her eyes on Haley, Medan spoke to John. Commanding him. And because of the ties formed by the temporal fluid, he could not disobey. “Pray to me, John. Pray to the only God.”

“Hail edan, ull o grace...”

The Queen smiled. "Very good, John."

John Tate worked his mouth and Medan fed him more. His head lolled to the side and his eyes rolled into his skull. John clawed at himself, digging one hand into the sack below his cock, while the other continued working until he climaxed.

"This is for you, Haley Night. How long do you think he can stand my pleasures before he begs me for death?"

Haley turned away. She couldn't help it.

"You will watch, Haley! He lives! Just as you wish, he lives!"

John's cries turned into piteous wailing. His eyes bulged from his head, and when the next wave hit him, he bit his tongue in half. And he still couldn't stop, clawing, stroking, coming.

Medan laughed, reared upward, caught her *chelae* on the marble, and threw sparks. "They want our pleasures, I will give them our pleasures. They want our gifts, I will give them our gifts!" She snarled at John as he screamed for her mercy. "That's right, John, pray to me. Fuck yourself and pray to me! Give yourself unto me, *chetrah*. Bear your soul unto me!" John threw back his head and smashed it into the marble. "More, John. More!" She kept laughing and John Tate kept screaming.

"STOP IT!" Haley started towards him, but Farley yanked her back. Medan's jaws shot forward with a deafening snap. One more step and the Queen would have bitten Haley in half.

"Stop what, Haley? His life? Are you asking me to end his life?" The sound of her voice and the power of her *Fear* took Haley to her knees. Farley held her.

The sob burst out of Haley. Tears burned her eyes and cut rivers down her cheeks. She shook, she trembled, she couldn't gather a rational thought. Farley held her so tight that the air wheezed out of her lungs. She stayed there, curled and unable to stand. The screaming from John Tate trickled away and was replaced by a rhythmic grunting sound and the pop and crunch of bone.

Haley didn't want to look, but she had to. John Tate suffered because of her. Medan had stretched herself out on the marble floor. Red blood pooled at her feet.

This was what she meant by ruining the rugs. Medan had planned this just like everything else.

Medan dipped her head and ripped one of John Tate's legs from its socket and chewed. As his arterial spray fanned across the floor, his strokes slowed until they stopped completely. His mouth opened once, twice, and he became still. Medan bit his torso, ripping him apart, stringing his insides across the floor. She was slow in her eating. Exaggerated.

When she was finished, she extended a bloody claw to Haley. "Come to me, Child. Let us become one. You are weak, where I am not. Come to me and I will protect you."

Haley couldn't do it. She couldn't will herself to step forward. To go to her. To become like her.

"I can't." Haley slid back, struggled to her feet, stumbled, and Farley caught her. "This was a mistake." She looked around, dazed. Which way was out? Which way took her away from this hell?

A small smile curled on Medan's scaled lips. "This is what you need, Haley. This is the power and the vengeance you do not possess."

"No." Haley shook her head. "No, I will not. I can't." She couldn't be cold and murderous to survive.

"So weak." Medan hissed.

Against her ear, Farley said her name. "She can protect you."

"No--no ... I--can't."

"If this is what it takes to survive--"

"No! Get me out of here, Farley. Please, get me out now!"

"This way." Farley pulled Haley to her feet and they ran.

In the tunnel Haley fell.

"Get up! C'mon, Haley!"

She tried, but her body would only shake. The images of John Tate crushed her like a physical force, making her weak, making her helpless.

Farley scooped her up. "Fuck it." The tunnel he took didn't lead back into the club, but connected to a brick and mortar causeway and emptied out over a grassy bank. Runway lights from the airport glittered on the horizon. An airplane roared overhead, making Haley jump.

"Shhh…" Farley sat down and held her in his lap. It was getting cold out but they were shielded from the wind by the lip of the tunnel. "It's okay." His gentle hands stroked her back and arms.

"No, no, it's not okay. It's not okay. She killed him. *I* killed him."

Haley's words were butchered by her shivering.

God of Man, if only she could get the images out of her mind. Medan had eaten John Tate, not just eaten him but broken him. It was a kind of brutality she couldn't understand. But then, that was the way, wasn't it? In the belly of the Hive it was survive or die. Why should it bother Medan to kill something that wasn't even hers?

But it should have.

No matter how badly Haley wanted to survive, she couldn't do it at that kind of price. Never in her life had she felt so weak, so lost, so out of control. All her time with Humans, she longed to belong to the Dens, and now she only wanted to blow-torch the memories from her head.

"Is that what it was like for you on the hatching grounds? Is that why it doesn't bother you? Is that why you aren't..." *Falling apart. I'm falling apart.* "Tell me."

Farley touched her cheek. "Yes."

"I never understood. Even with the white-scales, I never ... I never understood."

"I'm sorry." He stroked her head.

"I thought I knew. I thought..." A nervous laugh escaped her lips. "I thought I understood. I've read every book. I've studied every paper. But I don't, do I? I don't. I'm Kin, but I'm not. Look at me. I can't stop ... stop ... sh-shaking."

"You're not used to it. I always envied you, you know. I never tried to tell you because I was afraid it would change you."

"I'm cold."

"It's the shock." He moved, and his hand pushed against the back of her head. "*Feed.* It will help."

"I can't. I feel too sick."

They sat there for a while listening to the planes coming and going, their passengers free of the horrible knowledge of the Dens.

"I wish she'd just killed me."

Farley shushed her and rocked. "No, you don't. Live at all costs."

"And yet she killed him ... no ... she tortured him, she broke him ... that's not valuing life."

"It's surviving."

She looked up at him and his face was serene. Haley couldn't understand. And she didn't want to. "How can you say that, Farley? You knew John. You talked with him, and you saw him in the halls--"

"He sold you out." He pushed the lock of hair behind her ear. "I understand why she did it, even if I don't agree with her methods."

Haley studied him, trying to find some hesitation, some regret, but there wasn't any. "You really meant it when you said you would have killed him?"

Farley dropped his eyes.

"Who am I?" Haley leaned against him. "What am I?"

"You're Kin."

"No, no. I'm not. I don't want to be. I don't want to be..." God of Man, she sounded like Deshi. "Ah, Christ." New tears broke over her cheeks. "I don't know what to do ... I don't know..."

Farley held Haley while she fell apart all over again, keeping all her pieces from becoming lost in the grass. He shushed her, he rocked her, he kissed her tears, and when she was completely spent, he picked her up again and carried her once more.

Chapter 39

Well, if this didn't beat all. Dobson checked his phone for the third time in five minutes. Obsessive compulsive just wasn't him.

The Queen didn't call. And she always called. Or at least her mouthpiece did. That could only mean one thing.

The shit had hit the fan in a very big way.

His men had taken care of that Clinic east of the Dens, but then his men had disappeared. Seven in all, including that cop, Tate. Dobson wasn't sure what to make of that. The Queen hadn't called, and now his team was missing. And from his personal experience variation in the norm was never a good sign.

And the kicker? The Buckhead and East Point labs hadn't checked in.

Civilian operations were always like this. Full of pits and cracks to break an ankle in. In the field, things were better. There, if something got in your way, you shot it or blew it up. But the public has a tendency to get cranky about that sort of behavior, so Dobson was forced to keep his crayon marks inside the lines. Another couple of days though, and it wouldn't matter. He'd be a goddamned hero.

Dobson flipped open the phone and called. One of them had better answer or there would be hell to pay. When the phone picked up he didn't wait for a hello. "Richards, tell me something bad hasn't happened?"

"We're all good to go here, sir. Should I be concerned about anything?"

"Always be concerned, Richards. Never let your guard down."

Richards cleared his throat. "Yes, sir."

"Have the Buckhead or East Point labs called you?"

"No, sir."

"Me either." Not good. Not good. "Send an Alchemist team over there. Have them check it out." While both labs had the standard surveillance equipment, they were nowhere near as fortified as the ADF. But then, what was?

Voices floated up the hall and Dobson glanced out the door. This time of night the only thing crawling around the Center should be cockroaches.

Two janitors appeared around the corner talking back and forth in Spanish.

Scratch that. Cockroaches and Spics.

"I'll be leaving here in a few minutes, then heading home for a few hours of sleep. If so much as a rat's asshole hair is out of place in my lab, you call me. Do I make myself clear?" Dobson didn't wait for the lab lackey's stupid answer, he just hung up.

He went back to the computer sitting on his bare bones desk. Dobson didn't use this office much. Hell, he avoided the place as often as he could. Like the rest of the building it smelled like wyrm and pussy. Not a great combination.

Dobson opened his email and sent a message out to the Center for Draconian Research. He wanted them ready for the final phase. He checked his inbox. It was empty, None of the facilities had replied to him via email either. Fine. He stood and his phone rang. He checked the number. It was Dolby's. Lead man for the Clinic Job.

"Where the fuck have you been, Dolby? I've been sitting on my ass here waiting for you to check in. Where is Tate? He didn't report in either." He waited for a reply and heard nothing. "Dolby? Dolby ... fuck. I can hear you breathing, Alchemist, so say something."

It wasn't Dolby who answered. Hell, it wasn't even Human. The rich, deep, feminine voice could be nothing more than Kin, and the distortions made by an inhuman mouth meant it was a Kin in full form.

"Unfortunately, none of your team will be reporting back to you, Colonel Dobson." There was a sound like something wet being torn in half. A whimper echoed in the background.

"Who is this?"

"Medan, the Queen of Atlanta."

Dobson was quiet. The Queen never spoke to him directly.

"Where's your Link? Why didn't she call me?"

Something big moved. It came over the tiny speaker like a thunderstorm. When the Queen spoke again, her voice was louder, closer to the speaker. "Colonel Dobson, I do not have a Link, I have never had a Link, nor will I ever take one. *Chetrah* are not even worthy enough to scrape the scat of my hatchlings. There is but one place on this planet for your kind and that is as Food."

Dobson felt dizzy. Part of him wanted to accuse the voice of lying, but he knew she wasn't. He could *feel* she wasn't.

"If you're Medan, then who the fuck have I been talking to?"

A thick rich chuckle shimmied the cheap speaker. "See, so easy to lead. Cattle, that's all you are. Tell me, colonel, when I tear the flesh from your bones, will you pray to your God? Will you ask Him to save you? To protect you? I have found that all *chetrah* pray in the end. And yet you still die." Voices in the background rose and fell. Dobson heard the distinct sound of someone sobbing like a goddamned infant.

"What do you want?" It wasn't like he really cared. He was more or less trying to buy some time to organize his thoughts and figure out what to do next.

"I wanted you to hear the news from me."

"What news?"

"Surely you know by now."

What? That'd he'd been fucked? Yeah, that was becoming real clear, but the problem was, by whom and how. "Are you going to tell me who I need to kill, or are we going to keep doing this dance 'til daylight?"

Her laughed was accompanied by the sound of whimpering. "You need not be concerned with killing anyone. You see, I'm very good at this game. I never flinch. I never hesitate. So, when I realized Nidia was pulling your strings, I pulled some of my own."

"Nidia?"

"Yes, colonel. The Queen of North Carolina. Seems she enjoys playing pretend. And since you *chetrah* are so easily led..."

A scream came across the phone, desperate, pain filled, and Human. Dobson jerked the phone away from his ear.

"Oh God, oh God, please, nooo--." The voice was cut short by a snap, followed by more sounds of something wet and thick being ripped and torn.

"My hatchlings thank you for your gift to them. They are so hungry. Always hungry. You were a fool to lay any faith in Nidia. She knows you plan on killing her, and she will strike first."

"If you want me dead, why are you telling me this?"

"Because no one takes what is mine. And you, Colonel Dobson, are mine."

Chapter 40

Stuffed in a way-too-small bathtub, Farley cradled Haley's body with his own.

Steam curled and rolled from the water's surface. It was hot enough to scald, yet it still wasn't hot enough. He petted Haley in long languid strokes. Water slapped against his chin when she moved.

"Be still or you'll get water up your nose."

She blinked, looking confused. "Where are we?"

"Safe." At least for now. And if he wanted to keep her that way, there were things that had to be done, decisions to be made.

"How long was I out?"

"About an hour. I had to get you warm. Medan really did a number on you." He petted her cheek and stared into her haunted eyes. She was thinking about Tate. This close, it was impossible not to see the images whirling through her mind like a blender. Her regret, her fear. It burned in Farley's chest, but the need to keep her safe burned hotter. "Haley." Farley pulled her chin up. "Garrett called. He said something is happening downtown. Dobson is moving Alchemist teams and three of the Bureau's board members have gone missing from their homes. He wants us ready to leave in two hours."

"But Dobson will have him charged--"

"Garrett said we have to take that chance. With Dobson's behavior, and the missing board members, it's going to be hard for anyone upstairs to ignore him now. Dobson's world is crumbling, and you just have to stay hidden for a week, maybe two. He can't risk the colonel getting a hold of you. He's panicked and that means he's even more dangerous."

Haley made a face.

"What?"

"I'm having a hard time picturing that man panicking about anything."

But he was. That much Garrett had been sure about.

"What?" she asked.

"There's a good chance Garrett won't be able to get you out of the country."

"Wait. What happened to *us* leaving? As in you and me?"

Farley shushed her and pressed his cheek against the side of her head. He wrapped his arms around her and pulled their bodies as close as possible. "That's part of plan B."

"Plan B? We haven't even tried plan A yet. How come something tells me I'm really not going to enjoy plan two?"

Farley kissed her to make her stop talking. Now she was just looking at him with large dark eyes, afraid for him, when she should have been afraid for herself. He sighed. "I didn't know what to do when Garrett told me this might not work. If Dobson somehow gets to you, the only Kin strong enough to save you will be Medan. So I called Justice." Haley tried to look away, but Farley wouldn't let her. He kissed her again and rubbed his thumb over her windpipe. "You'll have to bond with her. Become her Enforcer. She can protect you, Haley."

"At what cost?"

He gave a little up down with his shoulders. "As long as you live, what does it matter?"

Haley shuddered. "I can't go back to her." A deep worried frown weighed down her full lips.

"You won't have to. I can act as your vessel."

"What? No! She'd kill you."

Farley plastered a mask of calm on his face. If he was lucky, Medan would just kill him. If he was unlucky she would make him kill others first.

He tucked a lock of hair behind her ear. "I won't go alone. Justice will be with me."

"No."

"Haley, please, let me--"

"I said no! I can't live through losing you." She buried her face into his neck.

Farley couldn't help but think the exact same thing. Well, almost the same thing. Not only would he not live through losing Haley, he wouldn't want to.

Justice had warned him that she wouldn't agree to this. Farley hadn't argued because he knew the Male was right. But this had to be done. He was too weak to keep her safe from Dobson, too weak to keep the Queens at bay. With a little flesh and a little blood, Medan could. Justice had been worried about him getting it. Farley grinned because if there was anything he could do, it was convince Haley to surrender herself.

Justice had promised to keep him safe, so that meant all he had to do was collect what he needed and get it to the Queen. The only problem was, he didn't trust Justice either.

That Kin was hiding something.

Farley took her mouth, parted her lips, and ran his tongue along the inside of her cheek. Every happy moment he'd ever had tasted like that. A growl licked in the back of his throat and he heaved her up and out of the water. Steam billowed and hissed off of his skin.

"Where are we going?" she asked.

"The floor." He held her to him, kissed her, moved her over the edge and onto the floor. The bath mat squished under his knees from the water running off their bodies. "I'd drown trying to do this to you in the tub." Farley eased her back until she lay on the rug. The bathroom was small and narrow. He couldn't stretch out his legs, and was forced to crouch. "Haley..." There were so many things he wanted to say, but this time wasn't about talking. Farley wanted something to think about if Medan decided to kill him. He wanted somewhere to retreat to in his mind.

Farley stroked her stomach with his fingers to remember the softness of her skin. He circled her bellybutton with his thumb and bent down to suck along the edge. He caressed her curves, following the lines of her body until he reached the juncture between her legs. He kissed her at the top, then slipped his tongue into the folds.

With one hand he pushed her legs wider; with the other he stoked her lower, lavishing in the wetness, the scent of her arousal, and the taste of her pleasure. He slipped one finger in and she arched her back. Heat bloomed over her, and a deep moan crawled out of her throat. The sound of her coming almost took him over the edge. Farley forced himself to keep control, even as she thrashed and cried out his name.

He moved up, positioning himself over her. He wanted more, wanted it now. But this might be the last time he touched her like this.

"Farley?" She looked at him, eyes glassy, her energy flaring. "I can't Roll you so soon."

“Shh--this isn’t about me. Just you.” He flicked his tongue over her right nipple and rolled the other between his finger and thumb. “Just you. I want you warm, Haley. I want you burning inside.” He looked at her. She was bathed in the crystalline light he only saw through dragon eyes. Her hands slid over his neck and between his shoulders. She pushed there and he barked in surprise. So close, so close. He willed himself back down. Haley surprised him by flipping him over.

“Wait, Haley ... oh God of Man...” Her mouth wrapped around the tip of his cock and sharp points grazed as she swallowed him down. Farley kicked, sending the heel of his foot through the layers of the pressed wood door. He came without warning, arching off the floor, trying his best not to scream.

And failed.

No more waiting. He couldn’t hold out anymore. He cursed the small room, fought for position. He finally just pulled Haley up and pushed her over the tub. She threw her hands out against the wall as he pushed himself inside. Her body clenched until it was a struggle to move. Farley wanted her closer, needed to feel her against him, so he pulled her back. The angle brought her quick, over and over, but Farley didn’t want it to end. Ending it meant this terrible thing was going to have to happen. That she might die. He might die and there would be a great void of nothing. An eternity without his own. Without her. Farley sank his teeth into Haley’s shoulder, consuming bits of muscle.

Farley’s mouth locked, his throat spasmed and he drank her down. He didn’t sate himself even though he wanted to. Justice had warned him that if he did that, his body would spend it instead of holding it for Medan.

Farley popped his jaws free, licked the wound and stayed where he was, inside her, the connection now more of a comfort than a needed pleasure.

After a while he pulled her to the floor so he could hold her while he sat propped against the wall. His insides ached, his sex ached, and every bone from the top of his skull to his toes was on fire. Farley shut his eyes and breathed in her scent. Relishing it, committing it to memory. He wanted to tell her he loved her, even though she hated the L word. Kin can’t love...

But Farley wasn’t so sure of that.

She looked at him and he knew. She felt it too--a burn so hot that it made the heat of metaphysics quiver. A Human emotion and they weren't Human. "Haley--"

A hard knock on the pressed board door cut him off.

"Hey, if you two are quite through in there, Garrett's here."

"Ken?" Haley looked at Farley with wide eyes.

Farley shrugged. "His apartment was close, and I didn't have any money for a cab."

From the outside Ken asked, "Oh, and by the way, who's going to pay for the hole in my bathroom door?"

Chapter 41

At least Garrett had sense enough to bring clothes from Haley's locker at work. They were only sweats and a flimsy t-shirt, but it was better than naked. No matter what Farley thought.

"I just think you should try going bareback more."

"I'm naked enough." No underwear, no bra. Yeah, this was about as publicly naked as Haley wanted to get.

They came through Ken's bedroom. It looked like a war between Apple and PC had taken place on his desk. Both computers suffering heavy casualties. The living room wasn't much better. Haley counted eight different game consoles, including a 1980's Atari 64.

"They still make games for this thing?" Farley poked it with his foot.

"Hey! Be gentle with that. It's an antique."

Garrett was at Ken's kitchen table. When he stood up his head whacked the overhead light, adding a second welt to the one popping up on his forehead.

"I brought you a couple of jackets from the PD. They won't miss them." Garrett nodded to the extra wide chair posing as a couch. "We need to hurry. The plane will be leaving in about an hour."

Haley picked one of the jackets and put it on. At least it covered her, unlike a certain pink T-shirt she was wearing. She handed Farley the other one, but he just held it.

"Put it on."

He shook his head. "I have to stay."

She looked at him, then Garrett, waiting for someone to tell her this was a joke. "Put the coat on, Farley."

When you're safe, I'll follow. Until then, I'm staying here."

"You can't be serious." But he was. The expression on his face was deadly serious. She remembered what he said; he could act as her vessel. And Medan would need her flesh and her blood to form a bond.

But he didn't have that. Did he?

You *fed* him, she reminded herself, because he'd made her. The same way Farley kept himself alive on the Hatching grounds, convincing Males he was worth keeping around by manipulating the *need*.

"You bastard! You think getting yourself killed will make all this better?" How dare he, how dare he use her like that, especially now!

Farley's gaze came up for a second. "I don't *want* to die, Haley." He scrubbed a hand through his curls. "But I know what it takes to survive. To make sure *you* survive. You're not safe yet. It would be stupid to think Nidia is out of tricks."

"Garrett..." Surely he could do something about this, talk some since into him.

"Two of you are more likely to draw attention. This is for the best, Haley. Let's go."

"I can't believe..." She choked on her words. Had they both planned this?

Farley stepped up to her and wrapped himself around her, pushed his face into her neck and thrummed. "Please, don't leave angry with me."

She wanted to. Instead she held him back, inhaled his scent and kissed his temple. "Don't you dare die on me, do you understand?" A part sob, part laugh broke loose from her throat. *God of Man, please don't die on me.*

It seemed wrong that Farley could laugh, even if it was half-hearted and kind of sad. "I promise you, that is one request I plan on doing my damnedest to follow."

Outside, the wind froze the tears on Haley's cheeks as she followed Garrett out to the car.

"I need your cell phone." He handed it to her. She wiped the tears out of her eyes, off her cheeks, sniffled and tried to compose herself. Crying was such a damn bore. She envied those who never impressed the behavior.

Garrett opened the door for her and she got in. Haley dialed. On the fifth ring Gregory answered, sounding wide awake.

"This is Gregory."

"Can I please speak to Justice?" Even over the phone she could feel the change in him. Or maybe it was just her imagination.

"I am here." So strange. It was still Gregory's voice, but the inflection and accent was all Justice.

"Was it your idea?"

His breath stilled.

"Tell me, damn it. Was it your idea for Farley to go to Medan?"

"No."

"Then who told him he could be my vessel? Which means what exactly? Because I don't even know what the hell it means."

"I told him. He asked me how it could be done. He is your Marked. That means he is an extension of you. He can carry your blood and flesh to Medan so you won't have to."

"Why would you do that, Justice? Why?"

"He wants to keep you safe, Haley. It's his duty as your First Marked."

Haley pressed her fingers to her temple. "That's not my point." God of Man, how could she expect him to understand? He had probably killed his way to survival like every other Kin.

"You are afraid for him."

"Yes! He's my friend, Justice. He's all I've had for a century. He was the first Male I *fed* from, the first Male I ever had sex with, the first Male I Rolled. I've never known the world without him. Can you understand that? Can you possibly comprehend what that's like? Survive at all costs? Survive? What the hell is it worth if there's nothing left to survive for?"

When she stopped screaming there was only the sound of the car engine, the wheels on the road, rain starting to tap on the windshield. Garrett clicked on the wipers.

Haley inhaled. The action made her hearts hurt, but there were no tears.

Finally, she wasn't crying.

Voice calm, Justice said. "Farley is not as weak as you think he is."

"I don't think he's weak."

"You do not?"

No. Maybe. Okay, fine, yes. "Quit trying to change the subject."

"The subject has not changed. The subject is still about Farley. You fear for him because you see him as weak. You see him as not in control of his temper. You see him as Kin. And you see yourself as something other. The weakness you fault him for is the strength it takes to survive. Farley understands that. Any Kin that has fought his way from the belly of the Hive understands that. It is more than eat or be eaten. It is about a willingness to sacrifice a part of yourself. And that is something that you have not learned to understand."

Haley dropped the phone, kicking and screaming. Her fist struck the dash and it cracked. Beside her Garrett sat motionless, his eyes straight ahead, his knuckles white on the steering wheel. When the tantrum subsided she picked up the cell and put it to her ear. Her breath rattled over the receiver.

"Better?" Justice's serenity made her want to gouge his eyes out.

"No. No, I'm not."

"I see."

"You won't let her kill him. Tell me you won't let her kill him."

"I will protect Farley."

"That's not good enough. I want you to swear to me you will not let her kill him."

He was quiet for a moment. "I swear to you, I will protect him with my life."

"Good."

The highway split, and they passed under a bridge. Up ahead the first exit for air-cargo appeared. They were getting there too fast. Everything was happening too fast.

"Haley?"

"Yeah?" Her reflection stared back at her from the passenger window, highlighted by the dash lights. *I look tired.* She felt worse.

"You will not be lost to her."

"Yeah, well. We'll have to see about that, won't we?"

"Be well, Haley Night."

Her hand dropped back into her lap, feeling like it weighed a million pounds. The light on the screen blinked out. In the darkness the sun flickered on the horizon. The orange and red glow ate out the stars.

Haley looked at the clock. It wasn't even six. The sun wouldn't start to rise for another half hour.

"Oh, dear God, Garrett, stop the car. Stop ... STOP!" Garrett pulled the sedan over into the emergency lane. Haley threw open the door and scrambled out. Fire danced on the horizon.

"Haley, get back in the car!"

She looked at Garrett. His face was a gray mask of fear.

He knows. He knows what it is, that's why he was in such a hurry.

"What is it?" She asked him.

Garrett shook his head.

"Tell me, Garrett."

He rubbed his face with his hand then scrubbed the top of his brush cut. "It's Niles. It came over the wire about ten minutes before I got to Ken's. He escaped the ADF."

"All those people..." The flames were huge. She'd never seen anything like it.

"He hasn't left the prison grounds. He's leveling the place."

"How did he get out?" She waited for her boss to answer.

"No one escapes the ADF." Well, obviously that theory had been blown out of the water. "They'll dispatch a unit."

And that meant they'd kill him. Niles Fury, the Male who had watched over her. Kept her safe. Kept her alive. A Male who owed her nothing. A Male she didn't even know.

"I can stop him." As the only Female employed by the CFKR, it was her job to stop him.

"No, what you need to do is get in the car, so you can get somewhere safe."

"And if I leave? Then what happens? When he gets done tearing apart the ADF, where do you think he'll go?" There were a lot of people in the heart of the city. A lot of Human flesh waiting to be consumed.

"Let the Alchemists deal with it." Was he serious? This close to people? When the Alchemist teams arrived even more life would be lost. This wasn't like Garrett, she knew that. He was being a friend and looking out for her. "Get in the car, Haley."

"I can't let innocent people die. Not when I can stop him. Not when it's my duty to stop him." Human life meant too much to her to turn her back.

She took off up the emergency lane.

"Haley!"

There weren't many things Haley could do at the speed and agility of her people because of her Human influences, except for the shift. And shifting fast meant the *burn* ran hot.

Metaphysical fire surrounded Haley. Rain boiled away on clouds of steam. Pleasure erupted from her upper *ulysiss* and leached into her muscles, where the firestorm of enzymatic processes began to catalyst. Bones popped, muscles moved and joints realigned.

The rush of cellular division spiked her temperature high enough to warp the air. In response, the lower *ulysiss* released, to keep her from burning up.

Haley's Human hands became claws, her body reshaped, while mass and form multiplied. Wings unfolded from her back, and scales dark as night fluttered, replacing Human skin. Silver highlights bloomed over blue-black armor and horns sprung from her head. It only took seconds before there was nothing left but a lithe Draconian form.

With one push from her powerful hind legs she was airborne. Her wings pulled taut, cutting the air like a blade. Below her, cars skidded on the highway and veered into the retaining wall.

The roar that erupted from Haley's throat thundered across the sky as she soared. Her tail snapped, her wings pumped, propelling her forward at breakneck speed. Haley's body churned with metaphysical power, turning the frigid air into an inferno. There was no doubt why her people lost themselves to moments like this.

Like sex, like *feeding*, the power of the shift was a pleasure all its own.

Haley's dragon sight turned everything into daylight, and details like texture and color were lost. What replaced them was the innate ability to judge speed, distance, and size.

On a wave of metaphysics, she moved at a speed that defied the physical. Within minutes, the ADF appeared on the horizon. While the prison was located below ground, topside contained dozens of I-O departments that employed hundreds of people. A wide stretch of buildings pinwheeled out from a single thick skyscraper, and clinging to the center piece was Niles Fury.

It was like a script right out of a bad B-movie. Monster vs. Concrete building. Only there was no popcorn or cheesy subtitles. Worst of all, people were really dying.

He spread his wings as she circled. Niles was nothing she'd ever seen. A grand mane of black horns spiraled back from his head and ran a deadly line down the center of his back. He was easily twice the size of Medan.

Terrifying didn't even cover it.

His wings pumped, fueling the fire he had set loose on the place. Niles opened his jaws and flamed. A liquid heat erupted from his jaws, coating the sides of the building and running rivers to the concrete yard below, eating through everything it touched.

"Niles!"

He raised his thick head and the sound of his roar shook the air, the earth, and the sky. One side of the ADF collapsed.

He went airborne.

In one powerful stroke, Niles swept past Haley, his wake of air almost knocking her from the sky. Moving all that bone, scale and muscle broke the laws of physics, and seriously tested the metaphysical. Propelled on preternatural energy, like an invisible solar flare, he moved faster than the eye could track, and with the grace of something far more delicate.

Below, people exited the buildings in waves. The candy sweet flavor of panic and fear rolled up through the air. True forms burned resources at an alarming rate, and the hunger that came with maintaining one was almost constant. And all those people were easy pickings.

Niles was too fast for Haley to stop him.

He swept over the running and screaming masses. The buildings were too close, but somehow he managed the maneuver. His body skimmed the ground, his head flicked up and to the side. With the kind of agility only seen in the ancient, he plucked Human bodies from the ground and swallowed them whole.

Haley dropped from the air screaming. She extended her *chelae* and caught him right behind his tympanic membrane in the only vulnerable spot on his head. Her smaller, lithe form cleared the oncoming structures. Distracted by the attack, Niles was a second too late. In his attempt to turn, his shoulder caught a concrete structure, snapping one of his wings at an unnatural angle. He rolled, first in the air, then on the ground. Cars around the ADF became crushed aluminum cans under his girth.

But the red giant didn't stay down. He headed back towards the center building of the ADF.

Haley could hear his breath deepen, smell the acrid burn of his fire mixing. Thick strands of fire gland fluid coated his jaws, ran down the sides of his neck. He dropped his head with precision timing and flamed.

The weight of the liquid made it fall fast. As the foundation became a pool of molten fire, the rest of the building collapsed in a heap and Niles dove in and started digging.

What the hell?

"Niles!" Haley landed at what she hoped was a safe distance. When he didn't acknowledge her, she thundered a roar. His bloody red eyes rolled up. "Stop this, Niles. You've done enough killing."

"So predictable..." His mouth stretched into a nasty grin. He laughed and it just didn't sound right. That's when Haley saw the ugly scar on his shoulder.

Niles was *marked.*

His red eyes flashed gold then black, and the scent of honey saturated the air. Haley breathed, tasting Queen dragon.

It could only be one. Nidia. Her hearts jack-hammered in her chest.

Niles tossed his head like he was trying to shake something loose. The darkness in his gaze flickered and was replaced by a second or two of recognition.

"Fight her, Niles." Was it even possible? Haley had no idea.

Nidia screamed in laughter, using Nile's voice and his mouth. "It's just me in here, Haley Night. There is no Niles anymore. I control him, I own him; I have crushed him completely, because without the Fury is he is weak! And now I will use him to rip you limb from limb!"

She didn't even see him move.

But she sure as hell felt the weight of him as he slammed into her. They rolled across the concrete yard, nothing more than a flurry of teeth and claws. Haley fought to keep Niles' powerful jaws away from her throat. His teeth hit her shoulder and sank to the bone. He slung his head like a rabid dog tearing loose a mouthful of flesh.

And in true form, healing just didn't happen beyond a normal biological rate.

Haley managed to struggle free of his grip and go airborne. The reprieve didn't last long. Older, faster, and powered by the metaphysical energy of an ancient Queen, Niles ate up the sky on wings wide enough to block out the rising sun.

If she could keep him busy long enough, his body would eventually burn out, and he'd have to shift back or risk death. But then, with Nidia in control, maybe she wouldn't care about things like that. Instinct told Haley to run, her Human ethics made her stay. Whatever Nidia was after, it couldn't be good.

Niles' jaws creaked as they jacked wide. Heat bloomed against Haley's back. In desperation, she folded her wings and dropped like a stone. The glow missed her by inches, but the fire was still hot enough to blacken the scales along her back and side.

Haley threw open her wings in an attempt to dodge the buildings, but one of her sails caught the edge of a steel tower. White hot pain raced down her wing fingers as one snapped and the leather shredded. The world did its imitation of a blender as her shoulder struck the rooftop on one of the long buildings. She rolled, snapping another bone.

Niles circled. The wounds she'd left behind seeped. Niles vomited heat and the dragon napalm splattered up, catching Haley in the thigh. She screamed as it ate through her muscle.

Flight leather flapped in the wind as she glided to the next rooftop, going even lower. She stumbled into another landing. Aching, bleeding and unable to fly, she was trapped. Niles hit the ledge right behind her, and his weight broke off concrete boulders into the prison grounds below.

Please be in there somewhere. She turned to face him.

Even though it was Niles, Haley could see Nidia through the darkness in his eyes. She wore him like a Human shape over her true form.

"Fear me, Haley. And know that I am your death." The mouth she used jacked wide and then the expression flickered out. The black bled back to red.

"Niles--"

"Run, Haley. My Brother is not strong enough to fight her." And just like that he was gone again.

The massive red lurched forward, wings rattling, jaws working the air. His fire glands dripped. The thick mucus hissed as it hit the wet roof top.

Nidia was going to kill her because she just wasn't strong enough to fight her. Haley tasted fear in the back of her throat, smelled it emanating from her skin. Then a rhythmic thumping sound joined the panicked beat of her own hearts.

Black points appeared on the horizon. Choppers.

And she'd thought things couldn't get any worse. But they were.

The Alchemists were here.

Chapter 42

Right after Dobson ended his phone call with the real Queen of Atlanta, the first of the Alchemist teams reported in. The three labs they checked had been wiped out. Everything in them was missing: people, equipment. The virus.

It took Dobson another fifteen minutes to call five more, and when there was no answer, he could only assume the worst. As in, everything he'd worked for had just grown legs and walked off.

How the hell?

Better yet, who?

Do you really have to ask, soldier? That fucking she-devil. She did this. She arranged this. If the colonel had been Kin, he would have *raged.* But the best he could do was hurl everything off his desk. It wasn't much, and it sure as fuck didn't make him feel better.

His phone rang. In his fury, Dobson had thrown it. Now it was lying under the broken bits of a flat screen monitor. He retrieved it, tried to see who was calling, but the display was cracked. At least the goddamned thing still worked.

"What?"

"Colonel Dobson, we're being attacked."

"What the fuck is that supposed to mean? Attacked? Attacked by who?"

"Niles, sir. The other half is trying to dig his way down into the holding area."

"Move everything, through the tunnels now. Get it out of there. Get *him* out of there, do you understand me?" The colonel didn't wait for an answer. There wasn't time. If the two halves became whole, they were more than just fucked.

Dobson tore out of the room, hit the first office he found, grabbed the phone, and dialed the Military dispatch office.

"This is Colonel Dobson with the Bureau KF Military Division, clearance number JF nine eighty-four twelve-C. I need everything. We have a full scale O-forty-one attack at the Atlanta Draconian Facility."

If that's the game the bitch wanted to play, her pet was dead, not just pinned. No, Dobson was going to take his head, and with any luck, the after-shock would kill her as well.

Dobson pounded down the steps with purpose. At times like this he felt like he should be wearing armor instead of a uniform, carrying a sword or pike instead of a gun. He exited into the underground garage, and a black military Hummer screeched to a halt. The door came open and he climbed in.

First lieutenant Charin was in the back and Don Walters was driving. He was one of the few Negros that Dobson felt he could rely on. The man couldn't shoot worth a shit, but put him in the driver's seat of anything on wheels, and he was as graceful as a ballroom dancer.

"We have three Super Cobras en route now, sir."

"That won't be enough." Dobson leaned forward. "I want all five Havocs on this, do you understand me?" Charin relayed the order. "And get my Rooivalk into the air." While the SCs and Havocs would give him fire power and transport for the Alchemists, the Rooivalk was a little piece of South African goodness that could be modified to carry out specific jobs. The versatility of the chopper made it easy to retrofit, and that's exactly what Dobson had done.

Three years ago, Dobson had acquired the Rooivalk to test out his anti-dragon weapons. Through a combination of Alchemy and technology, the thing had been fitted with eight short-range pin cannons containing well over a sixty pounds of liquefied Melatite metal, and a metaphysical pulse-radar. The equivalent of an EMF bomb to the Draconian neurological system. With the Rooivalk, he could knock them out of the air and the rockets would pump enough *oasiss* shrapnel into them that being pinned would feel like a hand job.

Texas had taught Dobson a lot about killing Kin. Specifically, Female Kin. Take a powerful Mark, and throw Alchemist magic down the metaphysical ties, and it was like dropping a lit torch into a tank of gasoline. The stronger the Kin, the stronger the backlash, and Niles was a nuclear warhead waiting for the trigger.

The Hummer barreled into the street, and the wheels ate up the pavement.

"They've got a chopper for you on standby, colonel." Dobson caught

Walters' glance in the rearview. "You sure you want to be on site when this goes down?"

Like a frat boy in the Playboy mansion. "Yes."

"Sir?" Dobson looked back at the other man. He had the sat phone to his ear. "I'm getting reports of a second unidentified O-forty-one. It appears to be fighting with our target."

It couldn't be. Yeah, yeah, it could. This was exactly the kind of thing that stupid cunt would do. All to save her people and protect Human life.

"Get a description."

"Dark blue, silver highlights, about fifty in length, with a one-fifteen wingspan."

The grin on Colonel Dobson's face almost cracked his skull in half. "Well, boys, it looks like Christmas has come early this year."

Chapter 43

An ear-splitting scream sliced the air as the first choppers fired their weapons. The twenty millimeter rounds hit Niles in the flank, followed by a barrage of machine gun fire that sent a cloud of green ichor into the air. Haley dove off the rooftop to avoid being hit. Chain link fencing, razor wire, and metal poles became a snare for her legs and wings.

Niles went skyward. The fire he belched slapped against the side of the first chopper, cutting it in half. Blade fragments hit a second chopper, and it was slung into the earth where it cart-wheeled toward Haley.

The shrapnel severed Haley's mangled wing, sending bolts of heated pain through her body. She keened in pain.

Niles landed just inside the tangle of fence bordering the concrete plateau. This close, Haley could see the visible changes taking place from the drain on his metaphysical energy. Changes that were starting to show in her own body--loss of muscle, loss of color. One of his legs was nothing more than a mass of shredded muscle. The red giant reached back to his mangled limb and ripped it from the socket. His jaws made short work of the meat.

Niles slammed his talons into the ground at the base of the crumbled building and resumed digging. "You will not keep what is mine, Dobson. I will have all of him. Both halves to the whole! Mine!"

Five more choppers appeared, spitting out high caliber ammo like rain. All around Haley the ground exploded as gunfire erupted, chewing up concrete. A stream of bullets slapped her across the back and blood leaked out of the holes in her gut, forming tributaries that joined with the puddles of rain.

Much more of this and Nidia wouldn't have to kill her. Agony became a heavy weight and the *burn* sucked up the last of her resources. She was done. Even if her Human *Impressed* ethics would let her run, she couldn't.

Lines fell from the side doors of the choppers and Alchemists spun down like venomous spiders. As they landed, they scattered, taking up positions around both of them.

And while Haley lay bleeding out, the red giant was getting ready for another round. Niles roared, and the sound rippled through the air, sending Alchemists to their knees with bloody ears and eyes. His massive sails unfurled. The right one caught one of the low hanging choppers across the tail. After a small hail of sparks, it whirled, cutting the air like a whip. It smashed into a hovering chopper, still dropping Alchemists. Snap-pop, and their black suited bodies were pitched into the air.

Fire boiled from Niles' throat, hit the concrete, and the ground opened up as the liquid glow ate into the first underground floor. At the same moment, a new mechanical heartbeat joined the others. Haley looked up to see another chopper tearing across the sky. This one was fitted with strange disks protruding from the nose. The high pitched tone it emitted hit her as solid as a fist. Her vision scrambled and she was instantly deafened by static.

A sharp prick blossomed in her neck, and her muscles caught fire. Another pin hit her between the shoulders, snuffing out her upper *ulyssis* gland. She rolled, trying to get them out, but nothing responded. Her body was no longer hers. The forced change back to her Human form made her beg for death.

Haley's head hit the tangle of fence as she collapsed. She caught sight of Niles as he turned in her direction, claws raised, mouth gaping. The cold of the rain made her shiver, and in those few seconds of forever, Haley waited to die.

As Niles passed under the new chopper, his eyes dilated, going from black to red. Something crossed his face. Even in the fog of pain Haley could see it. Niles Fury was there, and not the Queen of North Carolina.

"You will not have her!" The red giant moved into the line of fire, catching the spray of twenty-five millimeters between his shoulders. Blood and flesh erupted from his chest, smacked against the building, and clung like gruesome garland in the twisted chain link fencing. Haley could taste him on her tongue.

Red scales filled her field of vision as Niles went down. His black mane of horns rose and fell as his body shuddered and he heaved for air. One blood red eye stared at her, flickering like a star. His tongue slipped from between his teeth and grazed her forearm. The long forked ends curled and fondled her hand.

Black suited bodies flooded across the crumbling buildings, carrying a super-cell storm of magic in Human forms.

Niles dragged his destroyed body closer as he slipped back into his Human shell. His hand touched Haley's and a small tentative smile curled on his lips. It fit him, that moment of contentment.

"Forgive my Brother. He was not strong enough to fight her. He could not do what had to be done. His conscience made him weak."

The Alchemist descended and heaved Niles' broken Human form back. Haley tried to hold onto him, but there were too many.

Rain fell in a steady thrum, keeping beat with the thump of chopper blades mutilating the skies. Water covered everything, washing away the blood, washing away the fire. Haley could see Niles between the crowd of Alchemists, his massive arms pulled back, his chest hanging open, bones jutting from his one remaining leg, and still he smiled. It was a haunting expression on such a broken body.

Silver flashed and the smell of magic burned the air, searing Haley's lungs. Niles shuddered once, and his head fell.

Sound returned and the horrible ear splitting sound rattling Haley's skull was her own scream.

Niles Fury was dead.

Chapter 44

As weather sirens sounded off, Ken clicked on the TV. After all, what idiot could possibly come up with a tornado in the middle of September? Even for Georgia that was a bit of a stretch.

When the special report flashed on, Farley felt his stomach drop.

"Damn, that's just a little bit west of here." Ken sat down on his pseudo sofa. Some grainy footage snapped by a cell phone showed a massive red dragon taking out the top of the ADF, then a smaller blue making chase. It was less than thirty seconds of digital recording, but it was enough for Farley to know. Haley wasn't on the plane.

"Ken, I need your car."

"My car?"

Farley growled and Ken pointed to the hook by the door. "Keys over there, man."

Farley's shit kickers thundered as he stormed out of the apartment. He hit the sidewalk and pressed the keyless remote. Up ahead a green Nissan blinked its lights with a not-so-subtle beep. He slid across the hood of some white monstrosity, soaking his pants in the fresh rain, landed on the other side, and hop-skipped the distance to Ken's car.

Farley turned on the radio as he pulled into the street. Announcers came on in panicked voices warning people to stay indoors. The Alchemist teams had been called. Niles Fury had somehow escaped. Reports were sketchy. Some claimed he had gotten out of the ADF. Some claimed he had escaped en route to his execution.

Either way it was going to end the same. A lot of people were going to die.

Farley took a left, slinging the Nissan's ass-end. The rear wheel made an ugly grinding sound when he clipped the curb. He slammed the gas and after another moment, whatever was making the noise came loose.

Hopefully, it wasn't anything important.

On the narrow streets, Farley dodged in and out of traffic, never stepping on the brake, and barely letting off the gas. The RPM flared close to danger.

He pulled out his cell phone and hit redial.

"This is Gregory."

"Change of plan."

A breath hitched then deepened. "We saw the news report."

"She's going to be fine, Justice." Because why the hell would Niles try and kill her after watching over her so long?

"Nidia knew she would try and stop him. She knows Haley's affection for Humans."

"Justice, what the hell does Nidia have to do with this?"

"*This* Niles belongs to Nidia."

"Fuck. When the hell did this happen? When the fucking hell--"

"When is unimportant."

Farley took the next turn too tight and the Nissan Versa shimmied across the wet road. Then it hit the speed bump and went airborne. The front end skirted against the asphalt. There were no sparks; only a spray of plastic.

On the car radio, the newscasters were in a full scale reporting orgasm. Blips and sound bites came in from all directions.

Farley growled. "I'm going to Medan's."

"I understand."

"Can I count on you?" God of Man, he sure hoped he could. Otherwise there was a good chance he wouldn't come out alive.

Scratch that. He definitely wouldn't come out alive.

"I gave Haley my word. I never break my word."

The line went dead.

This time of morning the Dens were desolate. A few stragglers lingered outside the Pit doors, still too drunk or stoned to be worried about rain. Farley flicked on the wipers and they left little streaks of slush with each pass. The radio announcer interrupted his own update, to bring an even more important update. Niles Fury, escaped man-eater, was facing off with Alchemist soldiers who were trying desperately to apprehend the subject with minimal loss.

Farley flicked his gaze to the radio, as if glaring at the damn thing might send a few thousand volts through to the talking head.

Minimal loss. They really thought Alchemists care about minimal loss? Yeah, right.

A good three blocks down from the night club, he found what he was looking for. A shortcut into the Hive.

Farley parked at the curb and left the keys in the car. In the Dens, it was as safe as sitting on the showroom floor. Although, it didn't look very showroom worthy right now. Not with the scrape marks on the rear fender and the front bumper cracking up like Humpty Dumpty. Was something leaking underneath? He didn't look. It was better just not to know.

The doorway was located behind a grate set in the sidewalk. Farley had to shove the dumpster off of the top so he could pull up the wire mesh and slide inside. Unlike the Pit entrance, there was nothing comfortable about this place. Hell, there wasn't even enough room to stand. And wouldn't you know it, thanks to the rain, there was now a good three inches of street slough flowing down the center. Farley's shoulders bumped the side and his back rubbed against the top as he crawled through the corrugated pipe.

At the end, where he could stand again, he found the door. It was hidden by a brick facing. The surface was so smooth that even with his natural sight he couldn't see it. But the scent of the Queen breathing out of the cracks in the mortar was unmistakable.

Farley pushed and it gave way with a grind, revealing a much wider, taller passageway on the other side. The tunnel didn't feel like it had much pitch, but he could tell by the way the earth felt, smelled, and how the world above him seemed to increase in weight, he was going deep.

At the end, on the other side of a heavy curtain, was an all too familiar room.

The parlor with its priceless treasures appeared to have gained a new item. Granted, Farley was no car expert, but he was pretty sure the dark blue antique car was a 1931 Bugatti Royale. Even in the low light the paint on the thing gleamed.

"Do you like it?"

Medan eased from the darkness at the end of the room, bringing the shadows with her as her massive form smothered the pitiful light. It took everything not to run full speed out of there. Save himself. Survive. Farley melted on hands and knees into the fur covered floor.

"You did not answer your Queen, Farley. Do you like it?"

"Yes, Your Greatness." He struggled to keep his lip from trembling as her presence invaded his space. God of Man, where was Justice?

She hissed, clicked, and purred. Farley hated the sounds she made. They were the things of his nightmares. That and the face of a blonde woman with the word *chetrah* stamped across her chest.

"Have you come back? Perhaps you are hungry?" Her tone suggested the kind of sin that involved a lot of blood, screaming, and begging for life.

"I come to you on behalf of *To Whom I Belong*."

"Show me your *mark*, Little Gold. Let me gaze upon the brand you wear for her." Medan's breath hit the back of his neck and he yelped. Farley pulled his shirt off and crumbled it into his fists. He shivered, but it wasn't from the cold.

"Ah, yes. Her scent is strong. She has renewed the bite. Did you *rage*? Did you kill any of the *chetrah*?"

Something sharp pricked the skin along his ribs, chased by the sensation of feathers.

Farley shook his head. "No, no, My Queen."

"Too bad." The sound she made was indifferent. "You puzzle me, Farley." The petting stopped. "Stand." That was *so* not a request. Farley pushed himself to his feet but kept his head down. Medan's breath kissed the scarred flesh of his shoulder. "Even my strongest cannot do what you do. How do you suppose that's possible?"

What the hell was she talking about? Oh, yeah, that's right. She couldn't read him. Even this close she couldn't burrow into his mind. She could drown him in her emotions until he suffocated, but she couldn't glean a single thought. And boy-oh-boy did that seem to piss her off.

"I don't know." It was the truth.

Medan's golden eye came in close, and the fire behind it roared. Fear trickled in, pelting Farley like molten rain. His knees shook, his arms trembled. He clenched his eyes shut, hoping it would help, but it didn't.

"Why are you here, Little Gold?" She coiled around him. "Tell me, Farley, Marked of Haley Night. Tell me."

"I bring you flesh, I bring you blood."

"Yesss--" Her scales rose and fell with the sound of fall leaves. "So now my gift is wanted. Now my gift is valued. It is my gift to give and it is my gift to take away!" She thundered and bits and pieces of rock sprinkled from the ceiling. With a sharp tick and then a crack, spider webs formed on the windshield of the Bugatti Royale. "Look at me, Farley. Look me in the eye. Only then I will take the flesh and blood you carry. Only then will I decide to extend my gift. A simple task that even something as weak, pathetic, and useless as yourself should be able to accomplish!"

Fear flowed over Farley. He struggled to lift his head. Medan's laugh was a sound that spent dark nights in the sheets with madness.

"Look at me, Farley. Gaze upon your Queen!"

Farley's knees gave out and he went down. His stomach rolled and he threatened to vomit. Lungs burning, muscles writhing, he fought her *Fear*. The beat of his hearts became erratic. Ugly black bruises bloomed across his arms and he tasted blood in his mouth. Farley felt his bones creak, his joints threaten to tear.

Dear God of Man, hurling himself into a chipper shredder would have been easier than this.

Panic, terror, *Fear*, Medan's *RHage*, the power of a Queen, it filled him, it flowed over, it claimed his senses and rendered him helpless.

Farley cursed himself for being weak, for being Food. He was going to die, he was sure of it. And that meant Haley would die, too.

God of Man, Haley... He inhaled and smelled her, licked his lips and tasted her on his tongue. Across every inch of skin he felt her warmth.

Farley's head came up and he met the Queen's gaze.

Medan reared back.

Stop.

Behind that one word, was the promise of power.

Medan froze, her clawed hand raised. Steam billowed from her gaping jaws. The cover of tranquility lifted, and Farley fell back gasping, his entire body trembling.

Behind him something big moved. He whipped his head around to see Justice standing in the entrance of the parlor. In spite of the haze of darkness and shadows, his ivory form glowed.

He met your request, Medan.

"You helped him."

Justice inclined his head. *I did not.*

"Liar!" She roared. Her wings rattled, and her *chelae* shredded the furred floors.

Justice's liquid blue eyes pulsed. *I do not lie.*

Farley struggled to stand up. "'Bout fucking time you got here."

Medan spun on her heel and dove into the shadows, her golden eyes burning like high beams cutting through the blackness. "You are not welcome in my Hive. Get out."

After. Justice nudged Farley with his muzzle. *Go to her. Give her the flesh and Blood. Haley's time is short.*

Farley's entire body felt like it had spent a thirty second go round in a food processor ... on puree.

"The gift is no longer extended." Medan clicked and snarled.

Farley glanced her way, then at Justice. If he didn't know any better ... naw ... no way... Damn. Was she afraid?

Justice took a step forward and Medan's fire lung rumbled.

Farley, go to her now.

Farley went forward, his entire body trembling.

Justice sat back on his haunches and tucked his talons under his chest. He looked absolutely unremarkable in his simplicity. *No more games, Medan. Take the bond. Make her your Enforcer. It is what you have always wanted. Needed.*

Farley stopped just a few yards away. Medan flashed her teeth. "This is going to be excruciating for you, Little Gold. Why not tell the white demon you have changed your mind?"

Farley looked back at Justice.

He blinked once, but otherwise was frozen in time. *Yes. It will hurt.*

"Like how bad. Are we talking as in getting an arm ripped off or getting two ripped off?" Silence. "Shit. That bad, huh?"

Worse.

Farley knew Medan expected him to run, being a Male, Food, a survivor of the nest only because he was willing to be Dominated. Living only because of his willingness to hide, to bargain, to give whatever it took. No doubt, courage wasn't even a part of the equation in that kind of survival.

Her eyes widened when he gave her a crooked smile. "What are you waiting on, Your Majesty?"

The definition of a bad day is seeing your own insides. One minute Farley was standing, the next he was on his back staring up at the Queen.

Her talons came across his stomach, slicing him open. A scream boiled up his throat.

Be still.

He threw his head back and saw Justice sitting there like a goddamned Disney display, while she pulled out his insides. "Easy for you to say, fucking ... Christ ... Oh, dear God of Man," he wailed as she dipped a talon into the open wound, prodding, poking. His legs trembled and his bladder let go. Medan's long tongue slipped from her teeth and dipped into the gaping hole she'd carved just above his pelvis. She dragged a glossy bulge out of the wound and laid it on his groin. Farley fought the pain, the sense of his life draining out on the floor beneath him.

And Medan? Well, she took her time. The bitch.

She moaned as her tongue slipped into his stomach, collecting the contents. Lines of temporal fluid leaked from the sides of her head and she smelled of sex and pleasure.

Medan made strange clicks and whistles as she withdrew back into the shadows, wings sagging, feet scuffing against the floor. Farley looked down at himself and pushed his insides back in place. He held himself together, willing his body to heal.

Drink from me, Farley.

The Great White offered him a bleeding palm.

We must go.

Heat burned over Farley's body as he swallowed. There was something powerful and familiar in Justice's blood. Just when Farley thought he was going to figure out what it was, his jaws popped loose of their own accord.

Farley groaned and shoved his hands down the front of his pants, trying to keep his erection from grinding against the material, and instantly came.

"Fuck! What the hell is in your blood?" When he looked, Justice was already moving down the tunnel.

Hurry.

Easy for him to say. He wasn't the one sporting a woody. Justice must have been eating Viagra by the buckets. Farley scrambled to catch up.

"Wait."

There is no time.

"Shit, wait. I can hardly walk." Farley pushed himself forward even though his legs felt like rubber. As he entered the tunnel, Justice disappeared around a corner. Farley didn't think he was going to be able to keep up, but the more he moved the easier it became. It was like his body remembered there were other limbs that needed a blood supply.

Justice took him on a winding path down tunnels Farley didn't recognize, and they exited out of a gaping hole in the floor of an old factory building. Outside, the rain had turned into snow. It was too warm for it to stick, so it just formed puddles of not quite ice, not quite rain.

In the middle of the warehouse, Farley sank to his knees, his body spent. At least his insides weren't hanging out anymore.

You will be safe now. Justice turned to leave.

"Wait. Wait a minute. Damn it."

The Great White paused.

"Thank you." Man, Farley hated having to tell him that. He still didn't like him. Even if he did keep his word. "For everything. What you did back there. I don't know what was worse, her *RHage* or her..." He touched his stomach and shivered. If he never saw his own insides again, it would be too soon.

You are welcome, Farley. But I did nothing.

He laughed. "Yeah, sure. How did you lie? I didn't even smell it."

I do not lie.

"Bullshit. You told Medan you didn't stop her from unloading all that scary voodoo of hers, but I felt it. It stopped."

Justice lowered until one blue eye hovered in front of Farley's face.

It was not me that stopped her. It was you.

Justice slipped out of the over-sized garage door and around the corner. Farley went after him.

"Wait. Do you really expect me to..." The street was empty except for a few dumpsters and Ken's puke green Nissan. Farley turned the other way, jogged to the corner. He scanned the sky where the morning sun was losing the fight with the clouds. "Great ... just great." Well, if Justice ever lost his day job, he could moonlight as the next Criss Angel.

Not only could the Great White lie without twitching, he could disappear into thin air.

Chapter 45

Haley was cold. Which seemed to have become a recurring bad habit. And like two packs a day, it was seriously detrimental to her health. She opened her eyes and was blinded by white. White walls, white ceiling, white floors.

At first she thought she was in a hospital, because there was an IV port in her right arm. But wide bands crossed over her limbs, buckling her down with a combination of metal and leather.

Haley pulled against the straps. The pin in her back flared, and the acrid stench of burning magic made her eyes water.

The table she was on tilted forward until she was in an upright position, making her feel like a piece of very bad living art. Even though the room was vast, the sterility of it was suffocating and claustrophobic. A thump and grind brought her eyes up. The top half of the wall facing her receded, revealing a window and a room full of people and Colonel Dobson.

His voice came through a nearby speaker. “Good afternoon, Ms. Night. I hope you’re happy with your new living arrangements.”

“Funny, I don’t seem to recall that getting I-O clearance required a long stint in bindings.” She glared at the man.

“I am truly sorry about this. I didn’t plan on things going exactly this way. You have the Queens to blame. Their nature has forced my hand.” It might have sounded more sincere if the jackass wasn’t smiling when he said it.

“Are you referring to the fact that you’re so stupid you made a bargain with a Queen, or that you made a bargain with the wrong Queen?”

Dobson turned and said something to one of the white coats in the room. A side door slid open and two men and a woman entered, rolling in a small machine, square and indistinct. For no particular reason, Haley noticed that one of the wheels on the stand wobbled as it was pushed across the floor.

They surrounded her and began pulling out tubing, and prepping syringes. Their bland faces conveyed perfect clinical detachment.

Haley cursed when one of them grabbed her head and forced it to the side. She didn't know what was more frightening, not knowing what they were going to do to her, or the fact that they could hold her down to do it. Without her preternatural self, she was helpless.

Dobson said, "I suggest you be very still, Ms. Night. It's only going to hurt worse if you don't."

A small sharp sting hit the side of her neck a moment later. They let her go and went back to whatever it was they were supposed to be doing.

Haley watched as one of the men opened the side of the machine. He picked up each vial of fluid and held it up to the light before sliding it back into place. The woman moved in next, adding the blood she'd drawn, and the third man checked lines. They'd either choreographed what they were doing, or had done it a lot.

"So, is your virus still defective like it was in Beijing?" Haley could almost hear the click of a gun as his gaze flipped up and locked on.

"I see Dr. Meyer has been talking to you about things she knows nothing about."

"Dr. Meyer has a conscience, unlike you."

Dobson laughed. It was a hearty rich sound. Haley couldn't help but think the man would probably have a great singing voice.

She jerked when the woman hooked up tubing to the port in the crook of her arm.

Dobson said, "You know, you should be grateful that we even bothered to save you. You were pretty messed up out there. Did you actually think you stood any chance at all against Niles?"

"I had to try." She did. As stupid and useless as her efforts had turned out to be, she could have never walked away. Obviously Nidia had been counting on that.

"You are an enigma, Ms. Night."

"Yeah, that's what *impressing* on Humans will do to you." Haley pulled against the restraints, trying to move away from the fluid creeping up the line.

"My comment about you being an enigma has nothing to do with your *impression* of Humans. Which, by the way, I do find fascinating and want to explore at a later date. No, what I was referring to is your genetic code. Your genes are different, unlike any Kin, Male or Female, that I've sampled." He paced back and forth, his footfalls echoing over the speaker. "You may start to feel a little tired. Just relax. It will go better if you relax."

Haley looked around, trying to figure out who'd unplugged her brain and replaced it with cotton. "I don't want to relax." Holy crap, was that her voice? And did someone just crank the heat up about a hundred degrees? "Hot..." Haley panted.

"This next phase is going to hurt. The pain will only last for a little while, but you're going to scream, so I'm going to turn off the speaker."

"Wait!" Violence shot through Haley's bones, throwing her head back, smashing it against the steel table, and then yanked her limbs against the bindings until bones broke. Her muscles strained, her tendons ripped, and just when it couldn't get any worse, her hearts squeezed, crushing the air out of her lungs.

A tide of pain washed over her. Like a million gnashing teeth, it ate its way up her legs.

Blood erupted from her nose and sprayed across her chest as her body became a puppet to the seizure. It was like nothing she'd ever felt and she couldn't stop the woeful cries as they ripped from her throat until she could only make a gravelly hissing noise.

When the muscular spasms melted away, she was left with her shoulders dislocated and one hip broken. Haley struggled for breath.

Niles had begged her for death. Was this what he feared? If it was, she understood. 'Cause now she wanted to die too. Maybe God of Man would at least give her this, release, freedom, even if it only led to a vast nothing. How did that prayer go, the one John Tate said before Medan killed him? Haley couldn't remember.

Dear God of Man, help me. Kill me. Kill me.

I am here for you, Haley. Come to me, Child.

Haley never expected an answer. Not really. Humans were supposively made in the God's image. Kin were beast, excluded from the promised afterlife. But a spark fired in her chest. Maybe God had a place for Kin in his heaven, too.

But then the soft voice laughed and said, *Haley ... there is no God, only Queen dragons.*

Chapter 46

Dobson got the speaker turned off just in time. The alchemy used to isolate the gene sequences always caused seizures. Which was why they used the Glycation. It slowed the response time, reduced the severity. It took losing a dozen or so Males before they found something that would work. Even in Human form, the Kin metabolism burned at full throttle and normal opioids went through them like water.

The colonel checked the clock. Average time was six minutes, eighteen seconds. Much longer and the subject was usually too broken up to survive, because the pin blocked their healing abilities to barely above Human.

Once the protein binding sequence was complete, it would just be a matter of drawing out her blood and letting the computer isolate the correct stretch of nucleotides, tear them down, then transcribe them back into the RNA of the virus.

And Dobson couldn't wait.

Three minutes into it the blood started. The capillaries in the nasal passages were always the first to go. Reasons unknown, but it sure did make for a show. He checked the clock. Four minutes. The seizures stopped. That was a new record.

"Sir, I'm getting a weird thermal reading."

Dobson walked over to Mike, who was monitoring the room in infrared. By keeping an eye on body temps, they could actually see the temperature drop the virus created in each subject as it completed the RNA sequencing. "We're dealing with an unknown here. It's not going to be unusual to get some variations from the norm."

"But, sir, these aren't dropping. She just went from ninety-eight point seven to one hundred in under three seconds."

The picture on the screen showed Haley in reds and yellows with white in the core. The number one hundred point one blinked in the upper right hand corner. It went to two, then three. It was still well below the normal core temp for the species, but...

"Richards?" Dobson flicked a look in the man's direction.

"We're okay, sir. She's still well within the expected readings."

"Yeah, well, I want to know why it's going up and not down."

He shook his head. "I don't know. Give it a few more seconds."

Dobson went to the other station when Lisa Whitman, his metaphysical signature expert, motioned for him. She pointed to the monitor, which was nothing more than a psychedelic conglomeration of colors that didn't exist on a normal light scale. If he squinted hard enough, the faint outline of wings and head could be seen. But that wasn't uncommon. The metaphysical waves often formed shadows of their true forms.

"What am I supposed to be looking at?"

"Her signature, sir."

"What about it?"

Lisa turned back to the screen, punched a few buttons on the key board, and it changed. The new picture showed less color variation and a narrower field. "This was her fifteen minutes ago, when Paul, Kyle, and Margaret were starting the mix." She clicked another set of keys. The picture changed, growing brighter, larger. "This is her now."

The signal strength should have been dwindling, instead it was getting stronger. "Is she trying to shift?"

"No, sir. I've never seen anything like this before."

From the other station Mike said, "Colonel, her temp just went to one o' three."

"Richards?" But Richards didn't answer.

Dobson looked back at the window. Haley's head came up, wobbled, and fell back. When she picked it up again he could see her lips moving.

What the hell?

"Someone turn on the intercom, I want to hear what she's saying."

Mike reached over and clicked on the speaker. The language was fluid, beautiful, something impossible to form with a Human voice box.

"I need a translation!" Dobson threw a glare around the room. "Tell me that someone here knows how to run a fucking translation program."

"I'm on it." Mike rolled his chair backwards to one of the other computers. After a good twenty seconds the computer played out the translation in a poor excuse for a Female voice.

Blood of My Blood.

Flesh of My Flesh.

"What the fuck is that supposed to mean?" No one volunteered an answer. "Richards?"

The man had his nose glued to his computer screen, hands going at light speed over the keyboard. "She's probably got cerebral damage. Ignore it."

Ignore it?

Dobson looked at Haley. Her hair was matted. She was covered in blood and she had several broken limbs. The pain alone should have knocked her out. Instead she was wide awake and staring at him.

"Hello, Colonel Dobson."

Dobson had an odd feeling that something had just happened, but he wasn't sure what. Mike called out another temperature spike and Lisa barked orders for the rest of the team to start recording, but it was nothing more than a distant hum. Colonel Dobson stepped up to the glass.

"You did well, Haley. In a few minutes we're going to start the second part, then you'll get to rest for a day." Her eyes looked dark like a Human's, but something about them seemed wrong.

Well, for starters, she was on enough Glycation to knock out three Males twice her size, so the fact she was even coherent smacked of a problem.

"Tell me, Colonel, is this the last of your virus?"

Colonel Dobson frowned. "I'm not sure why you're so worried about that."

Haley showed fangs. *Shit.*

"Her temp is up to one ten and climbing." Mike sounded worried. Really worried.

"You don't have to tell me, of course." Haley inclined her head. "I already know the answer." Her gaze slid to Richards, who was running a printout. "Did you know Richards is gay?" That got the metaphysical biologist's attention. His head came up and his face flushed across the cheeks. He fumbled with the printout, scattering papers everywhere.

Dobson didn't like faggots, but the man was good at his job, so he'd let it slide for now.

"And what does Richards' inclination for dick have to do with anything?"

He stared at Haley. It had to be a trick of the light. Her broken body no longer looked as twisted up.

A seductive smile spread across Haley's lips. "Four days ago, he got drunk; a little party downtown with his friends. He had no idea of course, but he must have liked the new flavor because he's been back twice since. Tell me, Richards, where did you think that scar came from between your legs?"

"Who the hell are you?" Haley dropped her head and closed her eyes. Her face went slack. She was out. Dobson didn't like this at all. Either all the flopping around had seriously fucked her up, or someone was pulling a Linda Blair on him.

With his eyes still on Haley he asked, "Richards, what the fuck is going on?" Dobson turned to Richards, and the clip board he held clattered to the floor. Sweat beaded along the man's receding hairline and his hands trembled. Dobson's first reaction was to disregard anything the crazy cunt said, but Richards was displaying all the earmarks of a guilty man.

"So not only are you into dick, but you're fucking the wyrms?"

"She's delirious." He waved a hand. "We've seen the Females pull things like this before. They like to play with your mind, get into your head."

"Don't tell me what we've seen. They like to talk about *feeding* on us, crushing our bones, tearing out flesh. They insult, condemn, threaten, but this..." Dobson grabbed Richards by the collar. "Tell me you are not fucking them."

Richards sputtered a gasp. His eyes zipped around the room, but no one was giving him eyes back. They were pretending he didn't exist, because if he existed so did they. The colonel shoved him into the wall. The impact knocked his glasses off. They clattered to the floor and skidded under a desk.

"Look at me, Richards." It took him multiple tries to meet the request. "I couldn't care less if you like it up the ass, but if you're fucking the monsters we have a problem. They keep Humans as pets. You know this. You know it, damn it."

"It's not--it doesn't." He yelped when Dobson knocked him into the wall again. "I'm fine. I'm not *marked.* She's messing with your head. Don't you see? She's trying to screw things up. And it's working. You're letting her delay this. Just let me finish the results, we'll get the virus out."

"Drop your pants"

Richards froze. "Sir, I don't think--"

"I don't care what you think. I want to take a look at your equipment. I want confirmation that she's lying to me. I want to see for myself."

"Sir ... please ... don't."

Dobson pressed the barrel of his Glock to Richards' crotch.

"Either you drop them or I'm going to make a window." Dobson stepped back and raised the gun to the man's head. The biologist looked like a junkie coming down from a binge. It took awhile, but eventually Richards got his belt undone. His pants slid down around his ankles, and he stood there trembling head to toe in his tighty whities. "Richards..." Dobson made a motion with the gun. Richards pulled his underwear down. "Hands." He was slow to respond, but finally got them up. On the right side of the man's groin, cozied up nice and close to the base of his shriveled cock, was a nasty looking bite. It had that smooth aged texture, like it was years old and not days, an indicative characteristic of a *mark*. The wyrms could secrete a chemical into their saliva that cauterized the flesh, sealing it. After all, it doesn't do a hell of a lot of good if the thing you're feeding on bleeds out.

Dobson looked up at Richards. And damn him, the faggot was actually crying. A line of snot rolled down his upper lip.

"You know what pisses me off the most, Richards?" The biologist gave the barest shake of his head. "I really liked you. I really did." The crack of gunfire made everyone in the room jump. There was nothing but silence as Richards slid down the wall, leaving a red lumpy trail on the white paint. His limbs gave a few feeble twitches before he melted into a heap on the floor. Dobson holstered his gun and walked back to the window. Haley's lips were moving again. He clicked on the speaker.

"Blood of my Blood, Flesh of my Flesh." Her head came up and her eyelids peeled back. They were gold.

Not good. Not good at all.

Whitman made a scared noise, and Mike screamed something about temps. But Dobson knew there was no way the bitch was going to shift. Haley had a pin in her back. The air inside the room wavered, becoming hot enough to make the blood on the floor steam.

"Just so you know, Dobson..." A wicked smile spread across her face. "It wasn't Nidia that took your people and your equipment. She was actually sending her Link to warn you in person. She found out I had ears in the D.A.'s office, as well as the Center. Your phone conversations had been compromised. But sadly her *chetrah* pet had a tragic accident."

Haley laughed, but it cut off abruptly and she looked at him with real fear. "You need to run. All of you need to run. Please, she's going to kill you..."

Dobson caught movement off to the side. Mike actually had the nerve to stand up. And if that didn't beat all, he was grabbing his stuff. "Sit your ass back in that chair."

"Sir, she's going to shift." He turned the monitor so Dobson could see. The infrared was lit up like a snow cap.

"The fuck she is! Sit!" He pulled out his gun and Mike sat back in his seat.

"What have I done?" Haley muttered. Dobson watched her eyes bleed gold and her fangs lower. "I told you, Dobson, no one takes what is mine, and you are mine."

Even though he'd seen the process numerous times, it took him a minute to realize what he was witnessing. Haley's flesh rolled and her limbs began to twist. Inside the observation room, the fire alarm shot off and the sprinkler system let loose. Like rats, everyone inside the lab scattered. Except for Dobson. He just stared, mesmerized by the sheer power rolling out of her Human shell. The first strap snapped like a rubber band. It was followed by the cuffs. Her body warped, limbs elongated, dark blue scales burst from her skin.

Dobson knew damn well he should run, but dear God, to have such strength, such power, immortality, indestructibility...

The smell of burning magic flared. Haley twisted and turned, and a scream erupted out of her half human, half dragon mouth. She bowed forward and Dobson could see the pin between her shoulders glow white hot and lengthen until it was pushed from the *ulysiss*. He shouldn't have been able to hear it clatter to the floor. Even if the sirens hadn't already made him deaf, there were eighteen inches of sound proof polymer separating the rooms.

The only explanation was that he'd imagined it. Maybe he was imagining everything. Maybe this was all nothing but a nightmare.

The blue dragon standing in front of him shuddered like it was going to explode. Then, just like the change from Human form to dragon, it rolled again. The scales went bronze, the limbs became longer, wider, the muscles thicker until there wasn't any more space inside the room.

Fear, real fear, sent Dobson stumbling back. "Dear God!"

One blood red eye rose to look at him through the glass.

Medan laughed, "And that is just one of many names you will call me before I am done with you."

Chapter 47

Haley struggled against the tide of *RHage* she had invited into herself.

Fire erupted from jaws that were no longer hers, and claws decimated concrete. All around her people screamed. She crushed them with her strength, fed on their flesh and wallowed in their misery until she stank of it.

I am lost.

She didn't want to watch, but she had no choice. Medan controlled her, commanded her, and she was trapped, forced to bear witness to the rain of death the Queen unleashed.

Oh, Farley, what have I done...

Desperate for escape, even if it was only in her mind, Haley thought of home, and warmth formed in the darkness. She ran to it. Memories, good, bad, they flooded her with Human emotions, Human values, her Human *Impressions.*

Haley clung to the feelings, buried herself in them and drank of the scents and tactile sensations of her life. The brightest of those memories were of one Male. Haley immersed herself with thoughts of Farley.

And that's when she felt it. Something very Human. Something that shouldn't be possible.

Kin don't love.

But then, she didn't follow a lot of the rules, did she?

So she let herself feel it, believe it, and found it not so difficult. Farley's dark eyes, soft mouth, how he laughed, how he moved like liquid. The memory was so real that she could feel him, smell him, taste him.

Inside this cocoon of warmth, the *RHage* couldn't touch her. And when the Queen descended to claim the last bit of what was left of her mind, the power of that emotion erupted. Like the sun to the night, Medan was cast out. Screaming, *RHaging*, and still powerless to stop it.

Chapter 48

Farley was almost back to Ken's when the Versa flipped off the road and was tossed right through a store window.

Holy Fuck, the goddamned planet just exploded!

He was wrong. It was just the gas line under the street.

The Nissan rolled twice and landed on its roof, spinning like a turtle on its back. When it stopped, Farley climbed out.

His shoulder popped back into place and the cut on his chest sealed. Whatever was in Justice's blood was like rocket fuel, and he was still running on the high.

Outside the busted window, cars had come to a standstill and a MARTA bus dangled front wheels over the mother of all potholes. There was another sound, and fire erupted from the wall of the Center for Draconian Research. Only this time it was dragon fire.

Farley felt it then, the sense of *Belonging*.

Haley. Haley was in there.

While everyone else was running away from the crumbling structure, Farley fought his way to it.

Another gas main exploded and launched a VW Bug skyward. Farley ducked his head as shrapnel and glass showered the street. With a deep groan, the CDR building shifted on its foundation and the brick began to fold.

The deep roar of a dragon thundered and a wing tip wavered in the billowing dust clouds. Above, the sky opened up and sprung one hell of a serious leak.

Fire rolled upward and the rest of the walls to the CDR slid down. Rock, brick, and steel beams parted as the beast climbed skyward. A massive bronze body flashed and gleamed within the smoke. The spiral horns and sheer size were unmistakable.

Medan.

The Queen turned her blazing red eyes on him. She keened and windows on nearby buildings blew out, showering the streets with glass. Then she sank back into the rising black smoke and rolling yellow dust.

Medan, it was Medan.

And yet all Farley could feel was Haley.

"Haley?"

He screamed her name over and over as he made his way to the pile of rubble and people fled in terror all around him. Closer, he saw that most of the building had sunk below the street. Farley climbed upward, picking his way across the rubble. He slid, fell, slid again, only to jerk himself up and start scrambling over broken desks, walls, and the remnants of bodies.

"Haley!" Still no answer.

As he climbed higher, the rain fell harder, turning gaps and cracks in the debris into rivers. Only in Georgia could it rain like this in the middle of a five year drought. Farley slipped again and a bolt of white hot pain shot across his ankle. He squeezed out a juicy curse and was forced to wait for the bones to knit. It only took seconds, but it felt like years.

Suck it up and move! Which is exactly what he did.

A downdraft parted the clouds, just enough for him to catch a flash of alabaster skin among all the blackened gray.

Tossed over a crumpled beam, Haley lay abandoned. Farley struggled to weave through the mess of tangled steel beams and rebar. When he got to her, the rain was coming down so hard it was blinding.

"Haley, God of Man, Haley..."

He rolled her over and pulled her against his chest. Her head rolled to the side. Old blood caked her chest, and bruises covered her neck and arms.

"Haley?" Farley touched her neck, felt for a pulse. It was there, but barely. "Haley, wake up, it's me." He rolled her head forward against his neck and pressed his cheek to hers. "C'mon, wake up. Please, wake up."

Behind him fire trucks pulled up, red lights flashing, sirens full blast. Farley looked around. There had to be EMS somewhere, anywhere.

"I need help!" he screamed. "Please, someone ... anyone..." Haley was so pale. If only she'd wake up, he could *feed* her, but she wasn't moving and her skin was becoming like ice. Farley clutched Haley to his chest, feeling her heart beats shudder. The bruises on her body grew darker by the second. "Goddamn it, somebody help me ... somebody help me, please!"

Figures dressed in yellow clamored up the rocky slope.

Farley carried Haley in their direction. It was hard to move because the ground kept wanting to shift. "Please, I need help!"

The first of the firefighters and EMS yelled at him, then his gaze fell to Farley's arms and he froze. Farley realized the man was staring at his *nevus*.

"Please, you have to..." He took a few more steps and hoped they wouldn't run.

The EMS man tossed his chin. "Put her down. We'll take care of it."

Farley laid Haley on the ground and stepped back. They worked fast, loading her onto the backboard. A third one arrived with a medical bag.

"Wait," Farley said. "She's Kin. No IVs, her temperature is down." They looked at each other, then back at him like they didn't believe him. Farley pointed to the back of his neck. "On her neck, look." One of the men confirmed the *nevus*. Now they all stood there, staring, like they didn't know what to do. "Help her!" Farley screamed. He clenched his fists and willed his temper down. The last thing they needed to see was teeth and scales. "Please..."

The black man was first to move. He called for a Hypothermia Kit and pulled a line out of a bag. The other two men seemed to catch on and followed suit. One tapped a vein while the other connected the tubing. "Can you give her blood?" The black man looked at Farley with weary eyes.

"She can't feed."

The EMS guy held up a needle. "Blood's blood, my man. We just need to get it in her."

"Yes, hell yes!" Farley scrambled over the blocks. He fell to his knees next to Haley and held out his arm. When the man hesitated he said, "I won't hurt you, just do it. Do it, please."

The EMS guy knew what he was doing and hit the vein on the first try, then he connected the line to the port the other two had set up.

"I'm going to push on her chest, pump her hearts faster. It will draw the blood," said one of the others. Farley gave a nod. Two white hands, surprisingly dark against her skin, folded across her sternum and began to apply pressure. There was no counting. This was just about pulling the blood supply into her veins.

"Marty, heads up." The black man caught the toss and a woman joined the group. She ripped open packets and pulled out small brown squares. "Here." She held one out to Farley. "Put it under your tongue. It's high calorie protein. This will take a lot out of you. It's not like *feeding*, it's a direct line." Her tone was so clinical that Farley wasn't sure what to say. She dipped her head into the radio on her shoulder. "I need a double board up here."

Farley sucked on the bland salty block. It tasted like shit, but he'd eaten worse. When he tried to ease in closer to Haley, he drifted to the side.

"Don't move, my man. It's only going to get worse. The double board is on the way."

Yeah, a double board sounded great, whatever the hell that was. Farley put his hand over Haley's and laid his forehead down on her shoulder.

Close to his ear the lady EMS said, "I'm going to move you in a second. Just relax. You'll be able to lay right next to her. Don't worry. You're both safe. She'll be okay, you'll both be okay."

And Farley believed every word she said.

Chapter 49

Haley had the strangest feeling she was being stared at. She laid there a moment trying to remember what happened. When the feeling got stronger, she opened her eyes.

Lines of sunlight cut through the blinds on the nearby window and painted the room. She moved a hand, felt the softness of a bed underneath and Farley at her back.

The feeling of being stared at did not go away. She turned her head and saw a man dressed in a gray suit standing against the wall. Short brown hair framed a pleasant face. Nothing about him was remarkable--average height, average build.

A small smile pulled at his lips and his blue eyes softened. And while Haley had never seen him before in her life, every fiber in her body told her she should know him. He blinked once, slow, and tilted his head.

"Gregory? I mean ... Justice?" He came forward, moving like a Human, but with a strange elegance.

"It is." When he smiled, faint laugh lines outlined his Human eyes.

Haley looked around the room. It had all the hallmark details of a hospital room--a TV in the corner, a bed-table on wheels, and an uncomfortable chair sitting in the corner. She looked at Farley. They had matching gowns and ports in their arm. Her first instinct was to rip the damn things out.

"They were running his blood into you. Medan almost burned you up."

Yeah, that sounds like something that bitch would do.

Farley moved, pressing himself closer. Haley sat up on her elbow and tried listening to her body. To see if anything was out of place. She felt normal. She felt like herself. "What happened?"

Gregory's shoulders rose and fell with Draconian grace. He put a hand on the bedrail. "You are okay, Haley Night."

"I am?" After everything that happened, she had a hard time believing that.

"You are Medan's Enforcer, but you are still you."

"I almost wasn't. She had me, Justice. She had me and she was eating up everything that made me ... me."

"And yet you stopped her."

Haley wasn't so sure. Before she could put her concern into words, someone opened the door.

It was Garrett and he had ... flowers? Haley couldn't help but crack a smile. The sight of the man, football big and linebacker wide, carrying a little vase of daisies and baby's breath was just too much. "I didn't know what you liked." He set the vase down on the rolling table.

"Aww--Garrett, you shouldn't have." Haley laughed when he blushed.

"Yeah, well, it's not every day you have a building fall on you." His face was poker serious, which made Haley laugh again. "I'm glad you're okay."

Farley yawned wide enough to crack his jaw. His fangs extended and retracted. His eyes came open, swimming gold before bleeding back to brown. He glanced around like he was doing a head count. "What?"

Haley rolled and put a hand on his head. "Hey, you okay?"

"Me? You're the one who almost died." He nuzzled into her side.

Garrett made a face. Haley reminded herself he was only Human.

"What happened, Garrett?"

Her boss shoved his hands in his coat."Everything and then some. Someone sent a gift wrapped package to the head of the Bureau. It contained a detailed report on the mechanics of the virus."

Oh shit, she forgotten about that. "He dosed me with it--" Garrett stopped her with a hand on her arm.

"You're fine. I had them test you, you're clean."

"But he injected it..." God, the pain. Just thinking about it made her bones ache. Farley thrummed at her back. The sound sucked the panic right out of her lungs.

"Haley, trust me. You're fine. The administrator is reviewing everything that happened. Dobson's labs have all been located. They're doing a full scale I.N.I. investigation on several board members, and the military sector has been completely shut down until further notice."

Haley stared at Garrett, afraid to believe any of it.

Against her back Farley said, "Worry about it later. Sleep." He kicked the sheet off his legs and flashed a butt cheek.

Garrett cleared his throat. “Doctor said you should be out of here in a day or so. They just want to monitor your temperature a while longer. You’ll be at work on time Tuesday, right?”

What day was it? Never mind. She’d take Farley’s advice and worry about it later.

“Yeah, I’ll be there.”

“Good, and if you happen to know of a good Kin informant, I’m looking to hire one. I need someone I can trust. The hours are erratic and the pay sucks, but it’s a job.” His gray eyes were laughing even though his face wasn’t. “Oh, one more thing before I go.” He reached into his pocket and pulled out a set of keys.

“My Mustang! Oh man, I’ve missed my car.”

“No excuses. Don’t be late.” Garrett left.

Haley petted Farley down his side. He smiled, his purr rising and falling in a deep rumble. She lifted her gaze to Justice. “Thanks.”

“I did very little. I was more ... moral support.”

Farley was alive. That meant the Kin had done a lot.

She said, “So what now?”

“I go home. As will you. And we live life.”

“That’s it?”

He gave a slow nod. “It is. It is all any of us can do, Haley Night.” Justice gathered up the coat lying at the foot of her bed and slipped it on.

“But something’s changed, hasn’t it? I don’t feel different, but I just can’t believe it ends like this. Just like that.”

Justice fell still, almost vanishing right in front of her eyes. The expression in his eyes held a deep kind of sadness that seemed impossible for any one person to contain. “Nothing stays the same, Haley. Change is inevitable.” Life poured back into him. “Be well, Haley Night.” The door shut with a click.

Haley stared at the vacant space for a long time, feeling empty. It was like some great space in her chest had been filled up and then emptied again. Maybe it was Niles? But that would be silly, wouldn’t it?

Farley moved and pushed himself against her, making it real clear just how happy he was to be there. “I thought they were never going to leave.” Haley laughed and let him pull her over so they could face each other.

Gold flecked the brown in his eyes, but it was the look in them that made her hearts soar.

Haley ran a hand through his red curls. “I love you, Farley.” His smile went a little flat.

“You always say Kin can’t love.”

She kissed his brow. “And I’m not most Kin.”

About the Author

Georgia bred and born, Adrienne Wilder spent most of her childhood exploring fantastical worlds hidden in her own back yard among tall grass, and shadowed kudzu tunnels. When she was not dragon hunting, she spent most of her time, reading, writing, drawing, and digging holes.
Currently Adrienne lives in Dahlonega, GA where she shares her home with a variety of dogs and one cat. She still spends most of her time, reading, writing, drawing, and digging holes. Although now she calls the reading "research," the drawing "artwork", the writing "books," and the holes "ponds" and "gardens".
You can visit Adrienne on the web at www.theatlantadens.com or email her at cityofdragons@windstream.net.

Other books by Adrienne Wilder

Lesser-Bred Stained
To Adam With Love
Worth

Darwin's Theory
(a novella series)
Book 1: Pain
Book 2: Secrets
Book 3: Promises
Book 4: Lost
Book 5: Found

Coming soon:

Darwin's Theory 2.0
City of Dragons: Of Flesh And Blood